RIDING THE TEMPEST

LEE JACKSON

SEVERN RIVER PUBLISHING

Severn River Publishing
www.SevernRiverBooks.com

ISBN: 978-1-64875-481-4 (Paperback)

ALSO BY LEE JACKSON

The After Dunkirk Series

After Dunkirk

Eagles Over Britain

Turning the Storm

The Giant Awakens

Riding the Tempest

Driving the Tide

The Reluctant Assassin Series

The Reluctant Assassin

Rasputin's Legacy

Vortex: Berlin

Fahrenheit Kuwait

Target: New York

Never miss a new release! Sign up to receive exclusive updates from author Lee Jackson.

severnriverbooks.com/authors/lee-jackson/

To the brave Norwegian commandos of Operation Gunnerside.
Their sacrifices and dedication to duty and country were exemplary.

Joachim Rønneberg, leader of Gunnerside
Knut Haukelid, second in command
Jens-Anton Poulsson, leader of Operation Grouse
Knut Haugland, radio operator
Claus Helberg
Arne Kjelstrup
Einar Skinnarland
Birger Strømsheim
Fredrik Kayser
Kasper Idland
Hans Storhaug

Their sacrifices and dedication to duty and country set the highest examples of courage,
tenacity, and honor. They saved the world from incineration for decades.

They must always be remembered.

PROLOGUE

February 9, 1943
Sark, Guernsey Bailiwick, Channel Islands

The Dame of Sark, Marian Littlefield, sat alone in her kitchen, staring, a forlorn figure. On the table before her rested a poster she had retrieved from a message board near the German army headquarters at the center of the village. It informed of a new requirement, ordering certain named residents of the island to assemble on the following morning with their travel bags to be deported to mainland Europe for detainment in POW camps. Among them were children as young as eight, septuagenarians, and anyone who had ever held a commission as a British military officer, a total of sixty-nine people.

From the front of the house, Marian heard her two poodles barking and then the sound of the door opening and closing. She sighed, straightened her back, and turned the poster over while her husband Stephen returned the affections of the two dogs in the foyer. Then he clomped through the hall to the kitchen.

He leaned against the doorframe with a slight wry smile while gazing at Marian and then at the poster now resting under her arm. He remained quiet a moment, and then reached into his pocket. "I have some wonderful news. It's a Red Cross message from Lance, and it was posted from London."

Marian's head popped up and her eyes widened. "Lance? In London?"

Stephen nodded, beaming. "Apparently he escaped the POW camp at Colditz Castle and made his way home."

An obstinate expression spread over Marian's face. "Not home. He lives here." She raised her skeletal frame from her seat while his equally emaciated form crossed the floor to embrace her.

Stephen laughed softly and pulled her face to his. "You know what I mean. He's in London and out of German clutches."

He glanced at the table. "I've seen the posters," he said grimly. He took a deep breath and plastered a perfunctory smile on his face. "Keep your chin up. What is it that Claire always says? 'Things will get better. You'll see.'"

"Oh, Stephen," Marian cried. "Things can't get much worse here." She buried her head in his chest and fought back sobs. "Now you're going to one of those awful camps, and we can do nothing about it." She raised her head, her eyes furious. "And what kind of madness takes children from their parents and deports them to a prison camp? Old people too?"

"Evil of the purest form," Stephen replied softly. He held Marian for a few moments. Then he chuckled. "Where I'm concerned, that's what you get for marrying an American."

"But you're not American. You're a British citizen—"

"—who held a commission as an RAF pilot in the last war."

"You'd think being the co-ruler of this island would get us something," she muttered, and then stepped back. "I know that's being selfish. None of our people deserve to suffer."

"Nor do the Polish slave laborers of the Todt Organization building the big gun emplacements along our coasts. Those poor devils have been reduced to bare recognition as human beings, and the Germans work them until they drop dead."

"Which makes it even more of a travesty. Sark is already contained under Nazi thumbs in conditions that I imagine might approach a POW camp. Why can't they just let us alone?"

"Letting us alone doesn't seem to be in their natures."

Marian leaned back and locked eyes with him, a sarcastic expression crossing her face. "We're a tiny island two miles across with a population somewhat over four hundred people and just a few miles from the French coast. What possible threat could we pose to them, particularly with our roads and beaches strung all over with barbed wire, minefields, and armed sentries everywhere?" She reached up and brushed back a scraggly hair from Stephen's balding head. "You're the handsomest man I ever knew, but I've seen you look better, and at our advanced age, I doubt either of us would be a match against our occupiers in a tussle."

Stephen chuckled and leaned down to kiss her cheek. "And yet you've held them back with your wit and charm." He gazed into his wife's eyes. "I'm proud of you, Dame Marian, and so are our islanders. They stayed when they could have been evacuated because you asked them to, in order to preserve our culture. You have the love and loyalty of every one of them for the way you've met the enemy and protected our rights, and you've done it with dignity and grace—"

"Do you think this mass deportation is in retaliation for the raid back in October last year?"

Stephen smiled wanly. "That's the scuttle. But the Nazis need no excuse. They'll drum up a reason that seems plausible to appease world opinion."

"But the *island* was raided," Marian protested. "We didn't raid anybody."

"None of that matters to Adolf Hitler." Stephen shook his head. "Three of their soldiers were killed. The message to us and to those who care about us on the mainland is clear: someone will pay for future raids."

Four months earlier, twelve men from No. 62 Commando and No.12 Commando landed on Sark to reconnoiter and take German prisoners. They climbed the cliff at a rock protrusion called Hog's Back between Dixcart Bay and Derrible Bay, and then went undetected to Mrs. Frances Noel Pittard's house.

"She must have been terrified when they first arrived," Marian had said on hearing the story, "and so relieved and full of hope on realizing they were British."

Mrs. Pittard advised the commandos that twenty German soldiers stayed in an annex to the Dixcart Hotel, but she declined an offer to be escorted to England. However, she provided them with documents and a newspaper from neighboring Guernsey.

The commandos hurried to the annex, a long, low structure built to house German soldiers. Immediately, Lars Lassen, a Danish commando, dispatched a lone sentry with his knife, and very quickly, the Brits overwhelmed the Germans, tying their hands behind them without allowing them to dress. And to make running more difficult, they opened the Germans' trousers such that they had to be held up from behind to prevent them from falling and exposing the captives' privates. However, one man who had slept naked and was not allowed to dress managed to escape and ran across a field, yelling fiercely. His comrades joined him in screaming and shouting. In the annex, shoving and jostling started and became violent.

The commandos decided to beat a hasty retreat to their evacuation point, but in the ensuing melee, two more Germans were killed. Nevertheless, the commandos managed to escape back to Britain with the newspaper from Guernsey that Mrs. Pittard had provided, and one prisoner, *Obergefreiter* Hermann Weinreich.

"These deportations and a copy of the *Guernsey Evening Press* seem a heavy price to pay for the deaths of those Germans and the capture of one prisoner, I should say," Marian grumbled. "And now there's a big fuss about tying captives' hands behind their backs. Our chaps supposedly did it here during that raid, and now the Brits and Canadians are shouting as loudly about the practice as the Germans, who ordered it done after that disastrous raid at Dieppe. I suppose our people fear that if we do it, it could become commonplace in the treatment of our own captured soldiers."

"Yes, well, don't talk about that too loudly or often in my absence," Stephen cajoled. "Our captors are in no mood to be benevolent, and I've heard no such talk coming from them officially, so they will conclude that you could only have learned about it from the BBC. The penalty for possessing an unauthorized radio is still death."

Marian sighed. "I know. I'll be careful." She held both hands to the sides of her face. "The whole world has gone mad. The Germans have laid so many more minefields across the island since the raid and added other security measures."

Stephen sighed. "By my count, sixty-three of us with past officer commissions are being deported to camps in Germany. I assume that with the Americans in the war now, the Nazis feel like they are lessening their own risk by ridding themselves of anyone on the island with military experience. And poor Mrs. Pittard is among us, I suppose because she had the temerity to answer her door when the commandos knocked on it."

Marian shook her head and placed a hand over her mouth. "That's small comfort," she said, her eyes brimming with tears. "I'm afraid I've condemned everyone to their own early and painful deaths. The Germans have taken our food, our livelihoods, and now they're taking more loved ones—the ones who are not already in the war." She glanced around the room. "Our homes are falling apart; several farms go unattended because their owners are already taken." She broke. "I miss our children so much. I know Claire writes as often as the Germans allow the Red Cross to forward letters, but those Nazi censors don't let her say much. The same for Jeremy, and hopefully Lance too, now that he's safe on British soil. But where is Paul? I would have expected him to be as attentive to communicating with us as Claire is, but we don't hear from him."

"No news is good news, dear. Sorry to use a worn-out adage on you, but it's only worn out because it's true much of the time. I prefer silence to a Red Cross message bearing bad news. We've received nothing saying he's missing. I'm sure Paul's work for the war effort keeps him busy."

Marian nodded slightly and held onto Stephen for a few moments in silence before gesturing toward the poster on the table. "It says you're to leave tomorrow morning."

Stephen nodded. "We are to assemble at the dock, early."

"I'm going with you."

Stephen smiled. "That's all right if you mean you'll go to the docks with me. Don't get the idea into your head of joining me wherever it is they're taking me. Our people need you here, and in any case, the Germans won't allow it."

Still holding onto her husband, Marian nodded. "I'll be here when you come home."

"That's the Marian Littlefield I know and love. Always finding a way to be optimistic in the darkest hours."

She sniffed and wiped her eyes. "I'll go pack a suitcase for you."

Dawn had broken to a cloudy sky the next morning, when they opened the door to the *Seigneurie*, the stone mansion dating back to 1635 that served as both the Littlefield home and the seat of Sark's government. A horse-drawn cart awaited them, driven by a close friend, Ethan Boggs. "I'm sure you'll be all right, sir," Ethan said as they started off. He glanced back over his shoulder at them. "And we'll look out for Dame Marian. She won't be alone."

"I'm grateful," Stephen acknowledged.

As the horse clopped along the narrow dirt road toward town, other deportees and their families joined them, some in carts drawn by horses, some by tractors, the only motorized vehicles allowed on the island besides the German war machines. Others walked along with them, and ahead, those of Sark's citizens who would stay behind lined both sides of the road, bidding them tearful farewells, and waving flags and bits of cloth.

German sentries also stood intermittently along the road but were careful not to interfere. As the only British soil occupied by the Nazi war machine, Sark and the other Channel Islands were a propaganda boon to Hitler, and his orders relayed down through the chain of command to the commandant were explicit concerning the Channel Islands: be good ambassadors so that the British people will know that they have nothing to fear from the Third *Reich*. Nevertheless, the exigencies of war and the burden of sustaining an armed camp larger than the islands' capacity to provision it had reduced the population to a nebulous state above starvation. And today's actions would gain Hitler no British popularity points.

As the procession of carts and beleaguered pedestrians continued, those lining the road fell in and joined from behind, and soon they reached the top of a tunnel that descended through the cliff walls to the docks below. There, a *Kriegsmarine* ship awaited, and after weeping families bade farewell to their departing loved ones, the new POWs boarded, and the vessel cast off.

With the families of Sark singing the mournfully hopeful lyrics of "We'll Meet Again," Dame Marian stood at the edge of the quay until the boat had disappeared over the horizon. Then she comforted those around her as best she could, returned to the cart, and rode in somber silence along the barbed wire-lined cobblestone lanes back to the *Seigneurie*. Only when she was alone in her cold bedroom where she had spent last night with Stephen did she break down and weep.

1

Three Months Earlier, November 12, 1942
St. Georges Hotel, Algiers, Algeria

British Lieutenant Colonel Paul Littlefield watched closely as American Major General Mark Clark stared at the French admiral before them. Clark leaned his lanky six-foot five-inch frame over the diminutive US-appointed titular head of government in the French North African colonies.

"Why, in the name of all that is decent, honorable, and intelligent, have you revoked your order to oppose Axis movement into Tunisia?" Clark bellowed. "We were to have crossed that country unopposed by your forces, and now, not only are they shooting at us, but they are allowing German troops to land without resistance. From where I stand, you betrayed me. I made military decisions based on your word, and now you've gone back on our agreement."

With mental images floating across his mind of British and US soldiers falling in battle, Paul suppressed his own seething anger.

Despite Admiral Darlan's small size, the French officer carried himself well with a slender, muscular build, aristocratic features, and a full head of silver hair. Nevertheless, his blue eyes revealed fatigue and bewilderment as he recoiled from the verbal onslaught. "I had no choice," he insisted, his voice raspy and turning hoarse. "General Pétain removed me as his deputy and relieved me of command of French forces including those here in North Africa. He's sent General Nogues to replace me. Nogues' plane will arrive by 1430 hours. I'll meet with him this afternoon at 1600 hours."

"That's not good enough," Clark barked, dismissing Darlan with a wave of his hand. "The Germans are moving into position *now*, expanding, and consolidating their positions. Your soldiers are shooting at ours *now*." He spun and glared at the other men in the room. "I want a French leader with the guts to re-issue the order, and if that can't be done, I'll arrest you all and rely on General Giraud to get the job done."

A burly French corps general, Alphonse Juin, stepped forward. Though tall, he was half a head shorter than Clark, with a round face that usually sported an easy smile but was now taut with concern. "General Clark, you are correct, the order must be re-issued. But we are an army of discipline that observes its chain of command. I am with you, but Pétain appointed General Nogues as our commander, and we must await his orders."

Clark whirled on him, his brown eyes flashing, his large hand brushing back his thick, dark hair. "Do you understand that America no longer recognizes either the government of Pétain or the authority of Nogues? If I must, I'll establish a military government here. By President Roosevelt's directive, I've already appointed Giraud as commander of French forces, and I expect you to obey his orders."

"Then I will obey them, sir—"

Clark's eyes narrowed. "You're the first to make that commitment."

"—after we have met with Nogues," Juin said, completing his statement.

Clark glared at him and then at the other French officers. "You all say that you want to fight for France, but you don't jump at the opportunity when it's right in front of you. The Germans are entering French territory now, in Tunisia. You have an army there, but you don't oppose them. You say you're with the Allies, yet you order your soldiers to fire on us."

Darlan stepped in angrily. "We gave no such order. We only suspended the ceasefire until Nogues' arrival."

"Which amounts to the same thing," Clark retorted, "and means that our soldiers could be shot and killed in needless combat until he gets here. Yours too. I want that ceasefire reinstated. Immediately."

While he spoke, Darlan and Juin entered into a heated argument, and yet another French officer, Admiral Raymond Fénard, nudged Clark and beckoned to him for a private conversation. "You're getting everything you want," he said in a low voice. "I myself will obey Giraud's orders regardless of the meeting with Nogues. Everyone in this room is with you, but if you keep pressing, you could lose it all."

"I have no time for talk, talk, talk," Clark snapped. "It's time for action."

"General Clark," Juin broke in. "For your information, General Barre, the commander in Tunisia, received orders this morning from Pétain's Vichy government to put up no resistance to German advances. I instructed him to ignore those orders. His men are actively engaged against the *Wehrmacht* now."

Startled and only slightly mollified, Clark peered at Juin. "Why didn't you tell me that before? They've already taken at least three airfields." He glanced at Fénard, who nodded confirmation.

"They'll take no more airports or ground without a fight," Juin said. "We're trying to be a unified force under excruciating conditions. We all want to fight against Germany and with the Allies, but we are Frenchmen, and we hate to take action that could invite the Nazis to make things worse for our countrymen at home. If we side with you, the Germans will invade and occupy the rest of France."

"That ship has sailed," Clark snapped. "Germany is doing exactly that as we speak. The best you can do is fight to take your country back." He placed his hands on his hips and studied Juin. "All right," he relented with a toss of his head. "I'll give you time to speak with Nogues. But then, I want the ceasefire to go back into effect with Darlan recognized as head of government over your North African colonies, and General Giraud appointed as overall commander of your forces across Africa."

He paused, rubbing his chin in thought, and then glanced around at the vexed faces of the senior French officers around him. "Let me warn you that since our initial landings, we've brought tens of thousands more troops and tons of equipment ashore. We have the ability to enforce Allied will." Then he swung his face back to Juin. "And I want you continuing to command the French forces in Algeria, under Giraud."

A sense of relief settled over the group. Fénard nudged Clark again and gestured for the general to lean close. "I'm sure those things will be done as you stated them."

Clark looked into the taut smile on the admiral's face, acknowledged with a nod, and then strode across the room to where Paul stood by a window overlooking the city. The blue Mediterranean glimmered in the distance. "Let's go. We're done here for now."

Clark and Paul meandered into the gardens at the base of the hotel. It was a bulky structure, four stories high with northern European architecture accented with arabesque parapets, although the interior was strictly of Algerian design. The two men found an area in the surrounding gardens within the Allied security perimeter where they could talk freely.

"What did you think of that meeting?" Clark asked when they were seated and sipping mint tea, its fragrance floating on the air.

"I'm sorry to say so, sir, but you're going to pay hell for that deal," Paul replied. He was a lean, muscular British officer wearing a US Army uniform, of medium height with dirty-blond hair and brown eyes. "Darlan is known and hated around the world for his active collaboration with the Nazis. The world press is already calling your arrangement with him the 'Darlan Deal,' and they're not being nice about it."

Clark nodded. "I know, but it had to be done. Darlan was the number two man in Vichy France, and he was in charge of all its military forces and intelligence services until Pétain dismissed him for issuing that ceasefire order—"

"Which you forced him to do."

Clark cast Paul a sidelong smile. "Guilty, and no regrets. But Darlan has the support of French forces in North Africa, and whoever we put in charge had to be a Vichy official that the French here would follow. Like him or not, he's the only one present who fits the bill."

"What about Giraud?"

"He's a war hero with two spectacular escapes under his belt, one in this war and one in the Great War, but he hasn't commanded anything lately and he doesn't come from a current position of authority. The other generals don't take him seriously and some hold it against him that he disobeyed Darlan's orders. They see him as a prima donna with more guts than ability." He breathed in deeply. "Roosevelt wanted Giraud as overall commander, but the president has never been up close with him. Don't forget that the general wanted to be named supreme commander of all military forces for the liberation of the entire continent of Europe." Clark tossed his head. "That's tall arrogance. He's going to need strong backup and a tight rein to make his command work." Sighing, he added, "I don't like Darlan, but he came with authority—"

"Until the afternoon of the 8th, when he was relieved of command."

"Yes, until then, but our gamble is that with the Allies and particularly the US backing him as head of government in the colonies and Giraud as overall commander, we can make it work until adjustments are needed. With or without Darlan, the course we follow will be the same. He's just the guy who had the most French clout when we arrived, and with our backing, his authority will be restored. The main objective is to stop French forces from shooting at us, and then for them to join us against the Nazis."

An orderly approached them with a message. Paul took it and opened the envelope. He perused the note and then looked up with a smile. "It's from General Eisenhower. Congratulations, sir. You just made lieutenant general. He'll fly down to review progress, and he'll pin on your third star personally while he's here."

Clark smirked. "Well, how about them doggies? That's nice, but Ike got there first, and he's still never commanded a battalion in combat." He stood. "Let's go, we have more work to do today."

———

Late that afternoon, on receiving word that Nogues had arrived and was meeting with the other French officers, Clark and Paul escorted General Henri Giraud from his room in another part of the hotel to the conference room in one of the upper suites. Giraud was a trim man who dressed in an impeccably pressed and decorated uniform.

"How will I be received?" he inquired as they mounted the stairs.

Clark shrugged. "Doesn't matter. You have Roosevelt's backing. Two senior officers have pledged their support and Darlan said that he would work with you. Of course, that was before Pétain fired him. I have no idea how Nogues thinks. I haven't met the man."

They arrived at the suite door. Giraud stood stiffly before it and took a deep breath. Paul moved in front of him, opened the door, and stood aside to let Giraud and Clark enter before following them.

Generals Nogues and Juin and Admirals Darlan and Fénard stood to greet them, and then regarded Giraud with stolid expressions. Nogues was a thin-faced man with stern eyes who seemed slightly out of his element. His attention shifted from Clark to Giraud, where his eyes rested a moment in tense contemplation before he turned back to Clark. "I won't work with this man," he said, gesturing toward Giraud. "He is insubordinate and perhaps a traitor."

"I fight for France," Giraud retorted.

He started to go on, but Clark cut him off. "I don't have time for this," he growled. "General Nogues, this is not a negotiation. You have no say in any of this. We do not recognize Vichy France's authority or yours. Your choices are to remain with Vichy, in which case I'll arrest you, or you can join our side." He leaned over the man and scowled. "I want that ceasefire reimposed, and I want it done now. Otherwise, consider yourself under arrest." He pointed. "There's the phone."

With a look of defeat and drooping shoulders, Nogues moved to the phone. Clark turned to the others. "I'll leave you to work things out, but when I return, you'll certify to me that all of the conditions I demanded are met, most especially that the ceasefire order is in effect. Failing that, you'll be arrested, and I'll impose a military government. Am I clear?"

He peered into each of five sets of eyes staring back at him. Five heads nodded in unison. Then he turned, motioned for Paul to follow, and strode from the room.

"How do you think that will resolve?" Paul asked as they headed back to the garden.

"The way we want it to," Clark replied. "Unless they want to sacrifice their country forever, they really have no other choice. My concern was to get that ceasefire back in place. We don't sacrifice soldiers' lives for nothing."

When they were back in their seats in the garden, Clark reached across and slapped Paul on the shoulder. "You've served me well here, Colonel Littlefield, but we'll soon part ways."

"I understand. You're headed to organize the 5th Army for the push into Italy."

"That I am, Paul, but you're becoming a popular guy. You've been requested by name to join General Montgomery's 8th Army in Egypt. That's been approved by higher headquarters. You fly out tonight." He chuckled. "Now you're going to see what desert warfare is really like."

Later that afternoon, as Paul packed his bags, he heard a knock on his door. On opening it, he was pleasantly surprised to find his American cousin, US Navy Lieutenant Commander Josh Littlefield, standing just outside. "Come in," Paul said. He stepped aside to let Josh pass and then followed him to a seating area. "I'm glad to see you, but I'm afraid I won't have long to visit. I have a plane to catch in a short while."

"I heard," Josh replied. "I stopped by your office and got the news there. I hurried over so I wouldn't miss you. I'm sorry we won't be seeing each other. We need to stay in touch. After this war, I'd like to see our families spend more time together. I know Zack and Sherry would like that."

"Our side would like that as well. Have you heard from your brother or sister?"

"I have," Josh said, stone-faced. "Zack is a tanker in Major General Lloyd Fredendall's II Corps. He's landed in Tunisia, and Rommel is pushing in his direction."

"General Montgomery and the British Eighth Army are pressing Rommel from the east," Paul said. "We'll catch him in a pincer movement somewhere around Tunis. I'm headed to Egypt to join Montgomery's army." Seeing the worried look in his cousin's eyes, he added, "I'm sure Zack'll be all right. What about Sherry? What's she doing?"

"I don't know where she's stationed yet, but she's commissioned as a captain. She's one of those new nurses they're calling the 'flying angels.' They take care of wounded soldiers on flights back to hospitals in the rear."

"Does she actually go on the aircraft?"

Josh nodded. "Some men need immediate care; some need monitoring —they can't delay arriving at a fully equipped hospital. These nurses are trained to treat wounds in the air."

"Then they truly are angels. Kudos to your sister. What about you? How's your war at present?"

"Lousy," Josh groused. "I don't like to brag, but I'm a topflight fighter pilot, and I *was* a good flight leader. But because I knew tactics and could organize exercises before the war started, I got stuck in operations. That should have been a career-enhancer, right? But then, Pearl Harbor happened, I got sent to watch Doolittle's raiders while all my buddies flew raids against the Japanese in the Pacific. No problem. You'd think that would raise my profile a tad, but by the time I got back to my ship, Midway happened, and I got shot down on my only sortie. I'm not complaining. I'm alive.

"But then, while I recovered, the first attacks on Guadalcanal occurred. I got there *after* the amphibious assault, which really wasn't much because the Jap soldiers were much farther inland. Only construction workers and a light security force were at the site where they were building the airfield.

"I survived the first real battle at Edson's Ridge, and then someone decided that I was a Naval operations officer with expertise in amphibious assaults. Meanwhile in the European Theater, General Eisenhower was planning Operation Torch, and his staff put out a call for a naval operations officer from the Pacific with amphibious assault experience, and I got the honors that I did not seek. So now, here I am in a desert, the assault is over, I'm still in an operations office instead of flying, and I'm—" He broke off, flushed with exasperation, and laughed. "Well, I'm frustrated. Can you tell?"

"I had noticed," Paul said, laughing with him. "What do you plan to do about it?"

Josh harrumphed. "I've put in for a transfer back to the *Enterprise*, back to the guys I trained with and fought with for a short while. It's where my buddies are. Obviously, I'll go where I'm ordered, but I'd like to feel like I'm contributing."

Paul laughed a deep, full, belly laugh. "It is the scourge of all Littlefields that we never feel like we're doing enough," he said. "I recall that impromptu speech you delivered to the French general on the coast of Algeria late last year. I'm sure General Clark would say that you contributed to the success of that meeting, which helped bring the Vichy forces to our side."

"Nah, I doubt that's the case," Josh retorted with a grin. "I was put on the spot, and I tap dance well." He lifted one arm in the air and pirouetted in a clumsy imitation of a few dance steps. "Well, maybe not so well," he said, laughing.

"What are the odds of your transfer being approved?"

Josh shrugged. "I sent a letter off to Admiral Halsey through his chief-of-staff, Captain Browning. I copied Ike, the chief of naval operations, and General Clark. I asked Clark to put in a good word for me."

Paul glanced at him with amusement. "Are you sure that was wise? You must have jumped over a few heads in your chain of command."

Josh chuckled. "I'm sure I did. I tried to include them all. But I pointed out that I'm a top pilot wasting away in the desert for doing everything I've been asked to do without complaint when I could be useful flying off the *Enterprise*. I figure, at this point, they owe me, and besides, what are they going to do, send me to North Africa?"

Paul laughed and straightened from closing up his travel bag. "I'm afraid all I can do now is wish you the best. I'm headed farther out in the desert myself, to serve under a commanding general who's raised quite a bit of fuss. That should be a jolly time."

"I wish you the best too, Cousin," Josh said. "I'll walk out with you, and when this is all over, we'll have to get together for a drink."

"On Sark?"

"Done."

2

November 13, 1942
South of Tobruk, Egypt

Paul stepped off the transport plane into the wonder of an early morning sun casting a panoply of rose and golden hues against the desert sky. An orderly approached and took his bag. "This way, sir," the young soldier said, and saluted. "A transport vehicle is waiting. I'm Staff Sergeant Toby Yates."

"Where are we headed?" Paul asked after he had settled into a Humber, a British utility vehicle, and it sped off, kicking up billows of sand.

"To the Eighth Army field headquarters. You're to report to Colonel Grant in the operations section. He'll direct you from there."

Paul took a sidelong glance at Yates, who looked exhausted, his lined face darkened from sun and soot, his uniform filthy and crusted with dust. Yet he carried himself with confidence that belied his youthful form, giving the sense of someone who had assaulted the fiery pillars of hell and emerged intact, if battle-weary.

As they drove through the barren landscape, Paul gazed in shock at combat wreckage scattered as far as he could see, marring the majesty of the line where the colors of dawn met the grim reality strewn across the desert. Enroute, he had listened to BBC newscasts reporting headlines from various newspapers around the world: "Rommel Army in Full Flight," "US and British Fliers Deal Smashing Blows," and "British Chop Nazis to Bits." But nothing could have prepared him for the horror of what lay spread out before him.

Capsized tanks, blackened by flames, their main guns blown off or lolling at odd angles, sat in forlorn repose, most isolated from each other, but here and there, they were grouped in bunches, most of them bereft of human life. Other war machines, trucks, Humbers, trailers, armored troop carriers, motorcycles with and without sidecars sprawled upended or half-buried in bomb-craters.

Paul stared at an object in the distance where smoke still rose. Seeing a battered tail section canted to one side, he identified the item as an aircraft, although with its wings flattened, its nose plowed into the soil, and its skin scorched, he could not determine its national origin. Given its size and single propeller with mangled blades, he determined that the hulk had to be that of a fighter. Scanning the ground near and far, he saw other downed aircraft, including large bombers, with German black crosses on some, and the British tricolors on others. Scattered between the mangled war machines, low depressions cut deliberately into the desert floor and mounds of darkened shells bore witness to where infantrymen had dug in and defended now-empty ground.

Men climbed about on some of the wreckage, and nearby, vans marked with large red crosses stood ready to receive corpses carried to them on litters. And all about, swirled by a steady breeze, was the putrid smell of spent ammunition and death.

Yates glanced at Paul, noticing his reaction to the ghastly sight and loathsome air. "You get used to it, sir, when you've been here long enough."

Paul returned Yates' glance. "How long have you been here?"

"We rolled in last night, sir. We've been on the move for two days."

"From El Alamein?"

"Yes, sir." The sergeant grinned, his yellowed teeth stark against his darkened skin and squinting eyes. "We kicked the Fox's arse, we did. Chased him all the way back to Tobruk, and with Monty in charge, we'll push him right off into the sea."

"You seem quite sure. How long have you been in North Africa?"

The soldier cast a long look at Paul before responding. "A long time, sir. A lifetime, maybe. I've been here since the beginning."

"Since June 1940?" Paul asked in surprised awe.

Yates nodded. "I've seen it all, the bad, the good. The burning summers, the freezing desert winters, the sandstorms. The defeats." He grinned again. "I've crawled through barbed wire and cleared minefields, and finally, finally, we're winning.

"I was in that months-long siege at Tobruk before the Germans took it. Escaped there in the nick of time by a hair's breadth and got back to our lines. I was at Alam el Halfa, in both battles at El Alamein, and I can tell you that we were deathly afraid that we wouldn't stop Rommel there and he would drive through to Alexandria—and that was only sixty miles away. It would all be over by now if that had happened. That's what I think.

"But General Montgomery got here," Yates continued, "and he made clear that we would retreat no more." He swerved the vehicle to avoid a jagged piece of unidentifiable metal jutting from the side of the road. "To give credit where it's due, General Auchinleck fought Rommel to a standstill while undermanned and with dwindling supplies. Then Monty took over and outsmarted Rommel. Made him think that a map the Fox captured showed where the soft and hard ground was. Got him to shift several divisions to block us, and they bogged down in the desert because the map showed the opposite of where the hard sand really was."

He laughed uproariously. "That was a pretty good trick. Then Monty got a professional magician, Jasper Maskelyne, to create a ghost division in the south. They were all rubber trucks and tanks, and Maskelyne made sure their shadows were right when seen by reconnaissance flights. I was detailed to work with him, so that's how I know all this. And then we created a lot of radio traffic from that area like we was going to attack from there." He laughed again. "Instead, we attacked right through their front lines. Of course, we softened them up a bit with two hours of artillery, which gave us away, but that was too late for Rommel to get his troops back.

"That was the end of El Alamein. The press is calling it the most pivotal battle of the war in North Africa and Britain's first major victory against the

Germans. Since then, we've chased Rommel; slowly, I'll grant you, but we can't outrun our supply lines.

"I think Rommel's down to about forty tanks right now." He looked over and grinned again. "We took some hits too, but we've got all those shiny new Shermans on the way, and the Americans are coming in from the west. It's good to see that we've cornered the Nazis when their supplies are dwindling and ours are growing." He laughed. "Courtesy of our cousins across the pond."

Paul's thoughts flashed to his American cousins and then to his own siblings. "Do you hear from your family?"

"Not enough," Yates deadpanned. "They write when they can. The homeland has had its own challenges." He stared straight ahead for a moment. "To tell you the truth, sir, I don't know who I'll find among the living when I get back." By way of explanation, he added, "I hail from Coventry."

"Oh, I'm sorry," Paul said, recalling the reports of utter desolation heaped on the medieval town turned advanced technology manufacturing center. It had been a particular target of Hitler's mass bombings during the *blitz* to the extent that noxious fumes from the main cathedral's tower rose from the molten lead as it ran through the streets, melted by *Luftwaffe* incendiaries dropped to mark targets for follow-on bombers. The death toll had been in the hundreds.

Yates shrugged. "The war will end someday. We'll win it, and then we'll pick up our lives again."

"I'm glad to hear your optimism."

"I've had my dark moments, but now I don't see how the Jerries can win." While they spoke, he wheeled to the front of a group of tents. "And here we are, sir. I'll take you in and introduce you to Colonel Grant, and then I'll be off. It's been a pleasure to meet you."

"Likewise."

Colonel Grant appeared to Paul to be only a few years older than he and a congenial man, albeit with a harried air, and guessing from his loose uniform, he looked to have lost weight recently. He received Paul cordially, but something in his manner left a sense that Paul was not entirely welcome. "The CG will see you personally, but you'll have to wait. He's touring the battlefield at the moment." He sniffed. "He leads from the front, you know."

Without further word, Grant returned to what he had been doing prior to Paul's arrival. Paul looked around at the sparse furnishings within the tent. A map hung against one wall, and adjacent walls were lined with radio equipment mounted on field tables.

After a spell, Paul ventured to ask, "May I ask what I'm doing here?"

Grant peered up at him from his field desk where he had been working on a document with pen and paper. "I would have thought you knew. Let me see your orders."

"Sir, the only orders I got were delivered orally by General Mark Clark, who told me to report to Eighth Army headquarters and that I would receive further instructions on arrival."

"Well then, you have them. Wait." Grant resumed his work on the document.

"Sir," Paul tried again after a few minutes had passed. He had poured himself a mug of coffee and took a seat in an empty chair. "May I help? There must be something I can do while waiting."

Grant turned and faced him. "I'm sorry, but there isn't. Not until you've met with Monty—er, General Montgomery."

The wait was a long one. To relieve boredom, Paul walked outside the tent and once again surveyed what had been a battlefield. Teams of soldiers and lorries had spread out and were going through the vehicles looking for anything salvageable. The scene conjured in Paul's mind the horror of a night with explosives rocking the ground, artillery rounds hissing by overhead, machine guns rattling, and rifles reporting all under the blaze of muzzle flashes and the anguished wails of wounded and dying men in mortal pain. Even now, as he scanned about, he heard faint shouts and then blasts as engineers searched out and set off unexploded ordnance.

An open Humber speeded toward the headquarters and stopped at the center tent, and for the first time, Paul saw "Monty" in person, a wiry man of average height with a thin face and mustache. He wore his signature self-designed jacket and black beret with his standard Royal Tank Regiment badge and another of whatever unit he might have decided to visit that day. Popular lore regarding the beret was that Monty honored those units by wearing their badge.

Paul stepped back into the operations tent, and no sooner had he done so than Montgomery breezed in with an entourage. The general glanced appraisingly at Paul but went straight to the map where Grant had already positioned himself and prepared to brief.

"Is this current?" Montgomery asked in the high-pitched voice that Paul had heard so often on BBC reports.

"It is, sir," Grant replied.

Montgomery examined it. "What is Rommel up to now?"

"He's moving into proximity of the 5th Panzer Army. General Von Arnim commands it under Rommel, and he's brought Tiger tanks with him."

The general continued his study. He pointed to a position far south and a bit west of their own. "How are the Americans doing down there?"

"They've maneuvered around a Free French brigade, which is in a holding position. The commanding general of II Corps—Lloyd Fredendall, I believe his name is—has established a supply depot at Tebessa and is building a massive headquarters bunker in the foothills there. We still don't know how the Americans will be in a fight."

"Hmm. About as good as our chaps were when they first arrived in this ghastly desert, I should think." He straightened up. "All right, I've got a grasp. I'll be here—"

"Sir, Colonel Littlefield arrived—"

"I spotted him when I came in." He started back toward the command tent and made eye contact with Paul. "Come along."

Paul did, finding himself passing between a throng of senior officers who regarded him with dispassionate stares. He followed the general through a series of tents that had been joined together to establish the headquarters until they reached one that formed the general's private office and sleeping quarters.

"Take a seat," Montgomery said, indicating a folding chair and seating himself in another one.

When they were both sitting, Montgomery leaned toward Paul. "I'm familiar with your dossier," he said. "It's quite impressive."

"I've been fortunate, sir."

"I'm glad you see things that way because I quite agree with you. I read about your jaunts with the American, General Donovan, through the Balkans; your trek into Prague for the Heydrich assassination; and your excursions with General Clark into North Africa, among other things. But two years ago, you were a lieutenant, and now you're a lieutenant colonel and imposed on me by no less than Churchill himself."

Paul drew back in astonishment. "Sir, I had no idea—"

"I know you didn't," Montgomery interrupted, softening his strident tone. "It was Churchill's doing. He first put you with Eisenhower as his own direct liaison. Ike passed you on to Clark, who then made you available to come here."

Paul took a deep breath and steadied himself to keep his mind from reeling. "General, I'm dismayed. I had no idea I had disappointed or offended anyone. I sought only—"

Montgomery silenced him with a wave of his hand. "You've disappointed and offended no one," he said. "On the contrary, they all valued your service and your judgment. The fact is that, like Icarus, you flew too close to the sun."

Seeing Paul's puzzled look, the general laughed and stood. "Keep your seat. I don't drink, so I can't offer you anything beyond water, if you'd have some."

When Paul nodded, he crossed to a portable cabinet, removed a full canteen, and poured two glasses. "Here you are," he said, handing one to Paul. "Cheers."

He took a gulp. "Let me explain. You've sat in small conferences with Churchill and Roosevelt. You've been a protégé in New York of the man the prime minister calls 'Intrepid' doing secret work for British intelligence. You went to spy school at Camp X in Canada, and you've been out on special missions. Churchill knows you personally and feels guilty about what's happened with your parents on Sark as well as the Nazi occupation of the Channel Islands. As a result, he not only watches out for you, but he listens to you."

Paul started to respond, but the general held up his hand. "All of that is well and good, even admirable, but no commander wants a spy watching over his shoulder and reporting back to the boss."

"Sir, I wouldn't," Paul protested. "I couldn't—"

"And I believe you. Churchill told me that you said as much to him when he sent you to Eisenhower." The general chuckled. "Having now met you, I see that you're about as guileless as they come. Not healthy for a spy."

Color rose in Paul's cheeks, but he did not respond.

Montgomery drank another swallow of water. "Here's the issue. Churchill wants you here, so you're here, but what am I to do with you?" He picked up a document from his field desk. "Your dossier," he said, showing it to Paul. "I'm short of commanders, but I don't see here that you've commanded anything, and you haven't been in combat. So, I wouldn't put you in a leadership position. Your spy training does you no good here unless we come to hand-to-hand combat, and in that instance, it's every man for himself. My intelligence section is good—"

"Put me in combat, sir."

Surprised, Montgomery stared at him.

Paul took a deep breath. "Sir, because of state secrets in my head, for the longest time I was not allowed to leave England. When I was, I had to carry cyanide pills." He tapped his left shirt pocket. "I still have them and if I am about to be captured—" He arched his brows and left the sentence unfinished. "Meanwhile, both of my brothers have been in fierce combat, and one, Lance, spent two years as a POW before escaping. My guess is that he's back in the thick of things. And my parents have had to live under German occupation for going on three years." He inhaled sharply and let it out. "I've felt in a protected status that I didn't seek, and this might be my only opportunity to actually join the fight." He chuckled. "This is my chance to escape into the war."

Montgomery sank into his chair with a fixed gaze on Paul. "My, my, you are a different sort of chap, aren't you? No wonder those in the exalted company you keep think so highly of you. All right, I'll see what I can do, but assure me on one point first. Do you have a death wish?"

"Not in the least, sir." Paul laughed. "I had a childhood friend whose first name was Dan. His motto was, 'Don't get dead.' I subscribe to that philosophy. In any event, training at Camp X included how to fight. I'm an expert shot. I know demolitions. I'm qualified for commando missions. Give me something to do."

"Hmph. I hadn't added those figures together." Montgomery's eyes narrowed as he contemplated Paul in a new light. "All right, I'll confer with our special operations people and see what we come up with, but you and I must have an understanding."

Paul sat forward, listening intently.

Montgomery chose his words carefully. "I think we can make use of you, but you need to be clear that if I ever have an inkling that you've undercut my authority by sending an adverse report, I'll send you packing."

Paul stood and clicked his heels at attention. "Understood, sir. Where do I report?"

3

January 4, 1943
Paris, France

Tramp. Tramp. Tramp. The rhythmic tread of marching soldiers accompanied a German marching band with drums and martial music parading along Champs-Élysées, Paris' world-famous grand boulevard with its cafés and shops running between the *Place de la Concorde* and the *Arc de Triomphe*. It had fascinated visitors over centuries. The aroma of French roast coffee that should have wafted on the air was supplanted by the smell of a tepid brew that did little to satisfy Parisians' demanding palates. Absent, except in front of establishments catering to German officers, was even a whiff of French pastries.

Amélie Boulier tried to calm her racing heart by taking deep breaths, and doing so inconspicuously, as she appeared to meander along the famous boulevard. Many of the shops were open, but just as many were shuttered. Most of the cafés were operating, as Parisians continued to engage in one of the few loved recreations still open to them, whiling away hours in conversation with family and friends amid the dilapidated grandeur of what the "City of Lights" had become—a trophy of Nazi military might.

Coffee and wine were sparse, discourse guarded, but Parisians could still spend hours visiting with loved ones and remembering the way things had been prior to June 14, 1940, the day the *Wehrmacht* entered the city. Depending on time of day and where they sat, French citizens might catch a glimpse of the Tour d'Eiffel rising above the city on the other side of the Seine, to the south.

The large numbers of pedestrians walking along on the broad sidewalks and sitting in the wide terraces of the eateries did not seem to have diminished since Amélie had first visited Paris last year, although she was sure they were depleted from pre-invasion days. After all, hundreds of thousands of Parisians had fled the city ahead of the German *blitzkrieg* in 1940. She imagined that the ones remaining attempted to carry on as normally as possible, although how they could do so in the face of shortages of life's essentials, she could not fathom. Even now, as she sought obscurity within the crowds, her heart thumped as the German formations marched by from her front, the soldiers' chins held high, their long formations originating behind the iconic arch visible two blocks farther on where they strutted past *la Tombe du Soldat Inconnu*. Such processions, occurring frequently, were both a slap in the face for every French patriot and a reminder of additional tyrannical measures the Nazis could still impose.

Most people no longer paused to offer bitter obeisance other than to avoid being caught in the path of anything German. A grim equilibrium had overtaken the city's atmosphere. The *Kommandant der Stadt Paris* trumpeted every victory wrought against the Allies by General Rommel in North Africa and against Stalin on the Eastern Front. Thus, while Parisians held out hopes for rescue, their faces showed grim acceptance that the likelihood of deliverance was slim as they cast furtive eyes at the passing conquerors as well as those of French countrymen sitting among them.

Some citizens, those who envisioned a long-lasting accommodation with their German masters, still lined the street to observe the parade. Amélie moved along behind them, watchful for groups of soldiers meandering along the sidewalks in threes and fours to further reinforce control over the French citizenry. She had dyed her hair dark brown, covered it with a scarf, and wore loose clothing that made her slight figure look even smaller, belying the face of a woman aged beyond her years by the stresses of her current occupation, a courier for the Resistance.

As she approached a café near the last intersection before the rotunda around the *Arc*, her already sharpened senses grew more acute as she glanced about and listened for any sign that might give warning to exit the area immediately. She caught sight of the person she sought, Jeannie Rousseau, codenamed Amniarix, and her dread increased tenfold.

The young lady sat with a group of senior German officers, and she laughed with them, leaning forward at her waist in amusement at something one of them had said.

She was exquisitely dressed, her hair coiffed behind her head under a stylish hat, her full lips smiling below mischievous brown eyes.

The hat drew Amélie's attention. The ribbon interlaced in its brim was red.

Amélie's trek to this place was a routine task, the objective being to reassure Jeannie that her fellow Resistance fighters were present and watching over her. Amélie's next step was to walk past the café to ensure that the young spy saw her. Jeannie would signify that such was the case by rising and excusing herself to the restroom. No eye contact was necessary.

If all were well, the ribbons in her hat would be blue. Red ribbons meant that Jeannie must meet with her handler, Petrel, as soon as possible.

Without breaking pace, Amélie moved close to the row of chairs in which Jeannie sat, and from the corner of her eye, she saw the young lady stand and excuse herself. Amélie continued on past, her throat now constricted, her eyes looking straight ahead, and for a moment, she heard nothing as her sole thought was to put distance between herself and this café.

As her heart settled and her breathing returned to normal, Amélie started toward the safe house at 26 Rue Fabert near the Seine River's left bank, a walk of roughly half an hour. However, Amélie took her time and a less direct route, cutting through side streets and emerging on Avenue Marceau, doubling back on herself, entering stores and dawdling over sparse merchandise, watching for faces seen multiple times; and she moved along the streets amongst large gaggles of pedestrians.

Her nerves were once again strung tight as she approached the *Pont de l'Alma* to cross to the other side of the Seine. Armed guards checked identification papers at checkpoints before allowing pedestrians to pass over the bridge. Amélie waited until a line of people had gathered, and then joined its rear.

Her heart pounded as her turn to face the guard approached, and when she handed him her papers, she could only hope that he did not notice her pulsating chest. But as she had practiced many times, she smiled shyly with just the right amount of fear showing in her eyes. She had counted on the press of people seeking passage through the checkpoint to hurry the guard's inspection of her papers, and once again, the tactic succeeded. Breathing easier on the other side of the great river, she meandered under the tall trees lining *Quai d'Orsay* until reaching *Rue* Fabert, where she took a right turn.

The safe house was only two blocks away, but she walked on past it through a wooded park on the opposite side of the street, and after wandering with seeming purpose through the neighborhood, she returned to the park. She had detected no sign of being followed.

The upscale French provincial apartment house across the street stood eight stories high within a row of similar buildings. Barred basement windows lined the ground floor, and terraces graced most stories. An ornamental wrought-iron gate blocked entrance to an imposing double door.

Amélie took a seat on a bench under some tall trees, their branches still bare from winter's grip. She removed a book from her bag and pretended to read intently as she glanced about furtively for anything untoward. Although bright weather had characterized the day, dusk approached, and with it a biting cold that penetrated her heavy overcoat.

Both foot and vehicular traffic were light on the street, and when she was satisfied that she had not been followed and was not under surveillance, she put the book back in her bag, withdrew the keys required for entry into the apartment building, and headed straight to the front door. Her circuitous route had taken five hours.

Georges Lamarque, codenamed "Petrel," met her inside the parlor and, sensing her distress, he went to a cabinet and poured a goblet of sherry.

"You look like you could use this," he said as he brought it to her and kissed her on both cheeks.

"Thanks," Amélie said, and took deep breaths as she settled on a sofa and sipped the sweet drink. "Jeannie should be here soon."

"I'll like seeing her again. It's been weeks. Something must have come up."

Amélie nodded her agreement wordlessly. She sank into the sofa, closed her eyes, and let her head loll back into the plush upholstery. "I got so scared today," she murmured. "I don't know why. The Germans paraded while I was arriving at the café. Maybe that's what did it."

"You've been at this a long time," Georges remarked.

"I suppose. Jeannie was wearing a red ribbon, meaning she wants to see you."

"We'll wait."

Georges was a brilliant mathematician by profession, a tall man, solidly built with classical French looks, dark hair, and intense eyes. As a member of the faculty of the Paris Institute of Political Science, a prestigious university, he had known Jeannie for being an excellent student there who graduated first in her class and was fluent in five languages, including English and German. After war broke out, he had organized the Druids, an autonomous subnetwork of Madame Madeleine Fourcade's Alliance group with a reach into all of France. As one of her most trusted lieutenants, he had been instrumental in helping the Alliance recover after two *Gestapo* sweeps had all but eliminated the network.

He and Jeannie had renewed their acquaintance by coincidence on a crowded train traveling between Paris and Vichy. Neither had found a seat, and when they saw and recognized each other, they had moved to a passageway and stood talking for the duration of the trip.

The conversation led to the subject of resisting the Nazis. Jeannie had already been expelled from Dinard, a village occupied by Field Marshal Walter von Reichenau's 10th Army, and she had been banned from any French Atlantic coastal regions, both actions insisted upon by the *Gestapo* for suspicions of spying. Jeannie had been hired by Reichenau's headquarters as a translator and interpreter during the *Wehrmacht's* planning and preparations for *Adlertag*, the intended invasion of the British Isles. She was

saved from more rigorous interrogation and released at the insistence of
senior officers who had refused to believe her capable of spying. They had
demanded evidence to support the accusation, which the *Gestapo* failed to
produce. Her expulsion from the area had been a compromise solution.

Acting on a tip from British intelligence that a spy might be in Dinard's
German headquarters, Fourcade had sent Amélie there to contact Jeannie
and offer support. When the danger had reached a point that Jeannie's
arrest appeared imminent, Amélie had returned with a Resistance group to
rescue her. A friendship of deep trust had resulted in the successful aftermath, and when Jeannie decided to go to Paris for the express purpose of
infiltrating the German high command there, Amélie had taken on the task
of being Jeannie's main means of communicating, a mechanism that
continued even after the coincidental contact with Georges.

Going to work as an interpreter with a French industrial company on
Rue St. Augustin in Paris that supplied steel to the *Wehrmacht*, Jeannie had
soon worked her way into a similar job with an association of industrialists
meeting regularly with senior German officers on the commander's staff.
She visited there almost daily to resolve commercial issues such as discon-
tent over German confiscation of inventories or contracts to sell rubber to
the *Wehrmacht*. Her good looks, refined manner, and deliberately coquet-
tish ways had once again made her a favorite, and she soon found herself
invited to cocktail and garden parties at the Majestic Hotel, which housed
the German army's headquarters in France.

At the gatherings, with wine and liquor flowing, the officers spoke freely
of classified matters. Jeannie enticed them to reveal more by feigning
naivete and amazement and saying such things as, "No, that can't be so,"
and, "How can that be possible?"

The officers at every level, far from home and enchanted by her charm,
were more than happy to display their Aryan superiority and personal
knowledge of secret matters. Jeannie plied them for information subtly,
never displaying her most formidable intellectual power: a photographic
memory.

A knock on the door in a particular rhythmic staccato caused Amélie to sit up. Georges went through the foyer to the front door. She heard voices of greetings, and then both Georges and Jeannie appeared. Amélie took to her feet and rushed over to embrace her friend.

"Are you all right?" she asked. "I've been so worried."

"I'm fine," Jeannie said. Her eyes strayed to Amélie's sherry goblet sitting on a side table by the sofa. She turned to Georges. "I could use some of that, please."

"Of course," he said, and while he went to the cabinet to pour the drink, Jeannie and Amélie sat together on the couch.

"I can't stay long," Jeannie called loud enough so that Georges could hear. She said with a note of mockery, "I'm invited to a soiree of officers and their French vassals."

"Be careful," Georges said, returning to the seating area. He handed the sherry goblet to Jeannie and took an adjacent overstuffed chair. "We've pushed your luck already. Why did you want this meeting? What's happened?"

For a moment, Jeannie's face broke with emotion. "I get scared sometimes," she said, and took a gulp of her sherry. "If I'm ever found out, they'll do awful things to me."

Amélie reached over and squeezed her hand. "I can't imagine how you hold up."

Jeannie pursed her lips. "I've had some luck."

"What is it?" Georges asked, leaning forward. "We could use a bit of good news."

"Some officers I worked with in Dinard showed up in the headquarters a few days ago. I was worried sick that they would bring up my arrest and question why I was roaming freely in the *Wehrmacht* offices in Paris." She displayed a brilliant smile. "But none did. On the contrary, they were pleased to see me and spoke highly of the work I'd done for them." She chuckled. "If anything, they enhanced my credibility. I'm even more accepted now."

"That is good news," Georges remarked, "but I doubt that's the reason you wanted to meet with both of us." He leaned toward Jeannie. "I'm always glad to see you, but keeping you safe is our main concern. If there's something more urgent, we should get to it so you can be on your way."

A forlorn smile touched Jeannie's lips. "I know," she said softly. She took a deep breath and sipped her sherry. "Remember a few months ago, I had a particularly urgent message to get out. I couldn't reveal the contents to either of you."

Amélie froze. She well remembered the event. Despite Jeannie's caution, Amélie had overheard three words in context with Jeannie's message. Flying bombs. Rockets. Amélie required no other knowledge to grasp an inkling of the danger. Before being rescued from the Valence *gendarmerie*, Amélie had been within seconds of biting down on the cyanide pills to protect the secret.

"I remember," she said softly. She had refrained from divulging to Jeannie what she overheard and how it had terrified her.

"I cannot tell you the nature of what I'm learning," Jeannie said. "It's too dangerous. The Germans must never know that their secret is found out, or they'll accelerate their plans or shift their locations."

She turned to face Georges directly. "There are several rooms inside the Majestic Hotel that are off limits to most headquarters personnel. The whispers about what is discussed in them pertain to the information I brought out back then. I think I can get inside, and if I can see what I think is there, I can reproduce the documents from memory. If that happens, you must have a plan already in place to move the information into British hands with all speed." She paused, leaned forward, and lifted a finger to accentuate her point. "And at no point along the way must anyone know the contents of the documents until they reach London. It's too dangerous."

Dread spread through Amélie's limbs as she listened, but she maintained a blank expression.

"We have the plan already developed," Georges said with a nod toward Amélie.

Jeannie took a deep breath. "It could be weeks or even months before I have anything solid."

"When you give the word, we'll be ready."

Jeannie glanced at her watch and then rose to her feet. "I should be going. Who knows what other tidbits I'll pick up this evening?"

Amélie joined Georges to escort Jeannie to the door. They kissed each other's cheeks, gave grim warnings to exercise caution, and after Jeannie departed, Georges closed the door behind her.

In a daze, Amélie wandered back into the sitting room, took her seat, and sipped her sherry. She, Amélie, would be the courier to carry the deadly secret.

4

January 7, 1943
Office of MI-9, London, England

"I'm sending you back to France," Lieutenant Colonel Crockatt, the director of MI-9, told Jeremy. "And yes, you'll get to see Amélie." He chuckled. "That's if you've settled down enough to keep your duty paramount above your romantic inclinations." He added seriously, "I'm only half-joking. Amélie doesn't seem to have a problem keeping her priorities straight."

Feeling his cheeks burning, Jeremy nodded. "I'm properly chastised," he said. "I'll keep my emotions in check." He had been on the verge of refusing orders on his last mission to France in favor of an impulse to rescue Amélie from the French jail in Valence. Only Crockatt's terse order had stopped Jeremy, reminding him of his military duty and the consequences of being derelict.

"If I thought otherwise, I wouldn't be sending you," Crockatt replied. He was a tall man who had fought with the Royal Scots Regiment in World War I, as the Great War was now being called. Having left the army in 1927, he had returned to service as war clouds gathered. He was fit, with a high forehead, piercing eyes, and a well-groomed mustache.

He smiled as he watched Jeremy's futile effort to maintain a neutral expression. "Before you get too excited, I must clue you in on the serious-ness of this mission. I'll tell you up front that it's an SOE affair, but it's the type normally run by MI-6, and as you know, that section of British intelli-gence is particularly jealous of its turf. The reason we have the task is that all the people already in place were recruited by SOE and MI-9, but there'll be no bridges or fuel-tank fields blown up this time. This one must go smoothly with only the amount of violence required to meet its comple-tion. You are to be involved in no other mission for its duration."

Jeremy listened, trying to be attentive, but his mind flitted to Amélie. Six months had passed since he last saw her, just as she was returning to France, and now, a vision of her auburn hair and honey-colored eyes flashed in his mind.

"Are you listening to me?" Crockatt demanded, jarring Jeremy from his daydreams.

"Sorry, sir."

Crockatt frowned. "I was young once and at war then too. Pay attention. This mission is crucial. You're on it because you're already a known and trusted entity. Tight security is imperative." He paused to read Jeremy's expression. "Do I have your attention now?"

"Yes, sir. When do I leave for Marseille?"

"Not Marseille. Lyon. Madame Fourcade is already there, and Amélie will be there soon."

Seeing Jeremy's look of concern, Crockatt held up a hand. "They're both safe, and they know what they're doing. The groundwork for your mission is already laid out. Essentially, it's a security operation, but the information we hope to retrieve is related to what Amélie carried at the time of her arrest in Valence."

Jeremy listened with rapt attention now, recalling how helpless he had felt on learning that the *gendarmes* had arrested Amélie. That had occurred on the same day that the *Wehrmacht* descended on southern France in retaliation for Vichy forces having joined the Allies in North Africa.

Crockatt had ordered Jeremy home under threat of court martial if he did not comply. As it was, by the time Jeremy had learned of the arrest, the gentle giant, Maurice, vegetable vendor to the enemy and unsuspected leader of the local French Resistance in Marseille, had already organized and deployed a successful raid to rescue her.

"Ordinarily, we don't like to put people together on a mission who are emotionally involved with each other," Crockatt continued, "but the inevitable consequence of fighting a war is that people sharing tense circumstances form bonds irrespective of our preference. I say that by way of emphasizing that in this particular case, your personal feelings must not interfere." A very serious man by nature, his countenance took on an even more grim look. "Given a choice between losing the information or losing Amélie, you must choose against her." He enunciated his next words. "Am I clear?"

Stunned, Jeremy just stared.

"Listen to me, Captain," Crockatt said, his voice more severe than Jeremy had ever heard from the MI-9 director. "Others have had to make exactly that choice with family members, including husbands and wives." Crockatt's voice became steely. "A man you knew as Cricket is Colonel Edouard Kauffmann. He's become one of Fourcade's main lieutenants. His whole network's been broken, and the *Gestapo* arrested his wife and brothers. He received word to surrender himself in return for their lives. Fourcade convinced him that he could not surrender. He knew too much, too many people's lives were at risk should he be taken, and she told him that he had no right to take such actions under the circumstances."

Crockatt's voice broke. He took a deep breath and continued in a softer tone. "The status of his wife and brothers is unknown, but Cricket now serves as Fourcade's chief of staff."

Reeling with horror, Jeremy could only continue staring, speechless. Then he said, "I remember him, and I met his wife. I'm sorry to hear that she's been arrested, and I had no idea he was that high in Alliance."

Crockatt nodded. "You and Fourcade have grown close. She's very fond of you, and she's been a tremendous asset to us. One of her greatest talents is creating and building a compartmentalized intelligence organization in which elements usually know nothing of what actions others are taking, and only a handful know what all the sections are doing.

"As you know, she developed networks across France that British intelligence relies on, and while we acknowledge that SOE is her main patron,

MI-9 also looks to her to support our POW escape and evasion activities. Often, the same people are involved in missions assigned by either agency. So we cooperate as best we can, as when Alliance aided in your brother's escape.

"Besides organizing operations around Marseille, Fourcade established radio networks for thousands of Resistance fighters in Nice, Toulouse, Pau, Paris, and other places across France, and she was instrumental in opening our new escape route in Spain. The fact is, she barely escaped from an old manor house, the Château of Malfonds, at Sarlat. She was tipped off that the *Gestapo* was on its way and got out with her immediate staff only minutes before they arrived."

He paused and rubbed his hand across his chin. "Unfortunately, most of her network was wiped out by infiltrators and *Gestapo* arrests. We hadn't heard from her in weeks and had given her up for dead when she radioed in, but she could count on four fingers the number of operatives in close proximity whom she knew and could trust. They were code-named Ermine, Wasp, Petrel, and, of course, Cricket." He shook his head sadly. "She said hundreds had been executed, many of them close friends."

Crockatt reached up and scratched the back of his head. "Honestly, I don't know how she carries on. She's really a marvelous woman. She had decentralized Alliance and given orders to each cell to continue local missions until receiving further orders. Then, without radios, she re-established contact using those four trusted operatives as couriers. You'll be working with one of them, Petrel. I'll let Fourcade tell you about him. She's still rebuilding, but the former senior French military officers that she had recruited went underground. They helped others in their local networks avoid detection and were as eager to resist the Nazis as ever. They helped recover quickly. We're back in business."

Crockatt's enthusiasm rose as he spoke while Jeremy listened, transfixed. Now the director checked his passion with a somber demeanor. "Your assignment requires total dedication. Amélie is already in the mix. She knows the mission's nature but none of the specifics of what she'll be bringing back. If you can't accept that you might have to see her die rather than sacrifice her information, we'll find someone else. It's that critical. I'll give you some time to think it through if you like." He stood, folded his arms, and started to speak again.

"I'll go, sir," Jeremy interrupted. "Send me."

"That was fast. Are you sure, Jeremy? You can't do any second-guessing—"

"Sir, a decision to sacrifice Amélie had better be made by someone for whom the decision would be most difficult. There's no one more qualified for that than me. I'm tested and proven. You painted a rather stark picture of the risks. I understand them. If I said I'd do it—"

Crockatt studied Jeremy's face. Then he chuckled and extended his hand. "Yes, I suppose you do know the risks. The window for Lysander flights opens tonight. Let's hope the weather holds. Fourcade will fill you in on the mission when you arrive."

January 17, 1943
Thalamy, France

The Lysander, the plane of choice for covert night flights into enemy territory because of its ruggedness and short takeoff and landing capability, thumped on the ground to Jeremy's relief, then bumped across a rough field. From his seat inside the cramped fuselage with no windows, he could see nothing.

For a week he had waited restlessly for weather to clear sufficiently to make the flight, and finally on this night, the last of the window, he had arrived. He had made similar flights and parachute jumps into France before, but this time he remained particularly alert as the plane engine's roar built and then receded. The aircraft slowed, took a right turn, and taxied to a halt.

This flight had been Jeremy's first into Nazi-occupied France.

Almost immediately after the plane halted, he heard someone scurrying up the ladder affixed to the left side of the aircraft, and then the hatch yanked open. "Hurry, let's go," a man called. He was visible only as a silhouette against the moonlit sky.

Two other dark figures whom Jeremy had not seen until just before departure stirred next to him, groped soundlessly to the exit, and scurried down the ladder. Jeremy followed.

Almost as soon as his feet touched the ground, three more figures darted from the shadows, climbed rapidly up the ladder, and pulled the hatch closed. A hand in the darkness grabbed Jeremy's arm, tugging him. He turned and followed his unknown guide away from the aircraft. Seconds later, the Lysander taxied into the wind and lifted into the sky.

For the next two days, Jeremy traveled at night, courtesy of dark figures he did not know. During the days, he stayed holed up in damp cellars or drafty barn lofts with strict instructions not to venture out. With apologies, his hosts delivered scant food, explaining that there was no more to share, but they thanked him for coming to fight for France.

Finally, on the third day, he arrived in Lyon. On seeing him, Fourcade rushed to embrace him. "Ah, Jeremy, I've missed you. I'm sorry for the travel security arrangements, but they *are* necessary." She chuckled grimly, then a dark look crossed her face. "We didn't know how good life was at Marseille. Things are bad all over now. Since Germany took over the rest of France, the *Gestapo* has tightened up, and infiltrators are everywhere."

She saw Jeremy glancing around. "I'm sorry. Amélie hasn't arrived yet." She added quickly, "But she's safe. You have my word on it. We've had people watching out and reporting on her. The delay seems to have been caused by a real train breakdown. No sabotage, no explosions, just an old engine with too much wear and tear and not enough maintenance." She shrugged. "That's part of war too."

"*I'm* here," a lively voice called at the parlor entrance, and a teenage girl burst into the room, her face bright as she ran across the room and threw herself onto Jeremy. "I can't believe you haven't asked about me yet. It's been months since I've seen you."

Jeremy laughed and squeezed Chantal, Amélie's sister, and then stood back to look at her. She was now as tall as Amélie, and with her auburn hair and honey-colored eyes, she looked more like a twin than a younger sibling. Her clothes were old and worn: coveralls with a work shirt and thick leather shoes, the result of a world in which necessities had become luxuries.

She and Fourcade had spoken in French, and he replied likewise. "My word, you're all grown up. How old are you now?"

"Seventeen. How's Horton?"

Jeremy laughed, picturing the young sergeant who had escaped Dunkirk and worked together with Jeremy to help the French Resistance. "Are you still pining after that sod? You're as beautiful as your sister. Any boy your age would be mad over you."

"Why shouldn't I like him?" Chantal retorted. She twisted on her ankles the way she had three years ago when Jeremy first met the sisters. "He's handsome—"

"Some might argue that—" Jeremy teased.

"Hey, you're supposed to be his friend." Her face took on a pouty expression. "He's brave, he's strong, and he knows what he's doing. He's not a boy, he's a man. He faced the enemy head-on, and he went back into battle." She turned scarlet, and tears brimmed in her eyes. "And I've made up my mind, he's the only man I'll ever love. Where is he?"

"I wish I knew," Jeremy said gently, and cradled Chantal's head on his chest. "By the way, I know about the reconnaissance that you and Horton did together for a very sensitive mission. The value of the information you brought back was critical. You saved a lot of lives."

Chantal drew back, beaming. "I must do my part. My father taught us that, and Maurice says that I'm still the best at reconnaissance of anyone." Her expression turned to one of adolescent anxiety. "Do you think Horton still remembers me?"

Jeremy laughed. "You do have it bad, don't you? Honestly, I doubt he could ever forget you. I certainly could not."

Chantal bounced up and down with excitement. "Oh, thank you." She stood on her tiptoes and kissed Jeremy's cheek. "I'm so happy to see you."

Fourcade broke in, laughing. "Let me rescue you, Jeremy." She gestured to a set of French doors across the room. "We do have a veranda. And of course, you must meet Madame Marguerite Berne-Churchill, our hostess, but no relative to your prime minister. She's a physician and a stunning beauty, and this is her flat. She's already active in the Resistance, and she's put reliable couriers at our disposal: her own teenage children. She runs the headquarters for us, right here in her own home. We codenamed her Ladybird. Come along. I'll introduce you."

Jeremy had to catch his breath when he first saw Ladybird. Slender and lithe with long, dark hair, her small features were exquisite, as though sculpted from marble. She floated across the terrace to greet him with a warm smile. "I've heard so many good things about you. Welcome. I'm afraid I can't top Chantal's greeting. I heard it all the way out here."

Jeremy recovered his composure, took Ladybird's hand, and responded. Then, he followed as she led the group to a table on the veranda. "I'm afraid the view is not as dramatic as Marseille overlooking the Mediterranean," she said as they settled around the table, "but it's nice enough."

"It's beautiful," Jeremy replied. He pointed to a wide river running far below, lined on both sides with stately buildings. "Look at all the trees along the banks. It must be spectacular in the spring. Is that the Rhône?"

"No, that is the Saône. Directly in front of us down this hill, that bridge is Pont Bonaparte." She pointed it out. "But if you look farther beyond there, that's the Rhône." She indicated downriver to her right. "The two converge downstream." Then, she waved her hand to indicate the area behind her flat. "You can't see it from here, but when you go out and look uphill in that direction, you'll see the Basilica of Notre Dame de Fourvière, one of Lyon's most famous and prominent landmarks. Do you know much about our town?"

Jeremy shook his head. "I'm sorry to say that I don't."

"It's the capital of our Auvergne-Rhône-Alpes region and has two thousand years of history extending back to the Romans. We still have the *Amphithéâtre des Trois Gaules* that was built in those times, as well as medieval and renaissance architecture in the old section. We're quite proud of our city. It's been fiercely independent; some say the culture is more like Switzerland's."

"You'll see that Marguerite is very organized," Fourcade interjected, "and you'd expect that being a doctor. But that's a trait of the people living here. In 1793, the Lyonnaise staged a huge revolt against the new French Revolutionary government. They were met with merciless force and were soon put down, but the anti-government sentiment lingers to this day. Besides that, the town is large with lots of railroads running through, and any number of warehouses and cellars. That rebellious spirit and all the places to hide are exactly the reasons why so much Resistance activity is directed out of Lyon. There's a joke that you can't walk ten feet through town without seeing a Resistance leader that you must pretend not to know."

"But it's also the reason why the *Gestapo* set up such a large local head-quarters," Ladybird added wryly.

At mention of the dreaded German secret police, quiet descended on the group. Chantal broke the silence. "Did you hear how well Jeremy speaks French?" she asked Ladybird, who nodded and turned to him.

"Your accent is curious. A German won't pick it out, but a collaborator might. You'll need to be careful."

"I was born and raised on Sark, one of the Channel Islands off the coast of Normandy. You probably call it *Îles de la Manche*. We speak both English and French there." He chuckled. "I'm fluent in German too, courtesy of a very zealous mother while growing up." He grinned. "If need be, I can switch to it and be as haughty as the best of them, and since the Germans have so many dialects and accents in their country, I should get by."

Ladybird nodded grimly while raising an eyebrow. "Let's hope so."

"Do you still carry forged *Gestapo* credentials?" Fourcade asked. "He used them quite effectively the last time he was in France," she told Ladybird.

"I do, but I use them sparingly, to get out of a jam if need be. And then I leave the area before anyone can check me out thoroughly."

"Good," Fourcade cut in, "but you'll need a cover story for our purposes here, and we need to age you so you don't look of military age. The Nazis are pulling young men off the streets and sending them to Germany to work in their war factories. You need to look old and bent."

"I have trusted photographer friends who'll know what to do," Ladybird interjected. Seeing Jeremy's curious look, she explained, "I modeled years ago. I kept in touch with the photographers, and they all know good makeup artists." She appraised him critically. "You should wear an overcoat and look disheveled most of the time. Walk with a cane and grow a beard. We'll make it gray. You'll need a job too, one that gets you traveling about the city without undue notice."

"Vegetable vending worked nicely in Marseille," Chantal chimed in. "We got to visit all the major hotels, restaurants, and cafés, and listened in on conversations between high-ranking German officers. No one ever suspected us. I can work with him."

"Good idea," Ladybird interjected, and then sighed. "We have the contacts to bring that about, but unfortunately, the vegetable market is rather slim these days. The *Wehrmacht* takes the best, and a huge portion of it goes to feed their soldiers. Still, I'm sure healthy deliveries arrive regularly at establishments where Germans frequent."

Fourcade had listened to the suggestions. "Let's not get ahead of ourselves," she cautioned. "Jeremy, you're here for a specific task, which I'll go over with you in private. Chantal's suggestion is good, though, and we should pursue it. You've got to be seen coming and going. If you suddenly appear out of nowhere, you'll be noticed." She turned to Ladybird. "Marguerite, can you get him introduced to the streets as unobtrusively as possible?"

Ladybird nodded.

"Good. But Jeremy, you are not to linger or try to gain information beyond what you overhear coincidentally. We don't know how long your mission will last, but we need to plan for getting you into hiding and out of the country at a moment's notice."

"Here's the situation," Fourcade told Jeremy when the two of them were alone in her room that doubled as her office. She noticed Jeremy taking in the sumptuous furnishings. "This is Ladybird's bedroom, but it's the only one large enough where I can sleep, work, and hold private conferences. She very graciously offered it to me on my arrival."

They sat across from each other at a table that had been brought in for Fourcade to use as a desk. "As I was saying, we are expecting—I should say hoping—to receive some documents that will have a significant impact on the war. I don't know what they are, but I do know that as soon as we receive them, they must be hand-carried immediately to London. That's your job."

She took a deep breath before continuing. "Amélie doesn't know the details of what's in those documents, but she does have an inkling, and it terrified her." She paused, choosing her next words carefully. "Jeremy, Amélie will be here shortly. I should caution that she's been under tremendous strain. You might find that she's changed—"

"In what way?" Jeremy demanded, his brow creased with consternation.

"Not fundamentally. She's the same sweet girl we've both come to love. But she's a trained agent now, as you are, and more importantly, she's done extensive fieldwork. I can count at least five times that her life was in mortal danger, not including when she rescued you from the German soldiers at Dunkirk, and she was traumatized by her arrest in Valence."

Jeremy leaned forward in his chair, resting his elbows on his knees while he dropped his head and rubbed his eyes. "I feel incredibly guilty about leaving the country before we knew that she was safe."

"You can't do that," Fourcade chided. "I left with you. We'd have done no good for anyone by getting ourselves captured, and her rescue was already in the works."

"I know," Jeremy said somberly, lifting his head. "But the guilt remains."

"Listen to me, Jeremy," Fourcade said fervently. "You must understand this. We didn't rescue Amélie because it was her, or for your love for each other, or any other sentimental reason. The secret she knows is one the Germans must not find out has been blown. She cannot be captured again. She understands that. She was on the verge of taking her cyanide pills when her rescuers got to her."

Jeremy sat frozen at the impact of what Fourcade had just revealed. An unwelcome image intruded on his mind of Amélie sitting on a steel cot in a dim jail cell and slipping the poison capsules into her mouth. He shook away the thought and exhaled sharply. "I had no idea."

"And don't forget that after that event, she and Chantal escaped to Spain from Marseille just ahead of the *Gestapo*. All of those incidents have put an unbelievable strain on her."

Jeremy sat up, a haunted look in his eyes. "Can't we pull her out? She's done enough."

Fourcade shook her head. "Now is not the time, and she won't go anyway. She knows the importance of what she's doing and is determined to see it through." She rose from the table and paced by a window overlooking the rows of classically designed buildings descending the hill to the Saône. "I'll tell you honestly that I don't even know the nature of the information. I'm not immune to capture or breaking under torture, so I wouldn't let her tell me. I'll have to learn about their contents when they arrive to vouch for them to SOE. But what she gave London in that last round was enough to spur an immediate bump to highest priority."

Fourcade's demeanor became even more grave. "Jeremy, the success of this mission depends on absolute trust. That's why you're here. There's no one that Amélie trusts more than you, and at the other end of the operation, in Paris, the trust there must be just as absolute."

Jeremy gazed at Fourcade while tumultuous thoughts tumbled through his head. "Tell me what to do."

Fourcade smiled gently. "For starters, enjoy being with her naturally, as you would have without this conversation. She needs as much normalcy as we can provide. This is a rest and recuperation trip for her. She'll be going back to Paris."

A pang of mixed emotions swept over Jeremy: thrill at the prospect of seeing Amélie and dread over sending her back into an abyss. He sniffed as his throat constricted, and his eyes turned red as they filled with tears, which he wiped away.

Fourcade noted his discomfiture. "We'll get through this. We don't know who we'll lose along the way or even if we'll survive, but in the end, the tyrants will die. I believe that, and so does Amélie, or neither of us could continue on."

Jeremy took a deep breath. "I'll do my part. Tell me what it is."

Fourcade re-took her seat and faced him. "We've established a corridor for Amélie to travel between here and Paris. Whichever way she's going, our people are watching over her, prepared to step in, kill anyone attempting to detain her, and sacrifice their own lives to make sure she isn't captured. None of them knows why they're taking such risks. They don't even know who she is. They're given information about her travel schedule and clothing to be able to pick her out and make sure she travels safely. If anything changes, like the train breaking down today, they call ahead."

Jeremy blew out a breath. "Well, that gives me some measure of relief."

"When the mission is about to culminate," Fourcade continued, "which could be next month or several months from now, you'll travel to Paris. There, you'll rendezvous with a man codenamed Petrel. He's in Lyon now, and you'll meet him later. When we're ready to bring the documents out, you and he together will escort Amélie south through the corridor. If she is in danger of being detained, you'll take whatever action is required to *safeguard the documents*. You must understand that priority, Jeremy. Amélie does."

Jeremy shook his head as he let out another heavy breath. "Why not just have one of us carry them out?"

Fourcade scoffed. "We're relying on men being men," she said. "For all their touted efficiency, the Germans rely on poorly trained sentries and puffed-up bureaucrats to man checkpoints and examine papers. The best troops go to the front, and now they're fighting in the Soviet Union and North Africa at the same time that they're building and guarding the Atlantic Wall. They're spread thin, and the soldiers providing internal security are accustomed to seeing fear in the eyes of the people." She smiled slyly. "They're susceptible to pretty faces and shapely figures. They can't conceive of the notion of a small woman passing right through their scrutiny with damaging information. That's why women are our most frequently used couriers and radio operators."

She paused a moment. "Assuming you make it to Lyon without incident, Amélie will hand off the documents to you. You'll rehearse how you do that while she's here.

Once that happens, you'll be taken immediately to a safehouse to wait for a dedicated Lysander flight.

"Petrel will monitor. He'll be your backup to make sure the documents get to London safely. Know this: if you're in danger of being captured, he'll shoot you and anyone trying to detain you, and he won't hesitate."

She pulled a small box from her skirt pocket. "While we're on the subject, I'll sew these into a part of your clothing where you can get to them easily."

Jeremy stared impatiently as Fourcade opened the box, revealing two small capsules. "You'll carry these with you—"

"I've carried cyanide pills before. I know what to do with them."

Fourcade sighed. "You're not the first person whom I've loved that I've had to give pills just like these." Her voice quavered and tears formed in her eyes. "Take them if you are about to be captured. If that happens, think of Timmy, Amélie, and your family. Your sacrifice might keep them alive and safe.

"If you already have the documents, Petrel will be nearby. He'll save you if he can, but his priority will be the documents. Try to stash them before you're caught. He'll retrieve them. The two of you can work out your procedures for that eventuality."

Jeremy sat back and rubbed his eyes. "This is a lot to take in."

"And to execute," Fourcade agreed. "For context, think of the fact that the Germans have slaughtered thousands of civilians all across Europe, grabbing people off the streets when their soldiers or facilities are attacked by Resistance fighters. It happened after Amélie's rescue. The *Gestapo* executed twenty people they seized outside the *gendarmerie* in Valence. Our fighters know that if they attack and kill Germans along Amélie's route, their own families could suffer. That's their level of dedication."

Jeremy sat quietly absorbing what he had just learned.

"Only you, me, Petrel, Amélie, and someone at the Paris end of this operation know of its existence. Amélie's protectors along the way know only their pieces of it. She knows she's protected, but not the full extent of how that happens.

"That makes you, me, Amélie, Petrel, and Amniarix—that's the Paris contact's codename—the weak links. If any of us is captured, it's not just the operation that's put in jeopardy. It's also the entire Alliance network."

"What can you tell me about Petrel?"

Fourcade took a deep breath. "He's one of the most effective members of the Resistance," she said. "Before I go on, I must tell you that protecting his identity is imperative, even if it means biting down on those pills I gave you. He had already organized his own Resistance organization, the Druids, by the time we came into contact. Amniarix, whom you know as Jeannie Rousseau, went to Paris of her own accord to infiltrate the German command. She did that successfully, and Amélie went up to be her active support and courier. Then Jeannie ran into Georges quite by coincidence on a train." Fourcade continued giving Georges' background at the university and in the Resistance. "He's been invaluable to us in building and then re-building across France."

"So, not only must I be prepared to watch Amélie die, but I must also be prepared to sacrifice my own life so that Georges can live."

"I'm sorry, Jeremy. That's the way it must be."

Jeremy stood, crossed to the window, and looked out. "What a beautiful city," he breathed. "From here, it looks so peaceful." He turned toward Fourcade. "I didn't ask for war. None of us did. I first came to France to build roads and airfields." His face tightened with ferocity, and when he spoke again, he hissed. "I'm furious at the Nazis."

Fourcade rose and stood behind him, placing her hands on his shoulders and leaning her head against his back. "I know. It's why we must carry on."

At that moment, Chantal's excited squeal broke the somber mood. Jeremy's heart leaped as he whirled and exchanged inquiring glances with Fourcade.

"Go," she said. "I'm sure she's here."

Jeremy rushed for the door, but before he reached it, Chantal burst in with bright eyes and a huge smile. She stepped aside. Behind her stood the slight, weary figure of her sister, Amélie.

5

Jeremy had to choke back a gasp to keep his horror in check at his first glance of Amélie. Thin, her face lined, she seemed a shadow of the woman who had stood up to the Germans on the night they first met. Exhaustion showed in her eyes, and her naturally small frame had grown thin, her cheeks gaunt, and her normally lustrous auburn hair straggly. Standing next to her sister as if to provide contrast, Chantal appeared as Amélie had three years ago, notwithstanding the younger sister's shabby clothes.

Jeremy wrapped his arms around Amélie and held her close, not speaking, just swaying with her. Finally, he murmured, "I love you. I've missed you."

"I look a sight," she whispered. "I saw it in your eyes."

He squeezed her. "You saw horror at what I know you've been through. I couldn't love you more than I do at this moment, which is more than I ever have before."

Amélie pulled back to look at him. "I can't believe you're here. So many times I thought I'd never see you again."

Fourcade broke in. "We'll leave you two alone." She ushered the others out of the room, much to Chantal's obvious impatience, then closed the door.

"You're looking strong," Amélie said.

"Adding to my guilt," Jeremy said, leading her by the hand to a divan at the end of the bed.

"Hush," Amélie replied. "I don't want to hear that. You're carrying on the war as best you can, like the rest of us."

Struck by their contrasting physical conditions, Jeremy wondered about life in Paris. He recalled the long lines in front of food shops in London during the Battle of Britain and the *blitz* before the Americans entered the war and alleviated the German sinking of cargo ships with foodstuffs for the island nation on the brink of starvation. And as an MI-9 team leader in the Loire Valley in '41, Jeremy had seen the pillaging of the French countryside, and now he was hearing of similar conditions in Paris.

He sat down on the divan, pulled Amélie to him, and kissed her tenderly. "Let's enjoy the time we have."

They talked and caressed each other long into the night, and Amélie fought to stay awake. At last, she succumbed to profound weariness, and fell asleep against Jeremy. He waited until he was sure that moving her would not wake her up before carrying her to the bed, tucking the blankets around her, and tiptoeing out.

He found Chantal sitting alone in the living room. Everyone else had retired for the evening. "Madame Fourcade is in my bed," Chantal said. "I'll sleep next to Amélie, and you can be here on the sofa."

She faced Jeremy directly, staring into his eyes with unusual intensity. "Do you still love Amélie?" she demanded. "She looks awful, but that's no reason to desert her."

Jeremy laughed. "You've come a long way from the scared little girl I met three years ago," he said, and tousled her hair. "Of course I love her. I would say at least as much as you love Horton."

"That's not the same. You're both adults and have said you're in love with each other. I don't want her to be hurt more than she already is. I think I'll love Horton forever, but what do I know. I'm still very young." She chuckled. "Or so I'm reminded, repeatedly."

"I can only tell you this, Chantal. My heart is right where I left it when I went back to England—in Amélie's hands."

"Ah, that's so romantic." Chantal sighed. "We'll be telling your story long after the war. I hope mine turns out as nice with Horton."

"We've still got a war to win before our story can be thought of as nice—"

"I know. So much sadness. I try not to think about it aside from what I can do to help win it."

———

Jeremy, Amélie, and Chantal took a cautious walk along the streets the next afternoon. Amélie had slept late, and meanwhile, Ladybird had brought in one of her photographer friends with a makeup artist. By noon, Jeremy appeared as an old man. He practiced walking stooped over with a cane and he wore an oversized overcoat and a fedora. So complete was the disguise that on getting out of bed, Amélie did not recognize him and was in shock when she realized who the old man was.

Their first stroll in the city together was short by design, intended only to breathe fresh air and take note of immediate dangers. Chantal, who had already spent several weeks in Lyon, pointed out escape routes as they went.

At first, Jeremy found staying in character to be difficult, but as they encountered the danger of German soldiers on the streets, particularly at key intersections, he resigned himself to his role. The sisters helped, appearing to assist him across streets and stepping up or down from curbs.

They had dressed to accentuate their differences, Amélie wearing a loose skirt and blouse while Chantal wore her coveralls of the day before with a wrinkled shirt. Her small size made her look younger than her seventeen years and more like a street urchin. No one bothered them.

Jeremy was aghast at the scenes they encountered. The soldiers meandered down the wide boulevards among the classical buildings and statues in twos and threes, their rifles loosely slung across their chests. Their stern countenances evoked reactions of fear, avoidance, stoicism, and subdued anger from most of the citizenry, who gave the Germans a wide berth. A few people tried to be friendly, and their accommodation ran a spectrum from caution to obsequiousness. By the proud looks on the soldiers' faces, all but a few of them reveled in a sense of invulnerability.

At the streetcorner down the block from where Ladybird had her flat, large lines of women and girls interspersed with some men waited to enter a bakery. "We have ration cards for everything now," Chantal explained. "One for bread, another for meat—two ounces per week for adults. The list goes on, and people spend hours waiting in line. There's even a black market for stolen and forged ration cards."

"It's even worse in Paris now," Amélie said. "The soldiers strut around everywhere, stopping anyone to examine their papers just because they feel like it. No citizen has a right to anything, not even life. They'll take and shoot you for anything, like they did to a train porter in Paris right after they got there because he inadvertently jostled a German sergeant.

"Everyone, not just Resistance fighters, takes their lives in their hands just by stepping outside their doors. And sometimes you're not even safe in your own house—look what they've done to the Jews, turning them out of their homes with ten minutes' notice, and they've done it with Vichy help, rounding them up, stealing their possessions, and sending them off to who knows where in cattle cars on those awful trains. What they've done to our beautiful cities, our country, our people—"

She sniffed and wiped her eyes. "We shouldn't talk more about that here on the street. Let's keep looking forward and make no eye contact with anyone until we're safely back in the flat."

At the apartment, the three sat on the veranda overlooking the city and were joined by Fourcade and Ladybird. "Are things really that bad in Paris?" Jeremy asked softly.

Amélie's mouth quivered, but she forced her composure and nodded. "It's beyond comprehension. The Germans have taken over all the best hotels, and only they and their collaborators have plenty of food. The rest of us scrape by. Lyon will get that bad, but it's not there yet. And they're looting our national wealth. That criminal, *Reichsmarshall* Goering, sends a train regularly to take our artwork from the Louvre and the Notre Dame and any other place he finds priceless paintings. He takes them back to Germany for his private collection.

"We're seeing our capital die, and with it our country." She caught her breath as emotion overcame her, and she turned to weep into Jeremy's chest. "The horror never ends."

"It will," Fourcade broke in, rubbing Amélie's shoulder. "That's why we must carry on."

Amélie nodded and straightened up. "You're right," she said, wiping her eyes. "A moment of weakness, and we don't have time for that luxury. Let's go over our plans."

"There's time enough for that," Fourcade said gently. "Relax a while. You've earned it."

Amélie shook her head. "No. Every second that the Nazis are in power, they're killing someone somewhere. We should plan and start rehearsing now."

6

January 23, 1943
Marrakech, Morocco

"Ah, Winston. I'm glad I let you talk me into coming on this ride." As President Roosevelt spoke, he reached across the back of the open-air automobile and clapped Prime Minister Churchill on the shoulder. He breathed in expansively and glanced about, taking in his surroundings. "The weather is perfect."

The haunting vistas of the great Sahara Desert stretched away on all sides, the sun's reflection gleaming off the sand dunes. Beyond a rise, Marrakech's brown walls surrounding the ancient trading city were just visible, punctuated by the iconic mosque tower, Kutubiyya, its three golden orbs rising high above its domed crown.

Churchill smiled contentedly. "After coming all this distance and enduring the travails of the past two weeks, there's no way you should have undertaken the arduous return journey to Washington without first taking in the sweep of the Atlas Mountains from the rooftops of Marrakech at sunset. As you'll see, it's magical."

"And there they are," Roosevelt said as the car topped a ridge. Snow-capped peaks hovering over purple foothills under a deep blue sky came into view, barely visible beyond the brown city and desert dunes.

The president tapped the driver and muttered to him to stop. As the convertible sedan came to a halt, Roosevelt leaned back in his seat and relished the cool winter air. "Magnificent," he exclaimed.

"This reminds me of the ride when you drove me to your home along the Hudson River in New York. You and I don't get much chance to relax, Franklin, but when we do—" He took in the view and inhaled deeply. "It's, as you say, magnificent."

High overhead, a flight of fighter aircraft circled in wide orbits, the sound of their engines now breaking the quiet. Glancing about, Churchill saw that the combat vehicles that composed their security detail had halted, spread out on the desert in close proximity, awaiting resumption of their excursion into Marrakech. He sighed. "We'll have to do this again sometime, when we'll need no escort."

Roosevelt chuckled and indicated for the driver to proceed. "You know, Winston," he said as the car accelerated, "this is the first time in history that an American president has left the country during wartime. I hope we've done some good."

"I hope so too, for the sake of both our peoples. The news that London was bombed again last week while we were in Casablanca is quite unsettling. But if we're to think clearly, we must clear our minds, and this setting is perfect for that."

Twelve Days Earlier, January 12, 1943

Churchill arrived in Casablanca, Morocco, a day before Roosevelt. Having had rooms reserved in the names of Mr. P and Admiral Q respectively, the hotel staff had been startled when the two world-renowned statesmen appeared in the lobby of the Afna Hotel, a four-story edifice rounded at each end such that it resembled a ship. On seeing the famous faces, the waiters and attendants were at first frozen in place.

"You'll just have to mind your p's and q's," Churchill had quipped with an amused smile by way of setting the staff at ease. He then stuffed his long cigar into his mouth.

An American flag flew in front of the hotel, and surrounding the premises, the US Army had imposed a dense security perimeter. US armed combat veterans camped beyond the sentries at the main gate and around the entire compound.

The need for the two-week conference had arisen from differences between the British chiefs of staff and their American counterparts. Following a series of letters between Churchill and Roosevelt, the conference had been proposed with its primary aim being to map out the war objectives for 1943. The third main ally, Joseph Stalin, Communist Party Secretary of the Soviet Union, had also been invited, but he cordially declined, responding that due to the battle with Germany raging at Stalingrad, he could not leave the country. But he requested to be kept informed and wished his two counterparts well for their success.

However, he also reminded them that Churchill had promised a second front in France in the previous year, which did not occur, and both the prime minister and Roosevelt had promised the same front in the current year. Following the British re-taking of El Alamein from General Rommel two months ago, such an invasion of France had appeared within reach. However, Rommel, the Desert Fox, had consolidated his army at Tobruk, and Hitler had transferred in more than a hundred-thousand reinforcements from the Soviet front. As a result, the effort to dislodge the *Wehrmacht* from its last North African stronghold this year now appeared doubtful.

The conference and gathering of its participants had been arranged in secrecy. The president and the prime minister initially met in the sitting room of Roosevelt's suite where they could talk privately.

Roosevelt opened the discussion with a compliment. "Your General Montgomery doused the Desert Fox's reputation and sent him scurrying back the way he came."

"You're speaking of the battle at El Alamein," Churchill replied. "Yes, that was the end of the beginning of this war, a real turning point, but I suspect we haven't heard the last of Field Marshal Rommel."

Roosevelt chuckled. "That was quite good, Winston. 'The end of the beginning.' You should use that in a speech. If you don't, I will." He laughed softly. "Oh yes, you did say that in a speech at the Mansion House back in November, didn't you? Good speech, and I still like the quotation."

Churchill stared off into space momentarily as if he had not heard the president. "Oh, yes. I suppose you're right." He returned to his previous line of thinking. "You know, we cut Rommel's tank force down to less than sixty. He'll need massive reinforcements to pose a real fighting force again." He paused while he switched mental gears. "We must point that out to Stalin, and the diversion of hundreds of thousands of German soldiers from the Eastern Front to defend along the Atlantic Wall from Norway to the southern French Atlantic coast as well as in the Balkans, and now in North Africa. We should emphasize, too, the many tons of weaponry, supplies, and equipment you've sent him to defend the Soviet Union. Britain even passes along to the Soviets some of the equipment you provide to us. The deliveries of war materiel are our combined contribution to easing the pressure on his armies."

"Agreed," the president replied. "But his people are taking the brunt of the land war, and their casualties are in the hundreds of thousands while ours are in the tens of thousands, so I understand his anxiety, but we're helping in every way we can.

"I'm sure Hitler intended to embarrass Stalin by attacking the city named for him, but personally, I think that was a strategic misstep. Hitler could have captured Moscow by now if he had reinforced his armies there before last year's spring offensive. But he divided them, and I'm guessing he did it as a poke in Stalin's eye."

Churchill nodded. "Our signals decoders and analysts at Bletchley Park would agree. We intercepted a lot of radio traffic from the German high command while those discussions were under way and as the charge toward Stalingrad took place. Hitler's generals were not pleased."

Roosevelt huffed impatiently. "And yet they follow his orders. You'd think that sooner or later they would mount a concerted effort to remove him from power to save their own skins if not their country.

"You've turned the storm, Winston. Two years ago, your countrymen lived in constant fear and danger of a *Wehrmacht* invasion. Now it is the

Germans who have to worry about seeing their country overrun. The tempest will soon be upon them."

"And we intend to ride it," Churchill pressed. "Tell me about the war in the Pacific. I see that your troops are still bogged down on Guadalcanal."

"I'll brief you fully, but first, you mentioned Bletchley. We're incredibly impressed with the intelligence coming from that facility. We do a good job of decoding Japan's messages too. Tell me about the team I sent there last year to learn your methods and work in tandem with your folks. How are they doing?"

Churchill chuckled. "Long before the group arrived, we had spotted American professors and intelligence chaps roaming our backroads in Bletchley's vicinity, seemingly intent on learning what goes on there. I don't have any anecdotal support to answer your question either way, but I'd have heard if there were problems."

"I suppose you're right." Roosevelt smiled briefly, and then his expression turned grim. "Guadalcanal is a hellhole," he growled. "The Japs won't let it go easily. It's key to their defense in the Solomons and the Marshall Islands and to their further expansion in the South Pacific. Our Marines have been slugging it out with them for five months, and we see no end in sight." He harrumphed. "We need to be sure Uncle Joe knows that too, and remind him that while he badgers us about a second front in Europe, he has not yet declared war on Japan and takes no action against them off his coast in the Northern Pacific while they pummel our Aleutian Islands and even bomb his ships."

Churchill chuckled. "I told him he must face that his problems are of his own making for not coming to Britain's aid during the Battle of Britain and the *blitz*."

Roosevelt studied the prime minister. "As my Uncle Ted would have said, 'Bully for you,'" he muttered softly. "You and your people suffered through a lot.

"Now," the president continued, "let's get down to business and move this war along to a successful conclusion as quickly as possible, shall we? Who did you bring with you?"

"Of course, I brought General Sir Alan Brooke, chief of the imperial general staff; Field Marshal Sir John Dill, head of our joint staff mission to

Washington; and Admiral of the Fleet Sir Dudley Pound. I also brought along Lord Mountbatten. He's been elevated to chief of combined operations since we last saw each other. My son, Randolph, came over as well, from the Tunisian front."

Roosevelt arched his brows in approval. "Mountbatten was a good call. I'll look forward to meeting him. I was doubtful at first because he's so young, but his concepts about combined operations have proven themselves, particularly with your Operation Chariot at Saint-Nazaire last year. That action took the *Tirpitz* right out of the battle in the Atlantic, at least for the time being, and our convoys are getting through. And by the way, we've incorporated Mountbatten's concepts of combined arms operations into our own doctrine and planning."

"Good," Churchill rejoined, "and we're not done with the *Tirpitz* yet, not by a long shot. We'll sink her yet." He pursed his lips. "We should give Mountbatten credit for what took place at Dieppe as well. He's taken his lumps for its supposed failure. The Canadians hate him for it because their casualties were so high, but what we learned about German radar advances from that raid is key to gaining air superiority over Europe. That was an achievement we could not trumpet. Germany would have immediately developed countermeasures.

"We also learned a great deal about amphibious operations that we put to use in our landings here in North Africa. They should help too when we finally invade Europe." Seeing Roosevelt nod in agreement, he asked, "What about you? Who came with you?"

Roosevelt laughed softly. "General Eisenhower will be here to present plans for an operation, but then he'll get back to the war. Clark is here, and I'm sure you know that Patton arranged this whole shindig, but the discussions we'll have are a step above their levels." He paused while he eyed Churchill with a frank expression. "Let's address the elephant in the room, shall we? Eisenhower didn't take Tunisia, and he was supposed to have done that before the Germans could build up there. Now, they're entrenched just eighty miles southwest of Sicily."

Churchill returned his stare. "We all have our setbacks, don't we? You're kind not to mention Tobruk or Singapore. Von Arnim brought his Panzers in, and now we're in what is likely to be a protracted static position."

Roosevelt sighed. "The practical implication is that we won't be able to mount an invasion into France this year, just as you predicted, and you were right about not yet being prepared for such a venture."

"But we're not without progress here in North Africa," Churchill broke in. "Large contingents of our armies are ashore." He glanced out the window across the city and chuckled. "And we're sitting in a hotel in Casablanca. Did you see the movie?"

"I did. It was wonderfully dramatic. I suppose there must be some parallels to current reality in there somewhere. I think it might have educated our two peoples on who the Vichy are, or at least that they exist."

"Getting back to business," Churchill cut in. "I'd like to suggest our General Alexander as Eisenhower's deputy for the continuation of Operation Torch. I neglected to mention that he's here now too.

"You've directed Mark Clark to activate and command the Fifth Army and that leaves a vacancy for Eisenhower's deputy. Clark did an excellent job in bringing the French over to our side and that saved a lot of our soldiers' lives. He's a good choice to command the Fifth Army.

"Alexander's been responsible for Britain's overall success in North Africa lately. Putting him into that deputy command slot will give our combined forces the benefit of his experience without upsetting the French by having them report to a British commanding general. You know, many of them are still angry with us for bombing their fleet at Mers-el-Kébir."

Roosevelt scoffed. "You're proposing to kick Ike upstairs."

"Excuse me?"

"Word has reached me that your senior commanders and staff regard him as a highly competent desk clerk."

"Your own Mark Clark has been heard more than once saying that Eisenhower's never commanded even a battalion in battle until now," Churchill interjected ruefully. "And as you pointed out, that hasn't gone according to plan."

"You're right, but I'll also point out that Ike's senior staff consists of five senior British officers, and one"—he held up an index finger to underscore his point—"I repeat, one, American officer. Even Ike's sentry is British, and you have your own envoy there, whom my guys consider to be your personal spy. So, you should know that my own senior military is none too pleased with that arrangement, and it begs the question: whose advice is Ike receiving."

Churchill started to respond, but Roosevelt pressed on. "Let's not forget that our boys arrived on these shores green, while yours had been here for a while. Rommel ran circles around your troops for a long time, too."

Churchill's face had turned red, but he took a deep breath and then laughed. "As I stated earlier, we've all had our setbacks."

Roosevelt's expression softened. "We have the greatest respect for Alexander. I'm not opposed to your suggestion of assigning him as Ike's deputy. You were impressed with Ike in London."

"I didn't know the extent of his combat experience, and it has now come up in discussion."

"Yes, well, I'm hearing rumbles that Alexander does not hold our American fighters in high regard. If we agree to your suggested arrangement, you might have a word with him on that score. Remind him that Americans will shoulder the brunt of new manpower, equipment, and the money to pay for it, and your battle-hardened veterans can't win the war without all of that. Therefore, the supreme commander of Allied forces must be an American."

"He'll respond that our army makes up the bulk of manpower currently on the ground," Churchill responded pugnaciously. "It includes Brits, Aussies, Canadians, New Zealanders, and Indians, most of them battle-tested."

Roosevelt eyed the prime minister cautiously. "You play the cards you're dealt," he said, a steely tone entering his voice. "At the moment, Ike is in charge of the ongoing North African campaign, and no one's going to convince me that yours fought any better when they first arrived. Nothing improves an army like combat experience, which ours are receiving in spades." He took a breath and relaxed back in his seat. "Ike and Alexander should get along, and there's no question about Alexander's combat experience. His view of how to plan for combat at ground level will be invaluable.

"Now, to finish answering your question about who came with me, I've got the chief of staff, Marshall; the air chief, Hap Arnold; and the chief of naval operations, Admiral King. I didn't see a need for anyone from the State Department, but I brought along Averill Harriman and Harry

Hopkins as personal advisors. They can liaise back anything State needs to know."

Churchill nodded in approval. "Then before we get into the thick of things with our combined staffs, let's go over what we corresponded about to be sure that at least you and I are seeing things the same way."

"All right, Winston," Roosevelt said, breaking into a smile. "But I have to be careful dealing with you one on one. You got your way on 'Germany first,' and I already mentioned the numerical advantage you Brits have on Ike's senior staff."

Churchill started to protest, but the president held up his hand to interrupt him. "Then you got your Operation Torch here in North Africa when my military leaders were pushing for an invasion of Northern France. And you persuaded us to take our new M4 Sherman tanks away from our own line units at home training for this war and to ship them to yours in Egypt." He laughed. "My staff thinks you own me."

Nonplussed, Churchill at first could only stare at Roosevelt. "You know that's not the case," he said at last while sitting back in his seat. "At least I hope you do. You and I have had very open interaction. You don't hold back, and neither do I. The decisions we've reached resulted from thorough discussion. The objective is to win the war."

Roosevelt waved a hand in the air. "Agreed, Winston, and I'm not worried. The whole reason for this conference is to be sure that we—and I mean the United States, Great Britain, and our other allies—go forward with united objectives, a unified command, and that we marshal our resources for best effect. So, in that regard, what do we do about the French?"

Churchill took a breath. "In that regard, Admiral Darland was kind enough to get himself assassinated, removing himself as one point of contention."

Roosevelt chuckled with a note of irony. "He did at that. We owe him one."

"You offered the French full and equal partnership with our two countries and the Soviets," Churchill went on, "if they joined us with Giraud as their commanding general. They've done that, and their forces now fight the Germans with us. We have an obligation we must honor. We should invite them to join us here immediately and participate in this conference."

"You mean invite Giraud?"

Churchill stood and paced. "I mean invite both Giraud and de Gaulle. If by the end of this conference, we can show the world, in particular the French people, that those two are working together with us, we could relieve some deep divisions.

"Right now, de Gaulle's Free French are on the sidelines running their own Resistance operations in France. But when we invade there, we'll need those fighters, and we don't need enmity between them and their own countrymen who are now fighting in North Africa. We need all of them on our side."

Roosevelt sighed. "I just don't like de Gaulle. He was public and bitter in his criticism of me for having recognized the Vichy government after Germany invaded France. He's—"

"He's arrogant, opinionated, willful, and difficult to deal with," Churchill interrupted. "Bloody hell, I've received reports that his staff must continually remind him that the Germans are the enemy, not me, and *that's* after we've welcomed him, housed him, and financed and armed his Free French Resistance movement. But—" Churchill leaned forward to emphasize his point. "He's the only French officer at any level who escaped France, came to England, and began immediately rallying his people to resist the Nazis with everything in them. His followers number in the hundreds of thousands, and he already has ships and planes. In France, his fighters carry out acts of sabotage routinely, and they've helped our escaped POWs get out of the country." He took a puff on his cigar and let it out. "We need him and his organization."

Roosevelt listened attentively, and when Churchill had finished, he chuckled. "All right, Winston, you win again. Let's invite him."

Now the prime minister chuckled while removing his cigar from his lips. "I will, sir, and I can only hope he accepts."

January 23, 1943

Marrakech, Morocco

The two statesmen sat on the flat rooftop terrace of the house in Marrakech, watching as the blood-red sun glistened off the snow-covered peaks stretching across the horizon. On a small table in front of them, a servant had placed a silver tea set of Moorish design. The scent of mint tea wafted on a gentle breeze.

For a time, neither man spoke, both leaning back in their seats and taking deep draughts on their cigars as they contemplated the magnificent scenery. At last, Roosevelt broke the silence. He slapped his leg by way of indicating their emaciated state, rendered that way by the onslaught of polio years earlier.

"That was a good conference. We got a lot done."

Churchill agreed with a nod of his head.

"Getting up on this rooftop was a struggle," Roosevelt said, "but definitely worth the effort." He blew smoke circles and watched them dissipate in the air.

Churchill nodded. "The desert certainly has an effect." He chuckled. "It influenced General Clark in the way he handled the Frenchmen there in Algiers."

"It did at that. That's what I like about him. He goes in wailing away and doesn't pull punches. And a good thing too, or we'd have been fighting both the Germans *and* the French. As it was, we gained a whole army and a lot of territory with hardly a shot fired."

"We didn't make as much progress at the conference as we'd hoped for," Churchill said. "With the setbacks since then, the invasion of Europe this year looks doubtful to me."

Roosevelt frowned. "I'm afraid you might be right, but don't say that too loudly just yet. My senior military staff would have conniptions."

"They'll figure it out," Churchill replied, taking two fresh cigars from his jacket pocket and offering one to Roosevelt. "It's all a matter of resources and logistics," he said after they had both lit up. "Your army's been blooded. When decisions were made back before Operation Torch, it had not been." He settled back in his chair and blew smoke rings. "At least we're now agreed on the next major objective: Sicily. Preparing for that will require building up our manpower and logistics capabilities. That island is the logical target since it commands both sides of the Mediterranean. Anyone with an atlas can see that. We can't bypass it and leave a large German force in our rear."

"I agree," Roosevelt replied. "We've chosen the right commanding general for the invasion of Sicily, but you surprised us by even suggesting that action. It would be the first large-scale operation aimed at Europe since the fall of France. Resources are scarce, and the enemy is entrenched. My staff was opposed to it at first, but once again"—Roosevelt cast a wry glance at Churchill—"you persuaded us that the island is the springboard for invading Italy."

Churchill pondered carefully before responding. "I assure you that my glibness did not win the argument. The force of its logic did. We all came to the same conclusion, that we're not ready for a full-on invasion of Europe. More soldiers, weapons, war machines, and supplies must be assembled, not to mention we need more combat experience among the ranks. Sicily is a place where we can assemble and deploy all of that on a smaller scale while forwarding our overall strategy of taking the fight to the Germans in Europe."

Roosevelt frowned as if searching for a pertinent response. At last, he said, "Stalin won't be pleased. He's been raging for a cross-channel invasion since the beginning, and he makes a point, perhaps a valid one, that our forces will be greeted as a liberating force, aided by the French people."

"I'm sure he's correct in that latter respect," Churchill replied, "but we must have already established air superiority over Europe, brought over the right kind of landing craft in sufficient numbers, stockpiled supplies and equipment to sustain the invasion after the initial drive, and we must be prepared to pursue across France. We're not there yet, and we won't be in the next two months, much less the next year. But we have built those conditions for a more limited objective in Sicily, which is itself a necessary target to command the Mediterranean. The armada we amass and the fighting force to be carried there will be the largest ever assembled in human history."

Roosevelt waved a hand impatiently. "I know, I know, and the decision's already been made. In any event, Eisenhower did a phenomenal job in re-taking North Africa, and I'm sure he'll do equally well with Operation Husky in Sicily."

"Yes, well, he's got General Alexander to do his planning," Churchill interjected. "I'm sure that, together, they'll produce a strategy that will get the job done."

"With sound execution, I agree," Roosevelt responded impatiently. "And with our agreement to conduct Operation Husky, the notion that you're running me is reinforced."

Churchill sat forward in his seat to face the president directly. "Rubbish. No serious thinker would believe that." He chomped on his cigar and leaned further toward the president. "I'm sure the Axis perceives Sicily's strategic importance the same way we do. If they don't, they'll get an inkling of our intentions when we assemble our armada and a hundred and sixty thousand troops on North Africa's coast. But Hitler must be made to believe that we intend to strike western Greece and the island of Sardinia, and to follow on by invading southern France. Otherwise, he'll reinforce Sicily with reserves transferred from France."

Churchill continued, "We'll have to use sleight of hand to get him to shift his forces to Greece instead. It shouldn't be that difficult. According to our reports out of Bletchley, Hitler and his high command feel vulnerable in the Balkans. They believe that if we push there with the help of the Yugoslav Resistance, we could drive through and link up with the Soviets."

The president nodded. "That's a fiendish dilemma. How do you intend to accomplish the deception?"

Churchill smiled devilishly and blew out a smoke ring. "By inserting a man who never was."

Roosevelt regarded him sharply and waited for the prime minister to continue.

"We're going to play to German weaknesses." Churchill let out another puff of smoke and went on. "Bletchley has identified 'wishfulness' and 'yesmanship' as prevalent shortcomings within German intelligence. If their high command demands information they don't have, their staff will invent reports. If the senior levels see contradictory intelligence, they'll believe what suits their pre-formed conclusions. We'll exploit Hitler's wishfulness and his subordinates' yesmanship. They will participate in making our deception work."

Roosevelt pulled his cigar from his mouth and exhaled a puff of smoke. "I get all of that, but what specifically do you have in mind?"

Churchill regarded the president with furrowed brows. "We already have engineers fabricating a bogus army in the eastern Mediterranean; we've turned captured German agents who now feed false information to their *Abwehr* handlers; we're implementing orders for false troop movements, transmitting fake radio traffic, recruiting Greek interpreters and officers; and we're requisitioning Greek maps and currency. All of that is to suggest that we intend to assault the Peloponnese. And—" Once again, Churchill delivered a wicked smile. "We plan for a cherry on the top of this cake."

Roosevelt cast the prime minister a dubious glance. "Please explain."

Churchill did, and when he had finished, the president guffawed, genuinely amused. "Winston, if you can pull that off..." He reached across and slapped the prime minister's shoulder. Then his smile faded. "The other momentous decision from Casablanca is our condition for ending this war: unconditional surrender by the Germans and the Japanese."

Churchill acceded with a grunt, but otherwise did not respond. The president remained silent a moment, and then said, "You know, with everything going on at Casablanca, we never had the opportunity to speak of Tube Alloys or the situation in Norway. We should at least touch on it before we say farewell for now. Can you bring me up to speed?"

Churchill nodded sagely. "The subject had to come up, but we should define our terms. Tube Alloy refers to our own British effort to develop an atomic bomb, which is now joined with yours in the Manhattan Project. I heard that it's been moved to one of your western states—New Mexico, I believe. I think what you're asking about are our operations in Norway to prevent Hitler from getting the bomb first."

Roosevelt affirmed with a nod. "I heard of some tragedies in that regard. I'm sorry."

Churchill shrugged and sighed. "The losses always sadden me; the self-sacrifice of our young is magnificent."

Roosevelt regarded him compassionately. "Tell me about it."

Churchill stared into the desert as he continued. "We had sent an advance party, Operation Grouse, to a place called the Hardangervidda in Norway. That's a vast plateau high in the mountains between Oslo and Bergen. Dreadful conditions, especially in the dead of winter. It was a party of five Norwegian commandos that we trained. They know that country like you and I know our gardens. Their objective was to destroy the heavy-water production facility at Vemork."

The prime minister stared sadly into the evening twilight, and for a moment, he did not speak. "It was a debacle, Franklin, a terrible mess. They were only supposed to be there a week or so before the main body of British commandos of Operation Freshman was to land via towed gliders. But the weather kept being so fierce that the operation was postponed repeatedly, and the Grouse group was there for weeks with hardly any provisions at the beginning of what turned out to be one of the most severe winters on record in Norway. God only knows how they've survived. Then when the gliders' towing aircraft finally made it through, the pilots couldn't see the ground party's lights despite flying right over them. One of the flights turned back to England. The other crash-landed miles away from the target area."

He took a deep breath and sighed. "We lost them all, the entire lot of commandos. We learned from a local farmer that some in the crash-landing group were killed instantly. Others were badly wounded. All the live ones ended up in the hands of the *Gestapo* with no medical care, and after torture, they were executed, and their bodies tossed into a ditch and covered over."

He became silent once more, and the president turned to him. "What about the plane that turned back? Did it arrive safely home?"

Churchill grunted. "It did, but the glider did not. The towing cable iced up and snapped, and the glider plunged into the North Sea. We found no survivors."

Roosevelt leaned forward and touched Churchill's arm. "I'm sorry, Winston. Losing good soldiers is always hard. What's the status now?"

The prime minister pulled himself from a somber reverie. "Oh, the original chaps of Grouse are still there preparing for the next try. We've changed the name of their operation to Swallow."

"They're still there? Have you got supplies to them?"

"Very little. We don't know how they're surviving in the winter storms, blizzards, and sub-zero weather. But we hear from them over the radio. They remain in good spirits, ready and able to carry out their part of the next mission."

Roosevelt shook his head in wonder. "They're defending their homes, Winston. That's the key."

"You're right, Franklin, and they don't even know the stakes."

"So, when is the next try?"

"As soon as the weather clears enough to insert another commando group, Operation Gunnerside. This time, they're all Norwegian, and there are only five of them. Swallow and Gunnerside will join together to carry out the attack."

Roosevelt squinted as he studied Churchill closely. "That's only eleven men. Can they do it?"

Churchill took in a deep breath. "They must," he said. "That heavy water and its production facility must be destroyed. Hitler cannot be allowed to get an atomic bomb."

Roosevelt blew out a deep breath and nodded. "And meanwhile, we still have North Africa to contend with, and so far our boys are not doing so well."

"Be patient with them, Franklin. They'll come through. It takes time to develop battle-toughened soldiers."

"I know," Roosevelt said, clearly angry, although not at the prime minister. He spun one wheel of his wheelchair to face Churchill directly. "But how many will lose their lives?"

Both men lapsed into silence as the sun disappeared over the horizon and darkness settled. "You're headed to Turkey from here?" Roosevelt queried.

"I am. I'm meeting in secret with President İsmet İnönü to try to convince him to come into the war on the side of the Alliance."

"Do you think that's wise? You and I have long shared the opinion that Turkey's neutrality is good for the Allies. It blocks the Axis from Middle East oil reserves. The *Wehrmacht* has a strong presence next door in Bulgaria. If Turkey enters the war with a battered army, Bulgaria will do the honors on behalf of Hitler to overrun that country. It's been war-torn for years with civil wars and the like. A defeat on that flank could undo a lot of gain and be disastrous for us."

"In light of Axis victories through last year, I'm re-evaluating my position," Churchill replied. "Turkey keeps a good-sized army and air force, and if they opened a new front in the Balkans, that would be a good thing.

"And, if we can convince İnönü to at least let us base airfields there, that'll help us build air superiority over Greece and the Balkans. It's worth a try. We'd be able to come at Hitler from all angles."

"I don't see much chance of success, and I still worry about Turkey being overrun," Roosevelt said. "İnönü is sympathetic to his people's war fatigue. He's done everything possible to stay out of this one. Joining the Allies will enrage the Germans and invite Bulgaria's attack."

"We'll offer İnönü financial and military aid," Churchill countered. "As an ally, if he's attacked, we'd be obligated to do all in our power to help defend Turkey."

"Stretching our resources further," Roosevelt said with a skeptical note. "I suppose it's worth a try, as you say. We'll confer again if İnönü looks like he might entertain the idea."

"We'll do that, aside from the aid I can offer on my own authority, of course."

7

February 19, 1943
Kasserine Pass, Sahara Desert, Tunisia

Corporal Zack Littlefield stared in horrified shock at the field ahead of him through his rangefinder. All he saw were swirling clouds of sand-colored dust, but then he heard his tank commander shout for the second time from his cupola on the right of the Sherman M4's seventy-five millimeter, short-barreled gun, "Tank, twelve-thirty, three hundred yards, fire at will."

The high anxiety in the commander's voice could not be camouflaged, and it spurred Zack to faster, nervous action. He traversed the turret slightly clockwise as his tank continued its headlong charge through the eastern mouth of the Kasserine Pass heading toward its objective at Faid Pass. The sounds of large rounds hissing through the air and massive explosions shaking the earth all around broke his concentration, and as Zack searched for the target identified by his commander, he thought he saw the silhouette of a Panzer Mark4 in a break between rolls of thick dust.

He fired. His tank lurched from the recoil and continued to roll, but peering through the rangefinder, he saw no tell-tale flame, and he heard no explosion. He had missed.

He had no time for a second shot. The next explosion he heard was up close and the tank spun to the right and careened to a halt.

"The track's been hit," the driver called.

"Get out," the commander called, and just as he did, a burst of machine gun fire caught him in the face. Below, the driver slumped in his seat.

"Let's go," Zack called to the loader. He reached above, opened the hatch, and spilled himself over the rim, hoping for a soft landing. The loader followed but landed on his feet and ran. By the time Zack looked up, the soldier had disappeared into the dust.

Lying on the ground, Zack shook off his shock. Then he leaped to his feet, crouching by the tank that now spurted flames through the turret. With no time to evaluate a course of action, he ran a zigzag pattern as automatic gunfire erupted small sprays of gritty sand all around him. Reaching a small ridge, he dove over its crest and hugged the ground. Then, below his sliver of concealment, he listened as the battle raged on, unabated.

Zack spat the sand from his mouth and tried to look around the edge of the small desert protrusion. The ground trembled and tank engines roared in the distance on both sides of him. Those to his left were what remained of Sherman M4 tank formations; those on the right were German Panzers. On a ridge overlooking American positions, 88mm anti-tank guns still discharged devastating direct-fire rounds at fleeing American forces.

Zack wondered how long he could remain still and unnoticed in his current position. He had no idea if his buddy, the loader, had also survived. Only seconds after exiting the tank, another direct hit from the anti-tank guns on the ridge had finished it off. Now, black smoke curled away into the sky, and Zack saw in horror that the scene he had lived through had been replicated across a vast battlefield scattered with many M4s and a smaller number of Panzers.

He could not fathom the circumstances that had led to this turn of events. Even a green soldier understood that stirring speeches did not win wars. His instinct told him that whoever had planned this headlong charge through the Kasserine Pass had studied neither the terrain nor the comparative capabilities and limitations of the enemy.

Zack understood fully his own constraints. Sixteen years younger than Josh Littlefield, he idolized his older brother and had wanted to be like him, and even follow him into the US Naval Academy. However, Zack's talents were in athletics, not in academics, and his grades lagged those of his brother. The disparity in their academic abilities convinced Zack that he would not qualify for the academy.

Nevertheless, when Josh would come home on leave before the war, Zack listened rapturously to his brother's descriptions of flying and air tactics. Josh also talked of what he had learned about leadership, and what it took to be a good leader.

Despite Zack's deficit in technical subjects, he had a good mind and absorbed everything his brother told him. Bigger than most of his peers, he was a high-school football coach's dream: a team player, respectful, willing to push himself, and immensely coachable. And he applied lessons learned from Josh.

"Shoot, move, and communicate," Josh had told him. "All tactics come down to those three words. Doesn't matter if you're in the air, on the ground, or playing football, if you can do those three things, you can survive and win."

In high school, Zack applied Josh's advice on the football field and excelled as quarterback in his senior year. Zack was on his way to receiving offers for athletic scholarships from major universities when the Japanese attacked Pearl Harbor.

All thoughts of a future at college or an inkling of a later career in the pros had disappeared in a flash, and Zack joined the legions of men standing in line to volunteer for active duty. Self-doubts about his technical aptitudes steered him away from the navy or the Army Air Corps. He chose the army and tanks for the simple reasoning that if he could throw a football to his intended receiver, he ought to be able to hit a target with a tank. He eagerly told the recruiter his background and said, "I want to be a tank gunner."

Now, with his face scrunched into the hard-packed sand, he realized how naïve he had been. Once his vehicle was hit, and he found himself alone on the ground in the low-rolling hillocks of the high desert, he became a poorly trained infantryman with only the skills learned at basic training. He recalled letters he had received from his cousins, Paul and Jeremy Littlefield. Josh had told Zack in a rare telephone conversation after their mother's death last November that both cousins were officers. The call had occurred while Josh had been ensconced at Algiers as part of Operation Torch. In their letters, the two Brits had expressed condolences at the family's loss and offered encouragement as Zack prepared to enlist in the army. They both closed with the advice, "Keep your head down."

In training, Zack had heard the same lesson. He recalled a grizzled drill sergeant bellowing, "Get behind something that will stop a bullet. And if you can't do that, get under or behind something where the enemy can't see you. Don't look over a log. Look around the end it."

No logs were anywhere on this battlefield, nothing but scrub brush and patches of bare sand for hundreds of miles. Josh had ridden perched on his tank over the hard, crusty parts of the desert on the approach to this position for days, and he knew well that aspect of the terrain. And he had learned of the soft-sand parts of the desert too, where tanks would bog down if the monstrous machines ventured into them.

He peered around the end of the hillock again. The battle had paused. US tanks were beating a hurried retreat. German Panzers appeared to be re-grouping and preparing to pursue, which would surely bring them his way.

Zack took quick mental stock of his situation. His only weapons were his sidearm and a small knife on his utility belt. Aside from that, he had a canteen half full of water and a melted chocolate bar in his shirt pocket that had been part of this morning's rations for the day.

Slowly, careful to make no noise or draw attention by rapid movement, he slid down the gentle slope backwards on his belly. The ground beneath the scrubs was crusty, good for supporting vehicular traffic but not for hiding infantrymen. But when Zack had descended far enough that he was fairly sure he would not be seen by the Germans until they crossed the ridge, he turned and surveyed the ground behind him. Near the floor of the shallow gorge, several offshoots formed a series of low ridges topped with scrub brush.

From over the crest where he had been, Zack heard Panzer engines revving up. A change in their tenor warned that they had shifted into gear and were on the move. Within minutes, they would cross that ridge.

He pulled himself to his feet and ran the rest of the way downhill crouched over at the waist, noticing as he went that the sand was turning a lighter color and his feet sank in it. Reaching the bottom, he headed for the first offshoot and ducked behind it. The ground there was of the soft-sand variety.

Zack flattened himself against its surface and listened. When he was satisfied that the Panzers had not yet passed by his original position, he burrowed, and did not stop until his entire body was covered and he had blowholes allowing him to breathe fresh air.

Within minutes, the Panzers passed by on both sides of him, staying on the hard-crusted higher ground. He lay still, not daring the slightest movement until a seeming eternity had passed and all was quiet aside from the sound of a steady desert wind. Then he raised his head cautiously. Sand streamed into his eyes and the smell of spent ammunition still lingered in the air. He wiped the sand away, not daring to use the precious water in his canteen to rinse his eyes—he had no idea when he might be able to replenish his meager reserve. At this time of year, the air was cold and wet, and his uniform was still damp with sweat from his earlier exertion. Fortunately, he had grabbed his utility belt with his poncho as he had spilled out of the doomed tank.

When he was finally able to sit up and look around despite the rough scratching of granules plaguing his eyelids, he pulled the poncho around him and surveyed his surroundings. His heart sank. The vast desert looked just as it had while he was riding on the tank, but the context had changed. Then, he had ridden on a diesel-powered vehicle with his buddies on their way to "kick Nazi ass" in a formation of tanks that was part of a larger element that had deployed men by the hundreds of thousands into North Africa.

Only a few hours ago, his belly had been full, his thirst quenched. He had encountered fear on occasion over the past two months as his unit had closed onto the battlefield in fits and spurts, delayed by winter weather, but his misgivings had been subdued by bravado resulting from the certainty that the strong arm of America, equipped with the most modern weaponry and fresh troops, would romp over Axis armies, and send Erwin Rommel, the so-called Desert Fox, packing. The British Eighth Army had defeated Rommel in the second battle at El Alamein somewhere in Libya to the east, and the legend was retreating west toward Tunis ahead of the pursuing Brits.

Much of Zack's initial bravado and that of his battle-buddies had worn off during the ebb and flow of battle over the last few days as both opposing armies attempted to dominate the Kasserine Pass and thus control the main route north to Tunis. As Zack's company commander had briefed, the idea was for British troops to press their pursuit of the *Wehrmacht* from the east in a "Race for Tunis" and trap it there against the sea. Meanwhile, the new American 1st Armored Division, to which Zack's unit belonged, would close in across the Dorsal Mountains from the west in the M4 Shermans, the tanks that had proved decisive for the Brits at El Alamein. The division would maneuver around the Vichy French troops in the south, cut the supply lines north through the Kasserine Pass, and close the trap at Tunis. However, this was the 1st Armored Division's first combat, and they were going up against the most legendary of German commanders, Field Marshal Erwin Rommel.

Winter weather had not cooperated. During evenings at bivouacs along the five-hundred-mile march, Zack and his buddies had chuckled over letters from home that commiserated with their plight in dealing with blazing hot Saharan weather, and they informed their families that the climate in Tunisia at this time of year was biting cold and wet. Additionally, the farther east the Americans pushed, the longer their supply lines stretched, thus slowing their progress toward the enemy.

The trek across the winter desert and mountainous terrain of the Dorsal ranges during December and January had dampened their illusions of invincibility, and heavy rains had brought the war in North Africa to a pause. Although the north-south roads to Tunis were good, the east-west routes on which the 1st Armored Division traversed were not. Those latter roads wended their way through the mountains and constrained the movement of the opposing armies, which had reduced in size over the months such that neither could engage in major offensive operations. Small units on both sides guarded strategic high ground.

As Allied forces extended themselves over twelve hundred miles from Casablanca to Algiers, the *Luftwaffe* enjoyed air superiority by transferring huge numbers of fighters and bombers from Sicily to airfields near Tunis. Zack lost count of the number of times he had been forced to jump headlong from the side of his tank as ME-109s and Stukas descended from on high and strafed, bombed, and otherwise harassed US formations. And he recalled trudging past makeshift airfields where crews and mechanics dug the landing gear of Allied fighters and bombers out of thick mud in a push to secure the skies farther and farther east.

Word reached American troops that the Germans had transferred to Tunis the battle-hardened 10th Panzer Division of the newly formed 5th Panzer Army, commanded by square-jawed Prussian General Hans-Jürgen von Arnim. It now held ground on a line extending south of Tunis for two hundred miles, effectively controlling most of Tunisia.

Rommel had taken command of all of Von Arnim's units except for one, and he mounted a counterattack that succeeded in breaking through the Kasserine and thrust nearly sixty miles beyond, nearly to Tebessa, site of a huge American supply depot and an intricate bunker headquarters built by Lieutenant General Lloyd Fredendall, commanding general of II Corps, 1st Armored Division's higher command.

Two thousand American infantrymen now guarded the entrance of the floor at the western end of Kasserine Pass, supported by four tanks, thirty-six anti-tank destroyers, and eighteen field artillery pieces. The onslaught that came at them was four times the infantry strength, twenty-five times the tank strength, and nearly quadruple the number of field artillery guns.

The German *blitzkrieg* at Kasserine Pass was overwhelming. The 88 mm Flak36 guns, with their 4.9 meter barrels, high muzzle velocity, and long range, unleashed barrages that immediately killed the four American tanks.

Making matters worse, while the Sherman M4s carried seventy-five-millimeter cannons, their barrels were short and lacked the punch of the same caliber weapons of the longer barrels of the German Mark4 and Mark5 tanks, both of which were in the Germans' initial assault.

This morning, the Americans attempted an assault through the pass. The Panzer divisions had waited in ambush in the high ground on both sides of the eastern mouth of Kasserine with a full view of the American charge. They had picked off their targets one by one as the Americans, their own dust blocking their vision, fired back blindly until they reversed course and fled the battlefield.

As Zack sat in the shallow depression he had dug, his feet still buried in sand, he weighed bleak alternatives as he pondered the rumors that had circulated among the troops before the battle. He had heard that since the Torch landings three months ago, Allied warships had sunk nearly a quarter of German supplies sailing to North Africa; and the southern sector of the German front in Eastern Europe was in such dire straits that all their reinforcements were sent to bolster the assault on Stalingrad at the expense of Rommel's campaigns in North Africa, aside from Von Arnim's troops.

Those rumors provided little consolation for Zack. He had ridden over the muddy roads, encountered the breakdowns, and waited for hours with other dirty GIs to receive rations from late, ever-longer supply convoys bogged down from traveling over the same rough roads. Emblematic of the logistical difficulties, Zack recalled seeing a jeep's replacement engine being carried forward on the back of a camel. That memory was replaced this morning with the horrific image of his tank commander's head exploding in a red spray under a torrent of lead from a *Wehrmacht* machine gun. That fearsome sight was one that he knew would haunt him for the rest of his days.

This was supposed to have been a relatively easy maneuver. The British had pushed from the east, and the US from the west supported by the French in the southwest. But what Zack had heard of the Vichy French soldiers was unimpressive. They were strung-together remnants of the French colonial army from Morocco and Algeria, and they used antiquated weaponry left over from the Great War. Many of them rode on donkeys and mules. Since their chief function was to protect colonists from local insurrectionists, they had no tanks or anti-tank guns. Nevertheless, scuttlebutt from above attested to their tactical skill and reliability in combat.

Meanwhile, in the lead-up to this morning's battle, estimates of the Axis' current North Africa troop strength that Zack had heard bandied about were daunting: roughly eighty thousand German and twenty-six thousand Italian soldiers in the vicinity of Tunis. And a few days earlier, word reached the ground level that Rommel and his troops had vacated Libya and were conducting an orderly withdrawal back to Tunis, with the British in pursuit as fast as their supply lines allowed.

Zack's mind worked through the implications. The result of the German maneuvers must be that an even greater force than previously estimated would face the Allies. On this late February morning, he had seen only the spearhead.

When the battle had opened suddenly and with such fury, German troops, tanks, tank-destroyers, artillery pieces, and *Luftwaffe* fighters and bombers seemed to have appeared everywhere at once in massive numbers. And the Germans used cover and concealment effectively, hiding themselves from view until the moment of attack. Any illusions that Zack harbored regarding German competence in the field evaporated with the opening volleys that quickly annihilated the second American charge.

The sound of an engine alerted him that he still lived in immediate mortal danger. Hunger pangs further reminded him that many hours had passed since his last meal, and he had only his chocolate bar, melted and pressed into a gooey mess in his shirt pocket. A parched throat and dry mouth led him to wonder if he dared take a few drops of his now precious water. Staying put was not an option.

In late afternoon, Zack crept back to the top of the ridge that had hidden him that morning and peered around the end of the small protrusion at its crest. Only yards away, his tank still smoldered, its turret blackened with soot, the main gun sagging, and the tracks wrenched from their sprockets and roadwheels.

Glancing beyond the wreckage, he sucked in his breath at the sight of utter devastation, the plight of his tank replicated across a field of burnt shrubs and whisps of smoke rising above mounds of armored debris. In plain sight, charred bodies of soldiers lay naked in ghastly contortions strewn across the battlefield. Large black flies swarmed over them, and the smell of burned flesh rode a rising wind. Local tribesmen worked their way across the plain toward Zack, stripping the dead of their clothing and anything perceived to be of value while vultures circled overhead.

Zack retched, his breakfast hurled through his mouth and nostrils by an involuntary gut-level spasm. The nausea lingered, and he vomited again, now unable to unsee the horror over the ridge despite that he had slid down a few feet from the crest. His lungs heaved and he coughed uncontrollably as gastric acid and bits of undigested food caught in his throat.

Wrenching his water from his utility belt, Zack rolled onto his back, unscrewing the cap on the canteen with mounting desperation as his gullet burned deeper. He poured the cooling liquid down his throat and immediately coughed it up again. Then, deepening his despair, he realized that all the water was gone.

Resting with the gritty surface biting into his elbows, he let his head fall backward, his helmet just touching the ground as he choked back sobs. Gradually, his breathing slowed to a normal rhythm, his mind cleared, and he could think logically.

Survival instinct overcame the revulsion of what he had seen. Water, food, weapons, and ammunition lay close by in the gear carried by his fallen comrades not yet picked over by the tribesmen. If he were to live, he must secure enough to sustain himself until he could evade back to friendly lines.

Waiting until the sun cast long shadows, Zack crawled back to the top of the ridge. Steeling himself against the horror cloaking the landscape, he peered around the end of the sandy ridge. Selecting the most likely clump of burned-out rubble, he began a slow belly-crawl across the hard scrabble of the winter desert.

8

March 6, 1943
Tebessa, Algeria

Zack squatted on the ground in the front row of a large crowd of soldiers near the entrance to the byzantine bunker that Lieutenant General Lloyd Fredendall had built as II Corps headquarters into the steep hills near the village of Bekkaria, just inside Algeria's border with Tunis. General Eisenhower had visited there three days earlier, and word was that he had been less than impressed with a weak command environment; that he was distraught at the defeat at Kasserine Pass; and that as a result, a new commanding general was taking over the corps, one Zack had never heard of by the name of George Patton.

Word had spread wildly on the general's arrival that he breathed fire and kicked ass. He had rousted officers out of their bunks and informed them that they were expected to dress neatly and with neckties at all times. He expected soldiers to be clean and disciplined, and he made clear that he led an army that he expected to fight. No more retreat.

As Zack waited for the general to appear on a makeshift stage, he could not help reliving the events of the past two weeks. Fortunately, night had fallen before the scavengers had progressed to his side of the battlefield. Alone and crouching behind gutted tanks and low-crawling between positions, he had located two canteens of water, a few cans of C-rations, a serviceable M-1 Garand, several bandoliers of 30-06 cartridge clips, a field jacket, and additional rounds for his sidearm. He dared not look at the faces of dead soldiers he passed or searched for fear of gagging again, but he muttered a quiet thank you as he moved on. Then he headed for the same ridge where he had taken refuge initially, and feeling his way slowly in the dark, he made his way back to the vicinity of where he had previously buried himself in the sand.

He expected the night to be cold, so he put on the field jacket and dug into the embankment. Then, careful to muffle any noise under the poncho, he opened a can of spaghetti and meatballs with his P-38, and ate as much as he could stomach. Visions of the day muted his appetite. He drank sparingly.

At dawn, he woke suddenly, alerted to the sounds of engines. He steeled himself to be calm, wondering which side of the war they belonged to. Then a US Army jeep appeared, silhouetted on the ridge, and soldiers stepped out and stood with their backs to him while they observed the battlefield.

Blinking, unsure of what he was seeing, Zack hesitated.

The two soldiers on the near side of the jeep walked around to the other side, and then the four proceeded across the field and out of Zack's sight.

Zack tossed off the poncho, gathered it in a wad, picked up his rifle and other equipment, kicked sand over the C-ration can, and stumbled up the rise. Just short of the crest, he halted, lowered himself onto his stomach, and crawled forward with his rifle, leaving his other things behind. Then, peering around the sand protrusion, he looked across the floor of Kasserine Pass.

The burned-out hulks and dead bodies were still there. Their combined stench, mixed with the lingering smell of spent munitions, was now stifling. But among carcasses of men and war machines were myriad jeeps and ambulances with teams of soldiers in US uniforms picking up the dead on stretchers and carrying them to waiting vehicles.

Wondering if he was in a stupor and seeing a mirage, Zack watched for a few minutes. Then, he clambered to his feet and staggered over the crest toward the jeep. He tried to call out but found he had no voice, and when he arrived next to the vehicle, he collapsed in shock. Vaguely, he heard someone shout, "Hey, we got a live one."

He awoke in the medical facility deep inside the bunker at Tebessa. A medic attended to him, ensuring that he was hydrated and comfortable, and by degrees, Zack improved. Within a day, he was on his feet and taking short walks into the halls.

"What is this place?" he asked the medic.

"Corps headquarters," came the reply. "The CG says he built it to get soldiers out of the cold, wet weather, but we've noticed that he never leaves it, even when the battle's on."

Zack registered the comment but did not care to dig into further details. Vaguely recalling the jeep and the ambulances at the battlefield, he did not grasp how that could have happened with opposing forces so close by. "How did I get here?"

"Rommel offered a truce so we could collect our dead and wounded," the medic explained. "He's known for doing that. Decent of him."

A personnel officer came to visit. He had Zack's personal information, taken from his dog tags while he was unconscious. The news concerning Zack's unit was all bad. It had been wiped out.

"We're assigning you to the 601st Tank Destroyer Battalion," the officer said. "They're not tanks, but they shoot like them. You should pick it up easy enough. They lost some of their people in the first Kasserine battle, including a couple of gunners. You should fit right in."

Zack listened in further shock. His whole unit gone. Guys who had been through basic training with him, dead. Men he had spent weeks with on rolling Atlantic waves while they crossed the ocean on packed troopships, never to be seen again. Friends, pals he had entrusted with last letters to be sent home should he die in battle not only gone, but so were the letters he was to have sent on their behalf.

He sniffed to block the tears, but they came unbidden. The personnel officer, a lieutenant a few years older than Zack, clapped his shoulder. "It's all right, Corporal. Tears are part of war."

Zack rose painfully to his feet, almost at attention. "Tell me where to report."

Major General Patton strode across the stage, and Zack could not decide at first whether to be impressed. Tall at six feet two inches, he wore riding breeches over polished knee-high riding boots, a brown, waist-length jacket tailored to his trim figure, and around his waist was a leather belt with a gold buckle and a holster with a pistol.

The sidearm caught Zack's eye, a Colt .45 single-action revolver with Patton's initials clearly engraved in black lettering. Other men sitting around Zack also noticed it, some whispering that the white grips were made of ivory.

"He's sending a message," someone muttered. "'Don't mess with me.'"

"Message received," another man said, snickering.

Zack had seen the posturing of other military leaders as they took command. Some were arrogant, others loquacious, and most quietly confident. None that he had seen, however, addressed men who had just lost devastating battles and were about to face yet again the privations of constant motion over rugged terrain while their enemy lobbed large rounds that whistled through the air and exploded within yards, creating craters to their left, right, front, and rear. That enemy was intent on killing them and had already succeeded in killing their battle-buddies on a massive scale.

Quiet fell over the men as Patton stood poised to address them. Zack could not decide whether the pall resulted because of the general's rank or from his personal presence. The troops knew that Fredendall had been relieved of command. That a three-star should be thus humiliated would create its own sense of awe, not only for the event but also for the replacement. But Zack saw something different with this general, and he was sure that his fellow soldiers saw it too.

A light gleamed from Patton's eyes as he gazed across his new command. He stood straight, shoulders back, looking serene while he slapped a riding crop into his left hand. His oval face carried a stern expression under a polished combat helmet liner with two stars affixed to the front, and yet a hint of a grin formed at the edges of his mouth.

"Men," he announced, his surprisingly high-pitched voice ringing out over the assembled warriors. "You got your asses kicked."

The pall deepened as the men stared straight ahead, hardly daring to look at each other.

Patton took a deep breath. "That's not going to happen again." He took a few steps across the stage while he let the thought settle. "You taught those Kraut bastards a few things," he continued. "They rolled on through the Kasserine like you weren't even there, but when they got to the other side, they found fighting soldiers blocking their way to their objective, this depot, and headquarters." He spread his palms apart and looked beyond the men to the portal of the bunker and the military vehicles assembled in close proximity. "If they had captured this place, we might be beating a dusty getaway across the desert, bound for home with our tails tucked in."

The general paused and tilted his head while looking out sideways, catching the eye of individual soldiers, including Zack, who caught himself thinking that Patton spoke to him personally. Then the general pivoted to face his audience head-on and held his right fist high in the air, clutching his riding crop.

"But you stopped the Hun," he boomed. "You beat the Desert Fox."

Silence more pressured than any Zack had ever experienced descended. Then a cheer broke out, soldiers jumping to their feet to roar their approval.

Patton stood stock-still, watching while a slow grin spread across his face. He pumped his fist in the air until the cheering reached a crescendo, then he waited, his hands held behind his back as the celebration quieted and the soldiers once again sat cross-legged in the desert sand. His face became serious again.

"We won't win this war with blinders, so let's not kid ourselves. Rommel nearly had us. He thought so, and so did"—he interrupted himself as if searching for words and cleared his throat—"the previous management of Tebessa."

Patton swung around and stared into the desert toward the north. "I don't know why the Fox is pulling back. He was poised to attack again, and our defenses were worn down. But suddenly, he started withdrawing, that-away." He pointed with his crop. "That's okay. We wish his troops bon voyage and a safe return to their families to live out their days gardening, feeding the chickens, making babies—" He joined his men as laughter punctuated his comments. "If they don't do that, they're gonna wish they had, cuz otherwise, we're gonna grab 'em by the throat, we're gonna kick them in their asses, an' we're gonna send 'em to holy kingdom come."

The crowd was once again on its feet, roaring approval with fists pumping the air. The general waited for the men to settle down, and then he continued.

"Let's not take anything away from Field Marshal Rommel. He's a brilliant strategist and tactician, a worthy opponent. But let me remind you that the Brits beat him decisively at El Alamein, and then chased him clear across the Libyan desert so that we had to deal with him." A mischievous smile crossed Patton's face. "Of course, Monty had to use our Sherman tanks to get the job done."

He chuckled and strode a few steps. "You all know who Monty is, right? General Montgomery? He's that Brit fella who likes to strut around wearing a black beret with fancy silver stuff, a kerchief around his neck, and that silly growth of hair under his nose." He laughed. "Of course, no *real* soldier would posture like that."

Zack laughed with the crowd at the ironic humor of an officer who was obviously fond of military showmanship. The horrors he had seen receded into the back of his mind.

"Giving credit where credit is due," Patton continued, "the Brits proved that the legend of the Desert Fox was vulnerable. We're going to finish the job." Patton pointed to the southeast. "This morning, Rommel attacked the Brits at Medenine. Apparently, he thought the force there was small and he could prevent a British counterattack on his withdrawal to the north by attacking Monty's crew and driving it back to the sea." He grinned and lowered his voice to a stage whisper. "We were expecting him."

A ripple of laughter spread through the men, and they leaned forward, their faces expectant, eager for the general's every word. "The Brits reinforced their position with US-supplied M-3 tank destroyers and Shermans and let Rommel traipse into an overwhelming ambush. As we speak, he's trying to extricate out of what he got hisself into." He paused and then articulated his next words slowly, individually. "That's where you come in.

"The Fox isn't done yet, not by a long shot. He's got Tiger tanks with him, and in case you haven't seen one, let me tell you about them. They're rolling bunkers, weighing in at fifty-six tons. They're mounted with eighty-eight-millimeter cannons capable of breaching the forward armor of any of our tanks, and they're protected by three feet of steel on the front, making them impervious to most of our weapons."

After he had let that grim thought sink in, he grinned. "But they break down frequently, they eat up a lot of gas, and when they throw a track, their drivers can't jump down and fix it or any other part of the tank. They have to bring in a team of mechanics to get them going again." He paused and leaned forward as if to tell a secret. "Ya don't have to kill one to take it out of the fight. You just have to disable it."

The general pointed south again. "Rommel is trying to escape now, and his only route is through a mountain pass between here and Medenine at a place called El Guettar. The Fox'll be there, count on it. He leads from the front.

"We're going to dig in there, boys, just like he did at the eastern end of Kasserine, and when he comes through with his Tigers, we're going to hit him from the flanks and then from the rear. We're going to hit him high, we're going to hit him low, and then we're going to hit him again."

The men were on their feet again, cheering wildly. Then, Patton pulled himself to full height and his face turned to stone. "One thing we are not going to do is retreat." His stern tone matched his face. "The days of running are over." His voice rang out clearly over the crowd. "II Corps soldiers do not retreat. We advance."

Quiet descended once again on the soldiers as Patton's words sank into their collective psyches, still roiling from the pounding and losses taken at Kasserine. "We know the route they must take. It's much like the eastern end of the Kasserine Pass. We're going there now, and when we arrive, we're going to dig into that hard ground, on both sides, high up. We're going to dig foxholes and tank positions, and we're going to find the best places to put our tank destroyers."

The general paused again, and when he resumed, his tone was grave.

"While you're pounding through those very hard rocks, keep in mind that a pint of sweat will save a gallon of blood. Instead of breaking the corps up into small, unsupported units spread apart by distance, we're going to mass our weapons and kick those Nazi sons o' bitches clean off this continent. We're a team that lives, sleeps, eats, and fights as a team. Individual heroic stuff is pure horseshit."

He cocked his head to one side and peered through narrowed eyes. "I'll tell you my personal philosophy of war, and you might make it yours. That's up to you, but it helps me, and it is this: I'm a soldier, I fight where I'm told, and I win where I fight.

"Keep that in mind. Clear your memories of what went before. That's past. Put thoughts of home and hearth away. They get you killed. Your mind has to be on combat. You're fighting for the guy to your right and left because they're going to keep you alive. When they succeed, you succeed, and doing that will take care of family and home."

Patton stopped, grunted, and looked up at the sun as if suddenly aware that he had become long-winded. "This battle will be pivotal. We win this one, and we win the North Africa campaign. You've beaten the Fox once, and you'll do it again. Have no fear of anything. You're in good hands, and you'll come out of this on top. That's all." With that, and amid the cheers of his soldiers, he walked from the stage.

On returning to his sleeping quarters, Zack found a concerning message waiting for him. His battalion commander wanted to see him. Fearing bad news about Josh or Sherry, he made his way to the battalion headquarters, stopping on the way to confirm with his platoon sergeant and first sergeant that the message was legitimate.

"The commander likes to meet as many soldiers in his battalion as possible," the platoon sergeant told him. "Particularly his gunners, and you're new to the unit." He pursed his lips. "He's a little different, a West Point graduate, but he's from Cuba with a thick accent, so he's hard to understand sometimes."

"How do you say his name?" Zack asked. "I've seen it on papers. The spelling is different too."

The platoon sergeant chuckled. "Yeah, and his first name ain't easy either. His last name is Xiquez, but you pronounce the X like an H. His first name is Arturo, but most of his fellow officers have trouble saying that, so they call him Atcho. That's with a short A and a short O. He's Lieutenant Colonel Xiquez to you, though, so no need to worry about his first name. He's a personable guy, but a stickler for performance. You'll do fine with him."

With some trepidation, Zack presented himself at the battalion head-quarters and was shown into Xiquez' office. "At ease," the commander told him after Zack had reported. "I like to go into combat with men I know, so I try to visit with each one in my unit." He picked up a file on his desk and scanned it. "Your first sergeant told me that your unit was wiped out on the charge through Kasserine Pass."

"Yes, sir." Zack's eyes grew moist, and he coughed as his throat constricted.

Xiquez glanced up at him. "You're holding up well, soldier. We're proud of you." He glanced back down at the paper. "He also told me how you got away. Good thinking. You didn't panic."

At a loss for words, but finding Xiquez not so difficult to understand despite the Cuban accent, Zack merely replied, "Thank you, sir."

"I heard that you also suffered another loss recently," Xiquez said kindly, "that of your mother. That's a tough break. My condolences."

"Thank you, sir. I shipped out to Algeria two days after the funeral. I'll be fine."

Xiquez smiled and indicated a chair. "Have a seat. This needs to be more of a visit than an interview." He chuckled. "My life depends on my men wanting to keep me alive too."

When Zack was seated, Xiquez asked, "Do you have a girl back in New Jersey?"

Zack turned red and held back a smile. "Yes, sir. Sonja. She was my high-school sweetheart, and we were getting serious." He sighed inadvertently. "This looks to be a long war—" He looked away.

"Keep up your spirits, Littlefield. Jody won't get every girl."

Zack laughed quietly, recalling the marching songs from basic training about the figurative Jody who successfully chased after the girlfriends of every deployed soldier. "I hope you're right, sir." He arched his brows as a question entered his mind. "Do you mind if I ask about your having gone to West Point? My brother went to Annapolis—"

"Beat Navy," Xiquez interjected.

Zack smiled. "Of course, sir. I'm Army all the way."

"What's your question?"

"How did you get in there from Cuba? I didn't know it was possible—"

"I was lucky," Xiquez replied. "The US military academies have exchange programs with other countries to build good will. I was fortunate to be accepted and graduated. Quite a few of my countrymen volunteered for the US Army." He laughed. "I got to be an officer because of my classical good looks."

Zack laughed along with the joke, but he noted that the deeply tanned lieutenant colonel was fit, above average height, and indeed bore classical Latin features, including thick, jet-black hair. Xiquez turned serious. "I lost some gunners at Kasserine," he said. "I saw in the brief your first sergeant sent over that, since your recovery, you've familiarized yourself on our tank destroyers and you're an excellent shot with them."

"A fair one, at least, sir."

"Have it your way. Unless you have a valid objection, I'm having you assigned to my headquarters to be the gunner on my vehicle. I need one who can think on his feet, and you demonstrated that. The job comes with perks. You'll be promoted to buck sergeant, but there's a downside too. We'll be a sought-out target because the enemy likes to hit command vehicles, just like we do. What do you say?"

Stunned, Zack sat speechless for a moment. "Of course, sir, if you think I can do it. What about your jeep?"

Xiquez scoffed. "I ride in vehicles with firepower. I'll get plenty of use out of my jeep in other ways. Anyway, I told the companies to send their best for me to interview, and your chain of command sent you, so we'll consider this a done deal. Report to the sergeant major. He'll direct you from there."

9

March 9, 1943
Near Medenine, Tunisia

Wehrmacht Generalmajor Meier, a tall man with a high forehead, narrow face, and strong jaw, regarded his commanding general and mentor, Field Marshal Rommel, with troubled eyes. "What happened, sir?"

Rommel, the legendary field commander who had so dominated international news with his spectacular victories since the invasion of France three years ago, hardly looked beaten despite not being in the best of health. But by the action he had just ordered, the full retreat of his forces back to Tunis, he had tacitly admitted defeat. He smiled wanly at Meier and replied, "Do you want excuses, or the truth?"

Meier declined to respond out of respect. The two men had wandered a distance from the command vehicles and into the desert where they could speak outside the range of listening ears. Despite Rommel's indomitable spirit and military bearing, Meier knew that his commander was very ill. Two years of constant desert combat had taken its toll on the Desert Fox. Exhaustion, a liver infection, jaundice, and low blood pressure had etched deep lines on his face, and he suffered a chronic cough.

"What do you think of the American soldier?" Meier asked after a while.

Rommel chuckled. "You and I had a similar discussion about the British soldier fourteen months ago just after the Japanese invaded Pearl Harbor. When we first came to Africa, the troops we brought were battle-hardened, and the British soldiers were green. But they held us off at Tobruk for months, and by the second battle at El Alamein, they proved themselves in combat. They learned."

He sighed. "The Americans underestimated us. They thought they would roll over us with their Sherman tanks. But advanced technology alone does not win a battle. Perhaps a war, but not a battle."

He paused and gazed across the desert. "I underestimated the Americans. I sensed the indecision of their commanders typical of those new to battle. To borrow one of their expressions, they provided us a 'turkey shoot' in Kasserine, and I expected to roll through their defenses and take their depot at Tebessa with little resistance. But they had placed their defensive units well at the western mouth of the pass and along the route to their corps headquarters, and their soldiers fought hard. They learned fast, just as the British did.

"Now, we face not just blooded troops gaining in combat experience, but also a limitless supply of weapons, equipment, ammunition—" He laughed with a disbelieving tone. "Their soldiers get daily rations of chocolate and fresh cigarettes. And every time we destroy one of their Shermans, ten more show up. And if we disable one, the driver pops out, fixes whatever is wrong, including replacing treads, and the tank is back in the fight. Our tank crews can't do that." He shook his head and sighed. "The *führer* promised me, personally, forty Tiger tanks. That was back in November, and we received none until the 5th Panzer Army arrived with Von Arnim." He grunted. "I can fight a war, but I won't win with sticks and stones."

"What about Medenine?"

Rommel looked down at the ground and scraped it with his boot. "The British outmaneuvered me—it's that simple. I split my forces and attacked there to delay the Brits on my southern flank as the bulk of our army withdrew to the north.

"They had their tanks and anti-tank guns in place before we got there. I expected a small force that we could push northeast back to the sea. Instead, they were there in force with a massive ambush. Now, we're going to play hell getting back to the port in Tunis ourselves." He scoffed. "If I didn't know better, I'd say that the Brits intercepted our radio transmissions, knew my plan, and prepared accordingly."

He scanned the barren landscape once more. "I sense that we cannot win this war." He turned abruptly to face Meier, and when he spoke, his voice was tinged with controlled passion. "We have great technology. Our Tiger tank is better than the Sherman. Its longer barrel lets us take out a target two thousand meters away with one shot. They can't do the same. But the other side has so many Shermans, and more arriving in-country every day, and our drivers aren't trained as mechanics. They can't fix their own equipment.

"Using our anti-aircraft guns as direct fire weapons against British tanks two years ago was a great advantage, but the Americans developed their own anti-tank guns, and now the British and the Russians have them too. We fought outnumbered by our wits with better arms for most of this war, but our technological advantage is receding and the numbers against us are rising at a steady pace everywhere. So, the other element to winning the war is logistics, and we don't have the American industrial capacity to keep us in the fight." He laughed sardonically. "You could say that the war will be won in the American factories."

Rommel's tone became angry. "I'm a soldier. I look out for my men. I ordered the withdrawal because I cannot ask my soldiers to fight and die when we cannot win. I was criticized during our retreat from El Alamein for abandoning so many airfields that the Brits quickly occupied. But if we had defended them, we'd have lost more men than we'll lose by giving up those airfields. I joined the *Wehrmacht* to fight for our motherland, and I'll defend her to my dying day, but if we do not take care of our soldiers, there will be none left to fight for her."

"I understand, sir, and I agree with your points, but you had won against the Americans near Tebessa. Why did we retreat in that sector?"

Exasperation tinged Rommel's voice. "Because we cannot win in North

Africa. The Americans didn't expect our withdrawal, and before they detected it, we got more men to safety, alive to fight another day." He exhaled sharply. "We'll need every one of them if we hope to save our homeland."

Meier regarded the field marshal with concern. "You think it will come to that?"

Rommel harrumphed. "I don't see how it can't. That Operation Barbarossa against the Soviet Union was a foolish venture. It forced Stalin's alliance with Great Britain, and now the bulk of our resources go to the eastern front. The battle at Stalingrad has turned against us. We're retreating there just as we are here." He bowed his head and blew out another breath of air. "With patience, we could have broken the British ability to fight, taken Egypt, and proceeded north to the Iraqi and Iranian oilfields."

Rommel and Meier had wandered further into the desert, where they were free to share their most private thoughts. "We already know that Stalin didn't think we'd attack in the Soviet Union," Rommel continued, "and he didn't prepare for it. With the industrial capacity of the countries we've conquered, with England out of the fight and the US never having entered it except against Japan, and with plenty of petroleum, we'd have had no need to go into Russia. But if the *führer* still intended to do that, we'd have gone in with an intact and reinforced army. Now, we're scattered, our men and equipment are worn, replacements are thinning out, and they're coming to us poorly trained. We're destroying our own country."

Meier suddenly stepped close to Rommel, and when he spoke, his tone was bitter. "How long will we allow that Austrian corporal to rape Germany?"

Rommel regarded him sharply. "Until an opportunity arises to do otherwise," he replied with a cautious tone. "But now is not the time to speak of it."

"Then when?"

Rommel smiled and grasped Meier's shoulder. "You're a good man and a loyal soldier, *Generalmajor*. You've served your country well. Continue that while you contemplate the defenses that must be breached around this man if he is to be taken down. The best we might be able to do is bring the war to a close with our country intact. Remember that the *SS* was formed as the *führer's* personal bodyguard with loyalty sworn to him, not to Germany. It's just as large and well equipped as the *Wehrmacht*. The Nazis that surround him are completely loyal to him because their positions and power could disappear with one utterance from him. He is evil and a terrible military strategist, but he was brilliant in the way he set up his power structure to control it and protect himself."

Unmollified but respectful, Meier did not immediately reply. "I've heard rumors, sir, about *Herr* Hitler's personal physician. May I ask if you know anything about that?"

Rommel grunted and peered into Meier's eyes. "I've heard rumors. I have no idea how true they are. The high command despises him."

"They say the doctor might be poisoning him," Meier interjected. "Can we hope?"

Rommel stepped back and gazed into the desert again. "You are my friend, Meier, and a good one. I have no wish to endanger my friends."

The two were quiet for a few moments, contemplating. "What happens now?" Meier asked.

Rommel shook his head. "Our units in the north will complete their withdrawal. I ordered the destruction of anything and everything that could be useful to the Allies, including bridges and equipment we abandon. We'll bury their dead that we encounter, respectfully, alongside our own. Properly marked. That'll temper Allied rage against us. They already know that in my command, we treat prisoners of war as well as we can."

"And you, sir. What will you do?"

"I've been recalled to Berlin." Rommel allowed a small smile. "The *führer* ordered me home to recover from my 'ailments.' Undoubtedly, he'll summon me to explain my actions. That will be futile. I'll be relieved of command, *Herr* Hitler will find something for me to do, and Von Arnim will replace me." He chuckled. "You know, Von Arnim and I never liked each other, but he's a capable commander. He's from the Prussian aristocracy, and I'm an interloper, the son of a peasant school master. I'll predict that he'll seek an evacuation of German forces through Tunis not unlike that of Great Britain at Dunkirk. But since he lacks a flotilla of civilian boats, he'll likely fail."

He took a deep breath and let it out slowly. "The irony is that my first engagement with the Americans at Kasserine will have been my last victory in North Africa." He looked up at Meier and laughed. "All legends fade."

10

"I think you'll want to hear this," Claire Littlefield said, speaking to Commander Edward Travis in his office at the British intelligence decoding unit housed in the sprawling estate.

"Let's have it," he rejoined. He was a big man with a round face, bald head, and ready smile under round spectacles. "Commander Denniston spoke highly of your reports before he bequeathed this post to me and departed for greener pastures."

"That's nice, sir," Claire replied, "but this might be urgent. I believe we, the Brits, might have an operation under way to kill the *führer*."

"Where did you hear that?" Travis demanded sharply, steely-eyed and with furrowed brows.

"Sir, I work at the center of British intelligence. I hear things. Maybe I shouldn't, and to tell you the truth, I initially discounted the notion. I brought the matter to you now on the off chance that the rumor is true. If so, there's an aspect that might be pertinent, and I thought you should know it."

"Go on," Travis urged.

Claire hesitated. "This might seem a little outlandish—"

"Hmph," Travis grunted, frowning, and took a seat behind his desk. "What isn't outlandish about this war?" With a sweep of his hand, he invited Claire to take a seat in front of his desk. "Are we talking hard intelligence, or your instincts."

"A little of both, sir." Claire took a deep breath. "We think Hitler might be being drugged and poisoned."

Travis hauled his bulky frame straight up in his seat. "Excuse me, did I hear you correctly?"

"I believe so, sir, and we're not rushing in after the first inkling. I've personally decoded some of the messages and done the analysis on many of them. When I heard the scuttlebutt about an operation against him, I thought I should bring it in."

"Yes, of course. What are you hearing from the German side?"

"It's coming out of their high command in Berlin. Commander Denniston had assigned my team to concentrate there."

Travis nodded. "Continue."

"The generals closest to Hitler are concerned that he is acting erratically. There's a doctor, Theodor Morell, who's been treating the *führer* for several years. The generals, particularly Guderian and Goering, don't trust him. They call him a fraud, and he's always in close proximity to Hitler. They're appalled that Hitler gets up at ten o'clock on most mornings, and when he does, Morell is there to give him his first shot of the day. And apparently, he gets many doses of medicines throughout the day, particularly if he starts to feel depressed."

"How many is many?"

"I don't know for sure, but it's not ten or twenty. The number is closer to a hundred."

"Are you sure about this—"

"No, sir, I'm not, which is why I didn't come to you sooner. But I *am* sure of the German high command's concern regarding Hitler's behavior. We've been monitoring for a while, and he seems to be getting progressively worse. He's taken on a mantle of limitless brilliance and no longer listens to his generals. If he doesn't like their plans or considerations, he overrides them. They were furious when he divided his forces to take Stalingrad rather than mount another full-on attack against Moscow. Apparently, that was a decision taken for personal reasons to embarrass Stalin. It's cost the *Wehrmacht* tens of thousands of casualties and even more of their soldiers captured."

"I get that, but what is your point with regard to this rumor of an operation to assassinate Hitler. That *is* what you alluded to."

"Yes, sir. My point is that Dr. Morell might be doing it for us. Whether intended or not, he might already be shortening the *führer's* life."

Travis sat back in his chair, trancelike. "Could this be true? Do you think there could be a conspiracy to remove him?"

Claire also leaned back in her chair and let out her breath. "I don't know, sir. I haven't seen anything to indicate anyone else's involvement. Hitler's made bad decisions. We haven't known why. I think everyone conjectures on his narcissism and arrogance, and if that is accelerated by drugs—"

"He'll destroy himself and his organization as they turn on him, which, in the end, his generals must do if they hope to save themselves." He mulled in silence for a few moments and then instructed Claire, "Gather all the intelligence that indicates your premise. Bring it to me and keep monitoring. I'll deliver upstairs what you have so far and anything else pertinent that you bring on the matter."

He leaned back in thought again, and Claire started rising to depart. "Wait, Miss Littlefield. I'd like your opinion on another topic. About a year ago, the Americans brought in a group of intelligence analysts headed by a Major"—he looked down at a notepad on his desk—"Alfred McCormack."

"Yes, sir, I was here when they arrived and worked in the group that briefed them on our methods. They were astonished at what we'd done and were eager to learn."

"I should think so, although they'd already done a bang-up job of decrypting the Japanese codes. Good summation." The commander started to say something else, and then hesitated. "On another subject—"

"Yes, sir?"

"We have an ongoing operation in Norway's interior and expect action soon. Have one of your sections listening for unusual German traffic coming out regarding Norway, would you?"

"I can tell you that we've picked up some transmissions that might be along the lines of what you're looking for. The Germans are quite nervous after that failed glider attack in their mountains back in November."

Travis eyed her curiously. "What can you tell me?"

"Decoded transmissions we've received from an area west of Oslo informed us that the Germans believe a Norwegian man, or a group of them, is operating a resistance cell from a plateau they call the Hardangervidda. It's an area the Germans won't travel into for more than half a day because of the weather conditions; they fear that they might not make their way back out of deep snow. So far, there's nothing else to report." She chuckled. "Supposedly, they got a description and posted wanted notices looking for young men of ruddy complexions and blond hair. Of course, that could describe almost any Norwegian young man." She laughed. "I'll increase the monitoring—"

"One other thing," Travis interrupted. "Have you heard of any German transmissions coming out of Calcutta?"

"We have, sir, now that you mention it. That's somewhat far afield for Germans, but they have a few U-boats off the Arabian Sea coast of Goa, a Portuguese colony in India. The Germans are jubilant because they've been sinking our merchant ships quite regularly, apparently receiving messages from onshore about when traffic is entering or leaving the harbor. They chortle over our inability to stop them because Portugal is neutral and too important to us to interfere with the transmissions. We've passed along the decoded messages routinely—"

"Well now those messages are becoming critical. Treat them as high priority. At last count, they had sunk forty-six of our vessels." Travis rose, signaling the end of the meeting, and joined Claire to walk her to the door. "Denniston told me some things about your family," he said. "He mentioned that you had one brother return home recently after escaping from a POW camp, and another got back from covert work with the French Resistance."

"Yes, Lance and Jeremy. Thanks for asking about them, but we still don't know where our other brother, Paul, is or what he's doing." She stood and sighed. "But that's the war, and everyone must sacrifice."

Travis smiled kindly. "Denniston also told me about your parents, stranded on Sark. Do you know how they're getting along?"

Claire stood stock-still as emotion gripped her. Despite her best effort, tears filled her eyes. "I'm sorry, sir. I thought I was past this."

Travis reacted with chagrin. "My apologies. I didn't mean to upset you. I wanted only to express my concern."

"I haven't received word from my mother directly yet," Claire said through restrained sobs, "but I heard on the news two days ago that all the men on the island who had ever held an officer's commission in our armed forces were deported to a POW camp in Germany." Tears flowed, and she blurted, "That includes my father."

Travis stared at her with concern and then awkwardly put his arm around her shoulder. "There, there," he said. "Your father's a strong man. He'll pull through."

Claire sniffed and nodded while pulling away, embarrassed. "Thank you, sir. I hadn't mentioned it to anyone—"

"There is a limit to the stiff upper lip, you know. If you need time off, take it, and be with that little boy. Timmy, isn't it? I read about him in the newspapers. How is he?"

Claire wiped her eyes and gave a small laugh. "Growing and rambunctious. He's coming on five now, and honestly, he's what keeps me sane amid all the chaos."

Travis regarded her with respect. "You're a remarkable woman, Miss Littlefield. As I said, if you need time, please take it." He added, smiling, "If you don't need it, I'm sure Timmy will be pleased to occupy your afternoon."

Stony Stratford, England

Timmy ran down the gravel driveway of the home that Claire rented a few miles from Bletchley Park. Delighted with a sprinkling of snow, he threw his eyes wide as she scooped him up and held him.

"You like the snow?" she asked, laughing while she marveled at his growth and added weight since Jeremy had rescued him from a bombed-out ship at Saint-Nazaire nearly three years ago. The tragedy had orphaned the little boy, so Jeremy had brought him to Claire. The story of the ship's sinking, Jeremy's heroic actions, and Timmy's plight had caught the news and generated widespread attention, after which the kindly couple living on the estate had been more than pleased to offer the guesthouse to Claire for lease.

She had hired a nanny, and with the cooperation of her co-workers, she had made a home for Timmy. Inquiries regarding next of kin had revealed grandparents living in India, but whether for lack of interest or an inability to travel during the war, no one had shown up to claim Timmy. Now, Claire's biggest fear regarding the boy was that someday a legitimate next of kin would show up and take him away from her.

Timmy struggled to be let down to the ground and went to frolic in the snow while Claire looked on. The nanny, who had been watching from the door, came and stood by her. "He'll be entering school soon, I suppose," she said.

"Next autumn, I should say," Claire replied.

The nanny started to say something, but then held back.

"What is it?" Claire asked, concerned.

The nanny hesitated. "It's just that—well, once he's in school, I suppose you might not be needing me. I only ask so that I can make plans."

"Oh no," Claire cried immediately. "I had not thought at all about you going away, and I cannot bear the thought. You've been with us since Timmy came to us. You're family now, and I'll need you then as much as I do now." She frowned in somber thought. "It's wonderful that we're not being bombed regularly and that the threat of invasion has receded, but this war is global, and it's going to be a long one."

The nanny regarded Claire with a sad, respectful expression. "I'm more than pleased to care for our young war hero, and—" Her voice broke, and she hesitated. "I admire you, mum. I don't know what you do, but I know it must be something important in the war effort."

Claire smiled and then laughed. "You're more than kind. I assure you I'm a normal single girl trying to cope with this war like everyone else, and now responsible for a tiny tyke who puts a slight crimp in my social life, such as it is during a war."

"Yes, mum," the nanny said without expression. "You go on inside and relax. I'll watch Timmy and bring him in when he tires."

Thanking her, Claire entered the house and made a drink in the living room. Then she reclined on the divan. Soon, she fell fast asleep, exhausted.

11

Ten Days Earlier, February 27, 1943
Vemork Hydroelectric Power Plant, Norway

Second Lieutenant Knut Haukelid, second in command of Operation Gunnerside, peered through ambient light reflecting off the snow to see the line of eight commandos ahead of him as they approached the edge of the steep walls of Vestfjorddalen. The valley was so deep and surrounded by mountains so high that in deepest winter, direct sunlight never touched the floor. On the other side of the gorge, and visible by the light of an unwelcome moon, was the commandos' target—a long, seven-story behemoth that housed the Vemork hydroelectric power plant—perched on a plateau at the precipice of a frozen waterfall. Silhouetted against the snow-covered mountain wall behind it and lined on either side by tall fir trees, eleven massive pipes ran parallel to each other to the top and disappeared over the crest, reflecting moonlight off their silver surfaces.

The German *Wehrmacht* occupiers had mandated blackout provisions to confound potential air attacks, but in practice, the plant's employees, mostly from Rjukan, a small village roughly seven kilometers east on the valley floor, paid only perfunctory heed. Interior lights shone out at various windows along the front. Security was manned by poorly trained conscripts from Austria and German soldiers recovering from wounds inflicted at the Russian front.

Despite the obscure location among the rugged mountains of Norway that had made bombing the facility all but impossible, particularly when considering the potential hazard to Norwegian civilian casualties in the village, the commandos had been provided much intelligence about the site and its inner workings. Shortly after the Germans had invaded, Leif Tronstad, a co-designer of the plant's high-concentration heavy-water production unit, had escaped to Great Britain and offered his service to SOE, Churchill's special operations executive. The prime minister had commissioned the SOE to carry out sabotage throughout Europe and to recruit and train locals to do the same thing. In his words, the mission was to "set Europe on fire."

Tronstad now served as head of Section IV of the Norwegian High Command for the SOE and was the Norwegian commando unit's boss and chief contact in England. He had opposed Operation Freshman, the first attempt to neutralize the plant by the British commandos flown in by gliders, because he saw the effort as a suicide mission. He had argued that even if the men had succeeded in neutralizing the heavy-water production unit, they would then need to tramp over four hundred kilometers through deep, blinding snow to the Swedish border. None were from Norway or acclimated to the harsh mountain winters, nor were they equipped with skis.

Tronstad had explained the dangers and the tragedy of Freshman to the commandos prior to their departures, leaving out the significance of heavy water. He had no need to appeal to their patriotism, as each commando was eager to fight the Germans on their home turf. He had only to impress on them the importance of neutralizing the power plant, and he had built mockups of the plant's heavy-water production unit and drilled the commandos on their tasks until they could perform them in total darkness.

Like the other commandos of Gunnerside, Haukelid did not understand why this target attracted such attention, knowing that the plant's primary function was to produce fertilizer. But he recognized the urgency directed toward its destruction and knew that their British commando trainers had selected the toughest and most capable from among the thousands of Norwegian volunteers training in northern Scotland.

Chief among the requisite qualifications was that they must be Norwegian to avoid detection by Nazi sympathizers among the native population. They were also required to be expert skiers and outdoorsmen in superb condition and already acclimated to the living conditions of Norway's mountains.

Haukelid was among those chosen. And this time, rather than executing a frontal assault, the mission would be carried out by nine specially trained saboteurs.

The leader, Joachim Rønneberg, at twenty-two years of age, was the youngest among them, but no one questioned his leadership or skill. A big man with a narrow face and full head of dark hair, he could be both playful and serious. His superiors had found him to be "fully alive to all the difficulties and dangers of his position and demonstrating the virtues of steadiness and inspiration in a high degree."

Linking up the nine commandos of team Gunnerside with the five previously inserted commandos of team Swallow proved challenging. The men of Swallow—Jens-Anton Poulsson, Knut Haugland, Claus Helberg, Arne Kjelstrup, and Einar Skinnarland—had been dropped by parachute into the vast, frozen plateau, Hardangervidda, north of Rjukan and Vemork four months earlier in anticipation of receiving the commandos flown in by gliders.

Four months earlier
Hardangervidda, Norway

Second Lieutenant Jens-Anton Poulsson, the leader of Grouse, struggled forward under the weight of his backpack, parachute, and ancillary equipment to the edge of the hole in the bomber's floor. On takeoff from RAF Skitten near Wick in Caithness, Scotland, he and his teammates had been exhilarated that now, after all the months of training and waiting, they were finally going home to Norway to strike a blow against its Nazi occupiers.

Barely able to contain their excitement, they had looked together through the plane's portholes as the waves, illuminated by a bright moon, crashed against boulders lining the coast far below.

The aircraft had flown low over a fjord, and Poulsson had sucked in his breath at the nearness of the wingtips to the rugged mountains on either side of them. But the plane had lifted as the valley narrowed and then navigated among the peaks until the terrain leveled out on the high plateau that was the Hardangervidda.

"When I tell you to jump, you go," the grizzled British jumpmaster had told them at the pre-flight briefing. "We'll be flying at two hundred feet per second, so if you hesitate at all, you'll land hundreds of feet from your landing zone, and so will the men behind you. You could find yourself alone on that bleak wasteland with no gear." He had gestured toward the eight-foot-long steel canisters that would carry their supplies and equipment. "When we get the green light at the drop zone, I'll toss one of those through the hole, and the first man goes out immediately afterward. The rest of you move forward and drop through without waiting. Do you understand?"

The group had nodded in unison.

Poulsson's hands and legs tingled, and his buttocks tightened with apprehension. Now, as they approached the drop zone, lined up to shuffle to the hole, and hooked their static lines to a cable running through the bomber, he was glad that his back was toward his men and that his face was covered with goggles, his helmet, and a thick balaclava.

The weather was clear, but strong winter winds and irregular updrafts and downdrafts buffeted the plane as it flew between high peaks and deep valleys, causing it to creak and groan as it plowed through the air. Now, as it leveled off at jump altitude over the endless plateau shrouded in snow, the noise of the aircraft seemed to have receded, replaced by the sound of Poulsson's heart pounding in his ears. He wondered momentarily if his teammates experienced the same terror.

Inches away now, the hole seemed tiny, and Poulsson wondered if his giant frame could drop cleanly through without hitting the opposite side. A light in the cabin suddenly flashed from red to green, and the jumpmaster, poised on the other side of the hatch, shoved the canisters through the opening. Then he slapped Poulsson on the shoulder. "Go!" he shouted over the wind and the drone of the aircraft's engines.

Gulping a breath of air, Poulsson stepped into the dark void and dropped. Before he had enough time to gauge his fear, the static line attached between the top of his chute and the cable inside the aircraft jerked the silk canopy from its casing. When Poulsson looked up, it had spread, and he continued his descent at a gentler pace, albeit while being blown forward by a stiff breeze.

He checked around him. His four teammates' canopies had opened, as had those of the canisters, and he counted thirteen parachutes now descending against the moonlit sky. Then, looking down, he was once again exhilarated as Norway rose to greet him. He and his team were home and ready for the fight.

They landed without injury, but the canisters had been scattered, and one was carried along the ground as the howling wind caught its chute and dragged it for two kilometers before being wedged in an outcropping of rock. Two days later, after having spent the nights in sleeping bags and buried in snow holes for shelter, the team had recovered all the supplies and were ready to begin their trek to the area where the gliders were to land.

Poulsson had grown up in Rjukan near the southern edge of the vast Hardangervidda that covered nearly twenty-five-hundred square miles and was the largest such plateau in Europe. He had roamed its vast expanses as a boy. His knowledge of the area was one of the reasons he had been chosen for the leadership position, but other attributes had guided his selection. One training instructor wrote in his evaluation that he "showed a spirit of persistence that is beyond all praise."

He was happy to have on his team Knut Haugland, a wireless telegraph operator of rare ability and skill. Knut had served in a similar capacity aboard a merchant ship. After Germany invaded Norway, he had taken a job in an electronics plant and joined the Resistance, but after his second arrest, he escaped to England and joined the Linge Company, a unit of the best soldiers among the Norwegian volunteers.

Also on Poulsson's team was Claus Helberg, another Rjukan native who had sat next to Poulsson during their earliest years of elementary school.

Claus had been a member of the Norwegian Mountaineering Club, but he had left it to join the army when war broke out. Eighty-four days later, Germany invaded Norway and he was captured.

Known to have a propensity for getting himself into trouble and miraculously out of it, often by charm and wit, he had escaped to Sweden and joined the Resistance. His job, prior to wireless telegraphy being introduced into Norway, had been to run messages back and forth across the border. It was he who had smuggled the news through Sweden of Germany's intent to increase heavy-water production at Vemork. Subsequently, he was arrested but escaped to England and joined the Linge Company.

Arne Kjelstrup, born in Rjukan and raised in Oslo, spent many winters in the mountains of Telemark developing the skills to survive and thrive under the harshest conditions. A fierce fighter, he was known to have attacked an entire German column with the help of only one other compatriot.

The fifth team member was another Rjukan native, Einar Skinnarland, a champion skier and an engineer at the Vemork hydropower plant. Determined to help fight Norway's Nazi occupiers, he led several compatriots to hijack a ship and sail to England. There he joined the Linge Company. When the cadre learned of his background, they convinced him with minor urging to undergo intense training and return to Vemork to be an inside agent. Eleven days after his departure from Norway, he parachuted into the mountains and skied back to Rjukan. On arrival at work the next morning, he told his fellow workers that he had enjoyed a much-needed ski vacation.

With no landmarks to guide them, and having hundreds of pounds of supplies and materiel to bring along while often trudging against a blistering wind, Poulsson's team moved, at first on instinct, until they encountered a cabin. Rummaging through it and finding a map, they discovered that their instincts had been wrong and they had landed miles from the intended drop zone. With a known lake now in sight, however, they could plot their course and get back on track.

Moving the equipment raised an unexpected challenge. None of it was surplus, some of it was heavy, and they could not carry it all at the same time, but rather in rotation, carrying parts of it forward a few kilometers and then returning for another load. And some of their trek required tramping across the frozen lake that had given them direction. Although being on skis made the going easier, the weight of their burdens and the distances to travel sapped their strength.

Their feet became wet, and they took precautions against frostbite and hypothermia, but, having to conserve food and energy, they ate little. After days of constant exposure to the elements, and as the weight of their equipment wore them down, they got a lucky break—Poulsson found a sled. Fortunately, it was large enough to carry much of their equipment, eliminating the need for further rotations.

After eighteen grueling days, on November 5, the five men stumbled into Svensbu, the cabin that had been their original destination. Before them lay the intended landing site for the gliders of Operation Freshman.

As quickly as their numb bodies would allow, they built a fire, and Knut assembled his wireless telegraph and sent off a message to notify London of their safe arrival. Four days later, having received the message that the sabotage mission with the British commandos against Vemork was a go, they listened in dismay as the aircraft flew overhead, invisible to them because of the clouds. The sound of the planes slowly faded into the distance. A later message informed team Swallow of the twin tragedies of the gliders and the loss of the British commandos and aircraft crews.

12

As Lieutenant Haukelid approached the precipice of the Vestfjorddalen valley, he studied the five commandos who had comprised team Swallow. Gunnerside and Swallow had united only four days ago, and Swallow's commandos had been near starvation. Often burrowing into the snow to gather moss for their meals, the food of reindeer, Swallow had survived without re-supply on the Hardangervidda for four months after Operation Freshman's glider tragedy. Einar told the story.

***

Four months earlier

Team Swallow had sheltered in a Sand Lake cabin southwest of Vemork, and from there, they had run reconnaissance on the power plant. Two engineers had risked their own lives to bring what supplies they could as well as information concerning the inner workings of the plant. They stopped only when they ran the risk of exposing themselves and Team Swallow.

After celebrating a meager Christmas, Poulsson had led his men across the Måna River upstream of the target and then to another cabin farther away in Grass Valley, where they were less likely to be detected by

Wehrmacht patrols. They counted on German soldiers' practice of never venturing more than a half day's journey onto the plateau, leaving as much daylight as possible for their return trek. Team Swallow stayed at the Grass Valley cabin through the worst part of the record-setting Nordic winter, hunkered down with no chance to venture outside for days at a time, eating just enough of their dwindling supplies to sustain life.

They had been mere shadows of men when Haukelid had first seen them, hardened but also weakened by their long ordeal, and yet their spirits had been high, their determination to strike at the enemy for Norway unabated. He had learned that at one point, nearing the end of supplies and with no other food aside from reindeer moss, Poulsson had gone out alone to hunt for reindeer. At various times, the men of Swallow had successfully hunted the animals with mixed success, but never when they were so close to starvation.

Not expecting to find any prey, Poulsson stumbled upwind of a small herd, took aim, shot, and missed. He aimed at a second reindeer, and apparently missed again, for it remained standing and then bolted away with the panicked herd. Shifting his aim, Poulsson had time to take one last shot, but again, no reindeer fell into the snow.

Cursing his own weakness, he trudged toward where the herd had been and saw two trails of blood flecks leading uphill on a slight rise. With his remaining strength waning, he followed one leading over the crest, and there found a cow struggling to make her way through the snow. With one shot, he finished her, and after retrieving a tin cup from his backpack and filling it with the reindeer's blood, he drank in the warmth and strength, a time-honored Norwegian custom. Then he field-dressed the carcass, slicing open the stomach to harvest the rich, half-digested mixture of moss and other desperately needed nutrients. Stuffing the best of the organs and meat into his backpack, he also included the leg bones for their marrow. Then he buried the carcass in the snow to be retrieved later and made his way back to the cabin.

Einar wrapped up the story to a rapt audience of the newly arrived Gunnerside commandos. "We had a very good meal that evening and in the days after," he said. "And then the reindeer came by more frequently."

Haukelid, who had listened in wonder, asked Poulsson, "When you went out on that hunt, you were out of food?"

"I suppose we could have scratched around in the snow and found some more moss." Poulsson grinned. "I should have been a better aim. I was lucky."

Haukelid looked askance at him. "So that last shot you took saved your lives?"

"And the mission," Claus Helberg, the champion skier, chimed in. "We have no vitamins here. We were deficient in C and carbohydrates. The contents of that reindeer's stomach provided those things. We would not have survived otherwise. People on the Hardangervidda know these things."

Now, as Haukelid observed the men of Swallow maneuvering with those of Gunnerside behind snow drifts toward the edge of the valley, he was in awe of their tenacity and dedication. Only three days had passed since the two teams had united at Fetter Cabin south of Grass Valley.

Poulsson had immediately subordinated his men to Lieutenant Rønneberg, a prearranged chain of command accepted without question. The full team rested for two days, and on the third, they moved closer to Vemork, occupying Fløgsbudalen, a cabin where they could directly observe the plant across the valley. Then Claus, the best skier, set out to reconnoiter an approach to the target. He returned with the plan of attack now set in motion.

From Fløgsbudalen cabin, Haukelid had examined the ominous edifice first with curiosity, then with a military eye, looking for vulnerabilities. A touch of irony colored his observations as he remembered how, as a boy, he had shared the excitement of the villagers at Rjukan as the plant was being built. The industrial complex had generated an economic boom in the area and improved the lives of many thousands of people.

And now, Haukelid and his teammates were about to destroy it.

The two Vemork engineers who had previously supplied and informed Team Swallow reported that, following the debacle of the glider operation,

the *Wehrmacht* had reinforced the plant's defenses. The Germans had positioned anti-aircraft guns and three hundred crack troops to guard the
perimeter and the only road into the facility, which crossed a bridge span-
ning the valley to its front.

However, a railroad track skirted the mountain on the Vemork side of
the valley.

"We can get to the plant," Claus reported. "I found a way to cross the
valley nearby." He grinned fiendishly. "The train tracks are open.
Unguarded."

The difficulty had been the Måna River on the valley floor. It was frozen
over most of its length in the local area, but an unseasonable rise in
temperature that day had caused a thaw, bringing with it the danger of thin
ice across the river. Claus had found a path across the river at a narrow
juncture, and on the other side, he had observed intermittent stands of
trees tracing upward along the nearly sheer face of the rugged rock wall.

"If trees can grow there, we can climb it," he had pronounced, looking
around intently at his fellow commandos.

As they drew alongside the top of the valley wall they must descend
before climbing up the other side, they stared into the depths below. The
darkness was made more intense by light seeping from the stone structure
silhouetted against the snowy background on the opposite side less than a
kilometer away.

The hum and clank of large machinery filled the air.

Haukelid turned his attention to his original Gunnerside teammates. In
addition to the team leader, Rønneberg, there were four others, Birger
Strømsheim, Fredrik Kayser, Kaspar Idland, and Hans Storhaug.

Granted the privilege of picking his own team from the hundreds of
Norwegian commandos of the elite Linge Company, all eager to strike back
at the Nazis, Rønneberg had selected those who brought complementary
skills and who, in his judgment, were best able to cope with the treacherous
nature of the Hardangervidda. Birger, his first choice, was from Ålesund,
the team leader's hometown. Birger's SOE instructors had written that he

was "reliable as a rock." He had been a building contractor with a reputation for incredible craftsman's skills, an inexhaustible work ethic, and innate common sense. Like Rønneberg, he was excellent on skis, and he had escaped to Britain on a fishing boat. Because Birger was the eldest in the group at age thirty-one, Rønneberg relied on him for his knowledge and instincts.

Next was Fredrik, a thin and pleasant man, always cheerful even under the most adverse conditions, who had trained with Strømsheim through the parachute course. As a boy, he had participated in both cultural and sporting events, fishing, playing the mandolin, dancing, rowing, playing soccer, and participating in scouting—often finding that he was second best at everything. On finishing school, he had joined the King's Guard, returning home to clerk at an ironworks factory. He had fought the Russians when they invaded in 1939, and though wounded and suffering from frostbite, he went back immediately into the fight when Germany invaded, and then he escaped to Great Britain aboard a fishing boat.

Third was Kaspar Idland, an intelligent soldier and accomplished marksman. He was bigger than most of his peers even as a child, so his mother had nurtured passivity in him out of fear that he could hurt other children in school who mocked him about his size. But when the bullying became too intense, she relented and allowed him to fight back against his worst tormentors. He did so the next day and was never bothered again. Prior to the war, he had been a postman from a village near Stavanger. Idland had trained with Kayser and Strømsheim.

Hans, a short twenty-seven-year-old, was superb in the woods and at hunting and skiing. He had grown up in Hedemark, a district on the border with Sweden where the team intended to make their escape from Norway upon mission completion. His knowledge of local terrain would increase their odds.

Haukelid had been the last to join Rønneberg's team, and he knew that the leader, eight years younger than he, had viewed him with concern. Haukelid had been intended for the original Grouse mission, but he had shot his own foot in a training accident and was convalescing, to his deep chagrin, while Poulsson, Knut, Claus, Arne, and Einar had suffered through the winter storms of the Hardangervidda.

Prior to his escape to Britain, Haukelid had distinguished himself for courage, tenacity, and effectiveness within the Norwegian Resistance, and Rønneberg wondered whether the man, already known by the Linge Company leadership as a loner, would accept a position as second in command for the mission.

Although vastly different in temperament, Rønneberg and Haukelid had an unstinting determination to see Norway freed. Each had taken a risky trip to Britain to join the fight, and the leaders of the Linge Company had recognized both men's potential. But Haukelid was seen as a rebel, while Rønneberg acceded to rightful authority. Haukelid was a combat veteran, and Rønneberg, despite distinguishing himself in tactics and leadership while training in Scotland, had never seen enemy fire.

To establish his authority, at the start of the mission, Rønneberg had gathered his five teammates. He explained the mission as best he could, stating his ignorance of why the destruction of heavy water carried such a high priority. "It must be important, though, for SOE and our Norwegian high command to risk another go at it after so many lives were lost on the gliders." He paused and then looked into each man's eyes. "I don't know you all equally well," he told them, "but if there's any disagreement between you, put it aside until we're done with the job. Or get out."

No one bailed.

"One other thing," he added. "Any of you are free to refuse the mission with no bad feelings. We won't think less of you. We likely won't escape after we complete it, and if we're caught, the Germans will show no mercy."

When he had finished, he took each man aside to provide an opportunity to bow out. None did.

13

"Remember," Rønneberg had said grimly as the commandos prepared to leave Fløgsbudalen cabin, "if some of us go down on the way to the target, the others carry on to complete the mission. I still don't understand the significance of the heavy water, but I know it's crucial to saving Norway. That's all we need to know."

"*Ja!*" his team responded in unison, thumping their gloved hands together or stamping their feet in the snow. Only Knut and Einar would remain behind to man the wireless telegraph.

"Let's go."

With Claus showing the way, and Rønneberg immediately behind him, the men of the united Gunnerside team started down the steep, shrub- and boulder-strewn wall of the mountain that formed the north side of the narrow Vestfjorddalen valley. Haukelid brought up the rear, ensuring that no commando was lost to unobserved injury as they descended the rugged slope.

They had left most of their heavy equipment at the Fløgsbudalen cabin, but they carried five Tommy guns between them, and each man had his own pistol and knife, along with a few hand grenades. In their rucksacks, they carried the explosives for use against the heavy-water production unit, as well as essential survival gear in the event of a prolonged escape across the Hardangervidda. Each man also carried cyanide pills to bring about his own rapid demise should the *Gestapo* capture him.

Haukelid also carried a finely sharpened set of wire cutters.

The commandos concealed their skis and white uniforms on the crest near the place where they began their descent. Having filled their bellies and rested for two days, the Nordic men, hardened by their frozen circumstances, moved as swiftly and deftly as prudence and their skills as native mountain men allowed, clambering over rocks, stumps, and bushes as they made their way farther and farther into the void.

When they had reached the floor, Claus led them to an ice bridge over the river. The slight warming in the weather that day had softened the snow, and water dripped all around them. They stepped gingerly across, one at a time, until they were beyond the danger of breaking through and had scrambled safely over the rocks lining the opposite shore. Having just descended six hundred feet, they now faced the prospect of climbing up the same height. And the ice bridge might no longer be there on their return trip.

When they had gathered safely on the south bank of the Måna River, Claus pointed up at the snow-lined southern wall of the narrow valley where trees grew on intermittent clefts that formed an upward line. "There's where we'll climb."

Haukelid's eyes followed Claus' pointing finger as he gauged the danger. Despite the bright moon reflecting off the snow at higher elevations, the valley was shrouded in shadows. Any misstep resulting from poor visibility could result in serious injury or a long plunge to almost certain death.

After a brief conference, the commandos started the climb. Haukelid could see nothing in the darkness as each man made his own way up the steep slope, sometimes grasping at roots, sometimes clinging to impossibly narrow bits of ledges. He pressed upward relentlessly, his breath coming in short heaves, sweat gathering on his face and in his undergarments despite the freezing air, and his hands feeling every tiny slice and every contact with icy surfaces.

And then, at last, the men of Gunnerside were at the top of their climb, standing on the intended ridgeline and staring at the railroad tracks at their feet. The steel ribbons gleamed in the moonlight and disappeared into the night in both directions.

Haukelid looked at his watch. The time was just past eleven o'clock. An hour had passed since they had skied away from Fløgsbudalen cabin.

Now Haukelid moved to the front and, keeping to the shadows, led the commandos along the outside track, which had been blown clear of snow by the stiff wind. He thanked the Nordic gods that they would leave no footprints.

They came to a transformer shed covered in snow and paused. From there, they could observe the changing of the guard across the valley at the bridge, scheduled for midnight. Rønneberg would start the sabotage operation a half hour later when the new guard shift had settled into their normal routines.

While the commandos waited out of the wind behind the shed, they rested, snacked, and wandered away to relieve themselves. And one by one, Rønneberg went over the individual missions with each man, reinforcing that none of them could be captured alive. The potential damage from what they might reveal under torture was too enormous.

Haukelid reached up to pat the cyanide pills inside his right breast pocket.

At the appointed time, the nine men rousted from their rest. They rechecked their weapons, grenades, and explosives, and gathered for the final brief from Rønneberg.

"What we do in the next hour," he told them, "will be a chapter of history for a hundred years to come. Together we will make it a worthy one. Let's go. You know what to do."

Haukelid led with the covering party and crept along the tracks, recognizing that they were now within range of German minefields. Arne followed immediately behind him, with the others stretched back in single file. Snow covered their path ahead, but footprints, probably from employees, meant that they no longer had to worry about being detected from discovery of their own traces in the snow.

They came to a row of storage sheds, and gradually, the hum of the plant had turned into a roar. One hundred yards beyond was the gate.

It was a simple portal, not imposing in any way, constructed of chain-link fencing held together by a metal frame, and wide enough for a train. As the two engineers from the plant had reported, it was left unguarded. Apparently, the German security officer had counted on the ruggedness of the mountains to prevent an attack from that direction.

Haukelid scoffed. *The Nazis forgot that determined men built the plant and the railway in the first place.*

At exactly one half hour after midnight, Rønneberg signaled to Haukelid and Arne to cut the lock. Scurrying to the gates, Haukelid removed the shears he had carried and handed them to Arne, confident that the plant's noise would drown out their own. Once Arne had snipped through the lock, Haukelid shoved the gates open and motioned for the rest of the covering party to pass through.

Within moments, Haukelid and his teammates were in position, ready to neutralize the guards in the event the demolition team came under attack. Arne covered the approach to the sluice gates that controlled the flow of water. Einar took his station at the railway gate, protecting the path of escape. Storhaug scurried to a slope to watch over the road leading to the suspension bridge.

Haukelid and Poulsson hid behind two steel storage tanks fifteen yards from the barracks. Poulsson immediately aimed his Tommy gun on the barracks door while Haukelid prepared a row of hand grenades.

While the covering party was setting up, the demolition party— Rønneberg, Kayser, Strømsheim, and Idland—cut holes in the fence and a secondary gate as a means of escape. From his position, Haukelid watched his comrades' progress and breathed a sigh. So far, the mission proceeded undetected.

Rønneberg led the demolition team along the back of the plant to the northeastern corner and rounded it. He and Kayser covered for Strømsheim and Idland, the two men carrying the explosives. "They must be protected at all costs," he had instructed.

Peering stealthily through a small window, Rønneberg saw the room containing the heavy-water production unit. A lone man tended to the machines. With another quick glance, Rønneberg saw the offending canisters and the filtering apparatus that fed them. They looked harmless.

The commandos paused momentarily while Strømsheim handed nine bands of explosives to Rønneberg, and Idland handed the same number of bands to Kayser. Then they continued around the corner to the eastern wall.

The frozen waterfall glimmered in the moonlight just beyond. Whether the day's unseasonal warming had begun to thaw it, Rønneberg could not tell over the roar of the plant, but he guessed that the summertime thunder of water spilling over the rocks, added to the noise of the production facility, must be deafening.

He came to the basement-level door that the two engineers had reported as the best way in. Holding his pistol ready, he tried it.

Locked.

Peering through the scant light, he spotted a staircase to the first floor. He directed Kayser to climb the stairs and look for another door. "I found it," Kayser hissed on returning, "but it's locked, too."

"We've got to find another way in, and we can't blow a door or break a window. That might alert the guards." He paused, reflecting on a conversation with Tronstad, the plant's former designer who now headed the Norwegian section of SOE. The man had wanted to lead this mission himself but was considered too valuable to the overall war effort to be risked.

However, he knew Vemork intimately. "If you can't get in through the door, look for an opening on the eastern wall between the basement and the first-floor level," he had instructed. "It's the opening to a passage built to allow for the heavy electrical lines, water pipes, and the like. Essentially, a tunnel. It's narrow, but if it hasn't been blocked by German security improvements, you should be able to worm your way in there. Look for a ladder. It's always kept there to provide access into the tunnel."

"Come," Rønneberg called to Kayser. He explained their objective and began the search. The wall was coated in snow and ice, but by thrusting deliberately through it, Rønneberg found the ladder and, shortly afterward, the opening.

Minutes later, he and Kayser had clambered up the slick ladder and into the passage. As Tronstad had predicted, it was tight, but with much effort, they crawled through the gaggle of wires and pipes.

Then, too late, Rønneberg realized that Strømsheim and Idland had disappeared. They must have become separated while searching for the way in. Rønneberg and Kayser would have to sabotage the canisters and the production apparatus without them.

Ahead of them, Rønneberg spotted an opening into the room below, and upon reaching and peering through it, he saw that they were over the room that housed the heavy-water canisters. The lone attendant sat at his desk, poring over papers.

Counting on the raucous mechanical noises to cover the sound of his descent, he lowered himself through the ceiling, hung a moment, and then dropped fifteen feet to the floor, breaking his fall with a roll learned at parachute school. Kayser followed in the same manner.

The attendant heard them and whirled, startled to see two men in combat gear facing him. He rose from his chair and backed away in fear.

"Do as we say," Rønneberg told him in Norwegian, pointing to the British insignia on his uniform, "and you have nothing to fear from us. What is your name?"

"Johansen."

"Move out of the way and don't interfere."

While Kayser kept a weapon pointed at Johansen, Rønneberg hurried to the canisters and began attaching the explosive bands to their lower ends. He worked rapidly, knowing exactly what to do because Tronstad's mockups had been so exact.

"Careful," Johansen called worriedly. "You might explode them."

"That's what we intend," Kayser told him.

Just then, the window that Rønneberg had peeked through earlier shattered. Instinctively, he went for his weapon, but then was pleased to see Strømsheim and Idland breaking more glass away from the frame. He went to help them, and in the process, he cut his hand on a shard of glass.

Leaving Idland to use his body to block the light spewing through the window, Rønneberg rushed to finish attaching the explosives, with Strømsheim joining him. Working feverishly despite the blood still oozing from his hand, they were soon finished.

As they set the fuses, Strømsheim suggested that instead of using two-minute fuses, as planned, they use thirty-second ones. "That way, no one will have the chance to snuff them out. We light them and get out."

Rønneberg agreed. He glanced at Johansen, who watched them intently as they prepared the fuses.

"Where are my glasses?" Johansen said suddenly. "I need my glasses."

Rønneberg stared at him incredulously.

"They're hard to get these days, with the war and everything," Johansen said plaintively. "I left them on the desk."

Not believing that, after all the months of training, the lives risked and lost, and with the stakes attached to this mission, Johansen's glasses had suddenly become a priority, Rønneberg nevertheless rushed to the desk and glanced over it. "They're not here," he said.

"I left them there," Johansen insisted.

Rønneberg rummaged through the papers, leaving a bloody mess, and found the glasses inside a logbook. He hurried to give them to the attendant and then returned to finish preparing the fuses.

"We need a quick route out," Rønneberg told Strømsheim. "Get the key and unlock that back door we tried to enter." He glanced at Johansen, who offered the key from a ring on his belt.

While Strømsheim went to unlock the door, Kayser bustled Johansen from the room. "Get upstairs and lie flat on the floor," he instructed. "This room is going to blow."

Just then, they heard footsteps, and another man entered the room from the inside hall. As he took in uniformed commandos and the muzzles of Kayser's and Strømsheim's weapons trained on him, he yelped in shock and terror.

"Get them upstairs," Rønneberg hissed. "We're lighting the fuses."

Johansen and the new arrival needed no urging. Kayser escorted them to the stairs, where they bounded up unbidden.

Simultaneously, Rønneberg and Strømsheim lit the two fuses. Then, with Kayser, they sprinted to the door. There, Rønneberg paused only long enough to toss his bloody glove and a British parachutist badge on the floor.

From their position behind the steel tanks near the railroad gate, Haukelid and Poulsson constantly scanned the yard and tried not to fret. While they waited, Haukelid reflected on one of his first engagements against the Germans in the opening weeks of the *Wehrmacht's* invasion of Norway. He had been with a group of Norwegian soldiers surrounding a house occupied by enemy soldiers. When the Germans refused to surrender, Haukelid and his group had opened fire.

The house's thin walls provided no protection. All the soldiers inside were killed, some of them sprawled through broken windows, apparently having intended to escape.

Now, with his covering party positioned and primed with ready fingers on Tommy guns and hand grenades placed within easy reach to cover any move against them by the German security force, he contemplated the ugliness of war. No enemy soldier would escape the barrage that would meet them.

As the minutes ticked by, fear grew that something had gone awry. Too much time had passed since the demolitions team had gone forward.

And then they heard a distant thud.

They glanced at each other. "Is that it? Is that what we came for?" Poulsson asked.

Haukelid only shrugged, and both returned to scanning the yard.

At that moment, the barracks door swung open, and a guard appeared. He wore a heavy coat but no helmet, and he carried no weapon. He thrust his head through the door, turned it back and forth as if listening, and then wandered out into the yard, showing no signs of concern. Then he sauntered back to the barracks, entered, and closed the door behind him.

Haukelid and Poulsson exchanged glances of relief. Haukelid looked at his watch. Sufficient time had passed for Rønneberg to complete the demolition and escape to the rail line through the alternate route. He was about to suggest to Poulsson that they should fall back when suddenly the barracks door swung open and the same guard appeared, this time armed, with his helmet, and carrying a flashlight. He shined the light across the yard and then proceeded into it, casting the light in all directions.

Poulsson, who manned the Tommy gun, braced himself against the tank and took aim, squeezing the trigger ever so lightly.

The guard continued his rounds, shining light into various corners and working his way toward the tank where Haukelid and Poulsson hid. He shined the light over the tank from top to bottom, its beam striking within inches of the commandos' feet.

Poulsson held his weapon steadily, put more pressure on the trigger, and looked to Haukelid for guidance. Haukelid shook his head. Their instructions were to kill only if absolutely necessary. The plant's roar might muffle a shot, but perhaps not.

Poulsson returned his eyes to the guard, the sights framed on the center of the soldier's chest. The man shivered, coughed, and returned to his barracks. As soon as the door closed, the two commandos took off at a dead run for the railroad gate.

"Piccadilly," Arne called the password to them, but they were on him before they had time to give the response, "Leicester Square."

Arne was having none of it. "Piccadilly," he insisted.

"Oh, shut up," Haukelid and Poulsson said in unison, laughing. "Have you seen the others?"

Arne nodded. "Everyone's been through, and they're headed back down the mountain. I was instructed to wait here for you."

"That wasn't much of an explosion," Poulsson remarked.

"How would you hear it with all the other factory noise?" Arne said. "It worked, though. Rønneberg said they heard the explosion as they made their escape."

Haukelid's and Poulsson's eyes lit up. "We did it?" They exercised all their discipline to hold down elation and refrain from loud, celebratory yelps. "We pulled it off without firing a shot!"

Arne grinned and joined in backslapping, and then they hurried back along the tracks to descend the mountain.

14

March 5, 1943
Bletchley Park, England

Commander Travis was reading a message when Claire entered his office. He held it out to her, and she scanned it as she took her seat. It was very short and typed in all capital letters.

HIGH-CONCENTRATION INSTALLATION AT VEMORK COMPLETELY DESTROYED ON NIGHT OF 27TH – 28TH STOP GUNNERSIDE HAS GONE TO SWEDEN STOP GREETINGS.

Claire glanced up. "Sir, this is wonderful news. There's no mention of casualties—"

"Which is not to say that there are none, but I'd say the message is decidedly upbeat, telling us not only that the objective was met but also that the raiding force is making its escape. And it ended with 'greetings.' What are you hearing from that part of the world?"

"We've tracked the German communications, so we knew that the raid had taken place and our Norwegian commandos had done some damage, but we couldn't tell the extent of it. The *Wehrmacht* mounted a huge sweep on the Hardangervidda, but the soldiers are limited by their self-imposed practice of not risking a night in the snows. If our chaps can stay ahead of them, they have a chance, but from Vemork to Sweden is more than a hundred miles on skis through rugged terrain."

Travis arched his eyebrows and inhaled sharply through pursed lips. "That's a tall undertaking. Let's hope they make it. I understand, though, that two of them will remain on that plateau to help organize the Norwegian Resistance. I must say, those men were endowed with an extraordinary amount of pluck."

"I'd say so, sir. Do you want us to keep monitoring that area?"

"Yes. Also bring me immediately anything you hear about German reactions."

"We've already had some come in." Claire indicated a swatch of papers she had been holding. "Obviously, the Germans were furious, and the *Gestapo* security chief for Norway, Lieutenant Colonel Heinrich Fehlis, set about at once to exact retribution against the population. However, the *Wehrmacht's* commanding general in Norway, General Nikolaus von Falkenhorst, arrived on scene, completed his own assessment, declared that the operation had been conducted by British soldiers, and ordered the Norwegian hostages released."

"That's good news," the commander declared enthusiastically, "and a relief."

"That *is* the good news," Claire said, frowning. "Unfortunately, the rest is not so good." She sighed as Travis waited for her to go on. She took a moment. "Two things, sir. Falkenhorst ordered additional reinforcements for the plant, and now, they'll include some of his best troops—"

"Why? If the production facility is destroyed—"

"That's the worst part of the news, sir. He's ordered that it be repaired and operating at full capacity within two months."

Travis stared at her in dismay, and then slowly shook his head. "We thought that would take eighteen months."

"The Germans can be a decidedly determined lot."

Travis leaned his elbows on his desk and steepled his hands under his nose. "I'll have to get that bit of news upstairs immediately. Changing subjects, a few days ago I sent down a request for more information about those German messages coming out of Goa. Our triangulators assessed that they definitely come from a ship in the harbor at Marmagoa, and we're certain we know which ship. The *Ehrenfels*. Four Axis vessels are anchored in that harbor. Two are old German cargo tubs, the *Braunfels* and the *Drachenfels*, and the last one is an Italian freighter, the *Anfora*. But the *Ehrenfels* is a huge merchant ship that is designed to be converted into an armed cruiser very quickly, with heavy guns. Have you made progress with any of those messages?"

"We have, sir." Once again, Claire indicated papers in her hand. "They transmit almost daily but originate at different times of the day." She leaned forward to point out several entries. "They're detailed descriptions of Allied ships in the area, both merchant and warships. The information includes current positions, direction, and speed of travel, and for the cargo ships, they even detail what they're carrying."

"Hmm. Yes." Travis took the paper and compared it to an index card on his desk. He took a deep breath. "And those transmissions took place a short while before each of those ships was blown out of the water by submarine attacks. In the past six weeks, German U-boats operating in the Pacific have sunk forty-six of our vessels." He pondered a moment. "What conclusions do you draw?"

"That there's a spy or a network of spies operating in India collecting information about our Allied shipping and somehow getting it aboard the *Ehrenfels,* where it's transmitted to a waiting submarine. That's my best guess without further analysis."

"Mine too," Travis said somberly. "Well, thank you, Miss Littlefield." He rose from his chair. "That will be all for now."

After Claire had left, Travis returned to his seat and called his secretary on the phone. "Get me Sir Charles Hambro over at SOE."

When he heard the familiar voice on the line, he merely asked, "Is Operation Creek still on?"

"It is," came the reply. "Do you have something new on it?"

"No. But the activity out of the harbor at Marmagoa continues."

"Well, hopefully, we'll put an end to that within a few days."

15

March 9, 1943
Marmagoa, Goa Portuguese Colony, India

Lieutenant Colonel Lewis Pugh peered through the sea-salt-stained glass on the starboard side of the *Phoebe* into the night through the harsh glare and reflection of spotlights ringing the harbor. He easily spotted the four targets anchored in a dispersed group near the center of the wide waterway, away from the docks. He turned to the skipper, Bernard Davies, the retired Royal Navy commander from Wales who had piloted this hopper barge two thousand miles down one side of India, around its southern tip, and up the western coast from Calcutta. The barge had sailed through rough seas, far enough away from shore so as not to be detected by shore patrols.

Pugh gestured toward the largest of the four ships. "That's got to be the *Ehrenfels*," he murmured. Davies moved over to stand beside him and observe the vessel. "And that's where we believe the transmitter is located."

Both men were of medium height, but whereas Davies was graying around the temples and carried middle-age weight, Pugh was in his early thirties and lean. He nodded. "Last word from intelligence is that *Ehrenfels'* captain expects a raid. He's taken precautions, but we don't know what they are."

"I suppose his expectations are based on your having kidnapped the *Gestapo's* top spy in the area along with his wife," a third man, Bill Grice, remarked, joining them at the window. He was the colonel of the Calcutta Light Horse, a regiment with origins in 1759, organized to ward off Dutch attacks on a new British settlement and formally stood up in 1872 as a Cavalry Reserve unit of the British Indian Army. They still paraded as a reserve unit in Calcutta.

Grice was stocky, in his late forties, with a high forehead and thinning hair, and a pleasant though doleful expression. "What ever became of them, the spy couple?"

"That would be Robert Koch, codenamed 'Trumpeta,' and Grete," Pugh replied, "but I don't know what happened to them after we turned them over to British intelligence. They were quite cooperative, though, after they realized they were caught with no escape. They verified that a Nazi spy ring in India was delivering our shipping information to them for transmission via the *Ehrenfels* to German U-boats lurking offshore. Unfortunately, their removal didn't stop the U-boat attacks on our ships in the area. The spy ring replaced them and continued. Hence our current mission."

He turned to Davies. "Let's review our plan. You're going to continue on this northerly heading—"

"Right," Davies interjected. "If the *Ehrenfels* has any security posted at all, they'll already have spotted us. Once we're past the navigation buoy on the other side of the harbor, we'll cut our running lights and reverse course. The tricky part will be to enter the harbor without hitting the buoy, since we won't be able to see it.

"Once inside the port, we'll stay close to shore. Those waterfront lights shine far across the water but don't illuminate the shore itself. We're small enough to maneuver in the shadows behind them. When we've reached the shortest distance between the docks and the bow of the *Ehrenfels,* we'll turn and approach her directly."

"Good." Pugh turned to Grice. "Once we board, I'll lead a team to go after the transmitter. Are your commandos ready?"

Grice smirked. "Are you making fun?" He chuckled. "We're as ready as we'll ever be. Our chaps are familiarized on small-arms, and they'll put their all into it."

"I'm sure they will," Pugh replied grimly, "including Jock. Let's hope he can do his part." As the *Phoebe* floated into the harbor, he recalled the origin of the mission's title, Operation Creek. The men had themselves chosen it after one of them had joked loudly that the escapade would undoubtedly leave them "up a creek without a paddle."

Three Weeks Earlier

Pugh had not taken a suggestion seriously when it was first mentioned to him by Grice when the two had met for lunch at the Calcutta Light Horse Clubhouse. As colonel of the unit, Grice was a combat veteran and so were the members of his regiment. The two men had been friends for years, although at the time, all that Grice knew of Pugh's current occupation was that he was a professional soldier stationed at Meerut, a hundred miles west-northwest of Calcutta. However, given Pugh's relative youth and keen mind, Grice suspected that there was more to his friend's activities than the young officer let on. As it happened, Pugh was then head of SOE's India office and active in organizing local resistance against a potential Nazi invasion.

They dined together again now, and Pugh had brought along a colleague, Lieutenant Colonel Gavin Stewart. Both wore civilian clothes. "The last time we met for lunch, you needed a letter," Grice remarked after introductions and while enjoying drinks as they waited on their order. "What have you come for this time?"

"Must I need something in order to have lunch with my friend?" Pugh returned jovially. He could not then reveal that the letter had reinforced his cover as a tea merchant in Marmagoa when he and Stewart had gone there to abduct Trumpeta. Grete's kidnapping had been unintentional; she had appeared at the moment that Pugh and Stewart were hustling the Nazi spy into their car.

"When you've driven over a hundred miles specifically to see me and brought along an associate, a reasonable conclusion is that you have something on your mind, don't you think?"

Pugh smiled in amusement. Grice was an elegant man of impeccable manners, and he had held his position in the Calcutta Light Horse for many years. Although still technically a military unit, the regiment had evolved over decades to become a de facto social club wherein an evening at the clubhouse bar could be recorded in the regimental ledger as having attended parade. And for two weeks a year, the unit camped out and conducted training at Ranchi, a large army weapons training school two hundred miles northwest of Calcutta. For young British men on their first assignment at Calcutta, the Light Horse regiment was in essence a place to make contacts, enjoy sports involving horses, and climb socially. Most members were overweight, out of shape, and rusty on out-of-date weapons and combat tactics.

"The last time we met," Pugh began, and the tone of his voice arrested Grice's attention, "you asked me to keep your regiment in mind if anything came up where you could serve. You said your chaps would give their right arms to stuff it to the enemy—or words to that effect."

Grice stared at Pugh. "Seriously? Have you got something in mind?"

"Perhaps. But I have to tell you that when I proposed your unit for a mission, my boss was none too impressed. He says you're a bunch of pencil-pushing accountants and businessmen who like to pretend to play polo or participate in whatever gymkhanas you can conjure up, and that you particularly like to dress up in uniform for dances. Mind you, I've paraphrased his comments."

Grice threw his head back and laughed heartily. "Guilty, on all counts," he said. Then he leaned forward and grew serious. "But most of our members are combat veterans who've seen the hard side of war and feel sidelined in this one. We want to do our part."

Pugh gave him a long, searching look. "All right. I can't yet tell you what the mission is, and I'll need eighteen men, with you commanding them, of course—"

"Whatever it is, we'll do it," Grice enthused. "When is it?"

Pugh took a sharp breath and let it out. "They'll need two weeks to train, and they'll be gone for two additional weeks."

Grice regarded him with incredulity. "You would have us go somewhere unspecified to do something hazardous against the enemy and do it in short order." His face brightened and he grinned. "Sounds like a bargain. I'll put it to the chaps tonight. But with your needing that many men, we might not have enough among the Light Horse who can make the grade. We should invite the Calcutta Scottish too. They're another auxiliary unit." Then he added somberly, "I'll tell you this: every man in the room will volunteer."

"I have no doubt about that," Pugh replied, smiling. "Arrange the meeting however you want to. But one thing. When we make our presentation this evening, we must impress on the men that they must speak about what they've heard to no one. Not to wives, girlfriends, close friends—"

"I get the picture."

"I'll explain it all to you in due time. You and your men deserve to know why you're risking your lives."

"We already know why. For king and country, and that's sufficient."

Pugh chuckled. "Bill, you're always saying those high-brow things."

Grice's eyes twinkled. "That's why I'm the colonel of the Calcutta Light Horse."

The regiment's members were in high spirits bordering on rowdiness even before the formal meeting began at their clubhouse. They had each received a call encouraging attendance to hear a special announcement, and pint mugs overflowed with froth.

"There he is," someone shouted as Grice, Pugh, and Stewart entered. "And he's got that army regular with him. That can't be good. I wonder who the third chap is."

All three grinned and waved. Though not a member of the regiment, Pugh had visited the clubhouse sufficiently with Grice that he was known there.

"What's this about?" another man called, holding his mug high in the air. "You've got us all excited and expectant and everythin'."

Grice waved his hands in the air in a placating manner and climbed onto a makeshift platform. "It's been a while since the Calcutta Light Horse has fought as a unit—since the Boer War in 1900, as a matter of fact."

"Are they callin' us up for action now?" a voice exclaimed. "Are we losin' that bad?" The crowd burst into laughter.

Grice laughed with them and waited for the frivolity to subside. Then he struck a serious chord. "Tonight, I need eighteen volunteers for a secret mission against the Nazis."

All jocularity ceased. The men before him leaned forward in their wooden chairs to grasp his every word. "There's nothing I can tell you about it now," Grice went on, "other than that it'll take a fortnight and involve a sea voyage. And regardless of whether you go or not, you must never reveal what you've heard here tonight to anyone. That's it. Any takers?"

As soon as he had finished speaking, every man in the room raised a hand. "I was afraid of that," Grice announced. "We have more volunteers than we can take. All right, line up in front of that table over there"—he pointed it out—"and Lieutenant Colonel Stewart will take your information."

Then Grice's face turned glum. "I'm sorry to say that I'll have to eliminate some of you immediately for known health problems, and so on. I hate to disappoint you, but this is a crucial mission, and we must take only those who give us the greatest chance of success."

As the line formed and pushed toward Pugh, Grice walked along it, tapping men on their shoulders and shaking his head. Disheartened, they returned to their pints and wandered outside.

Within a short time, after the others had cleared the room, Pugh, Grice, and Stewart reviewed the remaining candidates, and based on Grice's knowledge of each man, they selected the final eighteen. Grice set out to inform them, but as he headed toward the door, an old man, Trooper Jock Cartwright, stepped back inside the room and approached him.

Seeing him, Grice's countenance became compassionate as he shook his head. "You know you can't go," he told Jock, wizened, white-haired, and in his sixties.

"But I must. My son—" He fought to contain strong emotion.

"This won't do anything to help find your son," Grice insisted gently. He knew the story. Jock's son had been caught in fighting the previous year near Rangoon, Burma, and was unaccounted for. Jock and his wife had been tortured with grief, and Jock had pursued a daily effort in attempting to learn news of him.

"But I must do something," Jock cried. "I'm losing my mind. Let me strike back somehow."

"I'm sorry, Jock. We need every man to be as fit as possible at the objective. With your heart, you might not make it that far. At least in that regard, the probabilities are in favor of the ones we chose."

His head drooping, Jock nodded and walked away.

"Wait," Pugh called from behind them. "I couldn't help overhearing." He approached the pair and turned to Jock. "There is a piece of the plan that you might be perfect for, if you're willing."

Jock stared at Pugh in disbelief. "Are you serious?"

"I am, if Colonel Grice approves."

"I'll do anything."

Grice looked askance at Pugh. "You've put me on the spot a bit, old boy. I'm to approve something I know nothing about, and you'll likely not tell me at the moment."

"You're spot-on," Pugh responded with a slight smile. "But he'll be in no danger, his role is crucial, and it requires no physical exertion. I'll fill you in before he executes."

"Huh, that's the operative term, isn't it: 'executes?'"

Securing a suitable boat proved more difficult and Jock more useful than anticipated. The vessel had to be large enough to carry its own crew, the Operation Creek team, and the explosives. But it also had to be small enough not to be regarded as a full-fledged ship. Seaworthiness was imperative to traverse the waves out of sight of land, but the boat should not appear to be recently built. An aging hulk was preferable.

Several alternatives had been considered, but only after a rigorous search, and the pickings were lean. Stewart mentioned the problem to Jock: "I need a ship for a voyage to Bombay. I'm willing to hire or even buy it. We've had no luck with our navy or any of the shipping lines."

"I might be able to help," Jock said. "One of my oldest friends works in the Port Commissioner's Office. I'll be happy to make introductions. We can go there now."

Jock's friend, Doug Lomax, greeted them courteously. He was a small, rotund man behind a big desk, and the comradeship between him and Jock was unmistakable. "He comes here looking for a handout when he needs more whiskey," Doug said. He fixed his stare on Jock. "What do you need this time?"

He listened intently as Jock described the issue. "Stewart wants a boat capable of sailing to Bombay and back, with twenty men aboard, excluding crew."

"These aren't just any men," Stewart broke in as Doug shifted his eyes toward him. "They're Light Horsemen, if you grasp my meaning." He hesitated, and then added, "I'm with the army on special assignment, and that's all I can say."

Doug's eyes bored into Stewart. "I've got it," he said blandly. "I was with the Horsemen for a time. I gather you can't use official channels for whatever it is you're doing, so you've come through the back door."

He watched Stewart's face closely as the officer nodded. "Is that all you need? I'm not in the business of hiring out ships or brokering them. Supposing I should find one, who's going to pay for it should something happen to it on its way to Bombay? And by the way, that's a round trip of roughly five thousand miles, give or take a few hundred. And you know better than I do what the German submarines are doing to cargo shipping."

Stewart did not hesitate. "I'll give you a letter right now accepting responsibility, in the event the vessel becomes a total loss, with payment in full at a price we agree to in advance, or otherwise cover full cost of repairs."

Doug raised his eyebrows and then leaned forward in thought. "You'll need a tugboat or a barge or some other battered vessel that shouldn't be floated any farther than the Hooghly River." He opened a desk drawer, removed a notebook, and paged through it while Stewart and Jock watched. "Here's the one," he said at last, "the *Phoebe*. It's thirty-one years old, built in Glasgow, two hundred and six feet long, thirty-eight feet across the beam, with an indicated engine capacity of six hundred and seventy-seven horsepower. It ran at nine knots when it was new. Probably won't do that now.

She's used for dredging and taking the silt out to sea and dumping it. That resolves the question of seaworthiness, at least to a limited extent.

"There's just one thing, though." Doug hesitated. "Well, two, really. *Phoebe* takes a crew of twenty. She won't carry the crew and your men that distance. You'll need a plan to rendezvous on India's west coast. I'd suggest you send the Horsemen by train."

Clearly dismayed at Doug's latter advice, Stewart leaned back and stared at the ceiling. Then he sat forward and offered his hand to Doug. "As the saying goes, beggars can't be choosers, and time is short. We'll take her. What's the other *thing*?"

"You'll have to find your own captain and crew. All the regulars are serving in the war somewhere." He paused in thought. "I know a sea captain who might be interested, and he can help you with the crew too. Commander Bernard Davies. He joined us after he retired from duty as a regular naval officer several years back. He's free now."

"We weren't expecting a fully-staffed yacht," Pugh said when Stewart and Jock reported back to him. "Did you speak with Commander Davies?"

"We did," Stewart replied. "He's a splendid choice and enthusiastic about joining us."

"Good. I'll look forward to meeting this fellow," Pugh said. "Stewart, you work with Davies to prepare the voyage and sail with him. We can pay enough to find good men on the docks to form the crew.

"I'll arrange the Horsemen's movement and travel with them," Pugh continued. "They'll go down in two groups by train to Madras and then to Cochin, a port on the southwest coast. We'll meet you there. We'll still have another four-hundred-mile sea voyage remaining."

He turned to Jock. "It's time that I provide you instructions and set you on your way. Mind you, I can't divulge the entire plan, just your part of it. But as I told you earlier, it's a crucial part. We might succeed without your part, but the odds are much greater for us if you complete what I tell you to do."

Pugh and Jock talked late into the night, after which Pugh handed the old man a thick packet of high-denomination rupee banknotes. "Use the money well, my friend."

"No worries, Colonel. I know what to do."

The next morning, each Operation Creek team member traveling by train received a letter with instructions purporting to direct them to their annual training ground at Ranchi. It directed that they should travel in civilian clothes but carry full combat kit, including khaki dungarees, web gaiters, and boots with leather soles and half an inch of felt glued to them. They were to bring along headgear, sleeping bags, and mosquito netting, as well as a change of clothing and mess gear.

Additionally, they were instructed to bring first aid kits, personal hygiene supplies, cigarettes if they needed them, and not more than one optional bottle of whiskey. Lastly, they were to withdraw their personal sidearms from the armory with eighteen rounds of ammunition. The letter stated that they would be issued Sten guns. Most ominously, they were to bring handcuffs and their special knives, designated SK for Silent Killing.

On reading the instructions, each Horseman perceived the truth: these were their mobilization orders. And they were not heading to Ranchi.

16

March 2, 1943
Marmagoa, Goa Portuguese Colony, India

Jock drove through the winding, narrow streets of Vasco da Gama, a village on the outskirts of Marmagoa. He caught a scent of the sea and beheld, beyond the palm-lined shoreline to his right, the azure bay with a most ironic sight: a British oil tanker at anchor in one of the finest deep-water ports on the Indian subcontinent, proudly flying the Union Jack. Behind it were three Axis freighters, two with red banners and black swastikas unfurled in the wind. The fourth vessel flew the Italian flag. Jock figured that the largest of the Nazi vessels had to be the *Ehrenfels*.

He continued into the thoroughfares of colonial Marmagoa, heading past the cafés along the docks, hearing music blaring in counterpoint to the flapping of the canvas roof of the used car he had bought for the purpose. The surroundings became more upscale as he drove past the Ritz and other grand lodging establishments and finally stopped in front of the Gran Palacio Hotel. He checked in using his wife's maiden name for ease of remembering, and then went looking for a particular local official.

Finding the man required Jock to drive into the countryside toward Panjim, and after an hour's trip, he found the house at an address that Pugh had provided, parked the car, and approached the front door. A servant dressed in white showed him into a sitting room decorated with mementos from foreign lands indicating that the official may have served overseas. Soon, a middle-aged Goanese entered. Jock introduced himself using his alias.

"I have an urgent request," Jock said after introductions, "and I was led to understand that you were expecting me." Pugh had mentioned that an SOE agent had preceded Jock to pave the way.

"Let's walk down by the river, shall we?" the man said. "We can talk privately there." The foliage was thick but neat with a gravel path. "What can I do for you?" he asked when they reached the river.

"I apologize for getting straight to business, but time is short," Jock said. "I believe you have two sons in school at Dehra Dun."

The man scoffed. "I do, but with inflation the way it is, I feel more like I'm paying for eight instead of just two."

"We might be able to help you to the extent that you would never have to pay their boarding costs again, if we can come to an arrangement."

"That would be grand," the man replied. "What must I do?"

"Well, I need your help," Jock said, edging into a gentle negotiation that must follow protocol. He knew that this man had been bribed before. The Indian needed the money to supplement his meager public servant's wages. "I'd like for you to use your influence to persuade the governor-general or another senior official to host a reception. His guests will be every officer working for the port authority or aboard the ships. It should be a diplomatic affair, and with Portugal being neutral, that should cause no international difficulties.

"I'd also like there to be a street carnival for the benefit of the crews of all these vessels. Can you arrange those two events? Of course, I'll pay all the expenses."

He sensed fear in the little man of being found out and the consequences.

"Neither of your events would be easy to arrange," the man replied, "and they would cost a great deal of money. You must know that the governor-general does not entertain often."

"I'll leave those matters to you, and if you cannot accomplish those tasks, I'll find someone else who can. But I must have an answer now. Yes or no."

"How will the money be paid?"

"Into a bank in India. No one will find out."

The man bowed his head slightly and then straightened. "Then I will make the arrangements."

Jock handed him a small packet. "Here are beautifully engraved invitations. They have Goa's crest and Portugal's colors. You can fill in the name of the host. And be sure to build up anticipation for the event. It should be one that no one among your elite or the ship's officers will want to miss. Bill the reception as being an expression of Portugal's desire for peace and neutrality while offering hospitality even in the face of war. Just be sure that it occurs in one week, at ten o'clock in the evening on the ninth. And the crews' street carnival must occur at the same time."

———

The following morning, Jock made his way on foot to the less savory streets of Marmagoa, where women clothed themselves to attract lascivious glances that they returned with come-hither sweetness. Some called to him, but he made his way past them, hearing jeers referring to his age and questionable ability, but he paid them no mind. He approached one of the establishments where men frequented and women's laughter escaped when the doors opened. A burly young man with dark hair and a beaming smile greeted him.

"Welcome, sir. You have come to the right place. Whatever your heart desires, we can accommodate. Let me show you in."

Jock shook his head and smiled back. "No thank you, though I've heard after making inquiries that yours is one of the finest such establishments in the city."

"It's a brothel, sir. No reason to pretend otherwise, and yes, our reputation is that it is the finest in Marmagoa. We have the most beautiful ladies, but if you desire something else—"

"No, no," Jock said, waving his hands in front of him. He sighed and glanced around the street. "You know, I spent a lot of time in the army and away from home during my life. I'm old now, but I remember those times. And now we have a war on and some men can't leave here, much less go home."

He swung back around and faced the doorman with a resolute look. "I've been out of the army for decades. I feel for these servicemen stranded here, and the other crewmembers too. They don't see their families much either." A big smile crossed his face, and he crooked a finger toward the doorman. "Well, I've become very rich as a businessman, and I'd like to do something to alleviate the stress on those poor chaps. I'll tell you what: for the next week, I'll pay for every man who comes here to spend time with your ladies."

The doorman reeled in shock. "Are you serious? When that word gets out, we won't be able to handle the crowds. Our girls will die of exhaustion."

Jock's brow creased as he contemplated the issue. "Well then, let's extend the courtesy to every establishment on this street. I'll leave it to you to arrange with the other such houses, and I'll even make it worth your own while."

The doorman beamed, obviously elated with his good fortune. He and Jock worked out payment details, to include a stipulation that Jock would hold back one third of the estimated payment until the week had passed. He left and returned to the Gran Palacio feeling certain that the young, burly man would complete the task in detail and enthusiastically while no doubt availing himself of Jock's generosity.

With preparations for the diplomatic reception and the entertainment of the ships' crews complete, Jock set about to prepare the finishing touches for the carnival. Back at the hotel, he retrieved his car and drove to the area where the festival would be held. There, he searched for suitable places from which to launch the contents of his car's trunk. *No festival would be complete without fireworks.*

That done, he reconnoitered along the coast beyond the docks and found a vacant lot far below St. Andrew's Church. It was ideal because it was separated by distance from both the church and the wharves, and the probability of anyone visiting this pathetic piece of land at the critical hour was diminished by the stench of bloated carcasses of dead cats and dogs swirling in the shoals, swept there by the tide. He had little fear that strollers or lovers would seek this place out at the exact wrong time.

Satisfied that all was prepared, he returned to his hotel and placed a call to his wife. She related that news had been received regarding their son.

After suffering through a train derailment and three boring days of keeping out of sight while divided between the Malabar and Harbour House hotels, the Horsemen were aghast to see the decrepit vessel that would carry them another four hundred miles to Marmagoa. But, amid jocular grumbling, they boarded and headed out to sea. They had been joined by Yogi Crossley, whom Pugh had introduced as a man who dealt with "explosive matters."

Phoebe's voyage had not been without incident. The main bearing had overheated. Fixing it had required a two-hour delay while the crew put a new shell around it. But it steamed into Cochin Harbor in manageable order and took on its passengers.

"As you can see," Pugh told the men assembled below deck as the *Phoebe* steamed beyond the Cochin horizon, "our flagship wasn't built for comfort. Find yourselves places to sleep, and then we'll gather, and I'll explain the mission. There's drinking water in the galley."

The "places to sleep" were sparse, a few square yards on the deck or below in the hold. Either way, they would rest on steel softened only by their bedrolls. The head consisted of an outhouse hanging over the edge of the deck.

When they had settled in, they crowded together once more for Pugh's briefing. "Our cover story, should you be captured, is that we are a bunch of middle-aged partiers seeking a good time in Marmagoa—and that is, in fact, where we're headed. The town is a popular destination for Continentals living in India and wishing for a vacation with a European flavor. You'll say that we decided to take a boat tour, drank too much, and then decided, for a prank, to raid a German ship parked in the harbor."

"That's it?" Grice asked.

"That's it." Pugh looked across the faces of the men of Operation Creek with narrowed eyes. "I must impress on you not to mention the Calcutta Light Horse or any connection with British involvement."

"Would you mind explaining why, sir?" someone called.

Pugh shrugged. "It's quite simple, really. Portugal is neutral in this war, but they lean toward the Allies. We can't disrupt that relationship. Marmagoa is not the only Portuguese colony. As you know, they own the Azores in the Atlantic near the mouth of the Mediterranean. Wherever they have port facilities, they allow us to use them for re-fueling, loading supplies, and repairing ships, including along their own continental coasts. We cannot upset Portugal and drive them to enter the war on the Nazi side. Therefore, this operation must leave no British fingerprints. That's why we're not sending a submarine or real British commandos into the harbor to do the job."

"Whaddya mean, real British commandos?" someone called. "What are we, laced tarts?"

The Horsemen erupted in laughter.

"Point taken," Pugh said, joining in the merriment. "We're doing a commando's job, so we can consider ourselves commandos. But"—he rose from a steel slab he had been half-sitting on and held a finger in the air— "make no mistake. What we are doing is dangerous. We're going against a force much larger than our own. Surprise is our critical element, but intelligence advises that our target expects something. They're just not sure what that is, but they've taken steps to harden their defenses. That information was supplied to our intelligence chaps by our consul general in Marmagoa."

"Good on 'im, sir," another man shouted above the sound of waves and the engine. "Now, do ya mind tellin' us what we're gonna do?"

Pugh straightened to his full height. Then he turned to Grice. "Would you like to do the honors?"

Grice stood with alacrity while Pugh leaned back onto the steel slab. "Gentlemen," Grice began, his voice both solemn and enthusiastic. "We'll be on this boat for two days, and during that time, you'll be practicing with your Sten guns. We brought along plenty of ammo. You'll need the practice."

His statements brought another round of cheers. He smiled and continued. "You'll notice in the hold that we've loaded a cargo of bamboo poles. They're hardened and won't bend. Over the time that we're traveling, we'll be cutting them and turning them into ladders. We have the tools."

A collective groan went up from the Horsemen. "That's fine," one of them called with pleading impatience, "but what are we going to do?"

"I'll tell you, but one more thing before I do." Grice was playing with his men now and enjoying it. "Well, two things. Before we go in, you'll hang old rubber tires with thick ropes from the sides of *Phoebe*. That'll keep her from clanging too loudly when we come to the target."

The men groaned again, good-naturedly but with growing impatience. "And what's the other thing?" a voice called.

Grice paused a moment, searching the faces. Then he pointed out Crossley. "Our new man here will instruct us on the care and use of specialized explosives we've brought with us. You'll all need to heed his instruction."

That brought an approving reaction among the men, and they glanced at Crossley with a new measure of respect. "That's good," came a loud comment. "He's into yoga and standing on his head for long hours, and we were about to throw him overboard for his weird habits. Maybe now we'll let him stay. Now, sir, would you please get on with the briefing?"

Pugh threw his head back and laughed. "Sir," he told Grice, "perhaps you should go ahead and tell them about the mission."

Grice smiled again and held out his hands, palms forward, fingers extended, in a calming manner. He took a deep breath. "The Nazis have a transmitter on a ship in Marmagoa Harbor, the *Ehrenfels*, and it's sending routes and positions of our own ships to submarines lying in wait offshore. They've been killing our vessels at the rate of one each day."

He turned to glance at Pugh, and when he again faced his men, he announced with bright eyes and a determined smile, "We are going to capture or sink that ship and three others, including one Italian."

For a brief moment, the Horsemen were quiet; only the wind, the drone of *Phoebe's* engine, and the sea breaking against the bow could be heard. Then her hold exploded with cheers, the men slapping backs, clapping shoulders, and dancing celebratory jigs on the curved floor of the dredging barge.

Grice waited for his audience to settle down and then pointed to the smokestack. "Notice our skipper, Commander Davies, had the funnel lengthened. That's so the *Phoebe* appears to be a small oiler or water boat. That's been important out here on the open sea. Enemies sighting this vessel will see a decrepit hauler near her last outing. That subterfuge could be crucial as we enter the harbor. It could gain us time if the enemy crews spot us.

"And I'm pleased to tell you that our man Jock Cartwright has also been busy on our behalf." He explained Jock's role. "So, if you find yourself in the water without an oar, swim to the south shore—as you face inland, that'll be the one to your right. Look for the church and swim to it—Jock will be there to pull you out of the drink, provide you with money, and set you on your way home."

"Good old Jock," one of the men observed. "We should have known he wouldn't allow this operation to go forward without him."

"I sure hope his son's all right," another said.

Amid murmurs, Grice turned back to Pugh. "Are you ready to brief the plan?"

Pugh nodded and regained his feet. "Let's get down to serious business, shall we?" He rolled out a map of Marmagoa on a makeshift table as the Horsemen gathered round. "We're going to divide into three groups, and then we're going to rehearse, rehearse, rehearse, and then rehearse some more."

17

March 9, 1943

Commander Davies guided the *Phoebe* past the navigational buoy at the mouth of the harbor, piloting the boat a few miles north before dousing her running lights. Then he spun the wheel and turned the vessel back in the direction she had come. Staying close to the shore, which was visible only as a darker blot against the sky, he guided the boat slowly, cautiously in the dark, navigating by compass, and watchful for the buoy.

He steered the *Phoebe* around the northern bank of the harbor entrance without mishap, and there before them was the full waterfront. Across the water was the town itself, and against its lights and those of the dockyards, the four Axis ships were clearly visible.

Then Davies noticed something and sucked in a sharp breath. "Look there," he called to Pugh, standing close by. "That's a British oil tanker. And look." He pointed. "Three cruisers are in the docks. I don't know whose they are."

"Must be Portuguese," Pugh replied, "perhaps sent here to reinforce neutrality."

"I hope you're right." He turned to Grice. "Tell your men that it's time for our special provision. All the men must drink one shot of whiskey, regardless of whether or not they're teetotalers. They are then to take into their mouths and spit out another shot. The remainder of the bottles, they are to dump all over themselves. And remind them that if we are about to be boarded, we dump all of our guns and ammunition and stick to our cover story—that we are a group of British middle-aged men having a party that went wrong. In no case should your regiment be mentioned."

"Got it," Grice said, "and I'm sure they do too, but I'll remind them."

Davies steered along the northern shore heading east and generally held course for four to five miles before turning south and starting to parallel the eastern bank of the harbor. Ahead of them, the dockyards loomed with huge lights casting wide beams across the water. But as he had predicted, they did not illuminate close into the docks, leaving a gap wide enough for the *Phoebe* to traverse in shadows.

As they closed the distance, dance music floated down on a breeze from the governor-general's house on the high ground to the west of town, accompanied by the sounds of partiers' revelry. From closer to the docks came less refined, raucous sounds of a festival in full swing with drums, brass horns, and loud cheering.

"I think Jock got the better end of this deal," one of the Horsemen muttered. "I wonder if there's time to trade places."

Another one scoffed, "You wouldn't know what to do with all those girls."

"You might be right, mate, but I could sure learn in a hurry."

Davies kept to the shadows while constantly gauging his distance to the *Ehrenfels*. "I'll be making the turn in about five minutes," he called to Pugh.

"Alert your men," Pugh told Grice.

The *Phoebe* puttered out over choppy waters toward the group of four Axis ships. "I'll steer as if we are going across the harbor on a course to pass near them," Davies said, "and when we're in their shadow on the other side, I'll power up the engine and come in from port side."

Pugh grunted an affirmative response. He turned to Grice. "Are the men ready."

Grice nodded, his face grim, and glanced at his watch. "It's nearly two o'clock."

"Now let's hope that Jock delivers the third diversion."

Crouched in *Phoebe's* hull, the Horsemen of Operation Creek were poised with their Sten guns, their SK knives strapped to their legs, their faces blackened, and all looking up as the large hull of the *Ehrenfels* slid into view. They had already hung the rubber tires on thick, knotted rope over the boat's side, and the men in charge of placing the bamboo ladders gripped them, ready to hoist them into place.

Davies steered expertly. The target ships were closer together than they had appeared, and as his vessel approached, he saw that the anchor chains had rusted, and large clumps of seaweed had gathered around them below the water level.

To get to the chosen entry point on *Ehrenfels,* he had no choice but to steer beneath the overhanging stern of the Italian freighter, *Anfora,* and as he did so, the Horsemen heard talking and music from the deck above. Apparently, no one there noticed *Phoebe's* passage.

Ahead of them now was *Ehrenfels.*

"Blimey, she's huge," a man exclaimed. "From Colonel Pugh's sketches, I had in my mind something much smaller."

"I'll say," Pugh breathed.

Ehrenfels' bridge towered four stories above its deck, its sides were lined with portholes, and the rail stretched into the darkness at the opposite end. Her masts rose above her superstructure and disappeared into the night. And although her running lights were on, curtains blocked all but the smallest shafts of light at the edges of the crew quarters' windows.

"Two minutes," Grice called.

Phoebe continued on under Davies' able guidance, and now the riveted black hull passed by only yards away to starboard. The men in the hold craned their necks to see anything at deck level on the big ship, but it was too tall. The bamboo-ladder carriers began to lift their equipment, ready to put it into place.

"One minute," Grice called.

"Who's down there?" an angry voice demanded in German from *Ehren-*

fels' deck. "What are you doing?" The silhouette of a head appeared over the side.

"This is a harbor barge," Pugh called back in German.

"Why are you running without lights?"

At that moment, the *Phoebe* sideswiped the *Ehrenfels,* and despite the rubber tires and thick rope, the contact was loud as it seared a deep, long, silver scar in the ship's hull that reflected the ship's running lights.

Two men forward near *Phoebe's* bow tossed grappling hooks to the cargo ship's deck and yanked hard on them until they gripped.

"Now," Grice ordered, and immediately, multiple bamboo ladders were hoisted in the air and pushed against the ship's side. Pugh was the first on the ladder, and he scurried up, grabbing the rails when he reached the ship's deck, and none too soon. The force of the collision had caused the *Phoebe* to bounce back a few feet, and Pugh was left dangling for seemingly interminable seconds until he managed to grab the ship's rail with both hands, swing his right leg up and over the side, and pull himself the rest of the way up.

Meanwhile, the watchman above had disappeared, spreading the alarm in loud cries, and was soon joined by other German shouts. Below, other men had climbed to the top of the ladder and clung there, leaning forward lest they be thrown backward and topple while the little barge once again narrowed the distance to the great ship.

Suddenly, a huge, bright spotlight shone down from above, bathing the Horsemen in white, blinding light. They halted momentarily, covering their eyes. Then one of the raiders aimed his Sten gun at the center of the circular frame and let loose a volley that did not cease until the light disappeared and darkness reigned. However, before the light was fully extinguished, Crossley, the demolitions expert, noticed a thick cable running from the main mast down inside the ship's interior. "That leads to the transmitter," he muttered.

The ladders once again rested against *Ehrenfels',* and then, all the mostly middle-aged, out-of-shape, erstwhile and current warriors of the Horsemen climbed, huffing, puffing, and elbowing each other to move ahead. Those tasked with carrying fire extinguishers struggled to clamber up the ladders with the heavy tanks strapped to their backs while also carrying their sidearms and Sten guns.

As Pugh rapidly surveyed the deck, one element became apparent. The ship was manned by a skeleton crew. Jock's ruse had worked. Most of the officers must have been at the reception, and the crew was enjoying itself either at the carnival or in the best brothels of Marmagoa.

However, one worrisome aspect immediately caught Pugh's eye. The forward deck was covered with metal sheets, on top of which bags of flour had been piled and interspersed with hand grenades. Near the bow, barrels of petroleum had been placed that could easily be upended, spilled, and set afire. Obviously, the captain had anticipated a raid and taken defensive measures that could injure or kill the attackers without inflicting serious damage to the ship. As the leaders of each team came over the rail, Pugh pointed out the hazards.

Shots rang out from the top decks of the bridge. Pugh and those Horsemen already aboard returned fire as their mates continued to climb the ladders.

Jock watched anxiously from his observation point at the lot between St. Andrew's and the docks. The place stank almost unbearably from the dead cats and dogs washed there by the convergence of the tide's cross-currents. He heard the first shots ring out and saw the muzzle flashes on the deck of the *Ehrenfels,* but he had not seen *Phoebe's* approach and there had been no explosions. Then he remembered that Pugh's first preference was to capture the ship and sail it out of the harbor. *So, no fire, no explosions might be a good thing.*

Nearby, on the road, his car sat, the tank topped off, pointed in a direction for a quick getaway. Jock's job now was to wait for any survivors from Operation Creek who might show up on this ghastly beach. *But where are the fireworks?*

Over the last few days, with a young Goanese man whom he had paid handsomely, he had laboriously laid the fireworks in several concealed places near the site of the intended festival close to the docks. After making final preparations earlier in the evening, Jock had handed the young man a ten rupee note. "When you hear popping noises coming from the harbor, that's your signal to set them off. Then, come to my room at the Gran Palacio in the morning and I'll give you another ten rupees, *if* you get it done right."

The man had smiled eagerly and set off to accomplish his exciting task.

Jock glanced to his right, where the fireworks should have already been arcing overhead. Then, as if on cue, they lit up the sky. Rockets soared up streaming fiery sparklers. The air hissed with fireworks shot high over the town and releasing wondrously luminous blues, reds, yellows, all the colors of the rainbow in unimaginable shapes. Jock had no doubt that the attention of the town, and those still in attendance at the reception and festival, would be fixed on the shimmering overhead display—and not on the *Ehrenfels*.

Passing next to Pugh, Grice pointed toward the waterfront. "Jock delivered," he shouted above the din as more fireworks streamed into the dark heavens.

Pugh pumped his fist, thumb up. "Spread the word about those grenades and the petroleum barrels," he called back. "Shoot to kill any crewman who moves toward them. Don't hesitate—just try not to hit the barrels."

"Roger."

Suddenly, from high overhead, an alarm siren sounded, its high-pitched shriek wailing across the waters. The mind-numbing noise was disorienting as it pierced the night, but the Horsemen shook off the resulting confusion and continued on, the last of them clearing the rail and spreading out on their assigned tasks.

Pugh and one of the Horsemen, Melborne, headed to the captain's bridge, climbing the gangway and navigating the narrow passageways cautiously. They found the bridge empty but heard noises from above and discovered a small set of stairs leading up. After climbing them in the darkness, they came to a door and tried the handle.

Locked.

Melborne beat the handle with his Sten until it gave way and thrust the door open. Inside, the captain stared at them while another officer clung onto a cord suspended through the ceiling.

The captain went for his gun. Melborne fired first, sweeping the room with automatic fire. The captain slumped, dead. The other officer let go of the cord. The siren's scream fell silent, and the officer fell, his body twitching in its last throes.

Pugh appeared and rushed to the captain's desk and rifled through the drawers, searching for the codebooks. Not finding them, he headed back into the companionway, calling for Melborne to join him. There, they crossed paths with Crossley and another Horseman, Breene, moving silently across the steel deck on the felt-covered soles of their shoes.

They traded the password, "Matharne." Then Crossley told Pugh in a low voice, "I saw the radio cable from outside. It led to a glass insulator by a cabin. That's got to be the transmitter cable to its antenna, and it must be this way."

He led them through the darkness to another cabin. The door was locked. Breene first tried to kick it in before shooting out the lock.

Inside, an officer scrambled to jam documents into a metallic cylinder. Surrounding him on the floor were several lead-covered books. When the two Horsemen entered, he threw one of the heavy books at them and scrambled to reach his weapon.

Breen aimed his Sten at the officer. It jammed.

Crossley tackled the German. An incendiary device exploded between them, sending a burst of white-hot flame across Crossley's face and one of his arms. It seared the walls and ceiling, which immediately ignited, turning the room into a cauldron.

Seeing Crossley incapacitated, Breene fought with the German. Just then, yet another Horseman, Red Mac, entered and struck the enemy across the head with his Sten gun. Meanwhile, having spotted a photo of Hitler on the wall next to a brass clock, Crossley shot Hitler's likeness in the face and grabbed the clock, which he thrust inside his shirt. Then he helped Red Mac and Breene pull the unconscious German officer out of the room and handcuff him.

With suffocating black smoke filling the passageway, Crossley stopped only long enough to wrap a first aid dressing to his injured arm and continued on with the others, in search of the transmitter.

At the stern, Manners and Squire encountered the starboard anchor and determined that they must blow out a link with explosives and let the heavy chain drop into the harbor in order to have a chance of sailing the *Ehrenfels* out of port. As Crossley had taught them, they mashed the plastic explosive around an enormous steel link at the eyehole through which the chain ran into the water. Dampness prevented the explosive from adhering to the steel, so they jammed it in a wedge between the chain and the eyehole and set the charge.

The loud concussion moments later deafened them momentarily, but they had managed to shield themselves behind heavy metal equipment. Emerging half-dazed into the smoke after fragments of metal had stopped pinging around the deck, they set about looking for the next anchor chain, but at that moment, Manners shouted a warning while leaning down to feel the deck and smell his hand. Kerosene.

A German crewman stepped forward on a deckhouse and fired a signal gun. The phosphorescent round skipped along the deck, igniting the fuel. Flames leaped into the sky and danced along the ship's aft deck and spread along its sides.

Horseman Manners fired his Sten gun at the deckhouse but missed, and his gun clicked harmlessly as he ran out of ammo. He grabbed another magazine from his belt, jammed it into the Sten, and sprayed the deckhouse.

The German fell into the sea.

Flames now prevented Manners and Squire from reaching the second anchor chain.

Below decks, Horsemen Lumsdaine and Hilliard ran through the passageways in the aft sections until they found the engine room and its control panel. Within moments, they had flipped on the lights and beheld a huge diesel engine in remarkably clean running order.

"How do we start it?" Hilliard called.

"Wait, I'm looking," Lumsdaine yelled back.

"Well don't take too long. The proprietors might object."

After a few moments, Lumsdaine's shoulders drooped. "We can't take her," he shouted. "The Germans have taken out the injectors and other critical parts. She's dead in the water."

At that moment, Grice entered, soon enough that he heard Lumsdaine's comment. "Don't waste time with it. We'll have to sink her. Look around for the transmitter. It must be around here somewhere."

"How about behind those bulkheads," Lumsdaine suggested, pointing them out and heading toward a sign emblazoned with a large skull-and-crossbones warning.

A heavy metal door behind the sign was held shut with six wingnuts. Lumsdaine turned them easily, but when he had removed them, the door still would not open.

"Blow it," Grice ordered.

"With pleasure," Lumsdaine replied, glad that he had paid close attention to Crossley's instructions. He set the charge and sheltered for the blast, which resonated through the ship's steel walls, and when the smoke had cleared, he entered the room, joined by Hilliard.

The chamber was strewn with debris, and no codebooks were on the shelves, but the radio they sought was still attached to a wall. It was black, and its attendant Morse-code key hung suspended by a wire below it with a list of frequencies. Hilliard grabbed it and thrust it into a pocket.

Meanwhile, Breen had been exploring the engine room and found another way out. Just then, an enormous explosion rocked the *Ehrenfels*.

Commander Davies alternated anxious eyes from the *Phoebe's* instruments to the small space between his boat and the giant ship, to the edge of the

Ehrenfels' deck far above him. The expected duration of the raid had passed. He had heard and seen the aft starboard chain crash into the water, but no sign of any such thing happening to the one forward. Meanwhile the stench of burned fuel and the thick black smoke rolled down into his small wheelhouse, impairing his breath. And when the huge explosion occurred on the freighter, the shockwave rocked *Phoebe*, threatening to capsize her.

He looked across the northern mouth of the harbor to where Portuguese soldiers at Cabo Fort at Dona Paula splayed spotlights erratically, focusing on one object after another but not dallying on any in particular. All that had to happen to upend the raid, even at this late time, was for the spotlight's beam to settle on the tiny hopper barge bobbing next to the blazing *Ehrenfels*, and they would be found out. A Portuguese cruiser would then be dispatched to round up the Horsemen as they sought escape.

Red Mac had made his way back to the top deck and secured one of the fire extinguishers brought aboard by the Horsemen. He commenced spraying down the deck, unaware that the ship could not be sailed out of the harbor. As he worked, he felt the ship listing to one side, and then he was suddenly attacked by three German crewmen. They dripped with water and ran through the flames unblemished, and in a flash, he determined that they must have opened the Kingston valves to scuttle the ship.

With no other weapon within his quick grasp before they reached him, he turned the fire extinguisher on them, immersing their faces in the white liquid. They screamed as they reached for Red Mac, but then the ship listed further, and they slid out of his reach.

Two more crewmen ran for him from the shadows, and he aimed the fire extinguisher stream at them, but it ran dry. He threw the red canister at them but they dodged. He reached for his pistol, but his lanyard prevented him from bringing it up to fire with speed.

They grasped him, and one German clubbed him over the head.

Red Mac went down.

Horsemen Melborne and Squire emerged onto the sloping deck in time to see Red Mac fall. Melborne attacked the man with the club, knocked him down, held him, and cuffed him. Squire tripped the second man, who fell against a hard steel slab and dropped, semi-conscious. Squire cuffed him.

The *Ehrenfels* listed still farther, and her imminent capsize became evident. The Horsemen, on whatever deck, headed to the top deck as rapidly as they could, panting, sweating, urged on by Pugh and Grice. They reached the main deck and slipped and slid across its oily surface to the side.

Far below, Davies saw the listing ship start to lean at an accelerating pace over the *Phoebe*. "Cast off," he shouted, and the barge's crew jumped to, untying the knots holding her to the doomed *Ehrenfels*. Davies threw the engines into full power astern, and her propellers thrashed the water as she backed away.

Still aboard the *Ehrenfels*, the Horsemen herded their German prisoners together. Others had been taken and secured with one end of the cuffs around the handrails. Squire unlocked the cuff on one of the Germans and handed him the key. "The ship's going down," he yelled in German. "Unlock your mates and jump."

Then he raced to where the Horsemen were already leaping. Having expected a long drop, he was surprised to see that the list had narrowed the gap between its deck and the *Phoebe* to a few feet. He vaulted safely into the hold.

Davies strenuously applied every maneuver to hold the *Phoebe* close, but the distance was widening, and already Horsemen were jumping into the water and swimming toward her. Germans had also jumped but were headed toward shore.

When all the Horsemen were aboard and reacting in disbelief at the reality that all were present and healthy despite some wounds, the *Phoebe* puttered to the mouth of the bay and then headed south. On the tiny bridge, Pugh and Grice had gathered with Davies. "We might as well celebrate now," Grice said. "We might not get the chance if we wait until we get to Bombay."

They leaned against the back wall of the cabin and watched the smoldering wreckage that had been the Ehrenfels. "Well, gentlemen," Pugh intoned, "to success." He produced a bottle of whiskey and three shot glasses and handed them around.

Just then, an unexpected explosion ripped the night. Looking back, they saw one of the other German cargo ships in flames and beginning to list. Then a second explosion lit up the sky, and the Italian ship was on fire, followed shortly by the remaining German ship.

Grice guffawed. "They must have thought we were the advance party of a much larger raiding force. They've scuttled their own ships."

The little *Phoebe* continued out to sea on a southerly course. When it was out of sight of land, Davies turned on her running lights and pointed the innocuous little boat north toward Bombay.

On shore, above the beach, Jock waited until pink fingers of dawn began to edge up over the horizon. Then he walked along the shoreline, staring intently among carcasses to make sure he did not miss any that might belong to one or more of his fellow Horsemen of Operation Creek. Satisfied that he had missed none, he walked back to his car.

He returned to the Gran Palacio Hotel only long enough to pay the young man who had faithfully ignited the fireworks, and then he set out for home. He wore a big smile, his contentment deep as he maneuvered back through Vasco da Gama. "We did it," he breathed. He thought of his last phone call with his wife in which she had delivered news about their son.

"He's a prisoner of war," she had told him.

"My son is alive," he now muttered as he started the fourteen-hundred-mile trek home. "My son is alive."

18

March 9, 1943
Bletchley Park, England

Claire knocked on Commander Travis' door and waited to be called inside. On hearing his voice, she entered and hurried to his desk, her eagerness showing. "Sir, I thought you'd want to know. The transmitter in Marmagoa is neutralized. All three German ships were sunk and the Italian one as well. Berlin is buzzing about it, looking for someone to blame. They suspect us, but they have no evidence. None."

"That is good news." Travis beamed. "What about casualties?"

"That would have to come from another intelligence section, sir, although I can tell you that the port authorities found no dead bodies."

"That's even better than we could hope for." Travis sat back to savor the moment. Then he leaned forward. "Have you heard anything more about Hitler's doctor and his possible malfeasance?"

"All the time, sir." Claire had remained standing. "I wouldn't say that we have anything new, but the notion persists among the German High Command that the doctor is a bad actor, from their perspective. And Hitler's unbalanced behavior continues. He lashes out more and trusts his close advisers less."

Travis pursed his lips as he contemplated the ramifications. "Based on your section's earlier reports in that regard, we've held back on any action against Hitler ourselves. Please keep me informed if anything develops."

"Of course, sir."

Travis arched his eyebrows as he changed subjects. "Speaking of Berlin, have you heard anything about special weapons development?"

"All the time, but nothing definite. It's more whispers than anything. My guess is that most of the conversations regarding them are held behind closed doors with the most strenuous security requirements, and everyone close to those projects is vetted in the extreme. Little need would exist to communicate about them on the wireless where we intercept our intelligence."

"Of course. I was just hoping."

"I'll bring you anything we hear."

Just before dusk that evening, after Claire had put Timmy to bed and settled onto her sofa to read a book, a knock on the front door startled her. She was expecting no one and had heard no approaching car crunching gravel up her driveway. Hurrying to the window, she pulled back the blackout curtains and peered out. Dread seized her.

A dark-haired young lady waited there, perhaps in her mid-twenties, tall, standing straight, and wearing a US Army uniform with captain's insignia. She looked about, and then knocked again.

Claire caught her breath, fearful of news that the officer might bring concerning one or more of her brothers, and then reminded herself that any adverse information in that regard would come through official British channels. With some hesitance, she opened the door. "May I help you?"

The young lady greeted her with a cheerful smile and melodious voice. "Hello, are you Claire Littlefield?"

"I am."

The visitor thrust her hand forward. "I'm so happy to finally meet you. I'm Sherry Littlefield, your cousin."

Claire stared, wide-eyed. Then, recovering herself, she grasped Sherry's hand. "What a surprise. Come in. I was hoping I might meet family from America. There are so many of you Yanks here now." She grasped Sherry's hand more firmly and led her into the sitting room, closing the door behind them. "How did you find me?"

"My brother, Josh, sent me your address, but he neglected to include your phone number, or I'd have called ahead. Someone in the village gave me directions. I hope this isn't a bad time—"

"Nonsense. I'm thrilled to meet you."

Claire prepared tea and the two talked late into the night. "You're a captain," Claire said. "I'm impressed."

"A nurse," Sherry replied. "I'm in a group that flies to the field hospitals and cares for our wounded as they're brought back here for more extensive care. Some of our patients wouldn't have a chance without medical attention while being transported."

"I've heard of your group. They call you angels, and from the stories I've read, you are indeed that."

Sherry blushed, and her face showed traces of strain. "We're just nurses doing our jobs like everyone else."

Claire noticed the slight dip in demeanor and that Sherry recovered immediately. "Are you all right? You looked stressed for a second."

Sherry sighed. "Oh, sorry. We try not to do that. We have a mandate we impose on ourselves: never let them see you cry."

Claire regarded her quizzically. "Who is 'them?'"

"Our patients," Sherry said hoarsely, and suddenly her eyes filled with tears. She sniffed as she wiped her eyes. "Sorry, we're not supposed to do that."

"You're only human—"

Sherry shook her head and fought for composure. Taking a deep breath, she said, "Our patients are the ones with more than superficial wounds. Some are missing limbs, some have gaping chest holes, ghastly burns, or multiple gunshot wounds. Some will die within a few minutes, and we know it."

Tears flowed again as she wiped them away. "They look to us for comfort, and sometimes that's all we can give—medicine won't treat them, and usually, they know it. They cling to our hands, gaze into our eyes through their agony, and the best we can do in those times is to smile down and tell them everything will be all right." She paused to catch her breath. "That's why our self-imposed rule is never let them see you cry."

As she spoke, she spotted the cocktail cabinet in the corner of the room. "Could I have some of that? The stronger the better."

While Claire went to pour her a drink, Sherry told her, "I'm sorry. I didn't come here for this. Josh was so excited about having seen Paul, and I wanted to make contact."

"I'm glad you did, and don't fret about telling me anything. Your job is insanely pressured. I can't imagine how you do it." She returned to the sofa and handed Sherry a glass of rum. "I'm afraid that's all I have at the moment. Supplies of anything are short these days."

"So I've heard," Sherry replied. She took the glass and downed the drink in one swallow.

"Easy there," Claire said.

Sherry closed her eyes as if savoring the warmth of the dark liquid. "We're bringing a lot of the boys out of North Africa," she murmured. "My little brother Zack is there. My biggest fear is that one day I'll be smiling down into his dying face. I have nightmares about it."

She took another deep breath and her face relaxed into an expression of distant stoicism. "I'll be all right," she said. "The drink helped. If I could have another, I promise to sip it like a civilized woman."

"I'll join you," Claire replied, rising and going to the cabinet. "What about your other brother, Josh. Where is he?"

"The last I heard, he was transferred back to the Pacific. That's where he was before being reassigned to air operations for the invasion into North Africa. He's a fighter pilot and felt strongly that that's what he should be doing. What about your brothers, what are they doing?"

Claire shook her head. "Who knows? I worry about them constantly, but the war is so fast-moving. Paul does something with military intelligence, but I'm not allowed to know what that is. Lance was a Dunkirk survivor who was captured and escaped from a POW camp. And Jeremy, the youngest, has been all over the map. He survived Dunkirk too, flew fighters in the Battle of Britain and then nightfighters during the *blitz*. He's done covert work in France, but at the moment, I don't know specifically where any of them are." She blew out a breath. "It's frustrating."

Suddenly, she looked directly at Sherry. "Where are you staying?"

Sherry glanced down at her watch and rose to her feet. "I should be leaving. I hadn't realized so much time had passed. I'll take the late train into London."

"When do you go back on duty?"

"The day after tomorrow. I got a two-day pass."

"Then you'll stay here," Claire said resolutely. "You're family, and currently the only one I've got in close proximity besides Timmy."

"Timmy? Is that the little boy that Jeremy saved? May I see him?"

"Of course. He's asleep now, but you can peek in on him. He'll love playing with you tomorrow."

"Then I accept," Sherry said firmly. "I wouldn't miss it. Thank you."

19

Jeremy approached the safehouse at 26 Rue Fabert cautiously, meandering through the park on the opposite side of the street to avoid a café at the northeast corner of the block and doubling back along Rue Saint-Dominique, the street that intersected to the south. When he was satisfied that no one paid him particular attention, he moved to the front entrance.

Georges had been watching for him and opened the door as soon as Jeremy approached. They greeted each other quietly and went immediately into the apartment. "It's good to see you again," Georges said. "This time perhaps we can talk."

Fourcade had introduced them briefly six weeks earlier when Georges had stopped by Ladybird's apartment for an initial meeting, but they had not had an opportunity to deepen their discussion. "I don't expect to move soon," Georges told him. "Jeannie comes here on a regular basis to make sketches and jot down the latest that she's absorbed in that amazing memory of hers. But we don't have enough technical data yet to make an informed case back in London—"

Seeing Jeremy's querying look, he said, "You don't know anything about what the mission is, do you?"

Jeremy shook his head. "Madame Fourcade thought I should not know, for security reasons."

"She and I don't see things the same way on that point," Georges said, nodding. "Usually, I would agree with her, but in this case, the implications are so grave that action must be taken, which means that the information must get through. If we can get our hands on key documents, then you must get back to London and convince them of their content and authenticity and the action to take. They know you. They'll listen." He gave a wry smile. "Do you have your pills ready?"

Jeremy tapped his sleeve. "Madame sewed them in the seam for me."

"And you're ready to take them, if need be?"

"I wouldn't be here otherwise."

Georges studied his face and then exhaled. "I'm the last resort. If the documents are captured, and you go down, then I'll represent Fourcade and Alliance in London. She'll vouch for me, and hopefully, I'll be heard in the right quarters."

He noticed a dark look cross Jeremy's eyes. "What's your concern?"

Jeremy took a deep breath. "If the documents are captured, that means the Nazis have taken Amélie."

Georges took a deep breath and let it out as he nodded slowly. "Ah, yes," he said somberly. "I understand that you and she are—" He tapped his index fingers together to signal his meaning.

"We'd be married if not for this damnable war," Jeremy retorted angrily. "I don't know yet what the information is that we're bringing out, but I've accepted that she could be killed in the process and that you or I might be her executioners. I also accept that she must be sacrificed before these precious documents. I came because I'll make damn sure that there's no other alternative before her life—" His voice broke.

For a long moment, neither man spoke. Then Georges grasped Jeremy's shoulder. "I understand. I'll contact Fourcade tonight and let her know that I intend to brief you fully on what we're doing. She might not agree with my decision, but she'll support it. I operate my network as an autonomous group under Alliance because Fourcade wanted to decentralize. That's how we survived the two *Gestapo* sweeps."

He studied Jeremy's eyes. "What are you thinking?"

"When do I get to see Amélie?"

Georges hesitated. "You won't like the answer."

"Let's hear it."

Georges shrugged with reluctance. "It's too dangerous for the two of you to have direct contact. She knows you're here—or at least that you're coming—"

"You expect us to stay apart for weeks, maybe months," Jeremy interrupted angrily. "Did you see the way she looked when she was in Lyons? The stress and lack of food is killing her already. And I'm supposed to sit in safety while she exposes herself?"

"It's not as bad as you think, my friend," Georges said. "And I am your friend. Amélie volunteered for this mission. She doesn't know the content of the documents she'll be carrying, but she knows their importance." His voice softened. "I told her you'd be here to watch over her with me. I can tell you that she was greatly relieved.

"I can also tell you that she is relatively safe until we move the documents south. She sells flowers in a market; she lives with a family whose only action for the Resistance is to house her. And we make sure she has plenty of food. She's thin because of stress. She hardly eats."

Jeremy closed his eyes and acknowledged Georges' statements with a nod. "Can I at least see her? Let her know that I'm here?"

"Yes," Georges acquiesced. "We have a system in place to do that, and she uses it regularly to give the same reassurance to Jeannie. But you must understand that you'll walk by her, not too close, and you cannot make eye contact. She'll know why you're there."

"How will I know she's seen me?"

"She'll sneeze and rub her forehead with her apron. Don't linger, though. She's as afraid for you as you are for her. Trust us. We have people watching out for her all the time."

After the fact, Jeremy could not recall anything as searing as seeing Amélie in an open market selling flowers to anyone who walked by. Later, in retrospect, he recalled the trauma of jumping hand in hand with Timmy's mother from the *Lancastria* as it was sinking after being bombed at Saint-Nazaire. He had held the toddler, but when he and Timmy surfaced, the mother did not.

The loss of fighter-pilot mates also came to mind. Nothing that had happened to Amélie today compared with those events. His visceral fear for her sprang from what might happen to her, exposed and alone in the marketplace. For her to complete her part of the mission and survive required that he keep a cool head, something he had failed to do more than once when Amélie's safety was at issue.

He had entered the area with Georges and then the pair had split up. Jeremy had followed Georges' directions, rummaging about in his old-man disguise among the wares on offer by various vendors until he spotted her.

He drew closer.

She had grown thinner, but she smiled and greeted people who stopped by to check her flowers. Jeremy noted a quality to the scene that was at once endearing and pathetic.

She sneezed. He fought the urge to look directly at her but saw her lift her apron to her face and wipe her forehead. Then she turned and entered into conversation with a customer.

With great difficulty, Jeremy walked on by and continued until he reached the other side of the market. There he found Georges waiting for him.

"She's very brave," Georges said. "You're a lucky man."

"I will be," Jeremy retorted grimly, "if we both live through this war."

Jeannie Rousseau, codenamed Amniarix, came to the safehouse that evening. She and Jeremy had met at Fourcade's villa at Christmas just after the Japanese attack on Pearl Harbor. "I am fortunate to have Amélie watching out for me," she told Jeremy. "And you are a lucky man."

"I keep being told that," Jeremy said wanly, "but I need no reminding.

You've heard the story of how she went into a storm to save me from German soldiers."

"As I said, Jeremy, you are a lucky man." Her bright eyes twinkled with mischief. "If I were a person who gambled, which you know I am not, I would bet money that she will survive this war, and the two of you will live long, happy lives together. And I shall attend your wedding."

"I'll hold you to all of that," Jeremy said with a low laugh.

Georges entered the room. "Let's get to it, shall we?"

"Yes," Jeannie agreed. "There is another party at the Majestic this evening, and I must be my most charming." She batted her eyes, and her voice lilted as she mimicked her side of an anticipated conversation with a senior *Wehrmacht* officer. "No, you cannot be serious, Field Marshal. How can that be? To think that an aircraft can fly so fast and so far and do it without a pilot. That cannot be so."

"All right, Mata Hari—"

"Not Mata Hari," Jeannie replied in a mildly reproving tone. "As soon as I do that, jealousies crop up, and I lose effectiveness. I flirt equally with all the officers, but I never let any get too close."

Before departing an hour later, she left behind detailed notes of pertinent conversations she had entered into with all levels of *Wehrmacht* command and staff officers at their headquarters housed in the Majestic. Her notes included observations regarding both her routine work and information retrieved at the most recent party held there. Much of the information she supplied was classified.

"I'll be back tomorrow evening with what I learn tonight," she said as she departed.

20

March 23, 1943
El Guettar, Tunisia

Sergeant Zack Littlefield peered over the edge of a high ridge at a gathering dust cloud to the south. As he watched, the cloud grew, and a far-off rumble accompanied it as it moved through the narrow valley between two mountains. The sound grew, and with it the squeak and squeal of armored vehicles on the move. Their vibration traveled through the ground, already creating a barely felt tremor at Zack's position.

He raised a pair of binoculars and focused them on the cloud. Dark shapes appeared behind the leading edge of the spiraling dust, but they could be seen with no clarity. To his left and right, infantry soldiers moved forward from assembly areas to take their positions inside foxholes dug into the rocky surface of the ridge. All watched the advance of the feared *Wehrmacht* Tiger tanks.

Zack shifted his view to the other side of the pass directly across from his position. A quick sweep revealed nothing, but he knew that thirty-six M3 half-tracks with their 75 mm M1897A4 field guns belonging to the 805th Tank Destroyer Battalion waited and watched in defilade, matching the strength and actions of his own unit on this side of the valley. Each vehicle carried fifty-nine M66 high-explosive anti-tank rounds, and munitions supply trucks were positioned nearby to the rear. Together the two tank destroyer battalions were poised, out of sight, ready for each M-3 to leap forward at critical moments and unleash their version of hell on the steel mammoths rolling their way.

LTC Xiquez had set up his headquarters just behind the ridge near an outcropping where he could command his battalion while observing the forward movement of the Tigers. Field telephone lines had been strung between the higher and lower headquarters on this side of the pass to keep radio silence, and the commander on the opposite ridge carried out similar actions. Runners traveled between the elements with longer messages needing greater explanation.

Zack watched one such courier arrive at his vehicle, panting from exertion. Zack hurried over and listened as the message was delivered. "One of our recon units just bumped into the forward edge of the German formation," the soldier said. "They counted seventy-five Tigers, and that's just the leading element. They're moving slow, about five miles per hour, and they're organized with four at the front of a sub-formation, four at the rear, one on each flank, and the command vehicle in the middle."

The tank destroyer commander glanced at Zack. "You know where your first target is for each formation, right?"

Zack nodded. "Affirmative. The command tank's gonna get it."

"They know we're here," the runner broke in.

"I'll alert the loader and driver that we're about to get busy," Zack said.

The forward Tigers emerged from the pass into the valley. Their rumble had increased to a distant roar, and motorized units in half-tracks and motorcycles with sidecars broke away on either side of the formations and charged toward the ridges.

The American tank destroyers held their positions behind the ridge. Zack watched the deathly procession from a foxhole near the battalion headquarters.

"Shouldn't you be with your crew, Sergeant?" a stern voice called down to him.

Zack looked up to see Xiquez frowning down at him. "Sorry, sir. I wanted to see what the enemy looks like."

"You've seen him, now—"

As he spoke, small-arms fire rang out along the ridge. Zack whirled.

The German half-tracks had traversed as far up the steep slope as they were able, and now pummeled the crest with eighty-eight millimeter anti-tank guns while disgorging hundreds of infantry troops. The soldiers charged uphill under a steady machine gun barrage, fired off their rifles, and sought cover farther up the hillside. Calling to each other and alternating rushes between them, they advanced toward the crest.

The American infantry returned fire, with M-1s, light and heavy mortars, M1919 Browning machine guns, and M1A1 man-carried recoilless anti-tank rocket launchers. The latter weapons, popularly dubbed "bazookas" by the troops, fired a rocket capable of disabling a tank, and its operators soon drew beads on the stalled German half-tracks. Within seconds, their loud reports and rocket smoke trails pointed to targets that had been hit and were now engulfed in flames. The din was joined by the far-off boom of field artillery sending their rounds followed by their concussive explosions.

Anguished cries of wounded soldiers arose from along the infantry line, and others ascended from the German ranks below. Medics, with red crosses painted against white circular backgrounds, hurried forward with first aid kits and started work even as soldiers carried their buddies from the field in stretchers.

Zack felt bile rising in his throat as it had at Kasserine when viewing the aftermath of that battlefield. He swallowed hard and took a deep breath.

"Seen enough?" Xiquez called. The commander's radio operator, standing a few feet away, nudged the officer and gave him the handset. Xiquez spoke into it and listened. "They're falling back in front of us, but they've overrun two infantry and field artillery positions farther south, and they're threatening the 1st Infantry Divisions headquarters."

On the floor of the valley, the Panzers continued their steady progress, with more and more of them spilling out of the pass into the wider flat-lands. Zack heard the heavy artillery guns, the hiss of their rounds through the air and the heavy thuds of impact followed by loud explosions. Plumes of dirt and smoke shot into the sky from the desert floor, adding to the swirl of sand kicked up by the Tigers. And the massive armored vehicles began to break formation.

Tiger elements veered right, others left, and some straight on, and they ran into a carefully laid minefield that allowed no forward move-ment. Their explosions were muted against the thick steel of the Tigers' armor, but they nevertheless derailed their tracks or caused internal damage that left the tanks sitting in place. In two cases, spalling must have occurred inside the Tigers and ignited their ammunition—they erupted in enormous blasts with flames and black smoke rising far into the air.

Xiquez, who had been watching the battle through his binoculars, nudged Zack and handed them to him. "You wanted to see the enemy? Look there."

Zack peered through the binoculars to where Xiquez pointed, watching as German crewmen scrambled through the hatch of a disabled Tiger. However, before jumping off, and amid the chaos all about them, they paused long enough to detach the machine gun from the commander's cupola with a tripod and boxes of ammunition, and on reaching the ground, they set up rapidly and began shooting uphill toward the crest where Zack stood with Xiquez.

"We're out of range," the lieutenant colonel said. "They'll hit their own guys before they hit us, but you've got to admire their guts." He glanced at Zack. "It's good to know your enemy."

Zack acknowledged the observation and looked down at his watch. Fifteen minutes had passed since the opening salvos.

Zack watched as the Germans pulled back south through the pass, out of range to re-group, their initial attack having been repulsed. In late after-noon, he saw the Panzers again emerge into view amid swirling sand, seeking to break through General Patton's defenses. He watched their infantry assault and retreat, leaving dead and wounded behind.

He watched the formations probe the minefield but find no way through and then suddenly split, each half facing the nearest ridge, before unleashing volley after volley of main gun rounds. However, they fired uphill, their targets invisible to them, with no way to know the effects of their salvos.

Zack raced back to his vehicle. "Our turn," he called as he settled behind the rangefinder.

The half-track commander, Jim, wore his headphone. Now that they were in contact with the enemy, radio silence was no longer necessary. "Warning order," he yelled. "Joe," he called to the driver, "crank up the engine. On my order, pull forward fast. Zack, targets should appear at twelve o'clock. When sighted, fire at will. Joe, reverse as soon as Zack fires. Bill, are we locked and loaded?"

"Roger."

The battle over the crest of the rim was invisible to Zack's crew, but the sound was explosive and mounted with the crackle of rifle and machine guns interspersed between heavy mortars, artillery, and tank fire.

"Go, Joe. Go," Jim ordered.

Joe mashed the half-track into gear, slammed on the gas pedal, and the vehicle lurched forward and rumbled up the incline.

Zack kept his eye on the rangefinder and his hands on the knobs that controlled the gun's traverse and elevation. He kept his aim straight to the front.

The crest disappeared from view. In the viewfinder, all he saw at first was smoke. But then he detected movement and what appeared to be a muzzle flash.

The tank destroyer halted.

Zack fired.

The vehicle buckled.

Joe threw the vehicle into reverse and rapidly backed down the hill. As they descended, Zack whirled to look down the line. As far as he could see, tank destroyers of the 601st were in various modes of delivering fire: climbing to the crest, firing, or reversing.

"Was that a kill?" Zack called over the clamor.

"Don't know," Jim yelled back. "I saw the hit and a flash. But I couldn't tell for certain. I'd call it a probable. Get ready for the next one."

"Roger."

Bill slammed another M66 HEAT round into the tube and gave a thumbs-up. Jim clapped Joe's helmet, and the vehicle lurched forward while Zack hovered over the gunsight and controls.

"Targets slightly to the right of twelve o'clock," Bill called.

Once again, as soon as the crest disappeared below the sights, Zack marked his target, fired, and held on as the tank destroyer bucked under the gun's recoil. Before the vehicle settled, Joe had reversed it, and Bill was re-loading.

"There's less sand in the air than usual," Jim called. "They must not be moving too well down there. But there's more smoke. Ya figure with thirty-six of us shooting on this side of the pass and thirty-six firing on the other side, we should be thinning the herd a mite."

"Did we hit?" Zack yelled.

Jim shrugged. "Same as before. I saw a flash and a plume, but I'd have to call it a probable again."

As they started up the hill again, Jim told Zack, "Your targets will be farther south, closer to one o'clock this time. They're thinning out by the minefield. They must've figured out that they can't get through that way."

Zack calmed his frustration at not achieving verifiable direct hits with a sober reminder that his success meant someone else's probable death. He thrust all such thoughts aside as the tank destroyer climbed the hill. He cleared his mind, controlled his breathing, and watched for the crest of the ridge to clear. When it did, his crosshairs came immediately to rest on the center mass of a squat, silhouetted Tiger tank. Recalling the one-hundred-millimeter thickness of the front slope of the turret and the unlikeliness of killing it with a head-on shot, Zack adjusted the reticle down and to the right, hoping to hit the seam between the hull and the turret somewhere near the driver.

He fired.

Joe reversed down the hill.

Jim erupted in loud celebration. "Yeeha! You did it. Direct hit. I see smoke. I see explosion. You killed it, Zack. That tank's doing no damage to anyone ever again."

Somber elation overtook Zack, and he wondered how the two sentiments could co-exist. He had no time to think it through because Joe had backed as far as he should, Bill had slammed another round into place, and Jim was feeding him target information.

For the next hour, Zack's crew, the rest of the guns of the 601st and the 508th Tank Destroyer Battalions, rained down high-explosive anti-tank steel on the hapless formations while farther south, other elements of II Corps delivered punishing blows. Late in the evening, General Von Arnim's 5th Panzer Army retreated from the field.

March 25, 1943

Zack stared forward, hardly believing what he saw along the road leading north to Gafsa, a town formerly occupied by the Italians, who vacated it with little resistance, and where Patton had since established a new field headquarters and supply depot. For the past two days since defeating the 5th Panzers at El Guettar, the men of II Corps had been busily re-supplying, cleaning and repairing equipment, and resting. Now, the two tank destroyer battalions were headed to assembly areas to prepare for their next engagement.

They had rounded a curve, and there, on the side of the road, was General Patton. He was alone, but he wore a huge smile and stood in a half-crouch, waving the line of vehicles and soldiers on. As Zack's crew passed, he cupped his hands together and shook them over his head, calling out to them, "You magnificent bastards."

Zack could not help the sense of pride that welled in his chest. Exchanging glances with his fellow crewmen, he saw the same pride reflected in their eyes. "We really did it, didn't we?" Jim breathed. "We beat the Desert Fox."

Later in the afternoon, they were called to assemble before another makeshift stage, and once again, Patton mounted and strode across it.

"Men," he began in his high-pitched, clear voice. "I'll keep this short." He halted at mid-stage and faced them directly. "You won the most pivotal battle of the North Africa campaign."

A cheer went up, and Patton held out his palms to quiet his audience. "I might as well tell you now, cuz you'll find out sooner or later and I don't want any of you calling me a liar." He paused as quiet descended. "I hate to say it, but the Desert Fox wasn't there."

"We painted his back yeller," a soldier called out to much laughter.

Patton smiled and shook his head. "I can promise that didn't happen. No, the information I have is that the *führer* wanted an explanation for Rommel's defeats." He gave a short laugh, shielded his eyes, and scanned across the soldiers with an exaggerated motion. "I can tell you right now, I'm looking at the reason."

Another wild cheer went up, and the general waited for it to subside. "You fought. That's the simple answer. You fought when you were green. You fought when you were poorly led. You fought when you were defeated, and you never gave up. All I did was come in and show you how to win, and you did that too.

"The Brits did their part, and they went through the same learning curve before we got here. Rumor has it that they didn't think much of American soldiers." Patton leaned forward and stage-whispered, "I think you changed their minds." Then he straightened up and boomed, "El Guettar was strictly an American shindig, and you showed what you could do."

As cheering resounded again, Patton held up a hand and continued. "So what if Rommel wasn't at El Guettar? You had already kept him from taking Tebessa before I arrived. And two days ago, you defeated his plan and his tactics." He paused and grinned. "You learned he isn't ten feet tall."

Amid guffaws, he continued, "What's left of the German military in Africa is beatin' feet north to evacuate out of Tunis as fast as their tired legs will carry them." The general laughed, his eyes exuding mischief. "We haven't seen the last of Rommel, but I suspect that the next time we meet, we'll be on European soil where we'll teach him another lesson in armored tactics—that's if that funny little guy in Berlin with the weird mustache is smart enough to let him fight again. He's the best they've got.

"But none of that is the reason I called you together now." He squared his shoulders and saluted. "Here's my thanks for a hard-fought victory. You are fighters, the pride of our nation. Besides telling you that, I came to let you know that I won't be staying with you much longer in North Africa—"

A collective groan went up.

Patton held up his hand again. "Hear me out. The war will soon move off of this continent. You did that. Ike'll be sending me somewhere to figure out the next big move. I'm sure you'll be part of it, and I'll be right there with you. And while you're still here, fighting the good fight, I'll be here with you in spirit.

"You're tested. You're proven. You can believe in yourselves and each other. You'll do fine while I'm gone because you're American front-line combat soldiers. I'm proud of you." He scanned the faces before him once more. "That's all."

Every eye followed the general as he strode from the stage, Zack's included. "Wherever he goes in this war," he muttered, "that's where I want to be."

Jim nudged him. "Me too."

21

March 22
Wadi Ziqzah, Libya

Under a moonlit sky, a terrible scream that had become all too familiar to
Paul Littlefield rent the night, and as the bomb it signaled impacted with a
dull thud followed by a thunderous blast, it was joined by high-pitched
whistling of hundreds more artillery rounds fired from far behind his position. They plowed the ground close to his front, throwing up bright flashes
and clouds of earth. Then, having traced the forward line, the artillerymen
who had unleased this hell on earth walked the barrage forward toward the
enemy.

Paul scrunched against the forward edge of the bomb crater he had
dived into an hour ago after being routed from a key piece of usually
insignificant terrain above Wadi Ziqzah. The broken gulch commencing on
the Mediterranean a few miles southeast of Gabès, Tunisia, cut inland with
steep seventy-foot slopes for three hundred miles, forming a natural tank
obstacle that limited forward maneuver against an entrenched enemy.

Along the western edge of the gully, the colonial French military of the
1930s had built the Mareth Line, an imposing series of supporting and
interlocking concrete parapets and pillboxes above a rocky ridgeline that

made passage by tracked vehicles impossible for most of its length. The French had lost the line to the Germans with the capitulation of the Vichy government of Occupied France to Hitler in June 1940.

To have a chance of breaking into wider terrain where the semi-arid coastal plains met the Matmata Hills, Montgomery's 8th Army must breach the Mareth at Tebaga Gap, a gully that bisected Wadi Ziqzah and the only place where tanks could climb up a rocky slope to the high desert. Once there, Montgomery could drive north on the single road leading to Sfax, a major Axis base on the coast sixty miles south of the final objective, Tunis.

North and west of Tebaga was the Chott salt lake; to its west were the Matmata Hills and the undulating sandstone crests and wadis of the low Jebel Dahar mountain chain; and farther west the burning dunes of the Sahara's six-hundred-square-mile Grand Erg Oriental. The challenging topography limited Montgomery's options for a line of advance, but he was resolute in his objective: to capture or destroy what was left of the *Afrika Korps*, which had been renamed the Panzer Army Africa and was the remnants of the *Wehrmacht* on the African continent.

The Tebaga Gap in the Wadi Ziqzah fissure, which regularly flooded during rainy seasons, was the only place possible to break through the Mareth, and also where Paul's battalion now held ground, waiting to counterattack.

Two days of rain had preceded the first assault. Water in the Wadi ran deep.

Paul hunkered down, waiting for the field artillery to soften up the enemy defenses sufficiently. He looked at his watch. Midnight was an hour away, and he had just received word that the attack was delayed until 01:00 hours. He had already checked with his company commanders and knew them to be ready, so he leaned back, interrupted by waves of artillery and the intermittent crackle of gunfire, and reflected on how he had come to be here.

True to his word, Montgomery had found something for Paul to do, and per Paul's request and assertion that he was qualified for commando missions, the general had instructed his staff to assign Paul to a long range desert group, a unit for conducting reconnaissance and executing combat raids. Given his rank, he was initially held at arm's length by the team, but within two days, his group had been ordered to assist the engineers in breaching a path through Rommel's minefield.

Once again turning to the magician, Jasper Maskelyne, Montgomery had fooled Rommel into believing that the 8th Army would attack in the south when, in fact, Montgomery intended to attack straight into the *Afrika Korps'* main body. Maskelyne had set about creating a ghost army in the south with dummy tanks there complete with heavy radio traffic and dummy supply trucks in the north that were the actual tanks in disguise. Under cover of darkness, two days before the battle, Montgomery started moving his real tanks forward. Meanwhile, Rommel had moved a major part of his forces south to reinforce against what he thought would be an attack on his flank.

On the night of the assault, Paul, ensconced with his small team, had joined the sappers, which headed into the minefields under blistering enemy fire, unrolling white tape behind them to mark safe paths for those who came behind. When they encountered any of the myriad barbed-wire barriers, a soldier wearing a heavy overcoat ran up and flung himself on top of it, landing on his belly with the collapsed wire beneath him. Then his companions jumped over him through the just-created gap and continued working their way through the minefield.

Paul volunteered for wire-breaching duty because it seemed the easiest skill to pick up without lengthy training. However, in practice, he learned that the duty was rotated, and he soon found himself kneeling in the sand and prodding through it gingerly with a bayonet, looking for landmines. When he found one, he held up his hand and yelled, and a specialist came forward to take charge of and dispose of the mine.

Thus they proceeded through the deadly field, cutting paths wide enough for infantry and then for armor, and sooner than he could believe, Montgomery sent his forces through in strength.

That attack had begun a four-month rout of Rommel, whose vaunted *Afrika Korps,* reduced to just thirty-six tanks and five thousand men, retreated across Libya, past Benghazi and Tripoli, and finally to an area between Kasserine and Medenine.

Montgomery had pursued. Some critics said he did so too slowly, but he stolidly refused to outrun his supply line.

Then, reinforced by the 5th Panzer Army, Rommel once again struck British forces at Medenine and was once again beaten. He did not know that the decoders at Bletchley Park knew his every order and forwarded them to Montgomery's headquarters. The British 8th Army was ready for him and delivered a devastating defeat.

Shortly thereafter, word trickled down through intelligence channels that the Desert Fox had been recalled to Berlin. Paul had wondered momentarily if Claire had been the person at Bletchley to intercept and decode the messages with the news of Rommel's relief from command, but he dismissed the thought. The organization and the war had grown too big for such a coincidence.

With the success of the assault and his own contributions, when a leader of another long range desert unit fell in combat, Paul was assigned to replace him. He saw Montgomery only a few times during those months, and then only as most of the soldiers did, from afar, as "Monty" toured the battlefield in his open-top Humber with his black beret and regimental badges.

Two days ago, Paul had received orders to report to 8th Army headquarters. On arrival, he was shown into Montgomery's tent.

"Come in, old boy. Have a seat," the general had greeted him. "Good to see you healthy and intact." He peered closely at Paul. "Although I would say perhaps a bit leaner and darker."

Paul smiled wanly. "The Sahara will do that to you, General."

"Indeed it will," Montgomery responded, chuckling. "Here's the thing. I'm short on officers. I have an infantry battalion needing a CO, and you've been recommended."

Taken aback, Paul had no immediate comment. "Sir, I hardly qualify as an infantry officer much less as a commander of a battal—"

"Rubbish," Montgomery replied. "Our entire military, including intelligence, came into this war as amateurs, and we learned on the job. You're trained, you've led teams—"

"But maneuvering a battalion in combat?"

Montgomery shushed him with a wave of his hand. "Ordinarily, I wouldn't get involved in selecting a battalion commander under combat conditions, but because of the sensibilities with you and your family and Churchill, I am this time.

"Various comments have come to me. You're known as the lieutenant colonel who threw himself over barbed-wire barriers so that ordinary privates could jump over you. You took your turn in probing for mines. You've proven yourself as a team leader."

"That's nice to hear, sir, but you'd be putting these men's lives in my hands—"

"It's like this, Littlefield. In two days, that battalion along with another one will undertake its most dangerous mission to date. You probably will not live through it. You know we're headed to Tunis?"

"That was easy enough to deduce."

"Yes, well, to get there, we must breach the Mareth Line. We were fortunate to consult with General Georges Catroux in Algiers. He was the designer and garrison commander of the Mareth Line in the '30s and provided information on its weaknesses and how to attack. Two infantry battalions will have to break through the Mareth on Wadi Ziqzah at Tebaga Gap and clear the way for the tanks. You know what the terrain is south of here on this side of the wadi. If we try a flanking movement, we'll bog down in soft sand. The Americans are coming from the west to attack Rommel's flank.

"Your battalion's mission is already ordered. The company commanders know what to do. This is a short-duration assignment. I need you to lead over the crest. The men will follow your orders with confidence. If we hope to spread out into the wider desert on the other side and drive what remains of the 5th Panzers back toward Tunis, we must break through that defensive line." He grunted. "Much as I hate to admit it, that prima donna Patton pared down their strength somewhat at El Guettar, and we delivered a decisive blow at Medenine. I suspect they'll be trying to get out of Tunis, and we can't let them."

Paul was silent a moment. "You're sending me on a suicide mission?"

"I hope it isn't that, but the probabilities are high. The battalion has a technically competent 2IC—er, that's the second in command—but I'm told that he's neither inspiring nor particularly well-liked. He can advise you.

"I don't have time for a thorough search, and I need you to perform only one function: lead by example over the crest of that wadi at the critical moment."

In a voice that seemed disembodied, Paul heard himself reply, "All right, sir. If that's what you need."

The next two days had been as extreme as any that Paul could remember. A Humber transported him to corps headquarters, then to division and brigade headquarters in quick succession, and finally to the battalion area.

The battalion sergeant major met him at the operations tent. "Welcome, sir," he said as he led Paul into the tent. He was tall and slender, and his round face was grim. "I've gathered the company commanders, and the second in command will be here too. The plan is straightforward. This battalion will go in on the north bank, and the other one will go in on the opposite side. We'll make our way up the embankment, probably under fire, and assault the German defensive positions at the crest. We'll fill you in. You might have suggestions of your own."

Nothing in Paul's experience had prepared him for the enormous sense of responsibility thrust on him of "leading" men in battle. Despite Montgomery's reassurances and the courteous if somber welcome received at battalion headquarters, now, with bullets and artillery rounds hissing through the air followed by massive explosions, a sense of dismay seized him.

He glanced at the soldiers to his left and right, their faces illuminated briefly by bright moonlight and flashes of detonating munitions. They stared anxiously into the sky above the rim of their low, gritty cover. Soon, they would clamber over the rise and counterattack to regain the objective taken earlier in the day and then relinquished. They had been made to realize that taking and holding the high ground was crucial to driving Rommel and his Tigers and Panzers from North Africa.

Paul wondered how many of his soldiers would survive. With only two days to prepare himself, no time had been available to gather the men in formation to meet him. Instead, he had traveled to their various positions to greet them. He had found them to be battle-hardened, grim but spirited, with gallows humor despite their spartan conditions.

"D'ya think we'll finish the attack in time for supper?" a soldier at one position called to him. "We're having shepherd's pie that night."

"Umm, my favorite," another one said. "I thought I'd ask Fiona to come over."

"Blimey, she's done with you," a third chimed in. "All it took to pull her away was the promise of a bottle of cheap wine and a pair of silk stockings."

"Really, shepherd's pie? Out here?" someone else remarked.

"Blimey! That was a joke, you clod. We'll still be eating sand in the wadi at dinnertime if we're alive."

The men had laughed uproariously, clapping each other's backs. Paul had laughed with them and then turned away to shield emotion showing on his face at the thought of ordering them into combat.

He had taken with him on his tour the sergeant major, the first company commander, and the 2IC, all of whom provided a running brief of combat status and the mission.

"We've simplified things," the 2IC said. "First and Second Companies will be in the lead, with Third Company in reserve. Your headquarters will move behind the lead—"

Mindful of Montgomery's guidance concerning his role on the mission, Paul interrupted quietly, "I'll need only my signaler and a dedicated runner with me. Put us with the forwardmost element and inform the men that I will be there with them."

The staff members stared at him. "Are you sure?" the sergeant major asked.

Paul nodded. "You developed the plan, and your company commanders understand it. I won't make any changes beyond where I'll travel with the battalion." He indicated the second in command. "If I go down, you'll follow the 2IC's orders as if they came from me."

The officer, a diminutive, bookish soldier with a habitual deadpan expression, glanced up in surprise. Over the two days that Paul had commanded the battalion, he had noticed that the man's advice was invariably sound and that he had quietly shaped the plan, but he lacked confidence.

The commander of 1st Company and the sergeant major looked doubtful. "That should go without saying," Paul told them. "The 2IC's a good man. He won't lead you astray."

The dedicated runner Paul had required approached him in the darkness. "Sir, the company commanders are gathered below."

Paul took a deep breath, slid backward on his belly until he was well below the lip of the bomb crater, then rose to his feet and followed the runner, accompanied by his signaler. He found the commanders near the floor of the wadi just above water level. Pulling a map from his pocket, he laid it on a smooth boulder and illuminated it with a flashlight. "We're going back in to take that same objective," he told them, "this time with a creeping barrage lasting for two hours. Once we're near the objective, it'll break so we can overrun and consolidate, and then commence again on the other side and continue to roll forward while our tanks cross the wadi and come up behind us. Any questions?"

"I could use some replacements," one of the commanders said. "We lost a lot of men on the first assault."

"I know." Subduing profound dismay, Paul turned to 3rd Company's commander. "Stay close and be prepared to reinforce on order." He looked at the grim young faces around him. "Tell your men that they performed magnificently, and I have every confidence that they'll do it again."

The order came down over the radio on schedule. "Execute."

Paul received it and relayed to his subordinate commanders. He waited only long enough to hear their confirmations, and then edged up to the crater's rim. The minefields had already been cleared in the previous assault, and two hours of non-stop artillery on the objective had thinned out the resistance there. However, supporting fire from other elements on

the Mareth Line, including the German's own punishing artillery, rained
down in front of Paul's position and increased in intensity as friendly fire
grew in volume, signaling the start of the new attack.

Paul looked to his left and right, waiting for a lull in the clamor. He saw
the eyes of the soldiers closest to him shining in the moonlight, fixed on
him, some fearful, some determined, all expectant. He gulped.

A break in the firing finally occurred. Paul jumped to his feet. "Let's go,
chaps," he bellowed, and as the soldiers streamed past him, he saw that on
either side of him, the company commanders also urged their men forward
and then joined them.

Paul faced the objective and ran hunched over, taking long, loping
strides. He called over his shoulder to the signaler, "Stay with me," but,
hearing a gurgled response, he whirled to find the soldier sprawled backward, his chest spurting blood, his eyes sightless.

The runner stood over the operator, his eyes wide in horror. "Get the
radio," Paul yelled, swooping to grasp the dead man's rifle. Then he
grabbed another soldier running past. "You, stay with me," he shouted.
"You're my runner now."

Ahead, flares cast an eerie orange glow across the sky. Within a minute,
Paul and his small entourage had rejoined the assault, clambering uphill
over boulders, scraping against rocks, stumbling, falling, forgetting fears of
bullets or shrapnel bludgeoning their bodies and ending their existence.

When incoming fire was most fierce, they sought cover, held ground,
shooting uphill past companions and then charging forward a few more
feet during lulls to repeat the process. Across the battlefield, wounded men
shrieked in pain and called for medics. Some men sprawled forward on
their faces or were blown back, and after twitching for some moments, they
lay still.

Paul took in the scene, blotting from his mind the worst horrors and
keeping up with the progress of his troops via the radio. The moment came
when his reserves had to be committed and the implications were clear:
many men had fallen, and many more would die in vain if he did not call
for the soldiers of his last intact unit to place their own lives on the line or
risk losing the battle, the Mareth Line, and the road to Tunis. The war in
North Africa could be prolonged indefinitely.

Operating now on instinct, he called to brigade operations and received approval to commit Third Company. Sustained uphill fire from his right flank signaled that it had entered the fray.

As the early morning hours before dawn slipped away, Paul's unit continued fighting toward the high ground, slipping, falling, but pushing ever forward until, as rose-colored clouds stretched above the horizon, they had reached and overrun the objective. As the battalion consolidated its position, Paul, rifle in hand, toured the perimeter, proud of what his men had accomplished and sickened at the losses, the wounded, and the spatters of blood and destroyed equipment visible in every direction. The last charge had been close, with hand-to-hand combat such that many German soldiers' bodies had collapsed across those of Brits.

As Paul wandered to the far edge of the position, he noticed a German soldier's body sprawled in the shadow of a FLAK 88mm anti-tank gun, his sidearm still in his hand across his chest. Pointing his rifle at the body, Paul edged closer.

His boots scraped the ground and his shadow fell across the man's face.

Suddenly, the soldier's eyes blinked open. He fired his pistol at close range.

Paul fired back, but too late. He felt searing heat burn through his upper chest and shoulder as his body jolted backward.

The German shot again, sending two bullets into Paul's right leg.

Paul collapsed on his back while hearing shouts, running footsteps, and a fusillade of rifle shots as if from afar. And then all went dark.

22

April 17, 1943
London, England

Paul glanced up sharply from a single sheet of paper he had just read and stared at Lieutenant Commander Ian Fleming across the table in a small conference room in the SOE headquarters on Baker Street. "You can't be serious."

Fleming leaned back in his chair with a slight smile. "I'm afraid I'm quite serious." He bestowed a frank look on Paul. "How are your wounds coming? I heard you had been messed up somewhat in Tunisia."

Paul shot him a dismissive frown. "Not enough to speak about."

"But sufficient enough to send you back to London to recuperate. Good show there, by the way. I understand Monty pushed the 5th Panzers off the Mareth Line and is now pursuing them up the coast road."

Paul shrugged. "It was quite a fight." He remembered the assault at Wadi Ziqzah in blurred flashes of men running toward enemy guns under the flickers of a seemingly unending artillery barrage. He vaguely recalled a German lying on the ground who had shot him. His next memory was waking up in a London hospital.

Not content to convalesce, he had left after a week against doctor's orders. He had made his way painfully to SOE headquarters and persisted there in a request to see its director, Brigadier Colin Gubbins, a large, no-nonsense man with combed-back straight hair and a well-manicured mustache. He had received Paul with some reserve.

"Your reputation precedes you, which is why I agreed to see you. I believe your brother is in France right now on a cooperative mission of MI-9's with our section. What can I do for you?" He looked over Paul's slinged arm and the crutch supporting his body. "Obviously, you won't be suited for field duty for some time."

Paul smiled faintly and grimaced as he shifted his arm in the sling. The action shot pain through a wound in the lower part of his shoulder and projected through his broken clavicle. Inadvertently, he leaned on his wounded leg and realized more anguish from twin wounds in his right leg. He blanched in agony.

"Sit down, for heaven's sake, before you pass out," Gubbins said. He pulled a chair behind Paul, who struggled to take a seat.

"You must mean Jeremy," Paul gasped through clenched teeth.

"Excuse me?"

"Jeremy, my brother. He must be the one in France. I didn't know he had gone back over."

"Yes, well, that's neither here nor there at the moment. As I said, you're in no shape for field work anywhere."

"Granted, sir," Paul intoned, recovering a degree of decorum, "but I'm a trained intelligence analyst with behind-the-lines and combat experience. My brain functions just fine, and I'm sure that you have plans in the works for operations that need thinking through. I can help."

Gubbins eyed him closely. "Shouldn't you be convalescing somewhere? Taking it easy?"

Paul shook his head, thinking of his mother, Dame Marian, still contending with German occupation on Sark and now alone since his father was somewhere in a German prison camp. "I can't relax, sir, not while this war is going on. Give me something to do."

Gubbins frowned with uncharacteristic uncertainty as he studied Paul. At last he said, "All right, I'll go this far with you. Go home or go some-where to rest and heal those wounds. Come back in a fortnight, and maybe

I'll have something for you. I'll pass around your name and circumstances, and we'll see what we come up with."

Paul had agreed, departed, and made his way to Claire's house, an hour away by train, noting along the way the looks of gratitude from Londoners and the wondering stares of young children as they took in his injured condition. On entering the train, passengers moved politely aside to let him limp past on his crutch and cleared a seat for him near the door. "Thank you," he said, somewhat embarrassed, "that's not necessary." But they insisted, so he took his seat and passed an enjoyable ride conversing with grateful strangers.

Paul arrived at Claire's front door shortly after she had arrived home from work. She flung open the door as soon as she saw him and was about to throw her arms around him when she noticed his crutch and wounds.

"You're hurt," she cried. "Are your wounds serious?"

Paul smiled resignedly. "They hurt some, but I'll survive them."

"I knew one of you would come home like this one day," she fussed. "When will this damnable war ever end." She helped him settle onto the living room sofa.

Timmy was overjoyed to see Paul at first, but as he took in Paul's crutch and sling, curiosity and unease caused the boy to be somewhat standoffish. However, coaxed along by Claire, Timmy eased up next to Paul's good left side on the divan, and minutes later, the boy brought out brightly colored Dinky cars and trucks to share.

While they played, Claire went into the kitchen. When she returned, her face was grave. She stood by the doorframe leading into the hall with sad eyes, watching Paul play with Timmy.

Paul glanced up and noticed. "Is something wrong?"

"I put in a call to Ryan. I thought perhaps she could come visit while you're here."

Paul's face brightened. "Is she coming? When?"

Claire shook her head as tears streamed down her face. "She was killed, Paul. Two weeks ago while ferrying a Fairey Barracuda torpedo bomber to one of the RAF bases in East Anglia. A *Luftwaffe* bomber raid flew over her in the opposite direction. An escorting fighter looking for random targets engaged her—" Claire lost her voice as she broke down in sobs. She rushed to Paul and held him in her arms. "I'm so sorry. I loved her too."

Paul sat in stone-faced silence. Images of Ryan flooded his mind, of when they had first met and worked together at the Fighter Command bunker during the Battle of Britain. Her China-doll face floated before his eyes, her voice teasing him about Churchill's matchmaking role in bringing them together. He recalled the night he had last seen her, looking into her deep blue eyes shortly before he had been caught in downtown London during an early *Luftwaffe* bomber sweep. He had almost proposed marriage to her that night. His only reluctance had stemmed from the possibility of making her a widow. Now, in light of the irony, he wished he had asked. *At least she would have died knowing I truly loved her.*

Without speaking, he struggled to his feet and limped with his crutch across the back garden to a lone bench under an ancient English elm. Claire followed, unsure of whether or not to leave him alone. When he sat down, she approached and sat on his healthy side while Timmy, sensing something amiss, looked on with big, worried eyes.

Claire saw Timmy's alarm and called to him, and the boy ran to lean into her lap. "What's wrong, Gigi?"

She picked him up and rocked him while holding him close.

Brother and sister sat in silence for an extended time. After a while, Claire slid closer to Paul. "You know," she whispered through tears, "this is the same place where I grieved when I learned of Red's death."

Paul seemed not to have heard. Then he turned and faced her, tears streaming down his face. He placed his good arm around Claire's shoulders and pulled her close. "Will this never stop?" he whispered.

"It must," Claire replied. She rested her lips on Timmy's head and kissed him. "For his sake."

Paul looked down at Timmy. Then he removed his arm from around Claire and rubbed the little boy's back. "Agreed," was all he said, but his eyes had grown hard.

Fleming's voice pulled Paul out of his sad reverie. "You seem to have recovered from that operation we did together in New York as well. I recall that you were a bit shaken, that being your first 'wet' mission, as the descriptor goes."

"That was a lifetime ago," Paul replied. "I don't dwell on it. The mission was necessary, or the Japs would have had the American naval codes. I don't like to think about it."

Fleming studied Paul's face. "You've hardened. I can see it in your eyes."

"Maybe I've come of age," Paul snapped. "War will do that to you."

An image of Ryan again meandered before his eyes as she had been the last time he had seen her. *When was that? More than a year ago, shortly before the Americans entered the war.*

With Claire's help, he had located Ryan's family and visited her grave. A wave of sorrow overcame him as he had placed fresh flowers on her tombstone. Now he coughed to ward off grief.

If Fleming noticed Paul's discomfiture, he did not let on. "I see anger burning in your eyes," he said, responding to Paul's comment. "When we last met, you were a man bent on doing his duty. It's become personal somehow. I can see it. What's happened?"

"Nothing I care to talk about."

"I understand. Well, let's get on with this mission, shall we."

The brusqueness with which Ryan's existence was shoved into the past all but took Paul's breath away. He heard Fleming continue as if from afar, grasping dimly that the officer could not be blamed for callousness when he knew nothing of the sad event.

"Brigadier Gubbins circulated information within the office that you were looking for something to do while you convalesced," Fleming continued. "I volunteered you for this project because we'd worked together before. My task is to bring you up to speed so you can brief Eisenhower. I understand that you've already worked directly with him, so you're a trusted agent. We'd like him to make an informed decision regarding going forward. As supreme commander, he'll have final say."

"So my job is to convince Eisenhower?"

Fleming shook his head. "No. Your job is to brief him faithfully and in detail and to answer whatever questions he has. The final decision is his alone, after it's been approved by the prime minister."

"And the title is Operation Mincemeat? That's a little gruesome, don't you think?"

Fleming blew out a breath of air. "What isn't in this war? But we follow two main criteria among others in naming an operation: that it gives no clue about the underlying mission, and that no mother should worry that her son might die in a shamefully named operation. In this case, there's no fear of that happening."

Upon reading the description of the operation that Fleming provided, Paul could barely hide his disgust. "So, you propose to take a dead body, dress it up in the uniform of a Royal Marines major, drop it into the Mediterranean with a briefcase chained to his wrist. The case will contain documents marked 'top secret,' but they are, in fact, false. You hope the body will float to shore in the south of Spain near a town called Huelva, that it will be picked up by Spanish authorities, and that they will violate neutrality by making German intelligence officials aware that such a body with the briefcase exists. You'll rely on Spanish perfidy to make the Germans privy to the documents' contents before returning the lot to the British embassy in Madrid."

"You've summed up the plan quite nicely, and I'll add that we're also relying on the fact that Spain's dictator, Francisco Franco, has routinely passed on intelligence to the Germans despite his formally declared neutrality."

Fleming's face grew serious. "This operation is being conducted as a shot in the dark. It probably won't work, but if it does, it could save a lot of lives. And it's more than a mere hope that the corpse will float to the desired landing point. Our scientists have studied the winds and currents extensively. The odds of beaching near Huelva are quite high."

"Can you tell me who dreamed up this caper? I don't mean to be disrespectful, but at this point, 'caper' seems to be the word that fits."

Fleming let out a small, involuntary laugh, and his lips stretched into a tight smile. "I'd like to claim credit, but that would be untruthful. Let me explain.

"I told you when we first met in Canada back in '41 that I intend to write novels after the war." He chuckled. "Maybe I'll fit you in as a character. I've already got one for your earlier boss, William Stephenson, and for my own boss, Admiral John Godfrey, the director of naval intelligence. In my books, I'll simply refer to him as 'M.'"

"I'm sure I'll be delighted," Paul said with a touch of impatience, "but could we get on with what I need to know?"

"You asked the question," Fleming said testily. He leaned forward. "You need to hear the entire plan before you summarily dismiss the idea. You've apparently gained the confidence of General Eisenhower, and you owe it to him to give a full, unvarnished report, and to do that, your own mind must remain open. Agreed?"

Paul nodded, but his expression showed that he harbored deep doubts.

"Look," Fleming continued, "we have a department of war deceptions. And it's not like we haven't done similar things before. We even have a name for the technique. We call it the 'Haversack Ruse.' You've been involved in some of those operations yourself on a large scale."

"Excuse me?" Paul broke in. "What did you call it?"

"The Haversack Ruse. It comes from a ploy by General Sir Edmund Allenby. Back in 1917, he attacked the Turks at Gaza, but found his way blocked by a large force. Deciding his next attack should be at Beersheba, he consulted with his staff on how best to pursue that course of action. He had an enterprising young major in charge of deceptions on his intelligence staff, Richard Meinertzhagen. The major believed that for a deception operation to succeed to its fullest, just causing the enemy to believe you are not going to take a certain action is insufficient. You must make him believe that you plan to do the opposite of what you actually intend.

"So, Meinertzhagen rode into the desert on horseback with a haversack stuffed full of false secret documents that purported to show his plans. He included a faked letter from his wife celebrating the birth of a new son, and he smeared the whole lot with horse blood. When he was shot at in no-man's land, he feigned being wounded, slumped forward, dropped his rifle, canteen, and the haversack, and galloped back to his own lines. Then, he mounted the appearance of a massive search for the bag and even left a sandwich wrapped in a paper with the day's orders printed on it directing the search near enemy lines.

"Of course, he also dropped several hundred cigarettes laced with opium behind Turkish lines, so who knows what really worked. The Turks might have just been stoned. Regardless, they moved two divisions away from Beersheba to defend against another reinforced assault at Gaza. Allenby attacked at Beersheba after the Turks had thinned the lines, and he cleared the road to Jerusalem."

"That's remarkable. I didn't know that story."

"There are others. One ruse we ran recently against Rommel in the desert during the battle of El Alamein. If you'd like to hear it, I'll make it short."

Paul's mind flashed to the story of a fake map that Sergeant Yates had related to him on arrival near Tobruk and 8th Army headquarters. "If you mean about the map showing where the soft and hard sand are, I've heard it briefly. Please go on."

"All right then." Fleming leaned back, obviously enjoying his story-telling. "In the desert, there are two kinds of ground surfaces: hard scrabble and soft sand. To maneuver tanks, you need the hard kind. We took a map, reversed the markings on it to show the soft sand to be where the hard stuff was, and vice versa. Then we aged the map to make it appear decades old and planted it on a corpse where it could be easily found with other papers. The Germans found the map, and the Desert Fox's tanks bogged down in the soft sand. We won the battle and the campaign partly because of that deception."

"I see. It's all rather ghoulish, but if it wins the battle and saves our soldiers' lives, I can hardly object."

"And as I recall, you're experienced in the dark art of deception operations."

"I suppose so," Paul said, remembering the ruses the American, General Donovan, had pulled with him in the Balkans to nudge Adolf Hitler to shift forces into that region and away from the Nazis' eastern front, thus relieving pressure on Stalin. And Paul's mind flashed over events in North Africa where he had watched General Clark turn the entire Vichy French army away from the Axis Powers to join the Allies without firing a shot, largely through force of personality. "Go on."

"You know, it's not like we haven't done similar things in the past. Not to get into the weeds too much, but Admiral Godfrey, who heads up SOE's deception section, is a fly-fisherman, and he sees successful intelligence operations as sharing similar techniques with that of his favorite sport. He wrote a memo a few weeks ago that's become famous in British intelligence circles, and he titled it, 'The Trout Fisher.' In his words, the angler 'casts patiently all day. He frequently changes his venue and his lures. If he has frightened a fish, he may give the water a rest for half an hour, but his main endeavor, to attract fish by something he sends out from his boat, is incessant.' So it is with intelligence, particularly of the actively deceptive type."

Paul started to say something, but Fleming stopped him with a raised hand. "Let me finish answering your question. In that memo, Godfrey requested every idea anyone came up with for how to deceive the enemy, no matter how lame. Most of them are harebrained and perhaps this idea of the cadaver is too. It was number twenty-eight on the list and my contribution, but the original idea was not mine.

"I told you, I want to write novels. I like novels. I read other authors for variations of style as well as enjoyment. One scribbler whose work I've read was Basil Thomson. He was a spy-catcher during the last war and went on to be a tutor to the King of Siam, the assistant premier of Tonga, and the governor of Dartmoor prison. He was head of Scotland Yard's Criminal Investigation Division and the Metropolitan Police Special Branch for a while, and in his spare time, he wrote twelve novels.

"In one of them, *The Milliner's Hat Mystery*, someone finds a body in a barn and reports it to authorities. Thomson's main character, Inspector Richardson, discovers while investigating that nothing about the deceased is genuine. Everything on him has been expertly forged including calling cards, receipts, his passport, down to the lint in his pockets.

"Now don't misunderstand, Thomson didn't write great literature, but he knew about deception, intelligence, and police work. And it was from his fiction that I found the seed of an idea that might work—with heavy emphasis on 'might.'"

Paul had listened attentively. "What do you hope to accomplish?" he asked while Fleming took a pause.

"Here's the issue. In six weeks' time, we'll put a hundred and sixty thousand British and American sons, brothers, husbands, and fathers on a hostile coast in Sicily. The Germans expect it, and they're reinforcing. Sicily is a military jewel in the Mediterranean, commanding its east-west traffic. Whichever army holds it possesses a massive advantage. The current estimate is that we'll lose ten thousand soldiers and three hundred ships. The aim is to reduce that number and get our army ashore quickly and decisively."

"Those are sobering numbers," Paul remarked. "How is our cadaver going to help? Does he have a name?"

"Yes," Fleming replied, rising to stretch. "We've had the chap since early January, and his name will be Major William Martin. We're building an appropriate background for him, including a fiancée."

"You've had him since January?" Paul interrupted, incredulous at the mental image.

"Yes, well, we put him in a special cooler that will retard decomposition but won't stop it. We can't freeze him, or his internal organs will swell and that would be caught immediately by any half-baked medical examiner. We're building a special canister to transport him encased in dry ice, via submarine, to the release point. Our scientists estimate that he'll float for about three days, and by the time the Spaniards fetch him out of the sea, he should have melted and look like he died five to eight days previously."

"Dry ice? Won't that freeze him?" Paul asked.

"That's a bit over my head. Our smart chaps assure us that the process has a high probability of working to give the desired appearance. Shall I go on?"

Paul assented, and Fleming continued. "One of the secretaries volunteered her photo to be placed in his pocket as his beloved, and we'll compose a suitably endearing love letter to press against his chest in his jacket. We'll also put used and dated theater tickets and receipts in his pockets, and his ID and wallet will be aged. One of our chaps, RAF Flight Lieutenant Cholmondeley, will go to a small village, Mold in North Wales, and stay in the Black Lion hotel. He'll post a letter there from Martin's father bemoaning the break-up of a long marriage and stating that he, the father, is staying in the hotel so as not to impose on his sister, Martin's aunt."

"I see. How did you pick the name William Martin?"

Fleming smiled as he re-took his seat. Paul followed suit. "That was easier than you might think. We know the Germans have a copy of our officers' roster down through the letter L. Martin falls under the next letter in the alphabet, of course, and there are many Martins in service. There's actually a Major William Martin, one of our best pilots, but he's in the US, training American pilots, so we doubt he'll ever get wind of the operation or that the Germans will inquire that far afield. They won't have time."

Paul regarded Fleming with a questioning look. "So you're anticipating that the operation will go forward."

Fleming nodded. "By agreement and as I mentioned, General Eisenhower has the last word, but our window is narrow. We had to plan as if he would approve. You know, acquiring a body is not as easy as you might think."

Paul glanced up at him in surprise. "With all the deceased filling our morgues these days, I should have thought that would pose no difficulty."

"The whole group on this project thought the same thing, but war casualties are usually in grim condition. People who commit suicide are typically in similar states, as are victims of accidents. Not that many drownings occur, and we can be sure that before the Germans are taken in, they'll order a thorough post-mortem and check for exactly that. Our challenge was to find someone who won't be missed, of an age consistent with a midlevel officer, and one who can be made to appear to have drowned after an airplane crash in the ocean."

"How would you do that?"

Fleming grunted. "Well now we're going to get into the gory details. Are you ready for this?"

Paul sighed. "I'll need to know for my report."

Fleming took a moment to gather his thoughts. "The cadaver had to be fresh and unharmed aside from an appearance of having drowned after a plane crash. This chap was a vagrant found in an abandoned warehouse, and the victim of rat poisoning. We don't know whether that came about by murder, suicide, or accident, but in any event, the dose was heavy enough to kill him, but light enough for it to be undetectable in an autopsy after he's been immersed at sea a few days."

"How will you make him look like he drowned?"

"The obvious answer is with water in the lungs and stomach, but that's not the complete answer. A death caused by rat poison would work because no trace amounts would appear with that much passage of time and decay.

"A drowning victim's lungs marble from inhaling water. If that marbling is not present, a pathologist would know our Major Martin did not drown. The solution is to ensure that the body decomposes sufficiently that the lungs would reasonably have turned to liquid already. The pathologist would be unable to conclude definitively that Martin did not die by drowning, and the seemingly obvious conclusion would be that he did. We're counting on that." He laughed. "We're even going to lengths to ensure that Major Martin will be wearing underwear. Since they're rationed, they're hard to come by, but no mid-level officer from an upper-class family would go without them."

Paul shook his head in sad disbelief. "What times we live in."

"You need to know that Mincemeat is part of a larger deception plan, which will lighten Major Martin's load a bit. Our aim is to convince the Germans that whatever we do in Sicily is merely a feint, and that our true objectives are Greece and Sardinia. In that regard, we're recruiting Greek fishermen as guides, developing maps of the Peloponnese, which is where the purported invasion would take place, and generating radio traffic indicating preparations for an operation there. We've even created a ghost army that looks like the real thing in aerial reconnaissance photos. If we can convince Hitler that Greece and Sardinia are the main objectives, he'll move divisions to reinforce in those places, hopefully taking forces out of Sicily."

Paul rubbed his eyes, red with fatigue. "This is bewildering. I need to know the wider plans as well. General Eisenhower will want to know. But first, assuming that Martin makes it to shore near Huelva, what are the documents he'll be carrying? And won't they be illegible from being in the water for so long?"

"We've thought through the problem of the ink. We can't use waterproof ink—that would give the game away at the start. But we've experimented with many regular inks. As it turns out, some will survive underwater conditions, particularly when on folded paper, inside an envelope, and pressed inside a jacket or briefcase. When dried, they might have run a bit, but they are still legible. Of course, there are no guarantees."

Paul sat back in awe. "I'm amazed. Is there no detail you haven't anticipated?"

Fleming exhaled. "If there is, it'll be the one that trips us up. But we're fairly adept at inventing personalities. We've turned all the known spies that Germany has sent over. They work for us now, and they recruit many more spies to help them here. However, those new spies are fictitious. We have a whole network of fictitious spies communicating with Germany, feeding all sorts of information, much of it real enough to be verified, most of it bogus, and all of it harmless. We have one real spy running twenty-seven imaginary ones, and of course each of those must have his or her personality, quirks, hobbies, families, and normal life's challenges. It's not an easy task, keeping it all straight, but they must never step out of character. Of course, the plus side with the imaginary ones is that they are less finicky or demanding than real spies; they're always compliant and ready to meet the wishes of their German masters." He scoffed. "It becomes a game, albeit a deadly one, and you might have heard of the very real mishap that almost tipped the Germans to the date for our invasion into North Africa for Operation Torch."

Paul frowned and shook his head. "No. I had not heard."

Fleming blew out a breath. "Ironically, it's a scenario similar to the one we're trying to construct. In September of last year, a British Catalina FP119 seaplane crashed on its way to Gibraltar in an electrical storm near Cádiz on Spain's Atlantic coast. The three crewmembers were killed along with a Royal Navy courier, Paymaster-Lieutenant James Turner. He carried a letter informing the governor of Gibraltar that General Eisenhower would arrive there to command the offensive, with the date set at November 4. Lieutenant Turner also carried a second letter, dated September 21, with other information about Operation Torch.

"Spanish authorities took possession of the bodies where they washed ashore at La Barrosa, south of Cádiz, and turned them over to our consular staff twenty-four hours later. Spain's neutrality tilts toward the Axis Powers. Our perception is that Spain first informed the Germans regarding the courier, but we don't know for sure. General Eisenhower was quite worried, as was the rest of the senior command. Regardless, our scientists, after examining the letters, concluded that they had not been rifled. However, the same was not true of a notebook carried by a fifth victim of that flight, a Free French intelligence officer, Louis Daniélou. He was on a mission for SOE, and his notebook contained targets inside North Africa and notes regarding command structure and personalities. We know from intelligence sources that the Germans received photos of the pages and considered the information inconsequential. After our success with Torch, we're counting on Germany to take steps so as not to repeat the error of not thoroughly analyzing captured material."

"So, what are Martin's documents?"

Fleming slid a folder on the table over to Paul. "They're all here. You can brief Eisenhower on their content, but you cannot take copies."

Paul assented and opened the folder. "You have an identity card already made up?"

"Issued by the admiralty with serial number 148228. We found someone who looks enough like the dead man to pose for a picture. We arranged for a death certificate from a bona fide undertaker, and after the cadaver's discovery and return to us in Spain, we'll post an obituary in the press. We'll also send a letter to the British consul from the bereaved family requesting that a large marble slab be placed on Martin's grave. The weight of the marble will complicate any effort to exhume the body should the Germans question the autopsy report. If you think of any details that we might have missed, please bring them to our attention."

Paul continued scanning the documents. "You've six letters here," he said.

"Yes, one is the aforementioned love letter. The second is one from Martin's banker relating to an overdraft. The third is the one from his father about the sad separation from his wife. Those will go inside the major's clothing and are there to lend genuineness.

"Our challenge is to make sure the Spaniards discover the operative letters. They might miss the ones on the body, as they did with Turner. That's why Martin will carry a briefcase, but it's too bulky for only two letters, those being for the commanding generals who'll execute sub-elements of Operation Husky, the invasion of Sicily. The letters use the name of the actual operation and mention Corsica and only allude to Sardinia, but we're fairly certain the Germans will pick up the implication. The letters essentially instruct the generals to plan for simultaneous invasions of Greece in the east and Sardinia in the west.

"We'll put them in the briefcase, but we'll also stuff several pamphlets in the case with them. The remaining letter is one to Eisenhower from Lord Mountbatten requesting his endorsement of one of the booklets, that one being about the history of the commandos, written by Hilary Saunders, the House of Commons librarian. The general's endorsement is sought, purportedly, to help with distribution in America."

In spite of the gravity of the matter, Paul had to let out a small laugh. "You certainly have prepared in painstaking detail," he said. "When will this operation execute?"

Fleming arched his eyebrows. "The timing is tight, but I must tell you that the credit goes not to me but to Ewen Montagu, a former barrister and scion of a notable family, and to the young lieutenant I mentioned earlier, Charles Cholmondeley. I merely nabbed the idea from the novelist and forwarded it. I'm briefing you because we have worked together before, but Montagu and Cholmondeley are the ones who worked it out, and I echo your admiration for a masterful job.

"Now as to timing, that is a bit difficult. The uniform's no problem because Royal Marine couriers travel in battledress, which are not close-fitting. The most difficult part will be transporting the body to the drop-off point. For that, we'll have a submarine in waiting, the *Seraph*. Her skipper is practiced at special operations."

"I'm familiar with Lieutenant Jewell and the *Seraph*," Paul interjected. "I accompanied General Clark aboard her on his mission to North Africa."

Fleming regarded Paul keenly. "I must say, you do get around. As I was mentioning, the timing is a challenge. When you plan backwards from Husky's D-Day at the beginning of July and allow two weeks ahead of that for the Spaniards and the Germans to do their part, that puts Martin in the water a few days before mid-June.

"We'd like for him to be discovered about two weeks before Operation Husky executes in Sicily. That's sufficient time for the Germans to react as we'd like them to, but short enough that they will be pressured to reach conclusions and act."

Paul shook his head sadly. "This poor sod, whoever he is, could deliver the greatest service of any individual in this war without ever knowing anything about it."

Fleming studied Paul's expression. "So, you're on board?"

Paul took his time to answer. "There are so many elements that must go exactly right. As you said, it's a shot in the dark. But if Mincemeat moves German divisions and saves our chaps' lives, how could I not be for it? I will certainly report faithfully as you've explained the operation to me. But how will you monitor the mission? How will you know if the ruse succeeded?"

Fleming deadpanned a single word. "Bletchley."

Paul's mind flew to his sister, Claire.

The two men finished their discussions. Then Paul called Claire.

23

Stony Stratford, England

Claire was surprised to see a Royal Navy officer accompany Paul as the two made their way through The Bull to the table she occupied. As Claire observed the officer, she thought him to be about six feet tall with a high forehead, wavy hair, and penetrating eyes flashing from a narrow face.

"Claire, this is Lieutenant Commander Ian Fleming, a friend, associate, and erstwhile journalist—"

Fleming bowed slightly and took Claire's hand. "I'm hoping to return to journalism when this war is ended. Very pleased to meet you, Miss Little-field." He straightened and looked into Claire's eyes.

Claire caught her breath as she felt dormant sensations stir. She hoped the rising warmth in her cheeks was not visible. Then her mind was flooded with memories of Red, the American pilot she had become enamored with, who was lost in the Battle of Britain.

"How's Timmy today?" Paul asked as they took their seats. "He's grown so big."

Claire replied, laughing, "And eating everything he sees. He's my bright spot in these days of gloom. Thank God they're not as bad as days of the recent past."

"Timmy is Claire's ward," Paul explained to Fleming. "Well, I should say that our younger brother Jeremy is his guardian and Claire stands in for him while he fights in this war."

"At this point, I'll fight Jeremy for custody, if it comes to that," Claire said, only half-joking. "Timmy's become an inseparable part of my life, and I'm sure the reverse is true. But we're all very proud of Jeremy for having saved him from a shipwreck."

"I remember hearing about that," Fleming said. "The two of you have a remarkable family."

"We have our warts like anyone," Paul intoned. "But we usually get along with each other, which makes life simpler, and pleasant."

The Bull's manager came over to greet them and take their order. As he walked away, Fleming looked around the pub, admiring its polished wood and brass and the pleasant ambience. "This is quite the place," he said. "I must remember it. The two of you seem to be well acquainted with it."

"The Bull holds many memories," Claire said, suddenly somber, thinking of Jeremy's fighter-pilot friends, now gone. Their group had spent many evenings here, drinking pints and singing while Claire played the piano in the corner. "I shall always cherish it." She roused herself from melancholy and smiled brilliantly at Fleming. "And now we have another friend to share it with."

If Fleming warmed to the comment, he subdued it. "Thank you," was all he said.

They chit-chatted until their food came, and having finished their meals, they conversed further. "Have you heard from Lance or Jeremy?" Claire asked Paul. "Do we know where they are?"

Glum silence followed. Paul shook his head, unsure if his knowledge of Jeremy's assignment to France was classified. Gubbins had not specified one way or the other.

"There's always at least one of my brothers unaccounted for," Claire grumbled to Fleming, "and now there are two. Turning to Paul, she said, "If I can't see Mum and Dad, it would be nice to at least see the three of you in one place and safe at one time."

"What about Dad?" Paul asked. "Do we know where he's being held?"

"I received a Red Cross message from Mum," Claire said. She had started to say that she had concentrated on intercepting messages from the vicinity of Ilag VII/Z and had been able to discern that, as internment camps went, it was a relatively pleasant one. Then she caught herself. The Official Secrets Act forbade her from revealing her employment at Bletchley Park or revealing knowledge she gained there, except in official capacity. Only Paul knew her status from previous intelligence work.

"He's in a prison camp, Tittmoning Castle at Laufen, in Bavaria," she said instead. "That's the main camp for detainees from the Channel Islands. I'm told by people who've visited the area that, as scenery goes, it's quite pleasant, and Father states that treatment of prisoners is not harsh." She scoffed. "He would say that."

Paul cast her a brief, searching look, which she avoided. Quiet descended.

After an awkward silence, Fleming placed his napkin on the table. "I should be going," he said. When Paul and Claire protested, he shook his head and rose to his feet. "I have an early meeting in the morning that I must prepare for."

Chagrinned, Paul walked with him to the front door. "We ran you off with our talk of family matters."

Fleming shook his head. "No. You have a close-knit family despite the war. I'm envious." Chuckling, he added, "Claire is dazzling. I see elements of her I could use in my books."

"That's nice of you to say. I'm afraid Claire's still a bit downcast over the plight of our parents as well as all the losses. She feels each of them."

"I understand. She carries the burden well." Fleming glanced back through the window to where Claire sipped her wine. "I must be off. When can I expect to hear from you?"

"I'll travel to Gibraltar tomorrow. If wind and weather cooperate, I could be there by the next day, even with the war-driven circuitous route. If not, getting there could take a week. Eisenhower has been apprised that I'm coming. I'll send back word first chance after briefing him."

"Brilliant. Cheers." Fleming sauntered away toward the train station.

Paul re-entered the pub and made his way back to the table. "I think Fleming was quite taken with you, Claire."

"Rubbish. He's a nice chap, though, and that navy uniform suits him. Where do you know him from?"

"Here and there," Paul said mildly. "And it's not just the uniform that suits him. He was a little bit of a lost soul when we first met. I think he's found a home in the navy. Did I tell you he wants to be a novelist after the war?"

"You mentioned it. What kind of books?"

"I dunno. War stories, I suppose."

"Then he won't amount to anything as an author. The world is tired of war." She sighed. "I dream of the day when everyone can share life openly." She gazed at Paul. "Well, big brother? Will you be disappearing again soon?"

Paul reached across the table and squeezed her hand. "I'm afraid so. I'll spend the night, and then I'll be off."

Claire fought off a frown and smiled through misted eyes. "Well, at least we have you tonight. I just wish we knew where Lance and Jeremy are and that they're all right." She raised her wine glass. "Better times will come. You'll see. Let's drink to that and to Lance and Jeremy. Cheers."

"To Lance and Jeremy," Paul said as he clinked his wine glass against Claire's.

24

April 28, 1943
Bokn, Norway

Despite the brisk weather, Lieutenant Lance Littlefield relished the wind across his face. After the two years he had spent as a POW at Colditz Castle and then four months of intensive training to be a commando, he exulted in finally exercising some control over his own life, which, to him, tasted like the essence of freedom. Granted, he was on his way to execute a mission for which the odds of returning safely were small, and in a tiny fishing boat no less, but he had volunteered for the commandos, he had survived the training, and he had eagerly sought out the chance to be on this mission.

All was quiet around him aside from the low hum of the motor on the fishing coble he and his mates used to carry the raiding team and their two canoes north from Bokn. The island was situated on the eastern side of the nineteen-mile-long Karmsundet Strait along the western flank of Norway, in Rogaland County, about fifty miles north of Stavanger. Eight members of No. 14 Commando had been transported to Bokn across the North Sea for Operation Checkmate by a motor torpedo boat, and with the help of the local Norwegian Resistance, they had set up their base camp on the islet.

Their targets were in the harbor at Kopervik, a town five miles north of Bokn on the opposite bank of the strait. Also on board the coble were a number of magnetic limpet mines to be attached below the waterlines of as many German warships anchored in the inland port as possible. That was their mission.

Lance had been disappointed at not being included on the assault team. He had relished the training at commando school in Scotland, climbing mountains, rappelling off cliffs, engaging in hand-to-hand combat techniques, detonating explosives, and learning to kill swiftly and silently with or without a weapon. He loved action and adventure, craving it while ensconced at Colditz, and was thus driven to escape over and over again until he finally succeeded in finding his way home. "With Jeremy's help," he muttered.

He had to admit to slight envy over the exploits of his younger brother. Lance had been the adventurous member of the family. All four siblings had engaged in active exploring and sports around Sark while growing up, but Paul had always been the staid leader of the pack and a bookhound, exercising cautionary influence over his younger siblings when their daring adventures approached the bounds of good judgment. Claire had delved into music, becoming an accomplished musician, and had been admitted to the Royal Philharmonic Orchestra prior to the war. And Jeremy, with a mild personality, had been a blend of the older three, always working quietly to keep up in their activities, including Lance's audacious exploits and Paul's studious habits.

Jeremy, like Lance, was a veteran of the Dunkirk debacle wherein a defeated British army had evacuated the beaches in northern France ahead of certain annihilation at the hands of the *Wehrmacht*. Prime Minister Churchill had raised the morale of the country by characterizing the evacuation at Dunkirk as a victory, but veterans viewed things differently. They had been routed and were lucky to escape with their lives, particularly those tens of thousands who had been left behind. Many, like Lance, had marched hundreds of miles across France into POW camps inside Germany where most still languished.

Jeremy's escape from Dunkirk led to his rescue of Timmy from the *Lancastria* bombing and sinking at Saint-Nazaire, a feat that brought him national attention. Then he had gone on to fly Spitfires and Hurricanes as a member of Churchill's Few, the small number of intrepid pilots who had held off the *Luftwaffe* during the Battle of Britain until a *Wehrmacht* invasion had become impossible. Jeremy went on to fly Beaufighters at night during the *blitz*. Since then, he had returned to France to participate in covert operations, including acts of sabotage. He had even found time to fall in love with a French girl with auburn hair and honey-colored eyes, Amélie Boulier, who was now active in the French Resistance,

Lance smiled at the recollection of how his brother had talked about her. "She's beautiful," Jeremy had gushed, "and brave."

Then Jeremy had turned somber as he worried about Amélie's current safety and that of her younger sister, Chantal. He told Lance about how, with the aid of a huge man by the name of Maurice who ran the local Resistance around Marseille, the sisters had escaped to Spain when the *Wehrmacht* had descended into the south of France following the capitulation of Vichy French forces to the Allied command in North Africa. They should be safe for the time being, Jeremy had said, as if reassuring himself, but he worried that they would return to Marseille and continue their Resistance activities.

Lance craved the action Jeremy had experienced. Long before the war began, Lance had enlisted in the army against his parents' wishes and worked his way up to sergeant. Paul, meanwhile, had taken a commission in military intelligence while Claire had joined the orchestra, and Jeremy had completed university studies and then took a military commission with the British army engineers. The youngest sibling had deployed to France to build roads and airfields, not to fight.

So while Britain had stood poised at the brink of destruction and Jeremy had done his bit for king and country, Lance, captured while trying to escape France after Dunkirk, had languished for two years within the cold stone walls of the POW camp at Colditz Castle. To be sure, just before capture, he had led a raid that blew up a field of fuel storage tanks at Saint-Nazaire, and at Colditz he had enjoyed the camaraderie of some of the best men anyone could meet. Nevertheless, pangs of guilt haunted him for not having done more to save Great Britain from the ravages that *Herr* Hitler had intended and still pursued.

Despite that most of his cohorts at Colditz were officers, and Lance had been a noncom, the POWs had accepted him as an equal, mainly because of his tenacity and success in breaking free of captivity multiple times. For that reason, the senior British officer had selected him from among the British POWs to be one of the members of the escape committee. On his last attempt, Jeremy, disguised as a Gestapo officer, had rescued Lance, and escorted him out of Switzerland to France and the relative safety of the Resistance. From there, a British Lysander night-flight had borne him to England.

Now, as the fishing coble puttered through the night on the dark waters with Lance and his teammates, his thoughts turned to Claire. He had noticed a change in her that worried him. She was still the fun-loving, caring sister she had always been, but the serious side of her seemed to prevail since his return from captivity. It manifested in a circumspect manner that he found puzzling. He admired the way she had taken over the care of Timmy, but he wondered about how she supported the child and herself in the home she rented on the estate. She was obviously no longer active with the orchestra. When he inquired, she had demurred, telling him that Jeremy helped out, but she otherwise avoided the subject.

Lance shook himself back to the present, pleased that, at last, he would strike a blow for Great Britain against the existential threat that was Nazi Germany. He had done well enough at commando school not only to regain his rank but also to be elevated to second lieutenant. He had hoped his achievement would put him in command of this raid but quickly realized that, at this point in the war, neither his sabotage activity in France nor his spectacular escape were particularly impressive among veteran commandos who had participated at Lofoten, Saint-Nazaire, Vemork, Dieppe, or any other of a number of raids along the French coast.

So, he humbly and willingly subordinated himself to Lieutenant John Godwin, a Royal Navy Volunteer Reserve officer who, though a British citizen, had been born and raised in Argentina. More pertinent to the current operation was that Godwin had completed training months before Lance had joined the commandos and had already proven himself in multiple raids. Lance contented himself with the thought that he had been embraced by an elite unit of men whose feats were at least equal to his own. He was pleased to support them and learn from them.

The plan called for the fishing coble to carry the canoes and the assault team under cover of darkness north in the strait as close as possible to the harbor at Kopervik. Before entering the harbor, Lieutenant Godwin and Able Seaman Neville Burgess of the Royal Navy would board one of the canoes. Two more able seamen, Keith Mayor and Andrew West, would take the other one. With their limpet mines, they would close the distance to the targets and attach the mines. Meanwhile, Lance and the support team—which included Victor Cox, who was attached from No. 12 Commando—and two Royal Navy petty officers, Alfred Roe and Harold Hiscock, would return to Bokn to prepare for a hasty departure once the raiding party had re-joined them.

The plan roughly followed that of a previous commando raid, Operation Frankton, carried out two months earlier along France's coast at Bordeaux. Many lessons had been learned from that one. It succeeded, but the cost in lost commando lives was high.

Conceived as a mission of ten men on five kayaks to attack ships in the Bordeaux harbor after several days of paddling, the concept had been upended at the outset when two canoes were destroyed because of high waves, one of them occurring as it was lowered into the ocean from the submarine that carried the commandos and their canoes to within ten miles of the estuary at Gironde.

Another canoe foundered in five-foot swells. Its two commandos swam ashore with great difficulty, and then set about to evade capture and make their way overland to Spain. However, they were betrayed, detained by *gendarmes*, and turned over to German authorities.

After five nights of paddling over sixty miles at night and sleeping during the day, the two remaining teams arrived at their targets at Bordeaux a night late, and set their limpet mines. Once finished, and as they hurried downstream, they heard the explosions behind them but could not assess the damage.

Lance and his teammates had been saddened to learn that only those four of the ten commandos who had started out returned home safely. To mitigate the difficulties of Operation Frankton, for this raid, Operation

Checkmate, Lance and his teammates moved across the North Sea on a surface ship and were delivered to Bokn in the relatively calm waters inside the Karmsundet Strait. There, they were met by Norwegian Resistance members who helped them prepare for the raid. The attack and support elements together steered the flat-bottomed fishing coble five miles to Kopervik. Then, while the raid was executed, the support team returned to Bokn, prepared to receive the raiding element after their sabotage was complete, and then, with the help of the Resistance, the entire party would make good their escape aboard the same motor torpedo boat that had brought them.

Godwin and Burgess set out from the coble in their canoe, trailed by Mayor and West in a second canoe. They had chosen a dark night but hopefully with enough moonlight to glimmer off the water and point their way, and they were gratified when that occurred. Staying away from shore, they paddled in long, synchronized sweeps, heading northward, navigating on a nearly full tide with the shush of a soft breeze on their faces bearing the scent of a salty coastline. All was quiet save for the water lapping against their tiny crafts and the occasional far-off calls of nocturnal wildlife or splashes of sea creatures breaking the surface.

They reached the edge of the harbor, detectable by the shoreline suddenly stretching away to the left. Ahead of them, dim blackout lights were barely visible around some vessels at anchor. Apparently feeling safe this far inside an inland waterway, the Germans had chosen not to keep an active watch over the harbor on a scale that included regular patrols and searchlight sweeps.

The commandos hugged the shore to avoid detection by shipboard sentries until they reached the harbor. Once there, they would traverse the anchorage, seeking targets. They spoke not at all, staying close enough together to maintain visual contact but far enough away so that if one of the canoes was spotted or fired upon, the other might be missed.

His throat constricting with sober anticipation, Godwin steered his canoe into the harbor. Then, as the pastoral backdrop merged into faint silhouettes of low buildings at the edge of Kopervik, they ventured farther from the shore once again, steering into the deepest shadows.

The impossibility of their task now bore down on Godwin. He had volunteered without hesitation for the raid without fully appreciating the difficulty of finding the target ships in a darkened harbor dotted with numerous islets and inlets. Although he had studied the maps and aerial photographs diligently, he now realized that spotting landmarks in a place he had never visited, shrouded in darkness, was next to impossible.

They passed several fishing vessels unseen until the canoes were almost upon them, and as Godwin peered through the night, his heart sank. Not a single warship was in sight.

They crossed the small harbor paddling rapidly, their breathing becoming labored. Reaching the other side, they took a short breather, reversed direction, steered further out, and started back. At the south end of the harbor, they rested again, and paused before starting back north.

"I think I saw the outline of a ship," Mayor whispered as the crews narrowed the distance between them. "If I'm right, it's about two-thirds of the way across to the east."

"Roger," Godwin murmured back. "Let's have a look, and if it's there, execute immediately. Burgess and I will take the far side. You and West place your mines on the near side. If we come upon it from the bow or stern, we'll go left; you go right. Set your timers for thirty minutes, and then clear the area. Head back to base. We've been here too long, and soon we'll be pushing dawn."

They checked to ensure their watches were synchronized and then started out again, using a compass to keep their bearing.

They came upon the ship on its starboard side, its identifying numerals barely visible in the ambient light: M5207. It appeared to be the size of a minesweeper, but without more light, Godwin could not determine that with certainty. However, given the bulk and configuration that he could make out, he was sure that it was a warship.

The two canoes separated, each going to opposite sides as Godwin had directed. Glancing intermittently up at the ship's deck as they approached, Godwin and Burgess set about arming and setting the timer on the first limpet, so named for its resemblance to a sea snail that clung to rocks and other solid surfaces. The mine consisted of a long handle attached to a round, thick, flat element that contained the explosives. It also contained strong magnets that, like its namesake, caused it to cling to its target. The explosive element had been made to create negative buoyancy, the effect of which was that should an enemy discover and attempt to remove them, they would detonate.

Gingerly, Burgess nudged the nose of the canoe against the ship's hull. Balancing carefully, Godwin then crouched forward and, having set the timer, held the limpet by its long handle, dipped it below the waterline, and maneuvered it to the steel skin. It attached with a dull thud that to Godwin and Burgess sounded for all the world like a loud clang.

Godwin sat back in his seat, and the two commandos hung in the shadows, listening, their hearts thumping as they fought to control their breathing. Hearing nothing amiss, they moved on to set the next mine, and then the third and fourth. Then, rounding the back end of the warship, they arrived on the other side in time to hear the thump of Mayor's and West's last limpet clasping against the side of M5207.

From above, a startled voice suddenly called out something unintelligible in German, and a flashlight shone down on the water. The beam of light caught the back end of Mayor's canoe as the two commandos dipped their paddles hard and deep, and with strong strokes, they slipped out of the light.

The beam circled around as German shouting ensued and resounded over the water, soon joined by other voices calling out in alarm.

The British commandos bent low and paddled furiously in the direction they had come, but not before a powerful spotlight switched on and probed the dark waters. It shone first at the place where they had been, close to the ship, then worked out in their perceived direction of travel before methodically traversing back and forth, extending farther and farther across the harbor in a southward direction. It shone ahead of them and behind them, but thankfully did not catch them in its light.

But then the rhythmic pounding of a large caliber machine gun broke the night, and small water plumes sprang up where steel bullets struck. The volleys shifted with the spotlights, spreading left and right as the commandos in the canoes pressed to the limits of their collective endurance to escape the deadly tracers.

At last, the commandos approached the mouth of the harbor and rounded the curve into the relative safety of the strait. But already, behind them, they heard the wails of sirens and the throaty roar of many engines, military vehicles in pursuit.

When the commandos had paddled far enough that Godwin was sure the spotlights could not reach them and that they were out of effective range, he directed his men to the opposite side of the channel. He had all but lost track of time, but he reasoned that most of the German vehicles would be on the finger of land on the western side of the strait, and if dawn broke before they reached Bokn, they would be in shadows longer by staying close to the eastern shore.

The minutes ticked by, and then, just as Godwin felt that his muscles could bear no more strain, a massive explosion erupted, shattering the night. It was followed by an even larger explosion as M5207's fuel ignited, casting an orange glow against the sky, clearly visible to the commandos. They took a moment to sit and watch while they rested their arms and caught their breath, and then pressed on, southward.

***

After dropping off Godwin and his raiding team, Lance and his support element had pushed the limits of the coble's engine, hurrying on a tide that began to recede as they headed back toward Bokn.

The Norwegian Resistance fighters were at the water's edge to help them beach the boat and prepare to receive Godwin and the raiding party. Cox quickly dispatched Roe to go farther down the beach to watch for the torpedo boat scheduled to rendezvous with them and take them home.

Then, shortly after reaching their camp, they heard a distant boom.

Exhilaration that comes with triumph surged adrenaline through their bodies, with attendant dread of having been discovered. The explosion would most certainly trigger an all-out search, starting within moments and in force.

Staring into the dark night, Lance watched myriad spotlights probing the sky and shining down along the water, and faintly, he heard the wails of sirens and the blare of horns. Even at this distance, the orange glow of a cauldron played against wispy clouds in the sky. Soon, the Germans' inland patrol boats would be heading their way under power. Although not overly religious, Lance breathed a small prayer for the safety of his commando brothers.

A husky Nordic man with a weathered complexion, ear-length blond hair under a knitted cap, and a week's growth of beard sidled up to him. Lance had met him briefly on first arriving on Bokn. "What is it, Leif?"

"You must leave now," he said. "The Germans are coming faster than we thought."

Stunned, for a moment, Lance was speechless. "But our torpedo boat. It's coming—"

"We have people far down the coast, watching. It's not in the strait, and if it came through the mouth now, it couldn't get here fast enough."

"But the raiding party. We can't leave without them."

"Our observers are spread on the roads and watching the banks on both sides of the straits to the north. We can intercept your men. But if you stay here, you'll be captured. We can take you to safety and bring the raiding party to you."

Flanked by Leif, Lance took only a moment to let his thoughts settle and then hurried over to Cox, who stood at the water's edge peering north into the darkness, straining to catch a glimpse of their brother commandos. "We have to go," Lance said. "Hide the coble and prepare to leave."

"Sir, we can't—"

"But we must." He turned to Leif. "Tell him."

Leif repeated what he had said to Lance.

When Leif had finished, Lance told Cox, "You were in charge on the water, and I followed your orders. We're on land now, and our task is to evade capture. Authority passes to me. Leif and his organization were vetted through the Resistance group on Hardangervidda via London, and they knew the right passwords. We don't have time for discussion. Assemble your men and prepare to march."

Cox stared grimly into Lance's eyes. "I'll gather our chaps," he snorted angrily after a moment.

25

May 13, 1943
Grini Fangelier, Bærum, Norway

The multi-colored charm of full-summer Nordic foliage, crystal clear streams, and surrounding low, forested hills did little to lift Lance's spirits or those of his teammates from Operation Checkmate as the troop transport lorry that carried them rumbled through the gates of the prison camp. When it came to a halt, German sentries rousted them at rifle-point to stand in front of the headquarters, a long five-story brick structure made ugly by the reality of the commandos' captive circumstances.

Behind and to the sides of them, as they stood in a loose formation facing the building, the camp stretched on flat, dusty ground to rows of huts and outbuildings. As Lance glanced around, he noted with curiosity that, as opposed to the prison camps where he had been held on his last capture, no group of prisoners gathered to see new arrivals and prepare to entreat them with questions of war or home news. The size of the camp enclosure and the number of huts indicated a large prison population probably numbering in the thousands, but aside from a few moving between buildings, no inmates were in view.

"*Raus*," a German guard snarled, and prodded Lance with the barrel of his rifle.

Lance stood in place deliberately for a moment, and while placing his hands on his hips, he turned to face the guard. He made eye contact and grinned insolently.

Next to him, Godwin nudged Lance's arm. "Come on," he called with forced cheerfulness. "Let's put our best face on this."

Lance held the guard's steady gaze a moment longer. Then he turned to Godwin, defiance still evident on his face.

Godwin's smile was beseeching. "No sense poking a rabid dog. Let's find out what we're in for before we invite more unpleasantness."

Lance stared back into Godwin's eyes for a second and then broke into an acquiescing smile. "Sorry, John. My natural obstinacy surfacing. I won't make trouble for you or the others."

"*Raus*," the guard ordered again, and this time he jabbed his rifle hard into Lance's kidneys.

A stab of pain coursed through Lance's side, and he staggered. But he caught himself, turned, and grinned once again at the guard. "I'm going," he rasped, and indicated the rest of the commando group already formed into a single line. "Can't you see?" And with that, he followed Godwin up the stairs into the headquarters building.

The two weeks that had passed since the raid at Kopervik had been trying but not unpleasant aside from the constant strain of evading capture. True to his word, Leif had moved Lance and the support team's members to a barn well away from enemy view. For days, they had hidden in relative comfort, fed by local Norwegian Resistance members and kept apprised of a massive manhunt being conducted by the *Wehrmacht* to find the culprits of M5207's sabotage.

As days passed by, Lance became concerned that whispers of Nazi reprisals against the population accompanied promises of monetary reward for information leading to the capture of British commandos now widely rumored to be in the area. Then, three days ago, Leif related the news that Godwin and the raiding force had been captured on Urter, an island off of Norway's coast. Apparently, the four commandos had made their way back to Bokn Island and, not finding the support group there, paddled south out of Karmsundet Strait, turned out to sea, and headed north to an established rally point at Urter. Arriving exhausted, they were soon spotted by German patrols and taken prisoner.

Leif moved Lance's group to safer places twice ahead of *Wehrmacht* search parties. But as word spread that the remaining commandos were still at large, German threats of reprisals increased, and with no boat to attempt an escape out to sea, their capture became certain.

Before the inevitable happened, Lance instructed Leif to remove his Resistance fighters from the area. Then he, Cox, Roe, and Hiscock waited for their captors to appear. Yesterday, that had occurred, and they surrendered without opposition.

"I'm sorry," Lance told Cox as they stood together while being disarmed.

"Silence," a guard barked at them.

"You did the best you could," Cox called back. "I'd have done the same."

The full commando group had been reunited on the way to Grini. No effort was made to keep them from talking among themselves while being transported to the prison camp, but once inside the headquarters building, they were separated and interrogated individually.

Lance refused to divulge details, providing only the information required by the Geneva Convention: name, rank, and identity number. Thus he was surprised when, after several hours of futile attempts, his interrogator released him into a bare room where Godwin, Cox, and three other commandos already lounged on the floor awaiting their fate. The heavy wooden door closed behind Lance, a key turned in the heavy lock, and, looking through a small, barred opening, he saw that a guard was posted just outside the room.

More hours passed. The remainder of the group trailed in one by one until the entire team was together once more. Too weary to talk, they greeted each other with nods, then took their places on the floor and either fell into restless sleep or sat staring into nowhere.

Multiple heavy footsteps tramped in lockstep, the key turned in the lock, and the door flew open, banging against the inner wall. An officer in full *Wehrmacht* regalia, including a knight's cross medal at his throat, riding breeches, boots, and quirt, stood studying them as if they were a newly discovered species of insect. He was an average-sized man, and when he removed his cap and placed it under his arm, his nearly bald head protruded through hair cut short on the sides.

The commandos eyed him but otherwise did not move. The officer was well known to them, *Generaloberst* von Falkenhorst, the commanding general who had planned and executed the German invasion of Norway and now commanded the occupying army. He stepped into the room, projecting his full aristocratic bearing when he spoke. "I believe a provision of your precious Geneva Convention is that all military courtesies are to be extended to captors' officers."

The commandos' eyes turned to Godwin. Noticing their unspoken acknowledgement of him as their leader, Falkenhorst locked eyes on him.

Godwin nodded to his men and rose reluctantly. The commandos followed suit.

"Sit, sit," Falkenhorst said, and as the men once again took to the floor, a slight smile formed at the edges of his mouth. "So, you are true soldiers after all." He placed his hands at the small of his back and strutted across the floor. "My compliments on an operation well-conceived and executed. Unfortunately for you, your withdrawal did not go as planned."

His tone was more matter-of-fact than mocking. "Your tenacity is admirable, your courage indisputable. You served your country well." He paused. "Grini is not the worst place you could end up. It's a work camp. The detainees here apply themselves in industry and agriculture."

Lance reflected on the scarcity of prisoners he had seen on arrival. Falkenhorst continued, "I'm truly sorry to say that you won't be here long." He paused and took in his tiny audience of fatigued commandos, their eyes already sunken into dark pits, wrinkles lining their young faces, their uniforms filthy and stinking. "I have a favorite saying, 'without valor there is no glory.' Consistent with that, my impulse is to be lenient with you, keep you here, and treat you as POWs to the letter of the Geneva Convention.

"Fortunately for the people of this area, you were caught, and the bombing of our ships was strictly a military affair, so I took no reprisals against them, just as I took none against the people of Rjukan after the raid on Vemork. Obviously, that was also a military operation, and conducted most splendidly, I must say."

Lance listened carefully. His nerves drew taut as his subconscious took in Falkenhorst's grave expression.

"However, I bow to the greater wisdom of our leader, and I'm not allowed latitude where you are concerned," the general continued. "Our *führer* considers you to be terrorists."

As a group, the commandos sat up and paid close attention. The tension in Lance's body drew his muscles tight as he anticipated what Falkenhorst would say next.

The general drew himself up straight and faced the commandos directly. "I have no choice in providing for *Herr* Hitler's wishes to be carried out. However, I can direct how they will be carried out."

Lance's mind flashed to an episode that occurred while he was at Colditz Castle. Another troop of commandos had been captured and were dealt with per the secret order Hitler had just issued on handling commandos. "You're going to execute us," he called out. "That's what you're going to do. Hitler secretly ordered the execution of all captured commandos."

A collective gasp arose across the room.

Annoyed, Falkenhorst glared at Lance, but said nothing. He snapped his quirt against his leg, and two soldiers stepped into the room, menacing the commandos with their submachine guns.

Godwin climbed to his feet. "Sir, we were captured in uniform," he said angrily. "We've provided all required identification."

Falkenhorst acknowledged with a curt nod and held up a hand. "The order states that whether or not commandos are captured in uniform is immaterial. You are deemed to be terrorists. I have my orders. You will soon be transferred to the custody of the SS and transported to the prison at Sachsenhausen, twenty miles north of Berlin. They can exact sentence as they will, and I wash my hands of you."

June 4, 1943

Sachsenhausen Concentration Camp, Oranienburg, Germany

Nothing in Lance's experience had prepared him for the sights that greeted the commandos when they arrived at Sachsenhausen Concentration Camp. The truck pulled through a short tunnel, passed some administrative buildings, drove through another iron gate, and came to a halt.

On climbing to the ground and looking around, the stark reality of the commandos' grim situation was immediately reinforced. Directly ahead of the truck, a corpse hung from a gallows, the victim's eyes wide and staring, his mouth forced open and tongue protruding, the ghastly effort for a last gasp of air frozen on the dead man's face.

The vast prison compound was laid out in an equilateral triangle, with its far corner roughly four hundred yards from the main gate and oriented eastward. Halfway along its northern fence, a guard tower stood manned by soldiers hovering over machine guns now trained on the commandos. The tower commanded fields of fire across the entire camp.

Behind them, the iron gates were still visible, as well as the countryside beyond the iron bars. Welded into the gate, large block letters spelled out the message, "*Arbeit Macht Frei.*"

"What does that mean?" Godwin asked Lance in a low voice.

"'Work makes you free,'" Lance muttered back, and then added ruefully, "like the freedom we're heading toward."

"Silence," a voice rang out, and a captain wearing the uniform and skull of the SS stalked rapidly toward them with a squad of submachine gun-armed SS sentries. When they had surrounded the commandos, the officer signed a paper accepting delivery of the prisoners, and the original *Wehrmacht* guards fell away, mounted the truck, and drove off.

Lance noticed a difference between these new guards and any others he had encountered in previous camps where he had been interned. Whereas the *Wehrmacht* sentries ran the gamut from harsh to friendly, the SS ones carried a cold, stern air.

"Take them to the headquarters," the SS captain ordered.

The squad of sentries closed in on the commandos and began prodding and jabbing them with their weapons, yelling and herding them toward the building.

They emerged late in the evening three days later, beaten up, faces swollen, some limping with visible body bruises, thinner by many pounds, and on the verge of dehydration. As their new guards ushered them across the compound, Lance stole a glance at the gallows.

Another victim hung in the noose.

Lance swallowed hard, and as he proceeded, he took in as much as he could while keeping pace. To their front, rows of long huts were arranged in a semi-circle. Concrete fence posts on the periphery curved inward at their tops and were crowned with electrified barbed wire. More such wire was strung between the posts, and at their bases, electrified rolls of it skirted the entire perimeter. A path on the other side of the fence provided space for armed soldiers to patrol with dogs, and beyond that, a concrete wall.

The commandos moved along, prodded by the guards' harsh treatment. As they drew closer to the barracks, they were aghast to see yet another occupied gallows, the body swaying in a gentle breeze. Flies swarmed at the dead man's eyes, nose, and mouth.

They passed the grisly sight. Reaching the front row of the barracks, the guards halted the commandos and turned them around. The commandos stood in painful silence, horrorstruck anew at the scene advancing toward them: hundreds of men in tight formation with shaven heads wearing white-and black-striped utility uniforms. Most were skeletal, with hollow cheeks, sunken eyes, and tormented demeanors.

Arriving in the wide courtyard, they formed along its width and stood for an extended period, many barely able to stand while the SS staff called roll. When at last those prisoners were dismissed, the commandos' guards once again prodded the British captives, this time toward the back of the camp.

Lance's group shuffled by a fenced area where POWs sat or stood in conversation, and as the commandos passed, these prisoners gathered at the wire and watched. One of the guards taunted, "You see those British and American pilots." He jeered. "For them, like you, the war is over. But not like you, they might live."

Lance looked over at the pilots with half-interest. His body ached, his mind in dull tumult, barely able to maintain a cogent thought. He lumbered past the pilots' section to another one just past it. There, they filed into hovels, where their beds were wooden shelves without mattresses or blankets.

"Sleep well," the senior guard said. "Tomorrow morning, you start work. Early."

The commandos were rousted from restless sleep before dawn. They were fitted with new *Wehrmacht* soldiers' boots and told to walk around a long cobblestone track. Their task was to break in new boots for German soldiers on the front line. At first a pleasant escape, the task soon became laborious as the stiff leather wore blisters on their soles and ankles, their feet ached from the uneven track, the SS guards constantly pushed them to go faster, and worst of all, they had to walk thirty miles per day. Hundreds more prisoners also walked the track, none that Lance recognized outside his own group, but the guards quickly stopped any attempt at conversation and kept the POWs trudging along, round and round.

On the third day, while the commandos broke in their third set of new boots, a man sauntered next to Lance in the regular workers striped uniform. "You're one of the commandos, yes?" He spoke in broken English.

"We're not allowed to talk," Lance growled. "I have enough trouble. I don't need more."

"No trouble," the man replied. "My name is Ondrej, from Czechoslovakia. I can help."

Lance cast him a sidelong glance. "I doubt that very much."

"Look," Ondrej said, and he turned just enough to show Lance a blue triangular patch sewn on his shirt over his chest. "I've been here almost from the beginning when they opened this camp. This patch tells the guards that I am trusted."

"And that's a good thing?" Lance said. "Get away from me."

"Listen to me," Ondrej replied. "I've never betrayed anyone, but I make the guards think I have. So I get the run of the place. I help them with facility repairs, and they think I help them with intelligence from the prisoners. Don't look around. They're watching us now."

"You're drawing attention to me. Go away."

"Listen to me," Ondrej persisted. "I talk to as many prisoners this way as I can. I tell them the same thing I'll tell you, and then I move on to the next one. It's my job."

"Some job."

"It keeps me alive without betraying anyone."

"Says you. All right, I'll go along. How does this work?"

"Tell me something innocuous. Something that sounds important but is harmless."

Lance scoffed. "That's like saying 'tell me something in French.' The mind goes blank, and mine isn't up to snuff as it is." He stopped talking to think even as he plodded along. At last, he said, "Tell me something about this camp I'm not supposed to know."

Ondrej almost stopped in his tracks. "That's a new one. Usually I get responses like, 'prove to me that you're not an informer.' How am I supposed to prove that I haven't told someone something? Let's do this. Shake your head and throw your arms up as if you're angry with me. I'll move off. I'll tell them that you refused to tell me anything. Then tomorrow, I'll come back around. I'll give you a piece of information. Meanwhile, you think of something you can tell me. Tomorrow, if what I tell you is valuable, you can tell me what you have.

"Think it over. Now, let's do our little charade, and then I have to move on."

———

Lance was shocked at what the Czech told him the next day. "This is a training camp for SS prison staff," Ondrej said. "It's also a place where they test methods, and if the techniques work, they spread them to other camps."

"Can you give me an example?"

Ondrej sighed. "This is dark information. Evil beyond comprehension. I have to block it out to keep my sanity."

Lance glanced askance at him. "What could be worse than just being here or being executed, which is what they intend for me and my friends?"

Ondrej drew a labored beath. "I'll tell you honestly that knowing what I know, sometimes I pray for death. Some inmates have thrown themselves against the electrified fences to escape this hell. But someone must live to tell about what goes on here."

"So tell me."

"There's a Jewish section by the front gate, opposite the administration buildings. The Nazis intend to exterminate them. All of them, not just the ones in this camp." He enunciated each of his next words gravely. "I mean they intend to murder every Jew living anywhere in this world."

In spite of himself, Lance whipped his head toward Ondrej and cast him a skeptical look. "Pshaw. Hitler might be a demon, but there's no way he could conceive of such a thing or pull it off."

"He's already thought of it and he's taking action to do just that. Look, there's a firing range on the south side of the camp. It's inside a wide trench dug into the ground, lined with concrete, and designed to muffle sound. At the southeastern corner of it is the mortuary, and above it is a pathology lab.

"They take prisoners to the range, mostly Jewish but also Gypsies or anyone else they deem undeserving of life. They tell them that they are taking their photographs for a new ID, but when the prisoners pose next to a wall, a small window opens behind them, and a guard shoots them in the back of the head.

"They always keep prisoners moving, doing things, and aside from the hangings, they do the executions out of sight so that the inmates don't panic and become unmanageable."

Lance was in such astonishment that he almost stopped walking. "You can't be serious. How do they dispose of the bodies? And why do the hangings in the open?"

"I've never been more serious. They've murdered thousands that way. The ones on the gallows rebelled openly somehow. The hangings are warnings to stay docile."

Ondrej heaved a sigh and continued. "To dispose of so many bodies, the SS built a crematorium, incinerated the corpses, ground the ashes to a fine powder, and buried them. They had a problem, though. The soldiers didn't like doing the killing. It was ruining their morale. So the SS built a gas chamber next to the crematorium. They herd hundreds of prisoners inside daily, telling them that they'll be taking a delousing shower. Twenty minutes later, the SS troops force other prisoners to empty the gas chambers and carry the bodies to the crematorium."

Horrified, Lance could barely continue his forward pace.

"Watch your expressions," Ondrej warned. He gestured slightly to the line of sentries at the edge of the track with their weapons loosely slung over one shoulder and pointed toward the mass of misery trudging the track. "And by the way," he said while glancing over the inmates plodding along ahead of them, "the barracks they sleep in were designed for a hundred prisoners. Four hundred live in each building now, and they share seven toilets. Think of the hygiene issues and diseases coming out of that."

He shook his head and went on. "I haven't told you the worst parts yet. Can you handle them without giving us away?"

Although reluctant to hear more, Lance nodded.

"I told you they use this place to develop methods and spread them to other concentration camps. They plan to refine the gas chamber process and build other camps to use the technique on an industrial scale. They might be doing it already."

Lance closed his eyes momentarily as his tired mind tried to cope with the enormity of what Ondrej had described. He re-opened them and kept trudging while soreness and blisters drove agony in his feet. "Is that all?"

Ondrej shook his head. "I mentioned the mortuary and pathology lab. There's also a clinic where they run medical experiments on inmates. Whenever any die from complications, they're sent to the mortuary and then upstairs to the pathology clinic for dissection to learn about what happened." His voice caught. "These are difficult things to talk about, but I have told about them many times."

"You've told this to others?" Lance asked with some skepticism. "Aren't you worried that someone might turn you in?"

"No." Ondrej shook his head. "I doubt I'll live to the end of this war, but what goes on here must be brought to light. The more of us who know about the atrocities, the greater the chance of getting the story out."

"I'm shocked beyond description," Lance said. "My mind is numb, and I can't think of a single detail to tell you that sounds important."

"We'll get to that, but there's one more thing to tell you, and it's horrific." He grimaced. "You must give me some tidbit of information, though. We've been speaking for a few minutes. I'll tell you what I have to say first, and then ask some questions."

Ondrej took another deep breath. "One of the most difficult diseases to deal with on the battlefield is gangrene. It kills, it maims, and is almost impossible to heal." He glanced at Lance. "Be sure to control yourself with what I have to tell you. You might throw up." He glanced at Lance and pressed on. "To try to find a treatment, doctors in the clinic cut long wounds into women's legs and inject them with gangrene. Then they try an experimental medicine on them. It hasn't worked, but they keep trying. At best, the women heal with horribly disfigured legs. At worst, they die in agony."

Despite his empty stomach, Lance's gut turned over. He felt his knees weaken, and he almost stumbled, but he caught his balance and continued on.

"Now, my young friend," Ondrej said, "let's find out about you. Where are you from?"

"What?" Lance said absently. "Oh. Sark. It's a small island off the coast of France. You've probably never heard of it."

"You're right, I haven't, and our German keepers probably haven't either. Anything else?"

Lance indicated that there was not. "Maybe I'll have something tomorrow, but my brain is overloaded with what you've told me."

"There's more, but that's enough for now." An urgent tone gripped Ondrej's voice. "Promise me that if you get out of this place alive, you'll get to the authorities, the newspapers, anyone who'll listen. Tell them about what's gone on here. It's hell on earth."

Overwhelming sorrow suddenly welled in Lance's chest, and he wiped tears from his eyes. "I promise. This can never be allowed to happen again."

Lance saw Ondrej on the track the following day, but the Czech did not approach him. The little man had proven his resourcefulness, so Lance concluded that he must have reasons for keeping a distance.

At dusk, he assembled with the commandos and the other forced laborers in the big square in front of the barracks. Another man occupied the gallows, and Lance guessed that yet another swung from the other gallows by the front gate. Three more prisoners hung by their arms chained behind them and lifted onto spikes driven into three poles, their feet dangling just above the ground. Labored breathing showed that all three were alive but unconscious as life drained out of them.

After roll call, the commandos marched to the camp kitchen for a daily ration of thin turnip soup and equally thin ersatz coffee. Then, they were returned to their special barracks. They had already found that sleeping on the hard planks was almost impossible and only occurred for short durations when the day's privations overtook their overtaxed minds.

For Lance that night, sleep was impossible as he wrestled with Ondrej's revelations, which he had not yet mentioned to the others. He wondered how he would endure walking his thirty miles over cobblestones the next day.

Then, shortly after midnight, the door to the hovel flew open and several SS soldiers entered, shouting incomprehensibly. They shined flashlights in the commandos' faces, and when they found Lance, they seized him and jerked him from his planks.

Godwin jumped to his feet to try to intervene. Two soldiers grabbed his shrunken figure and tossed him into a corner. Two more joined the two who had grasped Lance and forced him through the door. Once outside, one of them shoved a rifle into his side.

A *kübelwagen* waited outside the inner fence that separated the special barracks from the general population. Lance's escorts shoved him into the back of the vehicle. The engine ignited, gears ground, and the group sped toward the headquarters.

Minutes later, Lance found himself in the camp *kommandant's* office standing at attention. "You are Lance Littlefield of Sark Island?" the kommandant demanded, obviously not pleased with this unexpected interruption to his sleep. His English was excellent although heavily accented.

"I've given you my name, rank, and identity number."

"You are under a sentence of death. Your cooperation might serve you better."

Lance clicked his heels at attention and stared at a spot on the wall over the *kommandant's* head. "Littlefield, lieutenant—"

The *kommandant* shot him a patronizing glare. "Yes, yes. Duty and all of that, but you're being very foolish." He picked up a sheet of paper from his desk. "When we learned that you were from Sark, I did some inquiries. I was sent this document. It says that you were a POW at Colditz Castle and escaped last year. It also states that you are a *prominente*. My orders are to return you to Colditz immediately."

26

June 17, 1943
Oflag IV-C POW Camp, Colditz Castle, Germany

Emaciated and weary from the misfortunes that had overtaken him, Lance sat under the canvas cover against the cab in the back of a *Wehrmacht* supply truck as it rumbled over cobblestone streets through the town and the final uphill distance to the castle gates. He had pulled his feet onto the bench and curled his legs such that his knees supported his chin. Although he dreaded the thought of continued extended captivity, he welcomed the possibility of seeing old friends. "At least it's worlds away from the horror of Sachsenhausen," he muttered to himself even as the continued suffering of his commando comrades still laboring there under a death sentence plagued him.

On the other side of the cabin, in similar repose, another POW sat. Neither he nor Lance had spoken for the duration of the trip from the transit camp, Dulag Luft at Oberursel, and they barely stirred as the truck paused at the main gate. After conversation between guards, the truck lurched forward, turning left through a short tunnel and then right. It waited for a second gate to open, entered, and came to a final stop.

Lance had traveled the route so many times that he knew precisely where he was despite not seeing his surroundings. He also knew what to expect when he climbed down from the truck. He wondered if the same senior British officer, the SBO, was still there and who else among those he had left behind on his last escape would greet his arrival.

Even before Lance made a move to dismount, loud cheering resounded, the standard welcome by the current inmates for any arriving POWs. It brought a smile to Lance's face, and it grew in volume, echoing from what he knew to be stone walls many stories high surrounding a quad a little larger than a basketball court.

"*Raus*," a guard called from the rear of the truck. Lance and the other captive climbed from their seats and stooped under the canvas ceiling. When they descended, the cheering rose to a deafening volume, and when they came around to the truck's front, it exploded, resounding off the stone walls.

Lance glanced at the other prisoner. He was a slender man of average height, light-colored hair, and calm brown eyes. "You must be very popular here," he shouted over the tumult.

The man, another lieutenant, turned to respond, and Lance saw him do a double-take and stare. The lieutenant shouted something, but his voice was lost in the celebratory din.

In front of them, held back by the guards, huge numbers of POWs jostled for position to see them, and as Lance gazed about the courtyard, every window was open, and in all of them, men hung out waving impromptu banners.

The cheering died as a big British lieutenant colonel with a round, mustachioed face and short-cropped white hair emerged from the crowd and approached them. He first went to Lance. "Welcome, Lance. It's good to see you healthy. I'd have preferred knowing you were still at home." He extended his hand, but Lance stood at attention and saluted.

The lieutenant colonel returned the salute and scrutinized Lance. "I say, you do look a bit underfed, but otherwise no worse for wear."

He extended his hand as the other prisoner called to Lance, "So you're the one who caused all the hubbub."

"I'm the SBO," the senior officer told the newcomer. "Lieutenant Colonel David Stayner."

"Lieutenant Corran Purdon, sir. An honor to meet you, and I must say that the greeting lifts spirits."

"Sorry for the circumstances, but I'm pleased to meet you. Come along. Let's get you checked in. We'll head first into the British barracks."

He led them away against another chorus of cheers, and as they headed across the courtyard to a door at the center of the far side, Lance glanced around, recognizing the punishment cells, or "cooler," the delousing hut, the canteen, and the windows of the camp's theater on the topmost floors of the building to his left, the site of his first escape from Colditz. Below it was the chapel. He paid particular attention with some trepidation to a set of windows at the opposite end of the courtyard that looked into it from ground level. That was where *prominentes* were housed.

"I see you've been promoted," Stayner said to Lance, chuckling as he led him through the door and a maze of corridors and staircases. "Jolly good. Your peers will be happy about that. They won't have to listen to you call them 'sir' all the time."

He explained to Corran, "Lance is a stickler for military decorum. No one's been able to break him of that."

Along the way, lone POWs lounged against walls at corners and other locations that allowed surveillance of an otherwise blind hall. Lance recognized them as stooges, responsible to signal ahead if German guards were on their way.

They arrived in front of an open door that Lance knew only too well—the entry into sleeping quarters for a number of British pilots. It was the room in which he had been an occupant during his last long stay at Colditz. Although not a pilot himself, he had been accepted into the group as a peer early on because when he arrived, he had then been the only British noncom held there. His success at multiple escapes, including three from Colditz before the homerun on his last attempt, had earned him an added measure of respect such that he had been requested by the previous SBO to serve on the escape committee.

From inside the room, they heard numerous excited voices. On entry, momentary cheering resumed, until someone called, "Attention!" The noise quieted.

"At ease," Stayner said immediately. "Let's get down to business, shall we?" He turned to a solidly built, medium-sized lieutenant with straight dark hair combed back, and a thick handlebar mustache that fully covered his upper lip and was tapered at each end. "Is security set?"

"It is, sir. We can speak freely."

"This is Lieutenant Michael Sinclair," Stayner explained to Corran. "He's our security officer. He and Lance are already acquainted."

The officer's probing eyes studied Corran. Then he turned to Lance. "Welcome. Good to see you again."

"You're Michael Sinclair," Corran broke in, astonished. "You're a legend among POWs."

"Undeserved," Sinclair said blandly. "No homeruns." He indicated Lance. "He's the only one here who's made it all the way home."

"And back again," Lance interjected, irony in his voice. "I really must practice the 'staying free' part of this endeavor."

The room broke into light laughter, and Lance was warmed to see the faces of men who had been his comrades for so long. They looked gaunt, but their eyes still shone with the cunning spirit that had caused the Third *Reich* to gather these POWs in this particular place. The prison population was largely made up of men who made a habit of trying to break out, and undetected by their captors, Colditz had become an academy of sorts for prisoners to hone the art of escape and collaborate with other prisoners in their attempts.

"You got promoted along the way," Sinclair added. "That's better than any of us have done." More laughter erupted. "But I must ask what happened to you?" he went on. "You look like you've been worked over a bit."

Realizing how emaciated he was even compared to this room of underfed POWs, Lance hesitated to respond. "I was in a place called Sachsenhausen." He shook his head and breathed out a sigh. "Believe me, by comparison, this place is heaven."

The room fell silent as Lance's emotional agony became apparent. Then Corran turned to Stayner. "Before we start into business, sir, do you mind if I ask Lance—" He turned to Lance. "I haven't heard your last name. Is it by any chance Littlefield?"

"It is," Lance said, startled. "Have we met before?"

Corran shook his head. "No, but I know your brother, Jeremy, and your resemblance is so striking. He told me about you and all your family. When I heard your first name, I thought you must be the brother who was also trapped at Dunkirk."

"Guilty," Lance huffed.

Corran turned to Stayner. "Should we do this later, sir?"

"No, go ahead. I'm intrigued."

"Jeremy and I went through commando school together," Corran resumed, "along with another chap you know—Kenyon. We were on the Saint-Nazaire raid together, the three of us. Jeremy helped me when I was badly wounded. I might not be here otherwise."

A low, admiring murmur arose across the room.

"And you want to get even, is that it?" Lance joked amid another round of laughter.

"I never knew what happened to him," Corran said seriously. "The last I saw of him was when several of us were captured in the cellar of a building outside the town. Later, when we took accountability, he wasn't there, and no one knew whether he was killed, escaped—"

"He made it home," Lance said. "We spent Christmas together at my sister's house." He added with an ironic smile, "Obviously, I preferred these surroundings and the company of these men." After more chuckling, he said with a note of sadness, "I heard we lost Kenyon on that raid. He was a good man. No one ever had a better friend."

"I can vouch for that," Corran said quietly. Silence lapsed, and then he added, "At least I'm glad to hear that Jeremy survived and escaped."

"We should get on with things now," Stayner said. "I'm going to address my comments mainly to you, Corran. Lance knows the drill, and he helped us refine our methods before leaving us. Not much if anything has changed in our procedures since then. This session is not only to inform you, but it's also part of a vetting process. Don't take that personally. We do it for everyone. The Germans have tried more than once to infiltrate us either through a fake prisoner or by offering bribes to some of our own."

"I understand, sir."

Stayner shifted his attention momentarily to Lance. "There are a few checks we'll have to run where you're concerned—"

"I know, sir. I helped devise the system."

Stayner chuckled. "Right you are." He turned to Sinclair. "You'll take care of that?"

"I will, sir, and report back to you."

"In that case, gentlemen, this meeting is adjourned." He held up a hand as men started moving about. "However, I need the room cleared for a few minutes for a private conversation with Lance."

A pall descended on the room, the men glancing at Lance compassionately as they filed out. When the two of them were alone, Stayner started to speak.

Lance interrupted. "Sir, I mean no disrespect, but I needed to speak to you on an urgent intelligence matter. It must be passed to London as quickly as possible."

He told of his stay in Sachsenhausen, his treatment, the things he had seen, and those travesties Ondrej had related to him. Stayner listened, stupefied.

"You must be exaggerating," he said after a time.

"No, sir," Lance said firmly. "The things I saw are certain. The things I was told about, London must know about them at once. If true, those things must be stopped."

Stayner rubbed his face and nodded bleakly. "I'll get you to our coding officer immediately. Your sister will get some more nonsensical letters—"

"She knows what to do with them."

"Agreed. She's been effective, but we'll have to send to others as well, and develop a way for British intelligence to compile and make sense of them. As it is, London will have difficulty believing what we tell them. We'll get on it straight away."

"Thank you, sir. You had something to discuss with me?"

"What? Oh yes, of course. Your news was so earth-shattering that I almost cleanly forgot." He rubbed his eyes. "It isn't good news."

"I can guess," Lance broke in. "I'm to be housed with the *prominentes*."

Stayner sighed and nodded. "I'm afraid so. The *kommandant* has written orders."

"I'm about as prominent as your arse," Lance said, annoyed, "but that's the reason I'm here, and possibly the reason I'm still alive. We were under a death sentence, all of us on Operation Checkmate. My teammates still are. I didn't even get to say goodbye. Men who trained and fought beside me—for all I know, they're already dead."

Stayner took in the young lieutenant's grief quietly and the two sat in silence for a spell. Then he clapped Lance's shoulder. "You became a commando while you were gone. I sincerely can't decide if congratulations are in order. I'm just glad you're alive." He chuckled. "We'll get you fattened back up, at least as much as we are. You know the drill. You'll be in a cell by yourself where those ground-level windows look out onto the courtyard. You may be out and about with the rest of the prison population at eight in the morning, but you must be back in your cell by ten o'clock at night. There'll be a wooden door with a wide hole on it, and you must be visible to the guard at all times while in there. If you miss the curfew, the sergeant of the guard will send an armed patrol through the barracks, and you'll be punished."

A look of impatience flashed across Stayner's face. "It's quite the same as it was when you left. Need I go on?"

"No, sir," Lance said grimly. He faced Stayner with a frustrated expression. "Why are they doing this. Even if I were important, what do they hope to accomplish?"

Stayner leaned back and exhaled audibly. "The war is going badly for the Germans. They've lost Stalingrad and North Africa. An invasion of Italy is probably in the offing. The *Wehrmacht* is mounting a campaign against Kursk in the Soviet Union. I understand that's a tiny little village, but it's at the extremity of the Soviet thrust into German-occupied territory. But the *Luftwaffe* has already depleted their air assets, and their access to petroleum is waning."

Lance grinned. "I take it your access to the BBC in the attic hasn't been discovered?"

"Certainly not," Stayner said with a smile. "And that's augmented by coded messages from London. It helps keep up morale."

He hesitated with furrowed brows. "I think you know the reason for collecting *prominentes*, and it's happening all across the country. If Hitler can't turn the war around, he'll use all of you as bargaining chips to try to negotiate an armistice with better terms than he would otherwise get. It's that simple, and you're important to him because your mother is the Dame of Sark, and both he and Churchill have a personal interest in the final disposition of that island and the rest of the Channel Islands. They're the only British soil that Hitler has managed to occupy."

Lance nodded patiently, knowing that what Stayner told him was true. "What about escape?"

"The waiting line is months long. The Allies are growing confident of victory, but France will have to be invaded. Sooner or later, we'll be ordered to cease escape attempts. They could muddle invasion plans, and Resistance resources that would normally help escape lines will be needed to assist in preparing and executing the campaign. Besides which, your imposed living conditions complicate your probabilities immeasurably." Stayner furrowed his brow. "I'm afraid, old friend, that you and I might be right here in Colditz for the duration."

He stopped talking and looked at his watch. "Unless you want to spend tomorrow learning first-hand about punishment for missing *prominentes*, we'd best get you on over to your new quarters."

Lance inhaled, stood, and rubbed his hand over tired eyes. "Sir, I came traveling light. I have no bedding, toiletries—"

Stayner stood with a wry smile. "It's good to see that your roguish spirit still lives. We'll set you up."

"Lead on then, sir. I'm ready."

27

Five Weeks Earlier, May 12, 1943
The White House, Washington, DC

"That was quite an entrance you made in New York City this morning, sailing in as you did on the *Queen Mary* with your two-hundred-member delegation." Roosevelt laughed and tossed his head for a glimpse of Churchill as the prime minister wheeled him through the Oval Office to the president's private study. "If I didn't know you better, I'd think you were projecting British power."

Churchill chuckled. "And if I didn't know you better, Franklin, I'd think you said that in jest. But it's good to see you again. A lot has happened since Casablanca and Marrakech."

"Indeed it has, Winston. I'm glad you came." Arriving inside his study, Roosevelt wheeled himself behind the desk, spun around, and faced forward while Churchill sat himself in an overstuffed chair across from him. "We have a lot to talk about."

"We can start with the good news that our combined armies are today celebrating the end of enemy resistance in North Africa. We've driven the bulk of the *Wehrmacht* out of there and captured what remained, nearly two hundred and forty thousand POWs. Our problem there now is how to handle them all, but we'll get it done."

"Added to that," Franklin broke in, obviously pleased, "last month, our pilots took out the Japanese planning genius, Admiral Yamamoto. And communiques from the East report that initiatives on New Guinea and a scheduled recapture of the Aleutians will proceed." He searched his jacket pocket, pulled out two cigars, and offered one to the prime minister, who reached across the desk to take it. "Winston, our boys are performing magnificently despite early hiccups."

"I heard about Yamamoto. How did you bring that about?"

"Code-breaking," Roosevelt replied between puffs as he lit his cigar. "We got word that he was headed in flight to review defensive positions on one of their islands. Our fighters intercepted him and downed his plane. That's a hard blow to the Japs."

"Yes, it is, and kudos to your pilots and your intelligence lot."

When Churchill had lit his cigar, Roosevelt continued. "The big question now is, what's next? How do we capitalize on our advances in the immediate future? What's our long-term strategy?"

"We'll get that all hashed out with our staffs over the next two weeks," Churchill said between successive short drags on his cigar to keep it lit. "But I'd say that we must keep our forces in the Mediterranean active and not let them be idle.

"Sicily is our next obvious step. It's a springboard into Italy, whose defeat would be the downfall of a major Axis power. Hitler would be forced to pull troops into the Balkans, which would drastically weaken his Soviet front. Neutralizing the Italian fleet would allow us to threaten an invasion of southern France through Sardinia and Corsica and release major naval vessels to the Far East."

Roosevelt listened attentively, and when Churchill finished, he smiled and nodded. "I see the sense of what you're saying. Knocking Italy out of the war would certainly have its benefits, but I'll tell you that my staff is not on board with that approach." He drew on his cigar. "I have my own concerns about putting large armies in there. That figurative crocodile you like to refer to with its soft underbelly in Italy is a larger creature than you purport.

The belly was really North Africa with its head in Berlin, and it has a spine, and that's the mountains of Italy. A ground offensive there could lead to a war of attrition, with the Axis having the advantages of defensive warfare."

He leaned back while releasing a puff of smoke. "We're probably getting too far into the weeds until we've let our staffs hash things out. I've got you on my schedule to meet together every other day for the duration of this conference—and by the way, it's been dubbed the Trident Conference for some odd reason.

"I want to get you up to Shangri-La. That's a presidential retreat in the Catoctin Mountains in Maryland. We can do some fishing there." He looked down at his polio-ravaged legs and nudged one of them. "I'm not much good for hiking these days."

Churchill chuckled. "My, my. Whatever could you have become but for that calamity?"

Roosevelt swung his head up and fixed his eyes on Churchill's. Then he laughed, deep and long. "I'll never get any sympathy from you, will I, Winston?"

Churchill stared back blandly. "For what, sir?"

Four Days Later
Shangri-La Presidential Retreat, Catoctin Mountains, Maryland

Churchill waded into a shallow stream with a fishing pole while Roosevelt watched him from a bench along the bank. Only moments earlier, the two had posed for the press sitting side by side, each with a cigar in hand, and the president holding his rod out over the water. Then the Secret Service had shooed the gaggle away and retreated to a perimeter to ensure the safety and privacy of the two world leaders.

"I love this place," Roosevelt murmured, looking about. "This was a vacation camp for government employees and Boy Scouts. I needed a place for short jaunts. Going home to Hyde Park or down to Hot Springs, Georgia, requires too much travel, and by the time I get back to Washington, I need another rest."

He glanced at the dappling of shadows cast on the ground through stands of saplings and listened to the gurgling creek and the chorus of songbirds. "It's so restful here. I almost feel guilty for depriving the public of it, but—" He shrugged and chuckled. "Such are the burdens of state."

"I'm sure the citizens will not begrudge you a place to unwind and regroup, away from the demands of running a war. We've discussed Napoleon's advice of ensuring sufficient rest as a key to making good decisions."

Roosevelt nodded. "Unfortunately, we won't have such luxury. Our staffs meet again tomorrow, and they'll be looking for guidance from us. Should we discuss the issues of the past three days here, now?"

"This is a beautiful place." Churchill looked about. "It's as good a place as any, and we won't be interrupted. Then again, we won't be relaxing, will we?" He waded out of the stream and took his seat on the bench next to Roosevelt. "Where do we start?"

The president took a deep breath and frowned. "Not a pleasant place, I'm afraid. I'll tell you quite candidly that General Marshall worries that a poorly managed offensive in Italy would not only drain Allied resources but also jeopardize a cross channel invasion in the spring of 1944.

"He sees that supplying two simultaneous advances into Europe are close to a logistical impossibility. He thinks we might achieve the same end by a relentless air attack on the Italian homeland. And he points out that Allied air power is almost unchallenged in the Mediterranean now. We can attack as far east as the oilfields in Romania."

He paused to reflect, and then continued. "Marshall disdains a ground offensive in Italy, and I don't use the word 'disdains' lightly. 'Vehemently opposes' might come closer to describing his sentiments."

He turned to observe Churchill's reaction, but the prime minister sat staring into the babbling brook without response aside from removing his cigar from his mouth and blowing out smoke circles.

"Marshall thinks that you and your staff are too optimistic about your plans in the Mediterranean," Roosevelt went on, "and too pessimistic about the capabilities of Allied combined air power. He thinks that expending resources in an 'unrealistic campaign'—his words—in Italy at the same time that the build-up in Great Britain is slowing down doesn't bode well for a cross-channel invasion."

Churchill let out a chuckle. "My army chief of staff, Sir Allan, might be of similar mind in that last regard. He worries that Allied forces might bog down in Europe if insufficient resources are stockpiled ahead of such an operation."

"That's a concern we all share," Roosevelt interjected. "If we don't have the manpower, equipment, and supplies for the initial drive and then to sustain it, we'll send thousands of men to their deaths for no purpose. I lay awake at night over that thought."

Churchill turned to Roosevelt gravely. "We share the same nightmares."

They sat quietly for a spell, mulling their individual thoughts. Then Roosevelt said, "The guidance we give our staffs will be better if you and I are united in our views. Can we agree that our ultimate objective is to carry out a combined Allied invasion on the European continent as soon as possible?"

"Yes, yes. I think so. We certainly won't take back Europe and rid the world of that Nazi brute without such action."

Just as Roosevelt was about to nod his head, the bobber on his fishing line sank momentarily and then popped back up to the surface. "By God, I think I've caught a fish," he said excitedly.

Churchill rose to his feet, his eyes wide and eager. While the president pulled back on the rod, the prime minister hurried to the stream's edge to peer into the clear water. "I can't see him. Is he still on the line?"

"I think so. He's a small one." Roosevelt sat up as high as he could, moving his head about to try to see past low underbrush blocking his view of the creek. "Any sight of him yet?"

"None at all."

"I think he might have wrapped the line around a branch or something. I don't feel him pulling, but he's not coming up either."

After another minute of fiddling to no avail, Roosevelt called, "We may as well cut the line. The hook is caught on something."

Churchill returned to the bench, rummaged in a tackle box for a knife, and went back to cut the fishing line. He laughed as he once more joined Roosevelt on the bench. "Is that a metaphor—"

"It's a metaphor for nothing, Winston. It's just two old farts having fun with small things like we did when we were boys."

Churchill's chest shook with laugher as he sat down and caught his breath while rubbing both hands along his head. "I suppose you're right."

"Ah, that was fun, Winston." The president sat in reflection a few moments and then said, "You know, you and I met years ago when I was the undersecretary of the navy."

Churchill turned to him and shrugged. "I'm sorry. I'm afraid I don't remember."

Roosevelt formed his lips in an O-shape and breathed out a smoke ring. "I didn't think you did." He chuckled. "I didn't like you much at the time. I thought you were about as arrogant as they come."

The prime minister laughed gently. "Guilty, I'm sure, sir. I have my shortcomings, as many in the peerage would be happy to point out."

Roosevelt joined him in laughter. "We've come a long way, Winston. I've spent with you some of my best moments during this dark period. When you visited us the first time in DC, that same night you arrived, you spoke at the national Christmas tree-lighting ceremony right after Pearl Harbor. What you said then comforted a lot of Americans.

"Then, on the second visit, I picked you up from the airport north of Poughkeepsie to drive you in my modified convertible to my home in Hyde Park. Such a beautiful drive.

"And that sunset over the Atlas Mountains in Marrakech. That was pure magic." He chuckled. "But nothing can compare with watching the legendary Winston Churchill tromping around in this creek after a small fish neither of us could catch."

Churchill's head swung around, and for an instant, he seemed unsure of whether to laugh or be annoyed.

Roosevelt reached over and squeezed his shoulder. "You're a good friend, Winston, and I trust that you will always be so."

Churchill looked uncharacteristically perplexed. "You've certainly been a true friend to our people," he said at last. Then he grunted. "Where were we?"

Roosevelt chuckled. "Just determining our strategy for the conduct of the deadliest war in human history."

"Ah, right. Well, the laughter did us good, I suppose." Churchill paused in thought. "What if we were to issue a joint directive to our staffs that says something along the lines that we intend to concentrate as many resources as we can in an area still to be selected with the aim to execute a decisive offensive on the Italian citadel."

"You always like big words," Roosevelt said with a mock groan. He grinned. "I think that works. Marshall won't like it, but he'll live with it." He took a moment to reflect. "So we're agreed that Operation Husky in Sicily is the next major initiative, and after that, Italy, as you and I just discussed."

"You've won me over, Franklin."

Roosevelt cast Churchill a playfully rueful glance. "Let's not kid ourselves, Winston. You once more persuaded me to your thinking, and my staff will go to pains to let me know they've noticed. Now, I have a question. How are the plans proceeding for your man who never existed, Major Martin?"

Churchill half-smiled. "He's prepared to do his duty."

Two Days Later
Washington, DC

"This conference hasn't been all peaches and cream," Roosevelt told Churchill, "but I think we've hurdled some obstacles." They met again in the president's study off the Oval Office in the White House, and once again, cigar smoke filled the air.

"Yes, appears so," Churchill replied, "and soon we'll win the Battle of the Atlantic. Evidence is growing that such is the case."

Roosevelt laughed. "You mean like your voyage across the ocean on a luxury liner? That had to jab Hitler right in the ol' ticker."

"It wasn't all that grand an adventure," Churchill countered. "As you well know, the ship's been modified into a troop carrier, and we came the northern route under aircover via Iceland, Greenland, and Newfoundland. The course was a bit circuitous, but it got the job done and points out the importance of closing that abominable Azores Gap.

"Regardless, I'd say things have turned remarkably against the *Kriegs-marine,* largely due to your naval air assets providing cover for our Atlantic convoys along with your patrol boats and their anti-submarine mines. And our combined warships and subs brought the war to the U-boats."

The prime minister's face took on a look of impatience. "I'm a mite disgruntled with my staff regarding their intransigence on the Azores issue," he grumbled. "You and I have talked about the need to occupy those islands since before you even entered the war. Back in August of '41 at the Newfoundland conference, we agreed that the Azores should be taken by any means possible, diplomatic or otherwise, for their value as platforms for air and sea operations in the mid-Atlantic.

"You had your concept, Operation Lifebelt, and I had mine, Operation Alacrity. The Germans also had a concept—Operation Felix—that would have allowed them to position air and submarine forces there. That would have extended their range enough to threaten your eastern cities."

Roosevelt arched his eyebrows and locked his fingers together on his chin while regarding the prime minister with a skeptical look. "Are there diplomatic options? As the subject was discussed over the past few days, your staff was advising strongly that you exhaust diplomacy before we consider occupying the islands.

"The Portuguese prime minister, Antonio Salazar, is deathly afraid of appearing to support either side of the war for fear of inviting a Nazi 'protective occupation' of Portugal. He even allows German ships to provision at Terceira, the main island."

Churchill smiled mischievously at the president. "I might have a way, diplomatically, to pull this off, but it'll take some time."

"I hope not too much time," Roosevelt responded. "Unfortunately, diplomats and war planners seem not to understand the need to move swiftly—that every day means more deaths for our front-line fighters."

Churchill agreed with a somber glance. "You've stated very well the source of my annoyance just now." He took a deep breath. "Most Brits have forgotten that we have a friendship accord with Portugal known as the Windsor Treaty of 1373, the oldest such pact in the world. It commits the two countries to 'mutual friendship and defense.' It was signed by King of

England and France Edward III, and by King Fernando and Queen Eleanor of Portugal.

"It calls for either party to aid the other in war, the stipulation being that the assistance would not result in severe damage to the country rendering the aid. It was first invoked during the Peninsular Wars when Napoleon invaded Portugal and Spain. Fortunately, the Duke of Wellington vindicated the intent of the treaty.

"Before that, during Elizabethan times, British 'retribution pirates' attacked Spanish galleons laden with gold from the New World. Those acts were justified as avenging Spain's seizure of the Portuguese throne in 1570."

Roosevelt had listened intently, and when Churchill paused to draw on his cigar, the president leaned back in his chair. "Winston, you are a wonder. So, you're proposing to invoke that treaty with Salazar to give him diplomatic cover with Hitler?"

The prime minister shrugged. "I expect to open negotiations on that basis. If we don't get the desired result, we'll let him know that our bases will be built there one way or another, and that in no event will we allow them to be used by the Third *Reich*."

Churchill put an index finger over his lips momentarily in the universal sign for quiet. "Please keep what I just told you to yourself. When I invoke the treaty publicly, I'll have to do it before Parliament, and I'd rather avoid their meddling while I pull the pieces together. I intend to assemble a special negotiating team to bring this off."

Roosevelt pursed his lips. "Your secret's safe with me. Let's just get the Azores secured."

———

Two days later

"I feel like I'm becoming a fixture in your study, Franklin." Churchill took a long drag on his cigar and blew it out. He sat in what had become his regular seat across from Roosevelt.

The president tossed his head. "At least we've reached agreement, again, on a combined bomber strategy for an offensive against the Third *Reich* in preparation for a spring assault, as we'd agreed in Casablanca." He exaggerated an exasperated look. "How is it, Winston, that we come to what we think is a meeting of the minds, and then find our subordinates not only not in accord, but we're having to rope 'em back in from going their own way? It's like herding cats, and we're supposed to be the honchos."

Churchill laughed. "I've heard it said that democracy is a messy way to govern."

Roosevelt joined him in the humor. "Thank God we're a republic. But the military is supposed to be authoritarian." He laughed, and then continued seriously, "So, we've agreed to continuous bombing of the Third *Reich's* military, industrial, and economic centers to frustrate Germany's ability to fight, and to wear down its people's morale. Now let's turn the conversation to the Pacific, and this gets a little ticklish." He grinned briefly. "But what isn't about this war?"

"Yes," Churchill said wryly, "which brings us back to the conversation of who's really running things, us or our staffs. Your General Marshall seems to be trying to backtrack on the commitment to Europe first." He patted his jacket pockets, reached into one of them, and pulled out a note. "I wrote down what he said. 'If conditions develop which indicate that the war as a whole can be brought to a successful conclusion by the earlier mounting of a major offensive against Japan, the strategic concept set forth herein, beating Germany first, may be reversed.'"

He looked up at Roosevelt. "Franklin, I'm stubborn, but I'm not unreasonable, and we all want the same thing: to defeat the Axis Powers wherever they exist. We've already agreed on a Germany-first strategy and dispersed manpower and resources all over the planet to that end. To use an American truism, you shouldn't change horses in midstream. It would be calamitous."

Roosevelt held up a hand in a placating manner. "I know, and the overall strategy won't change. Marshall is pushing for greater British commitment in the Far East. The big question there is, how do we ultimately defeat Japan?"

Biting back annoyance, Churchill pressed, "I can defend British commitments backed by actions and resources anywhere, and I'll readily divert more men and equipment to that theater if the situation requires it.

In return I'd like to see a reinforced US commitment to the strategy we agreed on last year, our Germany-first solution, with the next step being the invasion of Sicily."

"We'll have to discuss more in that regard," Roosevelt replied. "Marshall's concerns are not without substance, but I understand he can be prickly at times. You know, he won't let me call him by his first name, insisting that I call him 'General' every time, and he's never voted in a presidential election. He says he prefers to remain apolitical. But he's a good soldier. In the end, he'll obey orders regardless of his personal feelings. We're still committed to a Germany-first solution."

"I'm gratified to hear that, sir. I respect General Marshall and will listen to his arguments closely. What other matters do we have to discuss?"

"I think that does it for today."

Two days later

The two statesmen sat together in the Rose Garden for their review of the previous day's Trident Conference proceedings. "I thought this setting might be more refreshing and conducive to clear thinking," Roosevelt said. "My study was becoming too stuffy, and the Oval Office is, well, too grand for productive discussion."

Churchill looked around while he spoke, taking in the serene beauty with the backdrop of the elegant White House behind him, the expanse of the lawn in front of him, and the Washington cityscape beyond. "It is beautiful."

A kitchen staff member brought out a pitcher of iced tea and poured two glasses, leaving them on a small table between the two men. Meanwhile, Roosevelt produced two cigars and handed one to Churchill. "We can't be expected to conduct sound policy talks without these," he said, leaning forward and lighting the prime minister's cigar.

Before he lit his own, he asked, "Preparatory to invading Japan, what do you think of the suggestion of a two-pronged attack with your forces leading through Burma and the Malacca Strait, and ours going through the Southwest Pacific and the Celebes Sea?"

"Hmph. Haven't thought about it much," Churchill replied with a touch of irony in his tone, "and frankly, I don't think anyone else has either. Not thoroughly. It's a complex plan with six phases, many unsupported figures and estimates, and lots of red arrows drawn on a map. But I don't see any serious, detailed planning for it."

"Those were my thoughts too. We all know that a full-scale invasion of Japan can't happen unless we launch from bases in China. That means that China must be kept in the war at all costs."

"Re-taking Burma will be no easy task," Churchill broke in. "We'd have to build new routes and re-open the Burma Road to adequately supply Allied operations on the Chinese coast and to prepare for a large-scale advance to re-capture Hong Kong. Our chaps would have little appetite for a massive offensive through that impenetrable jungle."

"And yet, three senior commanders in the region all requested reinforcements to do just that," the president replied, "including your commander-in-chief General Wavell, and our own Lieutenant General Chenault, as well as the supreme Allied commander of the China-Burma-India theater, General Stilwell. Those three are veterans of Burma and called for American reinforcements there."

"True, but your service chiefs weren't interested."

Roosevelt sighed. "It all comes down to resources and how we spread them out. We've had planning ongoing for some time for Operation Anakim to re-take Burma through Rangoon, but that's becoming less feasible as your resources and ours dwindle on too many fronts. The landing in Rangoon now seems like another logistical impossibility. My staff is advocating for increased air support instead."

He sipped his iced tea and took a puff on his cigar while gazing across the lawn. "Our chief of naval operations—"

"Admiral King."

Roosevelt nodded. "He's suggested a major push against the Philippines and the Marianas late this year to set the stage to destroy the Japanese Imperial Navy. He wants to sever their supply lines and isolate their holdings in the Southwest Pacific.

"Another proposal focused on seizing the Marshall and Caroline Islands and assaulting on the Solomons-Bismarck Archipelago with the same objective, cutting supply lines and isolating Japanese holdings.

"King's worried that we, the Allies, might be short on aircraft. But we have sufficient naval forces on hand in the Pacific now. His perception is that if the Allies could acquire a strong hold on the western Pacific, that could lead to Japan's surrender before being invaded."

Churchill frowned. "Hmm. That's a view worth pursuing, but maybe there's a quicker way. How goes the Manhattan Project?"

Roosevelt met Churchill's steady gaze. "It goes. Your atomic scientists and ours are busily working in utter secrecy near Los Alamos, New Mexico." He frowned. "Let's hope we can win without resorting to that option."

Churchill let out a long breath. "Agreed, but let's also hope that we have the ability before the other side does. My information is that Hitler's heavy-water plant in Norway is back up and running full tilt."

"I was informed, and that's a grave concern. We'll have to take action to stop it."

Churchill nodded in agreement. Then he leaned forward. "I appreciate you, Mr. President, and all that you've done to save my country and our shared civilization. I know you're sometimes put in difficult positions between your own views, those of your staff, and mine. Let me ease the pressure on you by consenting to your staff's estimates and plans for the Pacific theater. Britain will support as best we can."

Roosevelt smiled wanly. "I appreciate that, Mr. Prime Minister." He stirred in his seat. "Now unfortunately, I don't have a brandy cabinet out here in the garden to toast your statement, and I recognize that you're making no small concession. So I propose that we go back into my study and drink to it."

Churchill rose from his chair and circled behind Roosevelt's wheelchair. "Then if you please, Mr. President, let me do the honors."

Two Days Later

"I'm relieved, Winston. Despite the competing views of our staffs, we seem finally to have reached a consensus on the way forward." Once again, they sat in the Rose Garden. "To that end," Roosevelt went on, "I've had the brandy brought out here so that we can toast to our agreements in the sweet fresh air and sunlight."

"I share your enthusiasm, Franklin. Both of our chiefs of staff agree that recent successes allowed more aggressive actions against the Axis Powers. I'm gratified that they consented to launch an invasion into Sicily. That should come off soon."

"You and I didn't leave them a lot of choice." Roosevelt chuckled. "Sometimes, our orders work. But they were genuinely happy that you agreed to a fixed date range for a cross-channel invasion of France next spring, hopefully in April. My navy will go after Japanese holdouts in the Aleutians as well as attack in the Marshalls and Carolines, and we'll stage for further action against Rabaul."

"We still have the situation in China and Burma to resolve," Churchill noted, "but I don't think we'll get that done in this conference. The questions of manpower and logistics are just too great at the moment, and no one wants to squander resources. But this conference has been a huge victory for coalition warfare. Our insistence on unconditional surrender just became more feasible as a global strategy."

"You're right," Roosevelt said, slapping the arm of his wheelchair in enthusiasm. "I think we can win this war within the next two years. And that's a prediction, not a hope."

May 25, 1943

The two statesmen said their farewells under the shade of the White House's north Portico. "I really hate to see you go, Winston. I've enjoyed our tête-à-têtes. I shall miss them. It's good to share views with someone as a peer, and I don't know another way that you or I could have done that."

"Thank you, sir. I share the sentiment. You've been most courteous with your time and your hospitality. I hope that I might repay it someday in some small way."

"Never mind that. Safe travels home, Winston."

"The travel will surely be safer than before," Churchill said with a wry smile. "In that regard, Mr. President, I received a dispatch this morning through Bletchley. I wanted to share it with you first."

Roosevelt's head swung around, and he gazed at Churchill's face in anticipation. "I hope it's good news, sir. Let's hear it."

Churchill's lips parted in a rare, broad smile. "Admiral Donitz ordered all his U-boats out of the Atlantic. Aside from isolated incidents, the battle in that ocean is history. We won."

28

July 9, 1943
Off the Northern Coast of Tunisia

Paul Littlefield stood on the rolling deck of a ship where he had been transported during the night via motor launch through a storm, and he had no idea of the ship's name or numerical designation. He knew only that it was the flag vessel for a sub-unit of a large fleet. Lightning had broken the night sky during his journey, thunder had reverberated, and sheets of rain had driven down on the small transport vessel that had carried him. He had wondered if Operation Husky were possible at all to carry out on schedule.

On arrival, Paul had been granted permission to board, and after presenting a letter signed by General Eisenhower and climbing a swaying ladder, he had been escorted to the ship's captain. The skipper read the letter and regarded Paul with a less-than-impressed expression. "You're an observer, huh?" he growled in a rough voice. "Great. Just stay out of the way. We're busy."

Paul had studied the history of Sicily and the battle maps while at Allied headquarters in Gibraltar before flying to Tunis to join the task force. He understood the plan. He was with the invasion force to determine the degree to which Operation Mincemeat and Major Martin had accomplished their objectives.

He had already learned from intelligence received through the Enigma decoding machines at Bletchley Park and forwarded to the front that the Germans expected the Allied thrust into Europe to come via the Peloponnese. As a result, they had transferred two armored divisions there from Sicily. They had also transferred large troop formations south from Kursk under the mistaken belief that the Allies would come ashore in force at Greece and thrust north through the Balkans to unite with the Red Army. Those troop movements suggested that cadaver Martin had already done a remarkable job.

The proof of the pudding would come today when Allied soldiers landed on European beaches, in force, for the first time since the start of the war. Further, this was to be the largest amphibious operation in history, taking place on a ninety-mile stretch along Sicily's southern and eastern shore. The landing sites stretched from Licata, in the southern province of Gela, around the eastern corner of the island, and north to the port city of Syracuse.

Sicily had endured a long and difficult history. For centuries, it had been the site of bloody combat between competing armies, including the Spartans, Athenians, Romans, Vandals, Goths, Saracens, Normans, and, more recently, Spaniards, Germans, and Britons.

The main objective for Operation Husky was Messina, a city on the northeastern tip of Sicily across a three-mile stretch of water from the southwestern point of Italy. If the Allied armies succeeded, the Germans would look to escape in force. That could happen only at Messina. But between the one hundred miles of rough, mountainous terrain of the landing beaches and that port city, the volcano Mount Etna sat astride the route, overlooking the approaches from the south and the west.

The Americans had favored a pincer movement, with British fighters coming ashore on the east coast, the Yankees attacking from the west coast, and the main invasion force landing on the beaches between them. General Montgomery had argued against that concept, stating concerns that the center would be weakened. He preferred for American and British divisions to come ashore side by side at the southeastern corner, south of

Pachino. His concept was for General Patton's Seventh Army to drive west to Marsala and then northeast to Palermo. Meanwhile, he would push his army north along the hundred-mile-long eastern coast.

Montgomery's strategy won out, much to Patton's annoyance for relegating American forces to a supporting role. The plan called for Montgomery to drive the British Eighth Army north through Noto, Syracuse, and Catania to the main objective, Messina, trapping the enemy there against the narrow channel between Sicily and the Italian mainland.

Meanwhile, Patton was to sweep westward with the US 3rd Army, take Marsala, and then push his troops cross-country northeast to Palermo. From there, he would pressure the enemy to retreat east to Messina, forcing them into Montgomery's trap. The hope was that remaining Axis troops would be faced with a choice between surrender or obliteration.

As Paul contemplated the history of Sicily and the battle plans to liberate it, he felt sorry for the local population. Over the past century, as the Italian state had amalgamated into a country, Sicily had receded into poverty. Benito Mussolini had promised improved conditions for Sicilians but did not deliver, and now local citizens found themselves to be spectators in a war they did not want and from which they had no escape. Their only avenue for survival was to lie low, see which army prevailed, and adjust accordingly.

As the first light of dawn painted the eastern sky, Paul stood at the ship rail and watched in awe as the scene before him unfolded. He had wondered at the ease with which the boat that had brought him to the flagship seemed to have navigated through the storm between vessels of what he had been told was a vast armada, and now, as daylight filled the skies, his amazement expanded.

The wind brought welcome fresh air, and against the eastern horizon he beheld a sight he was sure could not be repeated in his lifetime. The invasion fleet spread out ahead of him to the left and right as far as he could see in both directions. The dull gray of the ships' camouflage paint blotted the skyline ahead, appearing as a great city bobbing on the choppy sea.

Paul had been amazed at the planning and coordination that had gone into organizing for this invasion. Three huge American fleets had embarked from ports, large and small, all along the North African coast to transport the invading force to Sicily. They sailed on coordinated itineraries, and each of the major formations was broken into smaller units and moved according to an intricately synchronized timetable.

An admiral commanded each of the three major fleets and carried on his flagship the commanding general of the ground forces being transported. In the war rooms below decks, operations officers and staffs worked from huge maps posted on the walls and sent and received messages from numerous radio operators at desks arranged around the room.

One fleet had come directly from America and arrived in Africa with barely enough time for the soldiers to stretch their legs on shore before embarking across the ninety miles separating Tunis from Sicily. Huge supply convoys had arrived to accompany the flotilla, and on reaching shore, they would be unloaded onto smaller craft stowed below, which would be launched and carry their cargoes ashore.

Enemy ground units were expected to mount counterattacks and aerial assaults, pummeling Allied forces and their supply ships. The *Wehrmacht* would destroy what it could and impede establishing a beachhead.

Paul was awed by the staggering effort required to place those soldiers on the Sicilian beaches with sufficient war machinery, ammunition, and supplies. Recalling his visits to arms factories in the United States, he imagined the construction of the big transport ships, the hundreds of ocean-going landing craft, fleets of seagoing tugs, mine sweepers, subchasers, submarines, destroyers, cruisers, mine layers, repair ships, and self-propelled barges armed with big guns.

From his days in Washington, he recalled the busy staffs of thousands of military and civilian workers coordinating deliveries, troop movements, and manufacturing schedules. They managed a mind-bending number of intricate details, any of which could prove crucial at unanticipated critical moments. They had pulled together the planning, coordination, and delivery of this particular operation in five months.

"A miracle," Paul muttered to himself as he contemplated the impossible feat.

A naval officer standing at the rail nearby overheard him. "And yet, people will be disappointed. They thought we'd go into Italy, France,

Greece, and Norway all at the same time." He sighed. "They don't realize the enormous effort to pull this off."

Paul agreed and sucked in his breath at the magnificence of the sight and the immense power of the formation. Still, he was plagued by the question that was his reason for being there: had Major Martin done his job?

The navy's mission was to pound the shores with tons of ordnance and then deliver flesh-and-blood young sons, fathers, brothers, uncles, even a few grandfathers into the shallow waters of Sicily's beach by the tens of thousands. If Mincemeat worked as planned, casualties would be relatively few; if not, there would likely be a bloodbath.

The flagship Paul rode caught up with its section of the fleet. Signaling frequently by lights and semaphore flags, it herded its subordinate warships and supporting vessels into their appointed positions within the formation.

As Paul observed throughout the day, other command ships to his left, right, and front mirrored the actions of his host vessel until the seemingly disorganized mass of ships that had greeted him at dawn formed into floating clusters by dusk, all moving northeastward at uniform speed. The great cruisers and destroyers had moved to the periphery and raced about to protect the flanks of the assembled troop carriers, landing craft, and supply vessels, while overhead, massive Allied fighter formations orbited to provide air cover.

All day, as the mighty formation plowed ahead, officers and crewmen crowded at the rail where Paul watched. They marveled at the fleet's vastness, wondering how much the Germans had perceived about the colossal force heading their way. Surely, they speculated, the formation's front edge must be visible as a dark form on the sea's surface approaching the Gulf of Gela on Sicily's southern coast. The ships' forms must be identifiable through binoculars by now, and if not, then *Luftwaffe* reconnaissance flights must have spotted them. The men on the deck also contemplated what being on the receiving end of the initial bursts from this armada might be like.

"Something like what their raids did to us in the harbor at Tunis while we loaded up," someone remarked. "I'll never forget the loud booms and the ship shaking and groaning and bobbing furiously up and down. I was so seasick afterward. I thought we were goners then."

"At least you wouldn't have worried about being killed in this shindig we're about to pull off," someone else replied, laughing. "Anyone know where we're going in?"

"Not a clue," said a third voice.

Paul listened, amused at the jaunty chatter while admiring the courage of these men who knew that they might not live much longer. He dreaded the thought that many of them might not survive through the next twenty-four hours. Then as night fell, cautious exhilaration stirred in his chest as he recalled that if Major Martin were successful, the Germans would have no time to reverse their transfers of whole divisions to Greece and the Balkans.

29

July 10, 1943
Off the Southern Coast of Sicily

Sergeant Zack Littlefield struggled to avoid inadvertently stepping on one of his fellow soldiers in his rush to empty his gut again over the side of the landing barge into the roiling waters of the Mediterranean. The night crossing from Tunis to Gela had been tumultuous because of the dark storm that arose from nowhere amid thunder and lightning. Crowded together in the craft's hold, the soldiers rode fifty-foot swells and then plunged into deep troughs, wondering if they would founder before surfacing on yet another wave.

The soldiers next to Zack were no less seasick. Those unable to reach the gunwales in time spilled their dinners of hours ago on their unlucky comrades, whose only consolation was that sheets of rain soon washed the bile onto the floor of the vessel. The stench was only partially mitigated by the howling wind.

While staggering back to his seat, Zack glimpsed a few ships of the vast armada that had formed up earlier during daylight. And just over the upright ramp at the front of the barge, he thought he saw land.

Adrenaline coursed through his body. The invasion was imminent.

Then, just past midnight, while the troop transports halted and waited, a terrible roar erupted as cruisers and destroyers, in a line parallel to the shore, unleashed their main guns' explosive rounds, which hissed into the skies followed by tracers lighting up the heavens. The latter flew in high, bright red arcs that receded to effervescent dots streaking north and landing on higher ground some distance beyond the shoreline. Moments later, a low rumble of eruptions rolled out to the landing barge as the naval bombardment struck its land targets, accompanied by clouds of smoke.

The naval gun barrage continued for hours, and as time passed, the sea calmed. Zack's seasickness and that of his comrades waned as the stench from the floor was replaced with fresh air. The bombardment and associated noise continued incessantly. At dawn, Allied bombers flying en masse to their inland targets added to the din below, and when they dropped their bombs, Zack watched the destruction in eruptions of buildings and earth thrown into the sky. Squadrons of fighters joined the bombers, bent on protecting Allied air, land, and sea forces from *Luftwaffe* counterattacks, but so far, no German air opposition had been seen.

Suddenly, the landing craft's engine raised a decibel, its gear caught, and with a lurch, it started forward. The wind built, the soldiers faced forward, some with looks of determination, others with grim uncertainty, some blandly taking impending events in stride, while still others were visibly terrified.

The landing craft built up speed. Zack rose in his seat and glanced quickly to his left and right. Scores of vessels sped toward the shore, leaving white wakes behind them, and mixed among them were giant tank landing ships, or LSTs. He stole one more look to his rear, heartened to see larger ships spread out as far as he could see. They would be bringing in supplies and the trucks to carry them inland. *Food!*

The thought suddenly made Zack ravenous, the misery of last night's crossing forgotten. Then the landing craft suddenly slowed down, the ramp dropped, the bottom scraped across sand, and the senior leader, a lieutenant, yelled, "Go! Go! Go!"

Sitting back several rows and with his view blocked by soldiers already clambering through the front and down the ramp, Zack could not see how his first few buddies had fared. The firing from the big guns had abated, and off to his far right, he thought he heard gunfire, but if so, it was sporadic and ended quickly.

His heart raced as he moved forward in the line, and suddenly he was staring down the ramp. Ahead of him, the line of soldiers had spread out. They carried their MI rifles over their heads, out of the water, bayonets fixed, and proceeded to wade through waist-high water to the shore, roughly fifty yards away.

Zack glanced about, puzzled. All along the beach in either direction, hundreds of landing craft disgorged their soldiers and then backed away to make room for subsequent waves. Tanks were already rolling ashore from the LSTs, and even cargo trucks were being delivered. In front of him, a jeep that had already landed sat parallel to the water's edge with an officer and a noncom in deep discussion over a map on its hood. Beyond them, on a high ridge, another group of soldiers pointed in various directions as they went about orienting themselves to the terrain. And there, just off to his left, was the tiny village of Licata, just where Zack's commander had said it would be during the final mission brief.

The company first sergeant was already ashore when Zack staggered out of the cold water into soft sand. "Let's go, let's go," the noncom barked. "No time for lollygaggin'. Just cuz no one's shootin' at you now don't mean they won't start. Keep movin'. Find your platoon and get your positions dug in."

Zack caught the first sergeant's eyes and grinned. "Looks like we get to live a little while longer, eh, Top?"

"Keep movin', Sergeant. Get with your squad and get those entrenching tools workin' on your foxholes."

***

Gela, Italy

Paul stared about in utter amazement, thrilled at the sight that greeted him when he came ashore. Having found himself essentially a free agent with no one looking for him to report, in mid-afternoon, he had found a friendly boatswain who put him on a boat headed to shore with supplies. When he landed, he could not believe his eyes.

The navy guns and the first wave of ground troops neutralized enemy resistance quickly. That allowed the supply ships to beach themselves and disgorge immense quantities of field artillery pieces, ammunition, trucks, jeeps, C-Rations, and any and all items needed to conduct a sustained operation. Shore Patrols, wearing black and yellow armbands, directed the vehicle and foot traffic to destinations guided by color codes painted on large white placards. Along the beach, engineers laid miles of burlap topped with chicken wire to form a sturdy, if temporary, road.

Looking down the beach both ways, Paul saw no traffic jams.

Mixed among the soldiers, curious Sicilians of every age, including grayed and wrinkled elderly couples, watched with disbelieving and joyful eyes the Allied display of power and organization. Even before embarking for shore, Paul had heard from the ship's operations room that Licata, the village thirty kilometers to the west that marked the left boundary of this unit's area, had formally surrendered.

Suddenly exultant while walking through the sand between units organizing and moving off the beach, Paul turned and stared out to sea. Spread out over the Mediterranean as far as he could see, ships of every description were either sailing in to make deliveries, docked on the beach discharging their cargoes, or motoring away to make room for others. Aside from gunboats, all of them had shallow drafts and flat bottoms and thus brought their wares right to the beach.

A screaming whistle that increased in pitch sent soldiers and civilians alike seeking cover. An air attack siren wailed, matching the intensity and increasing panic among the civilian populace. Paul recognized the whistle, a *Luftwaffe* dive-bomber making a run, but before it could release its load, it was met with a fusillade of anti-aircraft, machine gun, and small-arms fire. The plane careened out to sea, but even before it splashed down, a P-51 Mustang zoomed in from the clouds and finished it off with a burst from its .50 cal Browning machine guns.

The townspeople, shaken at first, cheered as the Stuka smacked the sea's surface and plunged below. That was the sixth such attack Paul had seen that day with similar results.

A group of excited civilians forming perpendicular to the water's edge caught Paul's attention, and as he watched, soldiers mixed with them, and a similar group formed facing the first group, but with all eyes looking out to sea. A single landing craft sped toward that point of the shore, and as it drew close, it slowed and inched its way forward.

A tall figure with a shiny helmet bearing three silver stars across the front stood in the bow. When the barge came to a halt, the man clambered over its ramp and lowered himself into the knee-deep water. Two noncoms on either side of him took his arms to steady him, but he shook them off and strode ashore.

Paul took a deep breath. General Patton had arrived.

Paul surmised that someone from the public affairs office had tipped off people onshore of the general's arrival. He watched for a few minutes as soldiers gathered around the legend. Then, seeing a convoy forming to head inland, Paul sought out anyone in authority and requested to ride along.

Observing Paul's British uniform, one crusty middle-aged noncom with a thick Southern draw said, "A limey, eh. You lost? Your people are up the beach a ways."

Paul assured the man that he was not lost. "I'm in a liaison role, and I need to get a classified message back to supreme Allied command."

"You can ride along with us, and I'll drop you at our company headquarters. You can work your way up from there."

The sergeant drove over coastal dunes to flat agricultural fields beyond the beach. Paul was astounded at the vast metropolis of tents and military vehicles spread out over many square miles. Aid stations had been set up anywhere that suitable ground supported them, and medics busily tended to the wounded. Phone cables had been laid out on the ground between command posts established in schoolhouses, barns, old buildings, and under leafy orchards. Tanks lined a hillside. Jeeps dashed about in every direction.

Following placards posted along the corridors that now served as roads, the supply convoy made its way past a group of tents. "It ain't marked yet, but that's the CO's tent," the sergeant told Paul. "He's probably a tad busy, so he might not be there."

With that, Paul dismounted from the truck, thanked the soldier, and they parted ways. A first lieutenant spotted Paul at the entrance and moved quickly to intercept him. "Excuse me," he said coolly. "I don't know you, and I don't know British rank, but I do know that uniform—"

"Lieutenant Colonel Littlefield," Paul said, and repeated what he had told the noncom about sending an urgent message.

"Sir, I'm the executive officer," the lieutenant said. "Meaning no disrespect, we just took this ground from the Huns. For all I know, you might be one of them—"

"I understand, Lieutenant. Send an armed guard with me, if you like, but get me to the highest headquarters you can with the communications capability I need."

The officer stared at Paul searchingly. Then he turned his head slightly, and without taking his eyes off of Paul, he snapped at an orderly, "Tell Top to send me our two best infantrymen, ASAP." Then, he told Paul, "We'll bypass Battalion and send you on straight to Brigade, but if you pull anything—"

Paul smiled and removed General Eisenhower's letter from his breast pocket. "I'm sure they won't need to resort to violence," he said, and showed the missive with his ID.

The executive officer scanned it. Then his head jerked up. "I'd like to take you at your word, sir, but this could be a forgery. You'll have to be checked out. I'll have you taken to division headquarters, and I'll call ahead to advise them of the circumstances. The armed guard will accompany you. I'm sure you understand."

"Thank you. I appreciate your help and diligence." Paul glanced around. "I don't even know which division's area I'm in at the moment. Events have been—"

"We're the Third Infantry Division, sir, commanded by General Lucian Truscott."

An hour later, Paul was ushered into the communications section of the division headquarters. Once again, he was astonished at the organization that had assembled as if blown in from the sea intact. Groups of tents were joined together to form the various sections of Truscott's HQ. When at last, having been vetted through communications with Allied headquarters at

Tunis, and after consulting with the division operations section and learning initial casualty numbers, Paul sat down to compose a message addressed to General Eisenhower and General Gubbins at SOE.

As he composed the message, he reflected on the magnitude of Mincemeat's success. With the help of a corpse dressed as a British army major and carrying fake invasion plans, the Allies had convinced the *Wehrmacht* to shift divisions from Sicily and the Soviet Union to Greece and the Balkans. As a result, the US Army, transported by the US Navy and overwatched by the US Army Air Corps, had come ashore virtually unopposed. Paul imagined that a similar result had occurred in the British area of operations.

He jotted his message and handed it to the operator to be coded and sent. It contained only three sentences: "Casualties low. Major Martin performed remarkably and effectively. Mincemeat complete."

30

"We're ready," Georges Lamarque said. He looked up from the documents he had been perusing in the study of the safehouse on *Rue* Fabert. The light was dim, the room furnished with the forlorn finery of long ago. He gazed across the desk at Jeannie. Jeremy sat next to her.

"You've done remarkable work," Georges said. "I'll send a prefatory note vouching for its authenticity without revealing your identity."

Jeannie stared at him and then sat back in her chair. Her mouth quivered at the impact and implication of Georges' words. "I wonder whether anyone in England's senior authority will ever see the documents or understand their importance." She leaned her forehead into her hand and sighed deeply. "Carrying on the charm all these months knowing that I could be found out, or at least suspected—the constant, bone-chilling fear." She stood and paced across the floor, her voice uncharacteristically anxious. "We're left with only our wits for weapons—we listen, and we learn—but we can't just let the Nazis take our country."

Since her father had first suggested that she translate for the headquarters in Dinard nearly three years ago, Jeannie's sense of obligation had compelled her to the Resistance. She breathed in deeply. "Now, it's the waiting, not knowing whether the documents we risked our lives for—or worse, torture—will be seen as crucial. Will the couriers pass them along to London? Will the documents reach anyone who can act on them in time? Will anyone even understand them." Her voice faded.

Georges rose from his seat, crossed the room, and placed comforting hands on her shoulders. "The documents will be carried by our most trusted courier, Amélie, to Madame Fourcade in Lyon, who'll keep them safe as well. Then Jeremy will carry them to London. He'll put them in the hands of Dr. Reginald Jones, a scientific military intelligence adviser that Churchill holds in high regard. There's no one more qualified than Jones to understand what you've compiled and explain the implications to the prime minister. I'm certain these documents will receive the highest priority."

Jeannie's body trembled and she raised shaking hands to her face. "All this time, I've operated like this was a game of wits to extract information. But it's not a game. It's real. And I'm a recording machine, not a scientist or engineer. My memory is worthless if the documents I've seen and the information I've overheard are faulty or if I haven't reproduced them faithfully. I don't understand any of it. I just replicate it."

She rubbed her eyes and continued. "In one conversation I overheard, a general told a junior officer, 'It appears that the final stage has been reached in developing a bomb of an entirely new kind. It's ten cubic meters in volume and filled with explosives. It would be launched almost vertically to reach the stratosphere quickly—with its initial velocity maintained by repetitive rocket engine ignitions.'"

Jeannie glanced up in agonized dismay. "Of course I know what that means, but the technical details don't make sense to me despite that I recall them perfectly.

"Hitler said these new weapons will change the face of the war, and I overheard an officer estimate that just fifty to one hundred of them could destroy London. The Germans plan to destroy Britain's large cities very methodically during the coming winter." Her troubled eyes took on a shadow of despair. "And this is August."

Jeremy joined Georges in comforting Jeannie. "You've done your part," he said. "Now it's in our hands."

"But it's Amélie," Jeannie implored, her voice breaking into spasms.

"I feel it too, I promise you," Jeremy replied steadily, "but there's no one better to carry those documents. She knows what to do to keep them safe, how to get them through checkpoints, and what to do if things go awry. And if that happens, Georges and I will be nearby with plenty of help. We'll get her to Lyon safely with the documents, and I'll personally carry them to Dr. Jones in London."

"And I'm his backup," Georges interjected.

Jeannie wiped her cheeks. "I have to trust you. I have no choice."

Blocking his own emotions, Jeremy wrapped his arms around Jeannie and squeezed her. "We'll take care of her," he whispered. "I promise."

She caressed Jeremy's cheek and gazed into his eyes through her tears. "And we know how much you love her."

Georges grasped Jeremy's shoulder. "It's time to bring in Amélie."

Amélie sucked in her breath as immense relief and profound dread swept over her simultaneously. Jeremy had just come into view. Rather than passing by, he lingered near her flower stand in his old-man disguise, walking in a stoop but without his cane, the signal to advise Amélie that the time of waiting and supporting Jeannie was over, and the next part of Amélie's mission was about to begin.

Fearing she would raise suspicion by leaving early, Amélie stayed with the other vendors until their normal end of day. Then, exercising her practiced precautions, she made her way over the course of two hours to the safehouse.

Jeremy met her just inside the apartment door, holding her like he would never let go. "These have been the hardest days of my life," he murmured, "seeing you and not being able to be with you for all these months."

Amélie did not reply.

"You're shaking," Jeremy said.

"I'm terrified," Amélie whispered. "I've been terrified."

"We can do this another way."

"No." Amélie shook her head. "We've got to finish this."

Jeannie entered the room and rushed to Amélie. "My dearest friend," she said, embracing her. "You've been there for me throughout this ordeal. Seeing you come by always lifted my spirits. I knew that as long as you were there, others were watching out for me. I hope our mission will have been worthwhile."

"We don't have much time," Georges broke in. "The courier plan goes into effect now."

An hour later, Amélie joined passengers rushing below a large clock, similar to London's Big Ben, at Paris Gare de Lyon, the train station carrying travelers to France's eastern and southeastern destinations. Georges had perceived this to be the best time because, being a Friday evening, thousands of Parisians seeking as much normalcy as allowed by a tyrannical conqueror would be leaving the capital for weekend haunts. Sentries at checkpoints would be overwhelmed by the crowds and less diligent about scrutinizing papers or searching suspects.

Amélie made it through the first barrier with no difficulty, showing the right amount of stoicism, fear, and cooperation. She wore a straw hat with a flat brim, and she dressed such that nothing about her was extraordinary: a long wrinkled skirt, a light blouse, and a jacket draped over one arm. She also had a handbag and a suitcase. When asked why she was traveling alone, she responded that her mother was sick in Lyon, and she produced a perfectly forged doctor's certificate attesting that such was the case and identity papers showing Lyon to be her city of birth. The guards allowed her through with little fuss and were unlikely to remember her.

Amélie barely looked around as she followed the crowd to the train bound for Lyon, but she could not help wondering about the locations of the Resistance members watching out for her, or, for that matter, those of Jeremy and Georges. Georges had been explicit that she should ride on Car #32, but when she arrived beside it, an old man was having difficulty mounting the steel stairs, and a line had formed behind him as several people offered to help him.

Amélie waited patiently. Fear had left her. Mission concentration dominated.

A porter arrived and jostled people to clear the stairs. The old man climbed the rest of the way up, the line thinned, and Amélie entered the car. It was almost full, but she found a seat midway down the aisle and sat down.

Unfortunately, the benches were the type that compelled passengers to face each other, and Amélie saw, too late, that a *Gestapo* lieutenant in full black uniform sat across from her. He had placed his cap on a shelf above him. The silver eagle and skull emblem seemed to stare down at her. The heavy man reeked of arrogance and gave her only passing notice. To avert any notions of conversation, Amélie stuck a little finger deep into her nose, examined the extract, cleaned it off by scraping her fingernail against her skirt, and licked her finger to clean off the residue.

The officer regarded her with disgust and stretched his legs, causing her to pull hers uncomfortably under the bench. Then he leaned into the corner of his seat, folded his arms, and closed his eyes.

Amélie breathed a sigh of relief and relaxed into her own corner.

Together, a hiss of released steam and the locomotive's high-pitched whistle announced the impending departure of the train from the station. Amélie settled further into her seat, not quite relaxed, but suddenly strangely secure with the presence of the *Gestapo* officer sitting across from her, realizing that no inquisitive German soldier or porter was likely to ask for her papers while he sat there.

This far north, and with the train having left the station at just past eight o'clock, she still had roughly an hour and a half of daylight for a journey scheduled to last four hours, with a stop at Pontcharra-sur-Turdine. As the engine chugged out of the station and the rhythmic clackety-clack of the steel wheels rolling on the tracks lulled passengers into a light hypnotic state, Amélie fought to stay awake by soaking in the scenic landscape and villages that rolled by. However, the strain of hiding in plain sight for months, of being the trusted agent to stay in contact with Jeannie, and now, with the terrifying pressure of carrying the earth-shattering documents, she succumbed to exhaustion and fell asleep.

Rough poking at Amélie's ankle jostled her awake. Her vision was blurred as she tried to open her eyes, but the struggle was too much, and she lapsed back into sleep.

Another immediate sharp jab brought Amélie wider awake, and a man yelled down at her. Outside was dark, and she realized dimly that she must have been asleep for some time. In the dim interior train light, her eyes focused on the yelling man's face, and she came fully awake with a start.

The *Gestapo* officer stood over her, arms folded, his eyes glittering with anger.

In his hand he held Amélie's straw hat. He had pulled apart two flat layers that had been sewn together to form the brim. Exposed between them was a piece of paper with notes and sketches.

The *Gestapo* man reached forward, grabbed Amélie's blouse at the shoulder, and jerked her to her feet. Now fully awake, she glanced about and saw terrified looks on the faces of fellow passengers.

A door at the far end of the car thrust open, and three German soldiers hurried down the aisle, their rifles at the ready. Behind them, a *Gestapo* major in black uniform entered and moved swiftly to the scene of excitement.

He appraised the situation swiftly and took over command. Gesturing to the lieutenant to accompany him, they moved to a vestibule where they could confer privately in low voices. "What's going on?" the senior officer hissed in German.

"That woman sat across from me and fell asleep. Her hat was scrunched between her and the wall, and the train's vibration separated the straw pieces of the brim of her hat. When I glanced at it, I saw the corner of a piece of paper sticking out. I pulled the hat away from her, and when I peeled back the brim, this is what I saw."

He held out the paper.

The major took it and glanced at it. After a moment, he looked up sharply. "Has anyone else seen this?" As he spoke, he thrust the paper deep into his pocket.

The lieutenant shook his head.

"Good work. Clear out the other passengers. Send them to other cars and keep her in custody. This matter threatens German national security. When we get to Pontcharra-sur-Turdine, we'll confine her in the local *gendarmeries* until we can get a car to take her to Berlin. Meanwhile, do not let her out of your sight. She could be a link that unravels a significant Resistance organization. Get me her bags. I'll be at the other end of this car examining the documents you found and any others in her luggage."

Within minutes, the only passengers inside the car were the two *Gestapo* officers, the three soldiers, and Amélie. As the train rumbled through the night, her nerves tightened, jabs of pain pierced her calves, and she fought suffocating fear.

At the end of the train car behind Amélie, the *Gestapo* major proceeded to go carefully through her suitcase and handbag.

The train rolled into Pontcharra-sur-Turdine and hissed to a stop amid a cloud of steam. The *Gestapo* major had ordered that the arriving and departing passengers must have cleared the platform prior to his descending from his car with the lieutenant, the three soldiers, and their prisoner. He had further ordered that the train should depart immediately, and he sent the lieutenant to requisition an automobile.

From the time she was discovered until leaving the train, Amélie sat in a stupor, her nerves numb. Visions of her first capture in Valence had played in her mind until she blocked them for the sheer terror they generated. On that occasion, just before her rescue, she had been on the verge of ending her own life with the cyanide pills. She saw no reprieve this time. Despite all the precautions, she knew the basic content of the documents she carried and why the knowledge that Allied forces had gained access to their secrets could not be discovered by Hitler and the *Wehrmacht*.

She fingered a seam on her skirt. The deadly plastic capsules were smooth to her touch under the rough folds of the material.

The major stood in the shadows while the lieutenant went after a car. Amélie's three guards stood around her under a dim station light. The train signaled its departure and chugged out of the station.

Soon a lone Peugeot sedan drove alongside the platform, and the lieutenant exited. Obviously he had appropriated the vehicle from a local citizen. It was large enough to accommodate the group, although with some crowding.

The major emerged from the shadows and approached the Peugeot. "Open the door," he commanded.

The lieutenant turned to do as ordered. Suddenly, the major stepped behind him, cupped his left elbow around the officer's neck, and held it firmly while he drew the razor-sharp edge of a British commando knife deep across the junior officer's carotid arteries. When the major let go, the hapless lieutenant dropped. Only a gurgling sound evinced the man's violent death. Before the three sentries could react, three other men rushed from the shadows and delivered to them the same end.

Amélie had heard only vague noises, but then, seeing the bloodshed around her, she sank to the ground, nearly faint. Perceiving movement to her front, she glanced up to see the major advancing toward her. She shrank away in fear.

In the hazy light of the station, the officer removed his cap and took her arm gently. "It's all right, Amélie. It's me, Jeremy."

Stunned, Amélie stared at him, and then sank the rest of the way to the ground, shaking and sobbing. Jeremy stooped, scooped her into his arms, and held her tight, swaying with her. "Shh. You're safe, and we don't have far to go."

"You're among friends," another familiar voice said, and Georges joined them. "The car is waiting," he told Jeremy. "Let's go."

Softly, Jeremy closed the door to Fourcade's room in Ladybird's apartment.

"How is she?" Fourcade asked.

"Sleeping. Chantal is with her."

Fourcade took in a breath and exhaled slowly. "Such an ordeal." She brushed a lock of hair from her forehead. "I've been through the papers. I can see why I was kept in the dark until now. But my rule is that I must vouch for any information I send to London, which means I have to go through it. You and I know the source, but Georges insists that Jeannie's identity be kept secret from anyone else here or in London."

They strolled onto the veranda and took seats. "Was that paper in her hat the only one?" Jeremy asked.

"Not hardly," Fourcade replied. "She had them sewn into her skirt, under a false bottom in her purse, and inside the lining of her suitcase. It's a voluminous set of documents. And since I know the content, and with Georges' preface, I have no problem vouching for them." She darted a searching glance at Jeremy. "I gather you're familiar with the pertinent details."

Jeremy nodded. "I am. Georges insisted on it. His concern was that if Amélie or one of us was captured with the papers, at least one person should know enough of the details to give a good briefing in London, sufficient, hopefully, to spur action."

"Well, the mission's not complete until Churchill has seen it all, but the worst part is over. Now we have to get you and the documents back to London."

"When's the next flight."

"If the weather holds, tomorrow night."

They sat in silence, taking in the view of Lyon. "Where is Georges?" Jeremy asked suddenly. "He dropped us off here and then left."

"On his way back to Paris. He returned the car to Pontcharra-sur-Turdine and left it near the station. So far, we've heard of no repercussions against the people. His men cleaned up the blood at the station and dumped the bodies into a deep ravine. I doubt they'll be found. For all the Germans know, their men could have deserted."

Jeremy sighed deeply. "You know," he said in a low voice, "I've never killed a man with my bare hands before. I've shot them out of the air and in ground combat, but I've never had an enemy's body up against mine as I sliced his throat. Until now."

"Ah, but your Amélie is alive and safe because you did that. You have nothing to regret."

"But she might have seen me do it," Jeremy fretted. "I worry about what kind of people we'll be when this war is over. Look at what she's been through, and she's got to know that her husband—" He caught himself and smiled softly. "If that ever comes about. As I was saying, she knows I'm a killer."

"Stop it, Jeremy," Fourcade chided. "You're a defender. Good people live because of you. Amélie would be dead but for you, and when you deliver those documents, you might save thousands more."

Jeremy blew out a breath of air. "Perhaps." He furrowed his brow and turned to face Fourcade directly. "I want to take Amélie to London with me. She needs a rest, away from danger. She can stay with my sister, Claire. I can take Chantal too."

"That's a wonderful idea. I might have trouble getting all three of you on one Lysander flight, but I'll see what I can do. You and the documents must take first priority, though, even if it means going without them."

"Understood. No argument."

"I won't go," Chantal broke in from the French doors onto the terrace. "My place is here, and I won't rest until the Germans are gone."

Jeremy and Fourcade stared at her. "How long have you been listening?" Fourcade asked.

"Long enough. Look, I've been in Lyon doing not much for a long time while my sister has been risking her life daily for months. She needs the rest. I don't. I'm staying."

"What if she refuses to go without you?"

Chantal's face wrinkled into a bemused expression. "I'll convince her."

"How old are you?" Jeremy asked.

"I'm not the little girl you met three and a half years ago," Chantal retorted with an edge of defiance. "I'm nearly eighteen, and I've done some things for the cause."

Jeremy laughed heartily. "I haven't done that in a while—laugh." He trained his eyes on Chantal. "You've done a lot for the cause. Soldiers at Bruneval owe their lives to you, and so do a lot of pilots. Your reconnaissance did that. No one doubts what you can do."

He rubbed his chin in thought. "I have an idea. How about if you come back to London with us and I get you into that same training that Amélie took? When you come back, you'll be even more effective."

Fourcade regarded him in astonishment and Chantal looked uncertain. "You mean spy school? Would they take me? They'll think I'm too young."

"We can put in a good word for you." Jeremy gestured toward Fourcade. "She has a lot of pull in London, and I have a little."

"Don't let him fool you," Fourcade broke in. "He carries plenty of influence. I think it's a good idea. Amélie will get the rest she needs and you'll stay out of trouble."

Chantal cast her a rueful glance that immediately transformed to a bright, wide-eyed smile. "And maybe I'll get to see Horton? You'll see to that, won't you, Jeremy?"

Jeremy let loose a full-throated belly-laugh. "You never give up, do you." He shook his head in amusement. "No promises, but I'll see what I can do."

Chantal jumped up and down in excitement. Then, she extended her hand to shake Jeremy's. "Done."

31

August 15, 1943
London, England

"Are you certain I need to be there?" Jeremy asked Dr. Reginald Jones as they hurried through the main corridor at Whitehall, seat of Great Britain's defense ministry.

"I'm sure," Jones replied. "You might be asked nothing, or you might provide a crucial piece of information that no one else has. Key decisions will be coming out of this meeting, and all pertinent parties need to be there."

"But I'm hardly important. I was a courier only, subsequent to getting the documents out of Paris."

"Which is why, as I stated, you might have nothing to say. The questions asked will determine your participation."

"All right then, sir. I'll give it my best."

They reached a set of wooden double doors leading into a conference room. Dr. Jones took a seat at a long table and indicated that Jeremy sit in one of a row of chairs behind him.

Other participants trailed in, and as Jeremy watched, his consternation grew. As a captain, he was the most junior among those who arrived early, and they were mostly colonels and brigadiers. Then Jeremy was startled when everyone stood and clicked heels to attention, and General Alan Brooke, Chief of the Imperial General Staff, entered. He was followed by Lord Louis Mountbatten, Chief of Combined Operations; Air Chief Marshal Sir Arthur Harris; Director of Military Operations, General John Kennedy; Chief of Staff to the Minister of Defense and Secretary of the Imperial Defense Council, General Hastings "Pug" Ismay; Professor Frederick Lindemann, scientific advisor to the prime minister; and finally, Winston Churchill himself.

Jeremy watched the august men take their seats, undecided whether to sit up straight or try to recede into the woodwork. The latter option being impractical, he sat at attention with his most serious countenance.

"I've been over the documents," Churchill announced, speaking even before taking a seat and glancing about the room with his iconic pugnacious stare. "We have some fast decisions to make, gentlemen, and we can't be wrong on this one."

He gazed pointedly at Jones and gestured toward Lindemann. "I'll tell you quite frankly that my science adviser believes these documents are a hoax. The same with whatever we've seen on reconnaissance flyovers. He thinks the evidence of rockets and pilotless planes are mockups. You don't agree. We're here to hash it all out."

Churchill turned to General Ismay. "Review for us what we've learned about Peenemünde. Stick to the essentials."

Ismay glanced grimly at his audience. "We've known since 1937 from the so-called Oslo Report that the Germans have been experimenting with large rockets for some time. But Hitler was always skeptical of them. And we've known about the facility at Peenemünde where they produce and test-launch rocket-driven gliders.

"As I recall, the Oslo Report came from an anonymous source, delivered to the British Embassy in Norway, and contained so much information that it was viewed with skepticism on the basis that a single person could not possibly have known all of the developments described in the report.

"It's gained credibility because so many developments it predicted came true. Dr. Jones, I believe that when British intelligence received the report, you were the only person to give it any credence. In fact, you once told me that you consulted the Oslo Report in odd moments to see what might be coming up next."

"True, sir," Jones responded, "and the latest prediction to come true is that, per intelligence, last month, on July 18, the Germans successfully launched a V-2 rocket and hit the intended target. I understand that Hitler's doubts have dissolved. He now believes that he has in hand the weapons that will change the war to his advantage."

Ismay nodded and addressed the general audience. "The press even learned of the Oslo Report and published articles about its content, so the public is aware of the potential threat. It's not been circulated lately, so the fear of it has probably dissipated, but that doesn't decrease the danger." He grimaced. "When the report came out, we treated it like so much science fiction." He exhaled heavily. "From all indications, we'd better treat the matter as a bona fide threat, and this latest report with the utmost care."

He paused a moment to gather his thoughts. "A first-hand account of *current* goings-on at Peenemünde came from a conversation between two inmates we recorded secretly at Trent Park, a POW camp where we hold senior prisoners. General Wilhelm Ritter von Thoma mentioned rockets being tested at Kummersdorf, which he had observed while visiting there with Field Marshal Walther von Brauchitsch, the *Wehrmacht's* commander-in-chief. Thoma said that he was surprised that Britain had not already been hit by a rocket attack.

"We also received intelligence from an Austrian Resistance group on development of what they're calling the V-1 flying bomb and the V-2 rockets. Their report included information on a production site in south Austria called Raxwerke. The details are quite compelling."

"I recall distinctly that we received reports last year and the year before from the Polish Resistance too," Churchill interjected gruffly. "They included sketches and maps. Perhaps we should have listened more closely then."

"Agreed, sir," Ismay said, and continued. "We've carried out aerial reconnaissance over Peenemünde, and we've seen long, winged objects that appear like aircraft with no cockpits and others that look like rockets, but nothing definitive.

"And then, of course, there are these new documents that brought us together this morning. For that discussion, I'll defer to Dr. Jones."

The physicist began slowly, solemnly. "It was my study of those documents that led me to place the urgent call to the prime minister." He took a deep breath and fixed his gaze on Churchill. "I believe we are in danger of a massive aerial bombardment within months, if not weeks."

The room fell silent, every eye riveted first on Jones and then on the prime minister. Churchill took a cigar from his jacket pocket and lit it. "I'm aware of your concern and the depth of the gravity in which you hold it, Dr. Jones," he said, leaning forward, puffing on his cigar, and then jutting his jaw toward the physicist, "but if we judge you to be right, we'll divert huge bombing assets from other targets to destroy the facilities at Peenemünde. If you're wrong, the consequences could be calamitous. What's to say that such a diversion isn't exactly what the enemy desires? Maybe the facility at Peenemünde was built there for that express purpose? I don't need to remind anyone here of the deceptive methods we've used to acquire an advantage where we had none. Operation Mincemeat comes to mind."

Jones replied gravely, "Sir, the details of these documents are too exacting to be dismissed lightly. As you saw, the sketches were to scale, the fuel requirements, payloads, range estimates, initial velocities, aerodynamics—all the technical details line up with two weapons systems, both of which are feasible and, if turned into reality, could deliver the explosive power onto our cities as we've described.

"The technical notes are those of experienced engineers, not science fiction authors or propaganda purveyors. I am staking my professional career on their accuracy and authenticity. I believe without a doubt that operational V-1s and V-2s in great quantities either exist or are being built, and we are due for a cataclysmic attack if we do not take prompt action to destroy them."

General Brooke cut in. "What does the 'V' stand for?"

Jones took a deep breath. "'Vergeltungswaffe,' sir, German terminology for 'vengeance weapon,' and if the information just received is correct, the V-2 will hit targets two hundred miles away. Further, it will have the ability to reach outer space for a brief time. Of course, with more research and improvements—" He broke off with a shrug and left the sentence unfinished.

For a moment, all was quiet as everyone contemplated the implications. Then a murmur of commentary floated throughout the conference room. It diminished to expectant silence while Churchill, Ismay, and Brooke conducted a whispered aside.

"What is the essential difference between the V-1 and V-2?" Mountbatten asked.

Jones, who had remained standing, creased his forehead as he formulated a response. "The V-1 is a *Luftwaffe* project and is essentially a rocket-powered plane. It's much slower than the V-2, but it's also much cheaper, so it can be built in greater numbers. Its engineers are provided a target, they determine the azimuth and range, fill it with sufficient fuel to reach the target, and launch it. When it runs out of gas, it drops to the ground, igniting its explosive payload. That simple.

"The V-2 is a *Wehrmacht* project. It's much more complex, but according to these documents, the first launch into space occurred on October 3 of last year; and in fact, one of the rockets' developers, Werner von Braun, is on record in decoded transmissions stating that one day their rockets would carry men to the moon. He's not terribly popular with his army masters. They want him working on developing weapons, not thinking of flying to the moon. That seems a stretch presently, but who knows what further advances might bring.

"Right now, the V-2 is more accurate than the V-1, it can carry a larger payload, and hit targets at a greater distance." He paused and met Churchill's steady gaze. "Together, the two weapons systems are a direct and imminent threat."

Jeremy all but held his breath. The conference descended into stunned silence.

Churchill resumed the discussion. "No need to bet your career, Dr. Jones," he said with a grave tone. "Your credentials are well known in this room, and your successes with Bruneval and Dieppe, among others, speak for themselves. But we must be sure of what we are doing. What is the source of these documents?"

Jeremy was seized suddenly by overwhelming dread. He sensed that his hopes of surviving the meeting unnoticed had just disappeared.

"They are vouched for by the leader of Alliance, the French Resistance group that works closely with SOE and MI-9," Jones said. "Their authenticity is also confirmed by the leader of the Druids, a subnetwork of Alliance headquartered in Paris. The information was obtained by a source there working inside the *Wehrmacht* offices."

He picked up the first page of the document lying on the table in front of him. "This is a forwarding note to the documents from the leader of the Druids. It reads, 'This material looks preposterous. But I have total faith in my source.'"

"That's all well and good," Lindemann, the science adviser, broke in, "but what do we know about this source."

"I understand that the person is not technical," Churchill interjected, "but rather someone with supposed perfect recall or a photographic memory, and that the notes and sketches were done from memory of overheard conversations and casual viewing of the documents from which they were compiled. Is that correct, Dr. Jones?"

"That is correct, sir," Jones replied. "However, there is precedent. Remember that we had an operator inside the *Wehrmacht* headquarters in Dinard ahead of Germany's planned invasion of our homeland. That person also produced critical detailed documents from memory which we relied on to bomb French coastal targets. The information proved to be quite accurate and reliable."

"Hmph," Churchill groused. "I wonder if it could be the same person."

"Not likely," Jones replied. "Regardless, I believe we must act, and my strongest recommendation is that we bomb Peenemünde immediately."

Again, the room descended into silence while Churchill and his senior military advisers conferred in whispers. Then, General Brooke addressed the assembly. "I have a question. How did these documents come into our possession? I mean how did they make their way from Paris to London?"

Jeremy's palms were suddenly moist.

Dr. Jones glanced at him. "They were hand-carried by two trusted couriers, sir. One took them from Paris to Lyon, and the other brought them here. In neither case were the documents compromised or tampered with. The latter courier is here with us." He indicated Jeremy.

All eyes turned to Jeremy, including Churchill's, who did a double-take on seeing him. "I say, you look rather familiar. Stand up, Captain. I need a closer look at you. What's your name?"

Jeremy did as ordered, his mind awhirl. "Captain Jeremy Littlefield, sir, if you please."

"Of course I please or I wouldn't have asked." He peered at Jeremy over his spectacles. "You're Lieutenant Colonel Paul Littlefield's youngest brother, aren't you? From Sark."

"I am, sir, although I had no idea he had risen so far in rank. Some time has passed since we last saw each other."

"Yes, well, you can catch up later. You look like him." Churchill looked pleased. "I've had a few dealings with him. A good fellow. I'll have to visit with you another time. For now, we must deal with the matter at hand. What can you tell us about the source in Paris?"

Jeremy's heart beat faster as his mind flew through possible responses. "Sir, I can tell you that, as the leaders of both Alliance and Druid stated, the source is absolutely reliable and a dedicated French patriot."

"Yes, but who is it? What is the name of this person?"

Jeremy hesitated to speak, and Jones came to his rescue. "Sir, Captain Littlefield informed me that he was sworn to secrecy concerning the source's identity before being allowed to bring those documents out of France."

"Sworn by whom?" Churchill asked testily.

Jeremy spoke up. "By the heads of both Resistance organizations, sir. I assured them that I would not be pressured to break their confidence."

Churchill leaned forward and peered at Jeremy. "I want to know who the source is," he said in a low voice, "and I'm not asking."

"I can't tell you, sir." Jeremy's knees became unsteady and he suddenly felt lightheaded as blood rushed from his head. "If I do, I'm finished as an operative in France, and the confidence we've built with Alliance will be severely damaged."

"Captain Littlefield makes a cogent point," General Ismay broke in. "Alliance is the largest and most effective of all the networks we support.

They supply a vast amount of reliable intelligence. Further, we know the identity of the source for the Oslo Report. His name is Hans Mayer. He had been a German scientist on these weapons programs, but he's now in prison for having listened to a BBC broadcast. Indications are that the Nazis don't know that he was the source of the leaked document, but nevertheless, a good guess is that our current informant is aware of that situation and prefers to avoid a similar outcome."

Looking momentarily flummoxed, Churchill glared at Ismay.

Dr. Jones had stood quietly listening to the exchange. Now he spoke up.

"Mr. Prime Minister, the identity of the source adds nothing to our dilemma of whether or not to proceed. Even knowing who it is would not change the facts on which we must decide. You have the word of the heads of two key, reliable organizations as well as Captain Littlefield himself. My best recommendation is that we proceed forthwith. The time to act is now." He paused and then added grimly, "And our primary target should be the barracks that house the scientists. Without them, the program grinds to a halt. The secondary targets should be the production, research, and launch-test facilities."

Churchill drew back into his seat, apparently sobered further by the recommendation. "That's a rather stark proposal."

"But I think a necessary one," Jones responded without hesitation. "It's a choice between their people or ours; and I assure you that if they launch, our civilian casualties will number in the many thousands across all our major cities. If we are successful in stopping them by air bombardment, their casualties will number in the hundreds, but we'll at least delay further development of this program from hell."

All eyes shifted from Jones to Churchill, including Jeremy's, who watched as the prime minster sat quietly, the press of responsibility visible in his eyes. While others discussed in low murmurs, Churchill stared distantly. Then, as he drew himself back to awareness, his eyes fastened on Jeremy and he leaned forward. "Are you allowed to say whether or not you are personally acquainted with your source?"

Seeing Jeremy's reluctance to respond, Churchill's expression softened. "My thought is that this person might have other information that could be valuable if we had a chance to ask questions. I understand Dr. Jones' point about time being of the essence. As he points out, we can decide without the source, and the press of events dictates that we do so. But what if we brought that person here? Would that be amenable?"

Startled, Jeremy took a moment, choosing his words carefully. "I don't know, sir. We can certainly ask. If your invitation is accepted, you'd know the identity by the source's own free will."

"Then by all means, ask." The prime minister stood. "This meeting is adjourned." He turned to his senior military advisers. "Please join me in my war office." To Dr. Jones, he said, "You come too." With one last passing glance at Jeremy and across the others in the room, he said, "Dismissed."

32

Stony Stratford, Buckinghamshire, England

Jeremy took a late train from London and arrived at Claire's house in the evening, just as the sun was setting. Claire, Chantal, and Timmy met him as he walked up the driveway.

"I still can't believe you're here," Claire exuded.

"I can't believe *I'm* here either," Chantal exclaimed. They spoke in French for Chantal's benefit. "Such a beautiful country. Thank you for having us."

"You've thanked me enough," Claire replied, "and I'm happy for the company. Timmy is thrilled."

Jeremy, Amélie, and Chantal had landed at RAF Tangmere early the previous morning, and after brief stops at SOE and MI-9 headquarters, they had gone on to Stony Stratford and spent the night at Claire's house. Jeremy had gone back into London at Dr. Jones' urgent call to attend the early afternoon meeting.

Now, at mention of Timmy's name, the child puffed his chest out, twisted his mouth in a failed effort to subdue a smile, and clutched Jeremy's hand. Jeremy lifted the child into the air to sit on his shoulders. Timmy squealed in delight.

"How's Amélie?" Jeremy asked.

"Still sleeping, just as you left her. That must have been some trauma she went through."

Jeremy nodded with a glance at Chantal. "And the part we watched is less than half the story."

"Is there anything you can tell me about it? I'd love to help her."

Jeremy shook his head. "I can't reveal anything about the operation. Your friendship will count for a lot. So will being out of danger."

"I don't even know what the mission was," Chantal interjected. "They wouldn't tell me anything. But Amélie is strong. She'll recover quickly."

"And this little guy"—Jeremy reached up and patted Timmy's shoulder —"he could cheer up the worst kind of depression."

Timmy laughed and urged Jeremy to gallop the rest of the way to the house, screaming with excitement the whole way. Amélie met them at the door.

"Excuse the way I look," she said, rubbing still-exhausted eyes. "I just woke up." Her hair was tousled, her face lined, and to Jeremy she looked so small inside a white robe with a faded pink rose design. But she smiled, and as Jeremy lowered Timmy to the ground, she kissed the boy, and then reached up and circled her arms around Jeremy's neck. "I just can't believe we're together," she whispered, "and that we probably won't die within minutes."

"You're safe here," he said. "You have nothing to do but rest."

Chantal and Claire caught up to them, and everyone entered the house and gathered in the sitting room. "How was your meeting?" Claire asked Jeremy.

"Rough," he responded. "I could use a stiff drink. Make it a double."

While still in Lyon and presented with the idea of Chantal going to England to be trained as a spy, Amélie had not been receptive. "Isn't it enough that we lost Papa—"

"And we nearly lost you," Chantal cried. "No. It's not enough. I'll fight *les boches* until we win or until I die."

"But you're only—"

"Nearly as old as you were when the war started." She took her sister's hand in her own. "I'm going to be in this fight one way or the other. If you refuse to go to England to rest, I'll stay in Lyon and I'll be in the Resistance no matter what you say.

If you won't let me go to that spy school, I'll stay here, and I'll still fight.

"The best situation is that we both go to England, you rest at Jeremy's sister's house, and I'll go to training. Look at it this way: at least I'll be safe while I'm learning, and so will you. And you'll get to rest."

Amélie had agreed reluctantly. The Lysander flight, after the normal nerve-racking rendezvous and takeoff under a full moon from an empty field at Thalamy, had been uneventful. They had arrived without incident on the southern coast of Britain.

After seeing Amélie and Chantal off on a train to Stony Stratford, Jeremy had called forward after landing at RAF Tangmere to let Claire know to expect guests. Then he made his way to deliver the documents to Dr. Jones and answer as many questions about them as he could. After that, he visited Lieutenant Colonel Crockatt.

The head of MI-9 had been pleased to see Jeremy healthy and in one piece. Fourcade had sent a message ahead informing him of the plan to allow Amélie to rest at Claire's house while Chantal trained. Crockatt had been cautiously supportive.

"I'm constantly reminded that Fourcade belongs to SOE, not MI-9," he said, "so I'm guessing that Chantal would be primarily involved in SOE missions."

"But don't forget," Jeremy replied, "that Alliance, with Fourcade's full support, helped many prisoners escape and evade re-capture, including my brother. And she helped set up the new escape line through Spain. We owe her."

Crockatt had taken a moment to think through the proposition. "We'll do it," he said at last, "and I won't even demand that Chantal be primarily involved in MI-9 missions. But I will require that your main effort continues to support our missions."

Jeremy stood and extended his hand to Crockatt with a grin. "In the immortal words of Chantal, 'Done.' Now, please help me find out where Horton is."

On his way back to Claire's house after the conference with Churchill and Dr. Jones and before boarding the train to Stony Stratford, Jeremy once again stopped off to see Crockatt. He explained how the meeting at Whitehall had gone.

"The prime minister wishes to invite the source in Paris to come to London. He's hoping to learn more that might be helpful in the future."

Crockatt mulled the implications. "Well, if that's what the prime minister wants, then we'd best set things in motion. I'll send a message off to Fourcade and let you know when I receive a response. Meanwhile, take a breather. Enjoy your time with Claire and Amélie."

Jeremy and Amélie sat together on the bench under the English elm in Claire's garden at the rear of the house. The moon waned against a night sky but still cast down brilliant light.

"You knew what was in those documents, didn't you?" Jeremy asked after a time of murmurs and caressing.

Amélie nodded and shuddered. She leaned her head against Jeremy's chest, clinging to him. "I was so scared. I know what would happen to me if the *Gestapo* found out what I knew."

"Then why did you keep on? You'd done enough already. We would have brought you out long ago."

Amélie remained quiet for a time. "I had no choice," she said. "It was something I had to do. If not me, then who? The very life of France is at stake: the people we love, our way of life, the freedom that other generations fought for. I can't let that go, not without fighting with every bit of strength I have left. Papa taught us that. He lived it."

"He did," Jeremy said, sighing. "I loved your father. That night at Dunkirk, I thought I was done in, and then he appeared in that ditch and showed me the way out. And then you confronted those soldiers to divert them. You knew they would not hesitate to kill you, but you did it anyway, and in the middle of a storm, and I'm here now because of you and your father."

Jeremy felt Amélie shuddering, softly sobbing. "I'm sorry. I've made you cry."

She shook her head. "It's a good cry. I have wonderful memories of Papa, and he died saving the rest of us." She caught her breath. "When this war is over, I'll know it's because of him, you, and people like Fourcade, Chantal, and Jeannie, and people like me who did what they could. Nothing heroic. Just refusing to be conquered."

As a thought struck her, another sob seized her. "I'm so afraid for Jeannie. She's still in Paris, and if the RAF strikes Peenemünde, the Germans will know they've been found out. They'll be looking for the spy who gave away their secret. They'll search in all the *Reich's* occupied territories, including Paris. They'll find her."

Jeremy squeezed her against his chest. "We'll get her out," he said. "I swear it."

Then he sat up and pivoted down on one knee in front of Amélie. "Marry me. Now," he said with uncharacteristic urgency. "I love you. You know that. I can't even think of life without you."

Amélie gazed at him, but took moments to respond. "You're my life, Jeremy. But I can't. Not now." Tears streamed down her face. "I want to marry you, but when we can truly celebrate." She leaned down, pulled his head to her breast, and kissed his forehead. "I've already said yes. Is that enough for now?"

Jeremy raised his head and looked into her eyes. "When you're ready, I'll be ready."

Amélie brushed his hair from his face. "And when that happens, we'll be on Sark with Chantal, your parents, and our entire family."

Jeremy chuckled. "Should we invite Fourcade and Jeannie?"

"Of course."

33

August 17, 1943
RAF Wyton, Huntingdon, United Kingdom

RAF Group Captain John Henry Searby, commanding officer of Bomber Command's 83 Squadron, thrilled to the roar as one after another of his four Rolls-Royce Merlin engines on his Avro Lancaster turned over, ignited, and ran up. Their power built to a hum as sixteen propeller blades spun to invisibility in waning sunlight.

The bomber strained against the chocks restraining its rush to flight. Their deep-throated vibration shook the airframe, declaring the aircraft's combat strength, ready to deliver mayhem on any enemy.

Searby's momentary excitement stemmed from his love of flying, especially in this particular aircraft. Descended from a failed and underpowered two-engine version of the same airframe, the four-engine Lancaster had become a favorite workhorse of the RAF Bomber Command. Being narrow with dual rear stabilizers and an aircrew of six—pilot, flight engineer, navigator, bombardier, and gunners in the nose and tail—the quarters were cramped, but the plane was easy to fly, and once the bombs were away, it was remarkably maneuverable. That agility had already saved crew members' lives as gunners menaced and pilots evaded attacking enemy fighters.

Only three months earlier, one of Searby's former fellow officers, Wing Commander Guy Gibson, had led a special squadron of Lancasters on Operation Chastise. They executed a bombing raid into the industrial Ruhr Valley, the most heavily defended area of Germany, to knock out three major hydroelectric dams holding water back at the Mohne Reservoir, and on the rivers Sorpe and Eder. The giant turbines of each dam, turned by the spill of huge quantities of water, fed electricity to a myriad of armaments factories below them.

The one-off special squadron that had formed for the mission flew under radar, two hundred feet above ground. They navigated at night by the stars and compass headings to deliver barrel-shaped bombs onto the lakes formed by the dams.

To target accurately, the bombs were spun backwards by special motorcycle-like chain devices slung below the aircraft, spinning them to five thousand rotations per minute and dropping them from an altitude of sixty feet. At that point, the Lancaster flew at precisely two hundred thirty-two miles per hour.

Under the light of the moon reflecting off the lakes, the Lancasters found their targets, and on three successive sweeps, they unleashed grim punishment on the sleeping, almost endless stream of contiguous cities spread throughout the Ruhr. When the bombs fell onto the water's surface, they skipped like stones, coming to rest against the dams' walls.

No massive explosion had been required. The dams were too thick for that. The objective had been to fracture the enormous, forty-foot wide, steel-reinforced concrete structures. The millions of gallons of water held back by the dams and then released through tiny fissures would force rapid expansions of the cracks that would give way into wide fissures. The dam walls would disintegrate, and a torrent of water would flatten anything in its path. The resulting flood across the Ruhr Valley would finish the job.

Gibson led, and after dropping his own bombs, he flew parallel to each Lancaster through enemy anti-aircraft flak bursts to mark the targets and draw fire away from the aircraft currently making its bombing run. The Eder dam resisted the onslaught, but those at Mohne and Sorpe crumbled under the ensuing torrent, flooding roads and villages; knocking out bridges, railroad stations, and telephone lines; and even destroying farms, crops, and livestock scattered between the largely urban area. The operation cut electrical supply everywhere in the valley and demolished many of the arms factories.

The success of the mission had been celebrated across the British Empire. The special squadron was dubbed the "Dambusters." Gibson instantly became a national hero and was awarded a Victoria Cross for gallantry in battle.

The operation set back the German war machine eighteen months.

Now, as Searby contemplated his own mission, his thrill dissipated to sobriety. While Gibson's success had been spectacular, it had been conducted by a squadron of sixteen aircraft. Operation Hydra, as Searby's mission had been dubbed, had assembled an aerial armada of five hundred ninety-six bombers, including three hundred twenty-four Lancasters, two hundred eighteen Halifaxes, and fifty-four Stirlings.

Searby's most sobering thought was that he would command the formation.

He was a lean, pleasant-faced man of medium height with dark hair and a ready smile. His career had been steady but unspectacular as he did any job to the best of his ability while avoiding the limelight. Having joined the RAF in 1929 as an aircraft apprentice, he had qualified as a pilot after six years, for which he earned the rank of sergeant. He was offered a commission in 1939 and attended the navigation specialist course and then became an instructor, flying Blenheims. He spent time ferrying aircraft across the Atlantic and then occupied a staff position before being promoted to squadron leader. During his first operational tour, he served as a group navigation officer before taking leadership as a flight commander with 106 Squadron at Coningsby under Wing Commander Gibson.

When Gibson relinquished command to form the special squadron for Operation Chastise with the Dambusters, Searby replaced him. Two months later, Searby received a promotion to group captain and assumed command of 83 Squadron. And now, for Operation Hydra, Searby would command the largest RAF formation ever assembled.

He sensed that he was embarking on a mission that was momentous, but he had no inkling as to why. The sheer size of the formation, which pulled together the entire complement of Bomber Command's assets, had to mean that other missions had been canceled or delayed, diverting all the RAF's bombers for this run.

The target was Peenemünde, in the far northeast reaches of Germany along the Baltic coast. His regular command, 83 Squadron, had joined the overall formation as part of RAF 5 Group, with Searby selected to command the whole raiding force and be the "master bomber," a new RAF designation for a new bombing concept.

RAF 5 Group had practiced a new tactic termed "time and distance runs," directed by the master bomber. However, this mission had been cobbled together quickly, on a scale not anticipated, and not all the sub-units were versed in the technique. This would be the first large-scale use of the master bomber and the time and distance concepts.

The method called for marking reference points employing multi-colored flares dropped from the aircraft. Using a new ground-scanning radar system known as H2S that provided a view of contrasting areas on the ground and over open water, the aircraft's navigators could confirm their locations.

The master bomber would then direct and redirect the main body of the formation to the targets by reference to a specific flare color, direction, speed, and time of flight, measured in seconds. The bombardiers then released their bombs at the set time and distance from the designated reference point.

Gibson had employed the method during the dam raids, but that had been the only use of it to date. Now it fell to Searby to employ it on a scale more than sixty times greater than had been the case in the Ruhr Valley.

Searby's formation would fly and navigate at night. If he directed the formation to the wrong targets, the results would be calamitous.

The plan called for Searby's raiders to initiate their bombing runs from Cape Arkona on the island of Rügen. From there they would fly over Thiessow, using the town as a reference point to check time, speed, and heading, make final adjustments, and zero in on a timed run to Peenemünde, ten miles south across open water.

During their mission briefing, the aircrews were told that the target was a radar research facility developing improvements to German night air defenses. To emphasize the importance of the mission without revealing its main objective—to kill as many civilian rocketry scientists as possible and to forestall a sustained massive flying bomb and rocket attack on Great Britain—the operations order specified that if the attack were to fail, the mission would be repeated on successive nights, regardless of RAF casualties.

Searby set his brakes and pressed the throttles forward. The plane's wide wings shuddered as the airframe strained against its restraints. On his signal, the groundcrew pulled the chock blocks away. The Lancaster lurched forward slightly, held in place by its brakes. Then Searby gradually eased his foot off the pedals.

The bomber started forward and gathered speed. Searby taxied to his holding point, where he ran up the engines to test power and went through his final checklist, assisted by the flight engineer perched in a well beside the pilot's seat. To his left and right, other bombers performed the same actions, and already in the distant sky, huge numbers of aircraft loitered, awaiting Searby's order to proceed to the target.

Minutes later, all pre-flight actions completed, Searby's Lancaster rolled onto the runway, sped into the wind, and lifted into the air. He steered to his rendezvous point, took his command position within the formation, turned east, and flew out over the North Sea.

Expecting a seven-hour journey each way, the formation skirted well north of Groningen on the Dutch coast while maintaining an altitude of fifteen thousand feet. The wind buffeted the plane, and the moon shone brightly, but all that Searby could see below was a black expanse of water broken by whitecaps.

Below and behind Searby, in a nook off a narrow passageway filled with electronic devices, the navigator sat in darkness watching instruments and reading maps by his own small penlight. He continually checked his position against the stars through a sextant embedded in a tarpaulin-curtained glass dome over his head, and he fed course corrections to Searby via an intercom.

As Searby reflected on the mission, the faces of pilots, many of whom were friends and long-time associates, formed in his mind's eye. He knew the wives and families of many of them.

The formation was miles long and wide and varied in height by hundreds of feet. He had witnessed German formations of similar size during the days of the *blitz*. The thought brought to mind the terror and suffering that Hitler had wrought on the British people, but he took no comfort in the pain he was about to inflict. He saw his job as one that was necessary and his to carry out, but each of the bombers under his command carried flesh-and-blood men. The weight of responsibility for them bore down on him.

The formation turned toward Denmark, staying north of Flensburg, where the peninsula was narrow and the population sparse. It made landfall over Fanø, and after traversing the width of Denmark and flying back over water, they headed southeast and at last crossed over the coast of Rügen, an island ten miles north of the target. The navigator acquired Cape Arkona, the final reference point on the island before reaching Peenemünde, and relayed the position information to Searby. "There's a cloud cover," he added. "We won't be able to see the targets."

———

Flak bursts in and around the formation started as soon as they crossed the narrow band of water between Cape Arkona and Peenemünde. Although Operation Hydra had achieved surprise, the research base was well defended and on constant alert. When the type of incoming aircraft was identified, German soldiers jumped behind their guns and inundated the sky with hot lead and explosive bursts.

"Pathfinders, fan out," Searby ordered, and immediately two squadrons behind him diverged across the sky. Each aircraft flew to designated coordinates around Peenemünde and dropped their specifically colored flares, none of them the same as those carried by another plane.

At midnight, Searby made his bomb run, dropped his payload, and climbed to a position above the main formation. Then, one by one, he called forward the three waves of the main body with orders to orient on a particular color as a reference point. Each wave flew over its respective flares toward their individual targets, counting off seconds to the bomb release.

The first wave aimed for the community where the rocket scientists lived. The second wave headed to attack the factories. The third went for the experimental workshops.

Even from high above the base, Searby heard the muffled boom of explosions, and in the moonlight, billows of dust and debris blanketed the earth's surface. A smokescreen released from *Wehrmacht* generators cloaked Peenemünde, further obscuring the target.

Forty-eight minutes after the attack began, it was over. Searby ordered the formation back to the British Isles. On the way, images of his air crews formed in his mind again, and he wondered how many of them would be missing at breakfast the next morning.

34

August 20, 1943
Stony Stratford, England

Waving a copy of the *London Times*, Jeremy rushed into Claire's house looking for Amélie. He found her on the bench in the garden under the English elm. "Look at this," he exuded. "Your hard work paid off."

Amélie stared at the headline: "ROCKET BASE DESTROYED AT PEENEMÜNDE."

"You did that," Jeremy said.

A tear rolled down Amélie's cheek. "I helped a little," she said. "So did you, and Georges. But Jeannie did that. The risks she took—" Her voice trailed off. "I'm so worried about her. She's in Paris, still attending those parties and being charming, and by now wondering which of those officers might recall what he said to her about the rocket program and suspect her." The tears flowed more freely, and when Amélie spoke again, her voice broke. "I can't get her out of my mind. The images of her in *Gestapo* hands..."

Jeremy took her in a comforting embrace. "I stopped off at Crockatt's office this morning on my way here. He received word from Fourcade that, so far, Jeannie is safe. Georges and the Druids will look out for her, and as you know, she's quite capable of looking out for herself."

Through bleary eyes and over a broken smile, Amélie gazed into his face. Then she patted his chest. "That's some small comfort," she said. "But Jeannie is still in danger, and I'm here, living in safety." She sat up straight and her eyes took on a determined glint. "I must go back. My job wasn't just to be her courier. It was to encourage her, remind her that real people care for and watch out for her."

For a moment, Jeremy was silent. Then he pulled Amélie to him. "All in good time," he said soothingly. "I know I can't talk you out of going back; I think you've done enough. You've put your life on the line and nearly lost it many times."

Amélie shook her head against his chest. "No more than thousands of other French Resistance fighters, and they're still there, Jeannie and Fourcade included."

Jeremy did not reply immediately. He continued to hold Amélie, and then he pulled back and looked around. "Where's Chantal?"

"She left for training this morning shortly after you took the train to London. A car came by to pick her up. She promised to come see us first chance." More tears formed in her eyes. "I'm worried about her too."

"She's learning to take care of herself," Jeremy replied. "That's got to be a good thing. She'll be as determined as you are to get back in the fight in France." He glanced around again. "I suppose Claire is still at work?" When Amélie nodded, he asked, "What about Timmy and the nanny?"

"They left on a walk just before you arrived. They should be back in an hour."

Jeremy pulled back and gazed at her. Then he nuzzled his face into her neck below one ear while murmuring, "Unbelievable that for once, we are alone."

Bletchley Park, England

Commander Travis showed up unexpectedly in front of Claire's desk, his expression urgent. "You must have heard something out of Berlin by now regarding Peenemünde?"

Claire looked up at him grimly and nodded. "Despite the headlines, the news is not all good." She stood and glanced across her section of women sitting at desks, studiously reading documents or adding to the clatter of typing machines. "I could come to your office to brief you."

"Let's take a walk outside instead."

The day was sunshiny when they entered the gardens. Despite the war and the rows of uniform huts ringing the old estate, the groundskeeper kept up the care of the property. The outside premises offered brief and pleasant escapes from the realities of war realized from the volume of usually grim decoded and analyzed messages.

"Let me have it," Travis said as soon as they were outside.

Claire took a deep breath. "Our bombers did a remarkable job—"

Travis interrupted her. "Spare me the preface. What's the bottom line."

Claire hesitated while she gathered her thoughts. "Of course there's consternation in Germany about how we found out about Peenemünde, but on the other hand, the high command had expected that we would learn about it sooner or later. That was evident by the level of defenses they mounted immediately."

"Yes, yes." Travis' impatience was becoming pronounced. "Get to the point."

"Yes, sir. Most of the German-reported casualties were in a labor camp—"

"Excuse me? I'm sure that wasn't a target."

"I wasn't aware of the mission ahead of time, so I can't speak to that. I can just tell you what's being reported across German communications."

"Understood," Travis said, checking his impatience. "The reconnaissance flight we sent over yesterday reported utter devastation, with huge bomb craters, destroyed facilities—"

"I'm sure the people on the ground felt the destruction, sir. The *Wehrmacht* reports that as many as six hundred slave-laborers were lost. We killed their chief rocket motors engineer, Dr. Walter Thiel, and their chief rocket manufacturing facility engineer, Dr. Erich Walther. We destroyed hundreds of homes in the neighborhood where the researchers and scientists live—"

"That was the main target," Travis interjected.

Startled, Claire's head jerked around. "Excuse me?"

Travis regarded her gravely. "I don't like the idea either, but the fact is that we were on the verge of being attacked massively by flying bombs and rockets."

"I see, sir." Claire shook her head. "What a war."

They strolled on through the garden in quiet for a time. Then Claire said, "May I ask what our casualties were?"

Travis grimaced. "Our losses were high, even with the steps we took to diminish them. We sent a raid by our RAF 8 Group Mosquitos into Berlin shortly before we hit Peenemünde as a diversion to draw the *Luftwaffe's* nightfighters there. We ordered another mission to bomb the local airbases where the nightfighters are stationed to destroy as many planes as possible and damage their runways."

He heaved a sigh. "Despite all that, we lost nearly seven percent of our aircraft. Most of that was in the third wave after the *Luftwaffe* figured out that the attack on Berlin was a diversion. Then they shot down twenty-nine of our bombers. We lost another thirteen from anti-aircraft fire over the target. Final numbers are still coming in, but that's over two hundred crewmembers captured, missing, or dead."

Claire contemplated that piece of information and exhaled. "So many young people gone." She was quiet a moment, and then said, "Here's another tidbit for you. We got word that, because of the success of the raid on Berlin, *Reichsmarshall* Goering was all over the *Luftwaffe* chief of staff, General Hans Jeschonnek. We had detected tension between the two for some time, and apparently, Jeschonnek finally had enough. Yesterday, after the raid, he shot himself."

Travis harrumphed. "The German armed forces were a professional lot for the most part. Now with the Nazi party, the *Gestapo*, and the SS transformed into a fighting force with allegiance to Hitler instead of Germany, and leadership jockeying to stay alive or curry favor, the best we can say about them is that they are still a formidable enemy. Have you heard anything about their recovery or how long that might take?"

Claire nodded. "I'm afraid the news is not good there either."

"Spit it out."

"The German high command expects to move its production facilities into tunnels in the Hartz Mountains. They think they'll be back in production within two months."

Travis heard the news with a stoic expression. "At least we delayed them for that much time. I'll need to get that upstairs. Get me the written report right away, will you?"

"Of course, sir."

35

September 9, 1943
Gulf of Salerno, Italy

Paul peered through the dark mist over the front edge of his landing craft. He saw nothing yet, but having nothing else to look at, he continued to stare in a concentrated daze while past events and those anticipated to unfold rolled through his mind.

Images of Ryan floated before his eyes. His throat and chest tightened as a bout of fresh grief overtook him. Always bookish while growing up, he had not entertained notions of girlfriends or falling in love mainly because members of the female sex bewildered him. He had been too awkward to speak to them, certain that he would say something ridiculous that would invite peals of laughter. Although they enchanted him, he refrained from pursuit of relations with any girl beyond friendliness. Until he had met Ryan.

She had been so beautiful, a woman with a China-doll face, and yet she had carried herself with a no-nonsense mien and conducted her duties with such efficiency in the RAF control bunkers that her superiors had taken note and promoted her rapidly.

It was in one of those control rooms that Paul had met Ryan. She had been his official escort for a study he had conducted for British intelligence. He had been taken with her immediately, and she with him.

He recalled vividly the last time he had seen her, back during the *blitz* when he drove her home. He had almost proposed that night, but refrained for fear of making her a widow, and she, sensing his intention, had said that she could not marry him while he was sent on special missions from which he might never again be heard.

A bombing raid over London had ended the evening for them. They had stayed in touch, but each time they tried to get together, the war had subverted their plans.

He shook his head sadly as he realized that two years had passed since then.

After that farewell, Ryan had joined the Air Transport Auxiliary, the organization that provided pilots, most of them women, to fly new and repaired airplanes of all types from factories and repair shops to the bases where the combat pilots would take delivery and enter them into military service. An inherently risky job was made even more dangerous by the possibility of being shot down by a German fighter. Paul had feared for her safety, and now she was gone, taken in exactly that way.

His throat caught and tears formed in his eyes. He wiped them away as he blocked visions of her in the cockpit of a burning Barracuda torpedo bomber plummeting into the ground.

He took a deep breath and forced his thinking to recent events. After seeing Operation Mincemeat through to completion two months earlier, he had requested to remain in theater and was assigned to General Mark Clark's Fifth Army headquarters, which was then planning for the invasion of Italy. Once there, he had immediately requested to be assigned to a combat unit. Hearing of his arrival in a routine briefing that included a list of replacements, the general sent for him to renew their acquaintance.

"Ike told me you were down here," Clark said, shaking Paul's hand and inviting him to sit down. "He said you were the guy who briefed him on Mincemeat."

"Guilty, sir. I'm glad it seems to have worked out."

"I'll say it worked out," Clark had responded with a sideways grin. "Casualties were extremely light on Sicily, the Italian soldiers couldn't surrender fast enough, and the Germans moved forces to Greece and the Balkans because they were sure the Sicilian invasion was a feint. The Soviets are romping over the *Wehrmacht* to the west of Kursk because of all the divisions the *führer* transferred south out of there. Lots of our boys, British and American, are alive because of your Major Martin."

He sprawled his long frame in a chair across from Paul and studied his face. "You've come a long way since we were together in Egypt. You've been in battle, Paul. I mean real live shooting going both ways, and you were in the thick of it. You've hardened. I can see it on your face."

"I don't like to think I was ever soft, sir."

Clark chuckled. "Paul, you're the consummate gentleman if there ever was one. But that's beside the point. I made a few inquiries and saw that you were in the thick of things as a battalion commander at Wadi Ziqzah in Libya."

"That was a special case, sir. They needed a cheerleader at the front with minimal verbal skills, and I fit the bill. And I was carried from the battle on a stretcher."

Clark let out a loud chuckle. "If that's the way you see it, so be it. Your superiors saw it otherwise, and Montgomery himself sent over a good word for you. Let me ask you this. What do you want to do now? You requested to stay in this theater."

"Put me back in a combat unit, sir."

Clark interlocked his fingers in front of his mouth and peered at Paul. "We've been in some tight corners together, Paul. In that sub taking us from Gibraltar to North Africa, then facing down the Vichy generals in Algiers. I'm personally fond of you, but I have to ask, do you have a death wish?"

A slight smile played on Paul's lips as he shook his head. "General Montgomery asked me the same thing." He looked directly into Clark's eyes. "On the contrary, General. As you intimated, I've been in close combat. I've seen men die next to me. I don't think they had exalted ideas of keeping the world safe for democracy, but they did care about their fellow soldiers, and I saw the haunted looks of the survivors burying their mates. I can't go back to staff work when I could and should be on the front with our soldiers carrying the fight to the enemy. If we fail, our countries die."

Clark sighed and took a moment to respond. "You know the prime minister takes a personal interest in your welfare and that of your family, out of some guilt he feels over the situation on Sark."

"I didn't ask for that, sir."

"My point is that you could be safe back in London, far away from the shooting."

"But not far away from my duty, which I would be shirking."

Clark inhaled deeply and let his breath out. "All right, Paul. You'll get your wish. We're preparing for Operation Avalanche. We're going to land in Italy somewhere about halfway up the coast. I have the British Tenth Corps in my command and the American Sixth Corps. I'll send you to be with your countrymen, with my recommendation added to Montgomery's for battalion command, if you like, when one becomes available."

"If you think I'm qualified, sir."

"You got on-the-job training and came out alive. Most of our officers and noncoms at all levels are having to learn as they go. That's the nature of all-out war. We're short of landing craft, so we're going in light." He heaved a sigh. "Most soldiers don't get to bow out of front-line duty. For you, it's now or never."

"Send me, sir."

"Consider it done." He shifted in his seat. "You mentioned going out on a stretcher. How are the wounds?"

"I'd almost forgotten I had them."

Clark smiled. "Stoic to a fault." He rose to his feet and crossed to a map. "We haven't yet decided where we're going in. Montgomery's army is headed to take Messina on the northeast tip of Sicily now, and once he's consolidated there, he'll cross onto Italy's toe and start pushing up its boot.

"We're still searching for where my army will go ashore. Somewhere farther north to block the route that the Germans in the south will have to use to vacate Italy. Between the Adriatic on their east, the Tyrrhenian Sea on their west, Montgomery's army in the south, and Fifth Army in the north, we should pretty much box them in. It'd be good if we don't have to fight them up the full length of Italy with all its mountains."

On July 25, only days after Paul's conversation with Clark and Italy's loss of Sicily to the Allies, King Victor Emanuel III ousted Mussolini as head of government. *Il Duce's* firing startled the world, particularly the ease with which it had been accomplished once Mussolini's propaganda machine had been rendered ineffective by underground leaflets and other outlawed information outlets.

Italians met the news with wild celebration, demonstrating in the streets their contempt for the man and fascism. The king kept the former dictator under house arrest, ordering the *carabinieri* to move him between undisclosed locations; and he installed General Pietro Badoglio, 1st Duke of Addis Abeba and 1st Marquess of Sabotino, to succeed Mussolini as prime minister.

Paul had seen photographs of Badoglio. The general was a septuagenarian who had opposed Mussolini during the dictator's early days in power and had been banished to minor roles as a result. Prior to then, he had served as the Italian army's chief of staff for fifteen years. Despite his age, he was trim and carried himself in dignified military form.

After reporting to Tenth Corps headquarters, Paul was assigned to 46th Division. Within days, he had found himself taking over command of an infantry battalion. Now, as the landing craft carrying him to Italy's shores bounced through turbulent waves, he continued staring into the night, oblivious to the boat's creaks and groans from the sea smacking heavy blows to its sides. He wondered about the vacuum that must have opened within Italian-German relations resulting from Mussolini's hostile departure. Certainly that event must have raised questions about Italy as a reliable partner among the Axis powers. But no news stories had yet surfaced indicating that the country had or would capitulate.

And then, only hours ago, a radio message from General Eisenhower transmitted publicly and played for all the troops announced that Italy had surrendered unconditionally to the Allies five days earlier. The surrender included the Italian fleet, fifth largest in the world, which until then had posed a significant threat to Allied shipping in the Mediterranean.

Eisenhower added a statement to his public proclamation. "All Italians who now act to help eject the German aggressor from Italian soil will have the assistance and support of the United Nations."

Immediately afterward, General Badoglio had also transmitted a message to the people of Italy, telling them, "The Italian forces will cease all acts of hostilities against the Anglo-American forces, wherever they may be. They will, however, oppose attacks of any other forces."

Paul had sat in wonder at the news, taking note that Eisenhower now referred to the Allies as the United Nations. "The Italians have switched sides," he muttered to himself in disbelief, seeing immediately the advantages just gained. No doubt, Montgomery's forces would move to take possession of air bases in southern Italy and prevent air strikes against shipping in the Mediterranean between Gibraltar and the Suez Canal. In the north of Italy, the Allies would gain access to air bases from which to launch attacks against Germany and its Allies. And across Europe and Asia, German divisions would be diverted and tied down to deal with a new threat on their southern flank.

The mood among the troops in the hold of the landing craft suddenly changed. It remained somber, but gained in buoyancy. Rather than sensing imminent death, anticipation spread that the assault might resemble the one on the south beaches of Sicily. The troops had expected those to be deadly, and to be sure, there had been over four thousand casualties, but that number was far below the pre-invasion estimate. For the most part, the invading Allied armies had come ashore unopposed. Now, as another Allied invasion force approached enemy shores, the soldiers in the first wave hoped that history would repeat in their favor.

A Few Hours Earlier, September 8, 1943
Bletchley Park, England

Claire hurried into Commander Travis' office without knocking. "This is urgent, sir, concerning an operation about to commence in Italy. Salerno, to be exact, just south of Naples."

"How would you know about that? It's a major assault up the coast of Italy, but it certainly has not been broadcast publicly."

"You are correct, sir, but less than half an hour ago, just as our invasion force reached the Gulf of Salerno, General Eisenhower announced Italy's unconditional surrender. Berlin had anticipated that might happen and had a contingency plan in place, Operation *Achse*. Since Mussolini's arrest two weeks ago, they've been on pins and needles. That's been heightened by Montgomery's army landing on Italy's southern tip five days ago.

"The high command just ordered their contingency plan put into operation in reaction to Eisenhower's statement. It entails disarming and imprisoning the Italian military, confiscating all their weapons and equipment, occupying their fortifications and air bases, and locking down control over the country.

"*Luftwaffe* spotter-planes had already reported the invasion fleet forming in the Tyrrhenian Sea and made sporadic dive-bomb attacks. The high command has since determined that our target is probably Naples, for the port facilities, and that our landing areas are the beaches south of there at Salerno.

"Messages are flying about from the high command to *Wehrmacht* forces near the area. Additional units are already ordered there, and the local forces are on full alert. They're in the process of taking over Italian defenses overlooking the Salerno beaches, including the big gun batteries, and they have mechanized units moving rapidly to buttress where needed. They plan on stopping the invasion at the bridgehead and holding our troops on the beaches until reinforcements arrive. When our men land, the *Wehrmacht* will be ready and waiting."

"Bloody hell!" Travis reached for his phone. "Surprise is blown. I must report this higher."

36

Gulf of Salerno, Italy

A spastic jolt caused by the landing craft hitting the front of a wave snapped Paul from his reverie. He looked at his watch and his stomach gripped as he realized that the sea voyage was nearing an end. Landing operations were imminent.

He ran the operation plan through his mind. The American Fourth Ranger Battalion would be the first to assault the beach at the north end of the landing zone, three miles west of Salerno on a small sandy strip in front of the village of Maiori. The Rangers would move nine kilometers inland, seize the high ground northwest of Maiori, set up protective fire on the left flank, and block the mountain passes coming down from the north.

The British Numbers 2 and 41 Commando units would go next, landing at Vietri, less than a mile west of Salerno. They would push into the highlands overlooking the town, establish contact with the Rangers farther to the west, and reinforce the blocking positions for routes from the north.

Once the left flank was secured, Tenth Corps would initiate the main assault on the beaches south of Salerno, landing at objectives Uncle, closest to the town, Sugar in the middle, and Roger on the south end. Meanwhile, the Sixth Corps would remain offshore until Salerno and the objectives farther north had been secured, and then land its troops on the far south end of the beach and head inland. They were to seize the high ground southeast of Salerno and disable the heavy guns emplaced there to protect against a waterborne invasion.

Paul's task was to land at Sugar and move his battalion north and west into Salerno. Once there, he would establish and hold a position to provide protection for the British Seventh Armored Division. That force would move ashore on already secured terrain and prepare to support the Tenth Corps in its advance on the main objective, the port of Naples.

An hour after midnight, the landing craft slowed to a drift, its previously roaring engine quieting to a low hum sufficient to maintain its position. Peering once again into the night, Paul sensed rather than saw the vast armada of four hundred fifty vessels spread along the Italian coast west of Salerno awaiting final orders.

Suddenly to his north, pinpoints of light sparkled along the coast, and the explosive force of heavy onshore guns launched rounds skyward. The projectiles arced and plunged toward the sea. Almost immediately, more powerful naval main guns unleashed a volley of return fire that tore along the shore with brief, lightning-like detonations. The dull thuds of massive artillery rounds hitting their marks were followed by thunderous claps resounding across the water. Then, small arms crackled.

The Rangers had landed.

More explosions east of the first landing charted a similar pattern of onshore artillery firing at Allied vessels followed by a withering naval bombardment of shore targets. Then relative quiet settled, broken by machine gun chatter.

The British commandos were ashore and moving into the high ground.

The landing craft's engine suddenly roared to life and gained a high pitch as the vessel raced toward the beach at full speed. Paul turned to look back across the faces of anxious soldiers, but all he could see were rows of eyes reflecting ambient light from their whites while looking his way, some terror-stricken, others determined, all wondering.

The craft slowed; sand scrunched along its bottom. Then the ramp dropped, and Paul ran down its wooden slope into the foaming water. He stopped at the bottom and stood off to one side, waving the soldiers ashore.

In staging areas and over maps while at sea, he and his company commanders had rehearsed their landing actions. Paul had also attended similar rehearsals held by company commanders with their lieutenants, noncoms, and troops. They were as ready as they would be, but he feared that the news of Italy's surrender only a few hours ago would alter the course of events for the worse.

The beach sloped up slightly and then broke into a wide, flat plain. Beyond it, to the northeast, two prominent pieces of high ground thrust into the sky, joined by a third to the southeast. Suddenly, from behind those hills, the sky lit up with shore guns aimed at the landing force. Almost immediately, they were answered by the concussive sound and accompanying thuds of naval main gun fire bracketing the enemy field artillery. Meanwhile, scores of landing vessels disgorged thousands of British and American soldiers on Salerno's southern beaches.

Paul headed toward his first rally point where he would meet up with his company commanders. Minutes passed while onshore and offshore guns exchanged fire and seared the air with the cloudy stench of ammunition. And then the enemy's guns became sporadic and finally quieted.

Paul's radio operator grabbed his sleeve. "Sir, an enemy mechanized unit is moving onto our objective."

Paul motioned that he had heard. Two of his company commanders arrived at his location, and he huddled with them behind a low berm. Then the second in command of the third company arrived. Paul could not see his face, but the slump of the officer's shoulders silhouetted against the light sand hinted at tragedy.

"Major Brown won't be coming," the young captain said.

"Is he—"

"Gone, sir. At the bottom of the ramp."

Paul inhaled. "Right. You've re-established your chain of command?"

"Roger, sir. Number one platoon commander has taken over my job as 2IC, and his platoon sergeant has taken his place. We're ready to move forward."

"Right." Paul addressed all three commanders. "Let me know when you're in your holding positions. We're exposed out here. Keep your men spread out, heads down, and behind anything that gives them cover and concealment. The units on our right at Roger Beach are moving out to take the high ground to our front on either side of Battipaglia. As soon as we get the word, we'll start our move northwest into Salerno. A German mechanized unit is moving in there now, so we can expect stiff resistance. We'll call in a naval bombardment before we go in. Get your companies together and radio in with accountability. I must know our strength before we maneuver."

Sweating and breathing hard, Paul jogged along the beach in the half-light of early dawn. The sand crunched under his feet as they sank in with each footfall, slowing forward movement despite the hurry. Hours had passed since the landing, but Salerno was now visible, with large buildings reduced to rubble under the annihilating storm of naval gunfire and stifling smoke. Despite greater resistance than had been expected, Paul's battalion moved steadily forward along the beach and approached the south end, where the bombed-out hulks of fine hotels lined a thoroughfare across from a seawall overlooking the beach.

Stopping to observe his companies' progress, Paul looked back along the distance he had come. Strung along the beach were a great many landing craft bringing in additional soldiers, and out to sea as far as he could see, more vessels were either inbound or outbound, shuttling the troops. Interspersed among them were LSTs in various stages of delivering tanks and other heavy vehicles ashore. Many more supply ships loitered offshore, awaiting word to move forward once the initial wave had met its objectives.

Paul halted the battalion just beyond the range of the enemy's crew-served weapons and then instructed his radio operator to send a message. Minutes later, the offshore guns responded, raining steel on the enemy positions that the battalion was about to assault.

When the smoke cleared, Paul radioed his company commanders to proceed to their objectives. Then he watched as troops filed past him, no longer fresh-faced. He called words of encouragement to them while blocking thoughts of the inevitable consequences of close-quarters combat.

37

Still out to sea and farther south along the same coastline, Zack Littlefield waited anxiously for the forward lurch of the landing craft and the roar of its motor signaling that his unit was heading to shore. Like elsewhere across the Allied invasion force, General Eisenhower's announcement of Italy's surrender had been celebrated with loud cheers and raised spirits. Regardless, the soldiers in Zack's unit were apprehensive as they approached the Salerno coast and readied themselves for the violent chaos of battle.

As morning twilight faded and the battle raged to the north, they waited in their boats, pondering the ebb and flow of actions on the ground. Zack increasingly sensed that the momentum had shifted in favor of the Germans, based on his observation of the Allied force afloat. He had noticed that the number of landing craft, appearing as tiny dots on the sea's surface heading to the beach in the north of the bay, had slowed. Meanwhile, the volume of big guns firing from both naval and enemy onshore batteries had increased, with more building up from the enemy. But how could that be if the Italians had surrendered?

His inescapable conclusion was that the Germans were in the fight. There would be no easy walk out of the surf such as he had experienced at

Sicily. When he went ashore this time, the *Wehrmacht* was the force that he and his comrades would face.

While he watched, *Luftwaffe* fighters screamed in, strafing troops on the beach and the landing craft offshore, accompanied by Stuka dive-bombers targeting the ships. Some were chased away by Allied fighters; others engaged in aerial dogfights resulting in spectacular crashes into the sea or onto the beach. Zack saw one of the downed enemy fighters strike Allied troops when it hit the ground.

Then, late in the afternoon, the engine rumbled, the platoon leader alerted the platoon sergeant, the squad leaders rousted the few who managed to doze during the distant melee, and the landing craft leaped forward, thrashing through the waves at high speed. From out to sea behind them, the big main guns on the cruisers and destroyers once more let loose with a continuous barrage that hissed overhead to drop with concussive effect far beyond the landing site. Then the vessel's engine shut off, its momentum shoved the vessel closer in, the ramp dropped, and the soldiers rushed into the surf and made for shore.

Zack knew that the 36th Division, the unit to which he was assigned, was the only element of Sixth Corps that would come ashore today. The battalions in the brigade he was part of had been tasked with seizing the inland high ground at the south end of the beach and securing it to protect the right flank of the main assault force.

Because of his actions on Sicily, Zack now led a squad. His company's objective was the center of the high ground, and the specific mission of doing that had fallen to the platoon that Zack's squad belonged to. Zack was to lead his squad to the center of that hill mass and secure its peak.

As he ran for the beach, he pivoted to see his assistant squad leader directing the three-member machine gun team while the remaining seven soldiers of his squad moved swiftly behind Zack toward scarce cover. The platoon sergeant was already on the beach with the platoon leader.

Glancing ahead, Zack saw the hilltop he was to take. With no time for dread, he sized up his mission against the physical objective. It looked like the aerial recon photos he had studied, but much worse when seen life-size in three dimensions. The slopes were steep and barren, and imposing stone bluffs crowned its crest. Although his view from the front did not reveal a long stone spine that protruded through the surface and trailed to the southeast, he had noticed it from the photos, making the ridge even more fearsome to assault.

Agricultural fields lay between the beach and the base of the hill, and scrub brush grew up the sides beyond, but farther the ground was steep and bare. The peak rose two hundred feet above its base, and green ground-cover coated the upper portion to where the cliffs broke through.

After conferring with the platoon sergeant, Zack met with his assistant squad leader. He spoke rapidly between gasps for air. "Have we lost anyone yet?"

Receiving a negative response from the winded soldier, Lance briefed him. "Catch your breath. We're going straight in. The navy will keep up their barrage until we're on the right side of that hill. Air support is on its way to suppress ground forces.

"Word's come down that the Krauts took over and threw the Italians in prison."

Both team leaders groaned. Zack held up his hand. "We don't have time for that. The Germans are manning the heavy guns now, and they're moving more mechanized units into the area. But they haven't got them here yet. We're supposed to beat them to the punch. Have we got our machine guns from the weapons squad?"

"Roger that."

"We got 'em."

"Make sure everyone checks their weapons and get your teams ready. We'll move out in five for that Catholic sanctuary we saw on the map, Madonna del Granato. We'll move to the right of it and hold there until the navy and the air corps soften up the objective."

The rapid march to the bottom of the hill had been harrowing. The terrain consisted of furrowed farmland, much of it gone to ruin, hardscrabble unused property, and a few hard-surface roadways. Because a landing had not been expected in this area, and because the Italians did not have their hearts in the fight, landmines had been deemed an unlikely threat. Regardless, the possibility still existed, and it slowed the squad's advance. Zack monitored the progress of the units to his right and left to be sure his element stayed abreast of them. Within an hour, his men had covered the distance to Madonna del Granato at the base of the hill.

They reached a road in sight of the sanctuary and proceeded to cross it in tactical formation, one man at a time, until the far side was secure and all of Zack's squad members were across. So far, they had received no incoming fire, though sounds of the battle on the north end of the beach near Salerno indicated that it still raged.

On the other side of the road, the hill rose gently at first, but then it towered steeply into the sky, its rocky crest forming a distinct divide between the right and left side. Once across the road, Zack told his squad leaders, "Spread your men out and take cover." Then he instructed the radio operator next to him, "Call it in."

Ordinarily, an SCR-536 radio would not be assigned below company headquarters level. However, realizing the prominence of the objective and that, should Zack's squad reach their objective, they would likely encounter an immediate and furious counterattack, the company commander had assigned one to Zack with an operator. Zack's transmission would go directly to the commander's radioman who had instructions to relay on up the chain to battalion. The way had been cleared for immediate re-transmission to brigade, and on up to a joint assault signal controller who would call to the warships for the pre-positioned targets.

The soldier acknowledged Zack's order, pressed a button on his radio, and spoke into the mic. Minutes later, a fusillade of navy guns released their fury, their rounds hissing through the air and pounding the crest of the hill with mind-numbing concussions. The bombardment continued for nearly sixty minutes and then ceased.

Almost immediately, the high-pitched sound of dive-bombers and fighters filled the air as wave after wave of Allied aircraft flew over the objective dropping ordnance, firing machine guns, and circling around for additional runs. When they had finished, Zack called out, "Let's go!"

They tacked around to the right side of the hill where the climbing was steeper, but so far, no enemy artillery, crew-served weapons, or small-arms fire had been seen or heard. Already strained muscles screamed as Zack

LEE JACKSON

started up the hill, contouring to the right and then zigzagging to the left to come up behind the crest.

Looking back to see the progress of his teams and the squad that would protect the left flank, he saw his men struggling. Feet slid, knees scraped on jagged rocks, and heavy equipment wore them down, but they continued to climb, and as the sun accelerated its descent in the west, they arrived on their objective, unopposed.

"Dig in," Zack ordered his team leaders. "The counterattack is bound to come."

38

November 20, 1943
Over Betio Island, Tarawa Atoll, Pacific Ocean

Dawn broke golden against a deepening blue sky as Commander Josh Littlefield streaked across the sky in his SBD-5 Dauntless dive-bomber over the tiny island that had emerged as a major obstacle to Admiral Nimitz' developing strategy of hopping US forces from island to island across the Pacific in a westward campaign intended to finally threaten Japan's homeland. From twenty-five thousand feet, Josh dipped his aircraft's nose and continued pushing his stick down until he dived at a seventy-degree angle, targeting Betio, a tiny speck of land two miles long with barely enough land mass to support a Japanese airfield. Located within the V-shaped sliver of Tarawa Atoll pointing east among the Gilbert Islands, Betio was hundreds of miles from anywhere of significance.

To his left and slightly behind him, Josh's wingman followed, and behind them Josh's entire squadron of Dauntlesses screamed toward earth to deliver a repeat salvo that had been ongoing for half an hour by other squadrons. For four hours prior to the air assault, Admiral Spruance's Fifth Fleet, holding ten miles offshore, had delivered barrage after barrage of high-explosive bombs.

Wispy smoke rose to meet the dive-bombers as they descended and then thickened as the aircraft converged on the island where tons of ordnance had already exploded on the one-half-square mile of what had been a paradise island bounded by white coral reefs and azure waters. At its center, but now invisible to Josh for the smoke, was the airfield that the Imperial Japanese Navy had built a year earlier and was the reason for visiting such violence on an otherwise insignificant spot in the vast Pacific Ocean.

Josh's aircraft thundered down, rocking and vibrating from the stresses of compacting air resistance at stirring velocities. He raised his dive flaps to dampen the turbulence of wind rushing over his wings and prepared for the G-forces his body would absorb when he pulled out of the dive.

He aimed at the island's center, easily identified by the white coral reef surrounding the island and the full cloud of smoke rising to meet him under the blue sky. His altimeter on the instrument panel spun counter-clockwise as the aircraft dived lower and lower. He glanced at the indicator intermittently, checked his floating ball, and pressed on his right pedal slightly to adjust his flight attitude.

At somewhere between two thousand and fifteen hundred feet, he pulled the lever to release his bomb. The cradle that held it descended below his front landing gear to a locked position where the projectile could not hit the aircraft as it was released.

Explosions from anti-aircraft gunfire buffeted the Dauntless.

The bomb dropped, and the plane's nose swung up from the weight loss. Josh immediately pulled back on his stick and stomped on his left pedal while sucking in air and simultaneously tucking his knees into his stomach to force oxygen into his brain against the effects of G-forces.

Momentum carried the aircraft lower even as Josh's adjustments to power and flight controls forced the Dauntless to level out in a tight arc within feet of the frothing ocean and begin climbing into the heavens. Briefly, Josh's mind replayed the calamity of his first such maneuver a year earlier at the Battle of Midway, when his shot-up aircraft's engine had sputtered, died, and the plane had dropped into the ocean. Only the quick wits of Josh's gunner and the proximity of a Catalina rescue plane had saved him from a watery grave.

He blocked the memory, concentrating his attention on maneuvering out of immediate danger and watching the skies for any sign of Japanese Zeroes sent in to support the island's defenses. Within minutes, he was under the Third Fleet's air defense umbrella and headed toward a roiling touchdown aboard the carrier, USS *Essex*.

Josh's request to return to the Pacific theater had been granted, but on arrival from Algeria, he had found that Admiral Nimitz had devised a unique command structure to deal with a new concept of operations in the Pacific. The idea was to attack in succession the island groups held by the Japanese, always heading west, with the ultimate target being Japan.

To accomplish his aim, Nimitz alternated command of the US fleet in the South Pacific between the crusty commander of the area, Admiral "Bull" Halsey, and Admiral Spruance. While Halsey commanded the fleet, it was designated the US Third Fleet, and when Spruance took over, it was re-designated as the US Fifth Fleet. While one of the two commanders was in attack mode, the other was planning the next operation. The arrangement would receive its first test in Operation Galvanic during the battles for Makin and Tarawa.

Josh further discovered, on arrival back in theater, that he had been assigned to the *Essex* to command a squadron of Dauntless dive bombers. He glanced over his shoulder to try to catch a glimpse of his command, but he was in a steep ascent and could make out the noses of only one of his planes, his wingman.

Now he flew a circuitous route between Tarawa and the fleet to the point where he would begin his descent. Waggling his wings, he called for an accountability check, and was pleased to learn that he had lost no aircraft or pilots.

With Tarawa being a dot on the horizon behind him, the fleet appeared ahead. The sheer size of it awed him. It consisted of more than two hundred ships, including seventeen aircraft carriers, twelve battleships, sixty-six destroyers, and thirty-six types of transport with more than a hundred and seventeen tons of cargo. It also carried thirty-five thousand

American men with the Second Marine Division and units of the Army's Twenty-Seventh Infantry Division.

Navy intelligence had estimated that the Japanese had stationed forty-five hundred men on Tarawa, including twelve hundred engineers who had spent a year building the island's defenses. Indeed, decoded messages had revealed Admiral Shibazaki bragging about the impregnability of the fortress he had designed, built, and now commanded.

Josh had wondered about the rationale for pouring so much US lethal power into one tiny island far removed from anywhere, but as he sat in pre-mission briefings, he understood. The longer-term objective was to seize the Mariannas as part of Nimitz' island-hopping strategy, closing in on Japan itself. To do that, the Allies must first take the Marshall Islands. However, Tarawa blocked the communications and supply lines between the Marshalls and Pacific Fleet headquarters at Pearl Harbor. Thus it became the crucial target of the first US offensive at the beginning of the Central Pacific campaign.

Despite Shibazaki's bravado, naval intelligence assured that the island was lightly defended and should present little resistance. The coral reef, prohibiting a successful landing at low tide, would be covered with six feet of water during high tide, deep enough to allow the wooden Higgins landing craft to maneuver directly onto the beach.

As Josh and his squadron drew closer to the fleet, he gaped at the scene far below. Large transport ships had disgorged hundreds of Higgins boats. Many of those were filled with Marines and circling in a wide holding pattern, creating an almost perfect circle of white wakes on the blue ocean. The vessels held the pattern while they waited for still more boats loaded with Marine infantrymen to join them.

When the formation was complete, the attack would be ordered. Then, the landing craft would deploy en masse to Betio, and eighteen thousand Marines would assault in successive waves.

Josh led his squadron in a wide berth around the fleet out of the path of the renewed naval bombardment. The thunderous explosions of the battleships' and destroyers' main guns resounded even at this altitude, and became louder as the Dauntlesses descended to the stern of the aircraft carrier.

Josh lined up on the steel deck, checked the guidelines painted on the ship's deck, and then kept his eyes glued to a signal man stationed near the tail end. From this distance, the man was barely visible, but in each hand, he held round, bright, red and white placards that he used to signal small adjustments. Josh adjusted his aircraft's attitude to the signalman's motions. If the signalman saw that the landing could not be made safely, he would wave Josh off to circle for another attempt.

Fortunately, Josh touched down safely, and he immediately felt a jerk as an extended hook on the rear of his Dauntless caught on one of three arresting wires and brought him to a swift and sudden halt. Following a deck crewman's gestures, he taxied out of the way, waited for the deck crew to signal that they had secured the plane and that he could exit safely, and climbed down from the cockpit in time to watch the last of his squadron fly in without incident.

Josh made his way straight to the operations room to be debriefed and to gain an update on the current situation. He found that chaos abounded.

Owing to high winds, the air campaign had started at 06:15, half an hour late. The troop transports had arrived on time at midnight, and at 03:00 hours, they began loading the Marines.

The assault had been scheduled to hit the beach at 08:30. However, the late air attack had not been communicated to the amphibious force, and thus, rather than softening up the island, it had instead alerted the Japanese that an assault was imminent and had given them time to adjust their defenses.

Meanwhile, the first Higgins boats with their Marines had begun their ninety-minute journey across the tossing Pacific stretch to Tarawa, followed by wave after wave of the wooden landing vessels. Once the first Marines had been put on shore, the Higgins boat drivers were to back away from the shore and return to transport more fighters to the battle.

During the naval bombardment, the radios were knocked out of commission temporarily aboard the *Maryland*, the ship that was to commence supporting fires during the assault. While her crews worked to make repairs, the assault was delayed for another half hour, leaving the Japanese more time to prepare.

Shortly afterward, radio word came that the first Marine scout-snipers and combat engineers had reached a five-hundred-yard-long pier stretching past the coral reefs. "Ground force coming under enemy fire," a disembodied voice intoned over a speaker in the *Essex* operations room.

All voices stopped in mid-conversation and all action ceased momentarily in the tight quarters as ears strained to listen.

Josh had taken a seat out of the center of activity to listen and watch. Although the custom was to keep unnecessary personnel out of the operations room, Josh was known as an outstanding pilot, operations officer, and now squadron leader who had seen ground action on Guadalcanal and in the European theater, so he was allowed leeway. He was amazed when he overheard two officers in conversation. "That's four million tons of ammunition dropped on that island," one of them said. "This operation should be a cakewalk."

Josh wondered momentarily if there was any such thing as an easy target in warfare. "There's skill, and there's luck," he had murmured to himself while recalling the Japanese soldier who had been impaled on Josh's bayonet at Guadalcanal. Josh had been trained as a pilot, not a Marine infantryman. "If I have to choose between the two, I'll take luck."

He had just grabbed a fresh cup of coffee and raised it to his lips when the voice came over the loudspeaker. He swung his head around to hear, sloshing the hot liquid and burning his lips.

"Damage from air and naval bombardments minimal," the voice said. "Enemy forces reinforced on landing side of Betio."

A collective groan rose up across the room.

"Landing craft caught on coral reefs hundreds of yards from shore. Enemy fire heavy. Shore guns firing out to sea. Expect incoming."

A pall hung over the room as the implications sank in, confirmed by the next message over the loudspeaker. "Marines wading to shore in chest-high water under heavy machine gun fire. No choice. No cover."

39

First Lieutenant William Hawkins, commanding officer of the scout-sniper platoon attached to the Second Marine Division, led the unit to first hit shore on Betio at Green Beach. He did it from the front, the first man to clamber the length of the five-hundred-yard-long pier jutting into the ocean. He was immediately hit by a piece of shrapnel, but he shrugged it off and continued, urging his men forward despite the blistering wall of bullets that met them long before clearing the jetty. Days earlier while aboard his transport ship, he had told a war correspondent, Robert Sherrod of *Time Magazine*, "I'll pit my platoon against any company of soldiers in the world, and we'll win."

The sea water already ran red from Marine casualties, and Hawkins wondered how the navy weathermen had forecast the tides so wrong. As Hawkins stole a glance out to sea, he saw hundreds of Marines scattered across a wide area from the water's edge. Instead of being carried to shore on the Higgins boats, they were trudging in chest-high water, already shot up and wounded, or dead. Wrecked landing craft dotted the edge of the white coral protruding through the surface.

No stranger to challenges, Hawkins had suffered extreme burns as an infant when a neighbor had inadvertently spilled boiling water on his legs. His injuries had taken more than a year to heal, and thus, he had been late in learning to walk.

His mother had refused to surrender to circumstance and raised him to surmount challenges, a philosophy that served her and her son well; Hawkins' father had died when the boy was eight years old. Prior to the elder Hawkins' death, the family had moved to El Paso, Texas. After the tragedy, Mrs. Hawkins had worked as a secretary at her son's school, and he delivered newspapers and took other odd jobs including bellhop, ranch hand, and railroad laborer. Despite the hardships, the younger Hawkins skipped fifth grade and went on to graduate from high school with honors, including a scholarship to the Texas School of Mines where he majored in engineering.

Pearl Harbor had prompted Hawkins to enlist in the military services, but because the scars on his legs were so horrendous, he was declined by both the army and navy. However, less than a month after the surprise attack, he was accepted into the Marines as a private. After basic, he had shipped into the Pacific, but his tenacity, leadership skills, and combat performance at Guadalcanal had seen him rise rapidly, culminating in a battlefield promotion to second lieutenant just over a year ago. In the interim, having proven himself as a combat leader yet again, he was once more promoted, to first lieutenant.

Now, as Hawkins surveyed the carnage erupting with every volley of machine gun fire, he saw the unspoken reality that every one of the Marines struggling ashore must have recognized: either they go back into the ocean and drown or they proceed into searing enemy fire with only a slight chance of surviving. Without the ability to return fire, struggling in the water hundreds of yards offshore on sharp coral, weighted down by weapons, ammunition, rations, grenades, entrenching tools, and other equipment essential to combat success, they proceeded in water turned red with the blood of their comrades. Men writhed in pain, with no aid close by. Others moaned as life drained from them, and still more were floating corpses.

"Let's go," Hawkins yelled above the din, and he led his men behind the slight cover offered by the long pier. After many minutes of struggling over the sharp coral edges, he reached the shore and surveyed the ground ahead.

The flat terrain above the water's edge offered neither cover nor concealment, but observing the Japanese direction of fire and seeing that the volume of gunfire created its own smokescreen, Hawkins grabbed each of his squad leaders by their shoulders and pointed them in a direction at the left flank. They further directed their respective fireteam leaders, and then the platoon fanned out, crawling on their bellies when necessary, taking the risk of low sprints when possible, and holding their fire to avoid being spotted.

Hawkins once again took the lead in maneuvering forward, hardening himself not to look at the beach as he went, knowing that the massacre continued and that the Marines in the water were helpless to save themselves except by proceeding into the withering hail of bullets.

After an hour of hugging the ground while maneuvering, Hawkins' platoon reached a coconut grove that provided not only cover and concealment but also access to platforms from which his snipers could pick out targets. Furthermore, the ground had a slight slope, at the top of which was a Japanese machine gun nest. The enemy gunners faced to the left of their own front, away from the scouts who had thus far not been detected.

The lieutenant signaled to his first squad leader by holding up three fingers. Moments later, three Marines squatted next to him. He greeted them with a gritty grin. "I see your boss sent the best."

They nodded with grim reserve in their eyes.

"You," Hawkins said, pointing at one, "cover from the right."

"You"—he pointed to another—"cover from the left."

"You," he told the third. "Cover me, up the center."

The Marine gave him a broken smile. "I guess that makes me the best of the best."

"Or you need more babysitting," one of his comrades shot back.

"Time to go, gents," Hawkins said. He turned back to the first squad leader. "If we don't come back, you're in charge. Take out as many of these machine gun nests as you can find." Then he added, "We'll take the objective and go looking for the next one. You'll take over this one and give our guys on the beach some covering fire."

Turning to his selected three Marines, he ordered, "Let's move. Take your time. Make your shots count, and don't forget to use your grenades."

The four Marines crept through the sand, placing their feet carefully with as little sound as possible while keeping the Japanese defensive position in sight. At one point, Hawkins signaled to the first Marine and pointed out the approach he should take to the objective. "Go in when you hear our fire," he instructed. Then he and the two remaining Marines moved on. Hawkins chose another position within sight of the machine gun nest and stationed his second scout there. "I'll be right back," he whispered. "You'll overwatch me when I go forward."

Then he took the third man and positioned him on the left flank with the simple instruction, "You know what to do."

Minutes later, having moved back to the center and keeping his head down, he crawled toward the nest. It was a concrete structure built into the ground and surrounded by a dirt berm. Firing holes with wide angles of view had been built into the walls, but no weapons protruded on this side.

The loud thump-thump-thump of heavy automatic fire continued, but from his angle, Hawkins could only imagine the bodies that must still be falling on the coral. He wondered momentarily if anyone else had made it to the beach.

Slowly, he inched up the rise, pausing when a lull in the machine gun fire occurred. He started again when it reached full volume.

Arriving undetected at the base of the berm, he looked back the way he had come and saw that his men had hidden themselves well. They were out of sight.

As his heart raced, he glanced up at the wall. It was low, only three feet high above the ridge. He waited, sweat streaming down the side of his face. For the first time, he felt the pain of his shrapnel wound.

The guns inside the nest stopped firing. He wrapped himself against the back wall in case any enemy peered through a rear firing hole, and he listened as the crew inside the nest reloaded their weapons.

He waited, hearing the clink of metal as Japanese soldiers fed a band of ammunition across the gun's receiver. Then the lid slammed down and one of the Japs pulled the charging handle.

Without waiting for them to start firing, Hawkins leaped to his feet, thrust his rifle through a firing port, took aim at a soldier preparing to fire, and shot. The man crumpled.

With surprise still on his side, Hawkins sprang to full height and shot again.

A second soldier fell as he was about to fire on American Marines struggling through the coral.

Hawkins dispatched the third and then shot the fourth just as the man had trained a pistol on him.

Seconds later, Hawkins' three comrades vaulted into the nest. Looking around, the first one remarked, "Geez, sir, you could've saved some for us."

"No time for kidding," Hawkins retorted. "Figure out how to operate those guns and get some covering fire going along the beach. American Marines are getting killed out there."

The first squad leader arrived. "Get your security out," Hawkins told him. He indicated the three Marines who had accompanied him. "I'm keeping these guys."

"Aw, c'mon, sir," one complained facetiously. "Us again?"

Hawkins smirked. "You're the only ones I got with experience at this."

Turning back to the squad leader, he instructed, "When Stan gets here, pass along to him to follow that way." He pointed down the beach to his left. "Tell him to be prepared to man the next machine gun nest. Tell Mike that he'll get the third one."

Then, turning to his selected three Marines, he said, "We got some huntin' to do. Let's go."

40

Navy Lieutenant (jg) Edward Heimberger viewed the massacre along Green Beach in shock, unable to believe his eyes. Driving an empty salvage boat, he had followed the first wave of Marines, had seen their Higgins boats founder on the reef, and now watched in dismay as men he knew struggled forward in chest-high surf, rifles held high to keep them dry, ducking under the water when thick gunfire hissed by them and plunged below the surface with soft whispers.

Heimberger was a salvage officer. His job was to deliver a load of Marines to the shore, collect re-useable supplies, and salvage damaged equipment that could be repaired. Now, as he watched in horror, dead and wounded Marines by the hundreds floated in the water, and close to the beach, more fell as relentless gunfire mowed them down. Worse still, the tide had begun to rise, further imperiling Marines struggling to the beach under the weight of their heavy equipment.

Heimberger saw a Marine foundering, trying desperately to keep his head above water while blood poured from a shoulder wound. The lieutenant revved his engine and headed closer, careful not to cross over the jagged coral reef. He maneuvered alongside the stricken Marine and doused his engine. Then, as quickly and gently as possible, he pulled the man to the relative safety of the vessel.

Nearby, healthy Marines, seeing his actions, called to him. "Bring back more rifles and ammo. Ours are getting waterlogged. Radios too."

"I'll be back," Heimberger called to them. "Keep up your spirits." Then he turned his attention to the wounded man. "You'll be all right," he said in a soothing voice. "That's a surface wound. I'll get you back to the ship where the medics will patch you up."

He grabbed a blanket from his pilot's cabin and covered the man to prevent shock. That done, Heimberger searched across the water for the next Marine needing rescue. Meanwhile, the Japanese guns continued to blaze against the struggling invasion force.

Heimberger had already established a working relationship with US Army intelligence prior to America's entry into the war. For months, he had worked as a circus clown and trapeze artist in Mexico, reporting on the comings and goings of German submarines frequenting Mexican ports.

Slightly above average height, he bore a ready smile on a square-jawed face with long dimples on each cheek and brown eyes under a full head of blond hair. Rumor among the ship's crew was that he had acted in films opposite an up-and-coming actor named Ronald Reagan and other notable celebrities, but Heimberger avoided the subject, so most of his comrades gave the claim little credence, ascribing its origin to unusual good looks that could have made him a Hollywood star.

Nearly a year after Pearl Harbor, he had enlisted in the Navy. A few months later he was discharged to re-enter the US Navy Reserves as a commissioned officer and assigned as a coxswain aboard the USS *Sheridan*, an Ormsby-class attack transport ship. In that capacity, he had deployed behind the first wave of troops to strike at Tarawa.

Now, as his eyes swept the water, he spotted another Marine going under its surface and bobbing up again, gasping for air. Blood coated the water around him from a head wound. Heimberger pointed his landing craft toward the man, and a few minutes later, after accomplishing his second rescue, he looked for his next one.

In the operations room aboard the *Essex*, Josh's consternation rose to peak levels as he monitored commo traffic that had been pouring in. Clearly far from a cakewalk, the battle on Tarawa was going badly; the Japanese garrison was far stronger and better entrenched than had been anticipated. Then radio reports became sporadic as equipment carried by the invasion force was soaked.

"How in hell did we get the tide so wrong?" he demanded in exasperation of no one in particular.

A passing junior officer overhead him. "It's a neap tide, sir."

"A what?" Josh glared at the officer, bewildered. "What is a neap tide?"

"It's when the gravitational pull of the moon and the sun cancel each other. That would have been a high tide this morning but for the sun pulling in the opposite direction. It's a rare event, but it happens."

"And we didn't anticipate it," Josh muttered. He glanced at the officer. "Thanks."

For an instant, Josh thought about his earlier ruminations on the competing values of luck and skill. "Ya need both," he muttered.

Then he hurried over to the operations officer, who was studying a wall map with several subordinates. "Send my squadron back up," Josh interrupted. His eyes determined, his voice urgent, he added, "Those ground troops need close air support."

The operations officer spun around and stared at him. "I know what those troops need, Commander, but dive-bombers ain't it. You know that.

"We've managed to get a few Marines onshore, and some of them are on or near Japanese positions. Your dive-bombers start their runs from thousands of feet in the air. You won't be able to identify where you should strike and where you should leave alone."

"Then put me in a Hellcat, sir. That's what I flew before the Dauntless. We've had wounded pilots make it back to the ship by now with flight-worthy planes."

"You flew an earlier version with a gunner sitting behind you. In the model upstairs now, you'd be flying solo."

"With guns at my fingertips, sir. I've familiarized on the F6F. I know how to fly her and use her weapons."

The operations officer still hesitated.

"Put me in," Josh pleaded. "I'll follow any squadron commander's orders. We can strafe the hell out of the Japanese."

"Or get shot down by anti-aircraft fire or Zeroes," the operations officer muttered, but he had listened with a thoughtful though non-committal frown.

"Sir, those Marines out there need every bit of our support—"

"All right, go. There's a pieced-together squadron forming on deck now. We'll call upstairs to let them know you're coming."

The rush of adrenaline Josh experienced as he climbed into the cockpit of a Hellcat was tempered by the sight of hastily wiped-off blood droplets smeared across his instrument panel. He wondered how his predecessor had been wounded, but had no time to find out. He would have to rely on the judgment of the deck crew that the fighter was airworthy.

He had only a few minutes to take stock of his cockpit, but he had studied the aircraft, sat in them, and had even coaxed a reluctant deck crew supervisor to let him fly in one before leaving port. This F6F-5 was designed to take damage and return a pilot to his carrier. The windshield was bullet-resistant and its oil tank and cooler were surrounded with armor, as was the entire cockpit and the self-sealing fuel tank.

Josh fingered the trigger of six .50 cal M2/AN Browning air-cooled machine guns. His ammunition load included four hundred rounds per gun.

As he ignited the engine and the propeller spun to invisibility, he noted with approval the throaty roar of the Wright R-2800-10W engine under a streamlined cowling. His mental run-down of other modifications was interrupted by the signal from the deck crew to taxi into position.

Twenty minutes later and high over the ocean, he made out the flat wedge shape of Betio. A long line of rising smoke marked the dividing line between friend and foe.

Along the rim of white coral where it broke into the deep ocean, numerous landing craft rested in various positions, some facing the beach, others tossed at odd angles, some pierced by sharp coral, all immobile and easy targets.

Then, to his front right, a dot appeared on the horizon, zooming in from the west. As it approached, he identified the distinctive shape of a Zero, confirmed by a Rising Sun insignia on its side. Flying in from the east, the thrown-together US squadron had the advantage of the mid-morning sun at its back and shimmering off the water.

"Red Leader," he called on the radio, "lone bandit at two o'clock low, heading this way. He appears blind to us."

"Roger. You spotted him. He's yours. Red Team, fan out and climb. Watch for others. Looks like a strafing run."

"Roger," Josh replied. "Red Three out."

He pulled back hard on the stick and rolled to his right, belly up, to keep the Zero in sight as he climbed into the sun. As Josh reached his zenith and reversed his maneuver into a dive, the Hellcat's nose obscured his view momentarily.

Josh anticipated his target's direction and speed and quickly re-acquired the Zero. Given the enemy's obvious objective, a strafing run against the stranded Marines, he descended at thunderous speed.

"Red Three, more bandits on the horizon, in a line."

Josh recognized Red Leader's voice and squawked his mic to acknowledge.

"Hit your target from above," Red Leader transmitted. "If you come on a line behind him, you'll be the target."

"Roger. Too late. Keep his buddies off of me."

On impulse, Josh pushed his nose into a steeper dive. He had no doubt that the Zero's pilot had been radioed that a Hellcat was on his tail, because suddenly, the enemy fighter jinked erratically while still closing in on the beach.

Josh pulled his throttle wide open and pushed his stick to dive beyond the maximum safe angle. The plane rattled and shook, but he held steady until he had descended below the path the Zero must take if the pilot intended to hit targets on the beach.

Josh pulled hard on the stick, set his knees, and controlled his breathing to absorb G-forces, then climbed up from under the Zero's expected flight path. It was to the left of where Josh had expected it to be, but a slight adjustment to the stick and pedals put him on course to intercept.

Suddenly, Josh heard metallic plinking on his right wing. Another Zero must be shooting from above and behind him. He rolled left while maintaining his trajectory, leveled out momentarily to get his target in view again, and then jinked sporadically while headed in the same general direction.

"Red Three, we got the one behind you. You've got time to get your bogey. We're on his buddies."

Josh squawked his mic again to acknowledge. Sweat streamed from his forehead and into his eyes, stinging them. He wiped the salty moisture away and steadied his flight. The Zero was now above him and headed straight for the beach, less than two miles away.

The Zero's nose dipped, and it picked up speed. *He knows the jig is up, and he's all in for a suicide run. It's now or never.*

Josh leveled his wings on the expected flight path. Within seconds, the Zero descended ahead of him, passing in front of his gunsights. Josh opened up with a full volley from his guns and continued short bursts as he dipped the Hellcat's nose and pursued.

Smoke trailed from the Zero, and it spiraled earthward, obviously out of control, plunging into the surf with a great splash. Josh rolled to his left to see, but it had already dipped below the surface.

"That's a kill," Red Leader called. "You're trailing smoke. Head for home."

"No can do," Josh replied, glancing at his fuel gauge. "I'm flying on fumes and draining fast. I burned a lot with those maneuvers, and I think I caught a burst that penetrated the gas tank. I won't make it back to the ship."

"Roger. Ditch. Look, there's a guy in a Higgins boat down there. He might be a little crazy, cuz he's coming under fire himself, but he's circling around in front of the beach and picking up wounded. See if you can settle down close to him, but keep a distance from the shore. No sense in making yourself another casualty."

"Roger. I think I see him. He's out about five hundred yards from the beach and picking up a guy now."

"That's him. Fly over the top of him as close as you can, then head out a little farther. He'll see you, but we'll radio in just to be sure. We've held off the Japs at your rear. They won't bother you."

"Roger. Out."

Josh descended to less than forty feet, banked right, and lined up on the landing craft that Red Leader had mentioned. Waggling his wings, he headed straight for it, and when he could see the operator's face, he banked left and headed back out to sea.

The small fighter skimmed the choppy water, paralleling shallow wave-tops and troughs. Josh fed in power slightly, raised his nose, and lowered his flaps to bleed off airspeed. Then he backed off the power and let the plane settle toward the water.

The tail caught first, at the top of a broad, shallow wave. Josh lurched forward with the plane's momentum. Then he pushed the throttle full in and cut the engine.

Immediately, he reached up and pulled the latch for the canopy. Wind caught it, blowing it open. Then Josh punched the release to his safety harness and stood in the cockpit.

The weight of the engine dipped the nose into the water. Josh grabbed his Mae West, looped his arms through it, and was about to jump over-board when he heard a heavy motor roar behind him, and a friendly voice called, "Are you looking for a ride?"

Josh looked aghast at the sight in the salvage vessel's hold. Marines writhed in pain, their wounds oozing blood through hastily wrapped bandages that their rescuer had applied. Their wounds were mostly in their heads, chests, arms, and shoulders as their lower bodies had been under water.

Other Marines lay still with similar wounds. A few appeared to have passed on after having been pulled from the ocean.

Josh turned his attention to his rescuer. "This is a hell of a thing you're doing. Who are you?"

The man's face crinkled into a grim smile. "Lieutenant (jg) Eddie Heimberger, at your service, sir."

The vessel picked up speed as it headed toward the fleet. Josh indicated the wounded Marines with his chin. "These guys wouldn't have had a chance without you."

Heimberger tossed his head with a craggy grin. "Maybe I'll need somebody to rescue me someday. I'll probably get court-martialed, though. I disobeyed orders by coming back for more, but somebody's got to bring these guys in."

Josh stared at him in awe. "How many trips have you made?"

"This is my second. I'll keep doing it until we don't have any more live ones struggling on the coral."

Josh peered at him, studying him more closely. "I've seen you before. I'm sure of it. Where are you from?"

"Originally Brazil," Heimberger said, "but I've spent time in Mexico."

"Your accent isn't from either place. How long have you been in the Navy?"

Heimberger gave a cloaked smile. "Not long. I came in about a year after the war started. Where are you from?"

"New Jersey." Josh kept scrutinizing Heimberger. "I know I've seen you. It'll come to me. Anyway, this is a tremendous thing you're doing. If you get court-martialed, I'll show up as a character witness."

"Thank you, sir. I think I'll be all right."

"How many guys have you picked up so far?"

Heimberger arched his brows. "I'm not rightly sure. I suppose somewhere between ten or twenty."

"That's remarkable. Instead of a reprimand, you should get a medal."

Josh shifted his view toward the beach. The wind blew pink spray from the foam at the tops of waves. Floating pieces of refuse dotted the water, and among them were the bodies of lifeless Marines. On the shore, gunfire and smoke continued to ascend skyward, and overhead, Zeros and Hellcats dueled.

"Maybe you should call it a day when we drop off these Marines."

"Can't, sir. I owe a load of rifles and ammo to the ones wading onto the beach."

41

November 28, 1943
Tehran, Iran

Winston Churchill sat in a stationary, open-topped convertible sedan belonging to the British legation minister in Tehran. He nodded and smiled at a throng of Persians pressing within a few feet of the car on a dusty main thoroughfare through Iran's medieval-looking capital city. He had landed less than an hour earlier at the same airbase used to import lend-lease shipments from the United States for overland transport to the Soviet Union, and he had been discomfited by seeing a security cordon of Persian cavalrymen on horseback lining his way on both sides of the street. They were spaced fifty feet apart, with the area between them filled with friendly albeit reserved crowds.

Churchill turned to his daughter, Sarah, sitting next to him in the back seat. "I must have a word with the minister about security arrangements," he muttered. "This reception alerts any evil-minded person of the arrival of a target and the intended route." He glanced around. "And I see no foot-policemen anywhere about. We're easy shots at any range."

The minister, sitting in the front seat, turned around. "What's that, sir?"

Churchill smiled and shook his head. "Oh, nothing. I was just commenting to Sarah about the warm reception. We'll talk later."

The minister beamed. "We should be moving again momentarily. The cavalrymen are opening a route through this gaggle."

Churchill had been ill in the days preceding his latest trip abroad. Given that he had not fully recovered from fever and general bad health, and that he expected to be out of the country for two months, his senior staff had arranged for Sarah, a women's auxiliary air force officer, to accompany him as his aide.

Having just come from a conference in Cairo with Franklin Roosevelt and the Chinese leader, Generalissimo Chiang Kai-shek, he was buoyed by success there in reaching an agreement on dealing with Japan. An overarching concern was keeping China in the war with the objective of pinning down Japanese forces, and to that end, the three leaders had issued a declaration stating,

"The several military missions have agreed upon future military operations against Japan. The Three Great Allies expressed their resolve to bring unrelenting pressure against their brutal enemies by sea, land, and air. This pressure is already rising...

"With these objects in view the three Allies, in harmony with those of the United Nations at war with Japan, will continue to persevere in the serious and prolonged operations necessary to procure the unconditional surrender of Japan."

A fly in the ointment, from the prime minister's view, was that, as part of the effort, Roosevelt had promised Chiang Kai-shek to undertake amphibious operations against Japan in the Bay of Bengal. Carrying out that commitment would tie up landing craft needed in the European theater to invade France, whether in the northwest or along the Mediterranean.

Churchill hoped that the issue would not become a sticking point with Joseph Stalin, who insisted with increasing vehemence on opening a new front in France. As opposed to earlier in the war when he had only his irascibility as a bargaining chip, now, having routed the *Wehrmacht* at Stalingrad and Kursk, and with ever increasing manpower and equipment pressing westward against dwindling German resources, he showed signs of using his newfound negotiating position to press for priorities that he saw as crucial to winning the war.

This conference in Tehran, coming immediately on the heels of the one in Cairo, would include Stalin, and was one that Roosevelt had pressed to bring about for years. The Soviet leader had always before stated that the eastern front required his personal attention and he could thus not leave the Soviet Union while that remained the case.

"When he speaks of priorities for winning the war," Churchill told Sarah privately, "he means those for saving his own skin. He's never been known to venture anywhere near flying bullets."

Still, the prime minister bore a grudging respect for the man whom he had once characterized as an orangutang. In the years since Lenin's death, Stalin had reorganized his country into a manufacturing behemoth, and after Hitler had unleashed Operation Barbarossa against the Soviet Union, the Soviet leader had transformed the factories to churn out war materiel in astonishing quantities. Further, he had rallied his people to fight the "fascist pigs" and staved off massive attacks at Moscow, Stalingrad, Kursk, and all points in between.

Churchill had heard through reliable sources that Stalin had secretly built a million-man army to crush the *Wehrmacht* on the Eastern Front. The Soviet leader sought from Churchill and Roosevelt a date-certain for invading France, an invasion that would force Hitler to divert divisions to the Western Front while Stalin's forces would sweep toward Berlin.

Arranging a place to meet had been no mean feat. Roosevelt had proposed several places, Alaska being the most recent, but Stalin had turned them down, always citing the demands of the war. However, on the last overture, he had posited Tehran as an acceptable place to rendezvous. It was controlled jointly by the Soviets and the Brits, and it was close to the Soviet border.

A major difficulty had been the logistics of bringing Roosevelt to the conference. The trip to the other side of the world was arduous for anyone, but especially for a man in his sixties who was bound to a wheelchair. The president operated under the additional constraint that while Congress was in session, he could be away from the capital for no more than ten days, or any legislation passed during his absence would become law without his approval. Finding a narrow interval near the end of the year to plan Allied strategy for 1944 while maintaining the ability to scurry back to Washington, should the occasion arise, had been challenging.

"Ah, we're moving again," the minister called over his shoulder as the car lurched forward. "Our destination is just up the road."

"At last, here we are," Churchill told Sarah minutes later as they turned into the stately gates of the legation, a designation which was a step below that of an embassy. The main building was set back at the end of a leafy drive, an elegant edifice with a domed roof and multiple narrow columns.

"This is a pretty place," Sarah said as the sedan came to a halt. She was slender and pleasant-faced, looking like her father, but was decidedly feminine even in her uniform. "Is that the Soviet legation over there?"

She pointed at a white building of Grecian architecture barely five hundred yards away. Wide stairs ran the length of the front with large double doors at the center.

"You are correct," the legation minister cut in from the front seat. "Unfortunately, the American delegation is across town, which might present security problems for getting Mr. Roosevelt back and forth several times each day."

"Then he should stay here, with us," Churchill replied ruefully as he climbed out of the car. "I'm glad you caught that." He added, "I can't see how staying at the Soviet legation could be an alternative."

Later that afternoon, cameras rolled as the three world leaders posed sitting together in chairs at the top the stairs in front of the Soviet building. "It's good that we all made it here from Cairo in one piece," Roosevelt quipped, and while interpreters whispered his humorous statement into Stalin's ear, he told Churchill, "I've just accepted Marshal Stalin's kind invitation to be his guest and stay here during the conference. That should alleviate some security issues that could otherwise arise from irregular travel between legations."

Startled, Churchill peered at the president while wondering how many electronic listening devices had been planted in the president's quarters. But he merely said, "Yes, we had thought that could be an issue, but you've resolved it."

Roosevelt hosted a banquet that evening inside the Soviet quarters, and after routine diplomatic hoopla with toasts and pronouncements of friendship and cooperation leading to world peace, Churchill and Stalin strolled through the room together. "We're seeing the possible end of this horrible war on the horizon," the prime minister said, taking advantage of the moment to probe. He could provide Roosevelt with a full report of the discussion. "Perhaps we could talk about your view of post-war Europe?"

Stalin agreed, and the two men sat together on a sofa with their interpreters.

"The worst case, as I see things," Stalin began, "is that Germany could recover and start a new war within a few years. They have a long history of doing just that. We all thought that the provisions of the Versailles Treaty would prevent a repetition, but Germany built its economy and industrial base back rapidly."

"And you think they could do it again. How soon?"

Stalin shrugged. "Fifteen, twenty years."

Churchill's brow furrowed. "We must put measures in place to keep the peace for at least fifty years. We owe the oncoming generations that. The younger ones living through this war will have to pick things up from us."

Stalin nodded. "We'll need to put constraints on Germany's manufacturing ability. Its people are industrious and resourceful. If left unchecked, they could do it again."

"Agreed. We should deny them aviation, both civil and military," Churchill said, "and I would forbid them to have a general staff system, leaving them only enough military for defensive purposes."

Stalin pondered that a moment and then queried, "Would you also keep them from making watches and furniture? Recall that those types of factories camouflaged their building of the *Wehrmacht* and *Luftwaffe*. They manufactured toy rifles that they used to teach whole armies of men to shoot."

The conversation continued over related history and current concerns until Churchill said, "We, the Three Powers, should guide the future of the world. You'll have your great armies, and the US and Great Britain have our navies and air forces. We three must remain friends in order to ensure happy homes in all countries. I don't want to enforce any system on other nations. I look for freedom and for the rights of all nations to develop as they choose."

Stalin stared at him with a stony expression. "Control failed after the last war."

"We were inexperienced. We know much more now about what they might do in secret and the mechanisms needed to stop them. Our technology is much more advanced."

Both men sat for some moments. Stalin's demeanor had relaxed a bit, and he asked, "So what is to become of Germany?" He cast a sidelong look at Churchill, and without waiting for a reply, he half-smiled and said, "I visited with some German POWs, just to see what sort of men they were. When I asked why they fought for Hitler, some who came from the laboring classes said that they only carried out orders. I shot them."

Churchill controlled his shock at the diminutive man with the big mustache sitting next to him on the sofa, unsure whether or not Stalin was serious. Then the Soviet leader let out a burst of uproarious laughter and grabbed the prime minister's arm. He pointed a finger mischievously at Churchill. "Ah, you don't know if I'm joking."

The prime minister looked away, less than amused. When he turned back to Stalin, he said, "Perhaps we should postpone discussion of Germany's disposition for the plenary sessions, and instead talk about Poland."

"By all means," Stalin said expansively, a wolfish expression on his face.

Churchill studied his face a moment, and then began. "Poland is important to us. We came into the war because Germany attacked her, and we are wedded to her sovereignty. We've stood by that position since before Germany invaded your country."

Stalin harrumphed. "And you know our position, which is that we will require recognition of the Polish borders established prior to that invasion."

"Meaning that you intend to keep that part of Poland you annexed when you entered into the non-aggression pact with Germany."

"I've been explicit on that since we joined together in this war."

Churchill peered at him wryly. "I suppose we could move Poland's western border farther west, perhaps to River Oder. That would result in a country of the same size that it was prior to the war, and we'd look for a strong, independent Poland as a main pillar of European stability and security. The arrangement would step on a few German toes, but that's not something that bothers me at present. Do you propose to draw frontier lines?"

Stalin nodded. "Of course. We've never recognized the Polish government-in-exile and we haven't relinquished our claim to those territories. The part of Poland we annexed is now empty of most Poles, and we won't lay claim to villages near the border with us that are mainly populated by them. And, as you say, we don't mind stepping on German toes."

Churchill leaned in. "I have no parliamentary authority to draw those borders, and I'm sure that President Roosevelt doesn't have Congressional authority either. But if the three of us, acting as heads of state, can come to a policy agreement, we'd have a united proposition to take back to the Poles with a strong recommendation that they accept it."

"We'd negotiate without the Poles?" Surprise tinged Stalin's tone.

"Yes. We'd inform them later. But your acceptance of the River Oder as a possible western boundary is encouraging."

Stalin's eyes narrowed over a sly grin. "We want nothing that belongs to others, but I'll make an exception to that for the Germans."

The next morning, Churchill sent a lunch invitation to the president. He received back a note to decline, informing the prime minister that Roosevelt had invited Stalin for lunch.

"Huh," Churchill remarked to Sarah. "If I didn't know better, I'd think the president is avoiding me. I hadn't thought much about it until just now, but he and I hardly spoke last night."

"Then again, you did spend quite a lot of time with Stalin. Perhaps it's just coincidental."

"Then again," Churchill huffed, "he invited Joseph to lunch and not me. I'm beginning to feel that, instead of a Big Three conference, it's a meeting of the Big Two and a Half."

"Oh, stop it, Father. You and Roosevelt just saw each other in Cairo. The president probably just wanted time to take his own assessment of the man."

Churchill smiled and hugged Sarah. "You're probably right. Good thing for the world that you're here to keep my head on straight."

"Don't put that responsibility on me," Sarah laughed, and kissed his cheek. "The world has enough to fear with just the three of you to muck it up. What's on for this afternoon?"

"The first plenary meeting. Stalin's highest priority is a second front in Europe, and regardless of what's on the agenda, he'll steer that way. He's never done an amphibious landing and has no idea of what one entails. He made the comment that he had done many river crossings and offered his expertise on doing a cross-channel invasion. General Brooke promptly advised him that the key issue was landing craft. First, we have to get our men, equipment, and supplies staged, and then get them ashore.

"We learned at Dieppe that sufficient numbers of the right types of barges to carry men and tanks is imperative, not to mention all the other types of equipment. The ones we have are scattered all over the planet and must be transported to the staging areas. The US is building the landing craft as fast as it can, but getting them to the right place is the next issue. That problem is accentuated when you consider that they're mostly in the Pacific right now, and they're doing a lot of landings there—meaning that much of the equipment is in frequent repair. The boats wear out."

"I see the problem," Sarah broke in. "What does Stalin want?"

"He wanted a cross-channel invasion into northwestern France this year, and we had promised him one. But knocking Rommel and the *Wehrmacht* out of Africa took longer than expected, so we couldn't meet that commitment. One irritating aspect of Stalin is that he doesn't give credit for how our intrigues, maneuvers, and battles have diverted Hitler's divisions from the eastern front.

"He has a good military mind, though. I asked him how he thought the amphibious operation should be carried out. He described precisely how we do it now, down to softening up enemy positions with a naval bombardment, followed up by heavy air bombing, to landing the soldiers, and following up with materiel support.

"But he doesn't seem to appreciate the many important actions we've taken in support of the war effort. Without them, the Soviets might have lost the war. If that had happened, we'd now be facing the combined *Wehrmacht* and the Red Army backed by Soviet resources and industrial power added to that of Germany and all the other countries they've conquered."

"That's a frightening scenario," Sarah exclaimed with a vexed expression. She lifted questioning eyes to her father. "Should you be telling me these things?"

Churchill snorted. "You're my aide, and most of what we've mentioned isn't classified. Anyone with a pittance of a brain could figure out most of it. Frankly, it's good to have someone to hash out thoughts with who isn't part of high officialdom."

Sarah laughed. "I'll take that as a compliment. What happens next?"

"We have three plenary sessions—one today, one tomorrow, and the next day—followed by a state dinner each evening. Our military advisers are gathering ahead of those meetings to analyze whatever we tell them to and report back to us."

"And someone has a birthday on that third day," Sarah teased. "A big one. You're turning sixty."

"Don't remind me," Churchill replied blandly. "But I used that event and my status as the most senior of the three principals as well as being from the oldest of the three countries to insist on hosting the dinner here at the British legation that evening. Do me a favor and look over the legation minister's shoulder as those preparations occur, would you? I'd like to be sure he does a better job with the dinner than he did planning for security on our arrival."

"I'll do that, Papa." The tone of Sarah's voice changed. "One of the reasons that your staff insisted on bringing me along was to make sure that you got plenty of rest. So, off you go. Your staff has things in hand. Take a nap. I'll wake you in time."

Churchill cast her a chastened glance and headed toward his room.

42

November 29, 1943

Before the conference recommenced the next afternoon, Churchill presented Stalin, "by the King's command," with a huge, specially designed ceremonial sword bedecked with precious stones, the "Sword of Honor," awarded for the glorious defense of Stalingrad. Stalin accepted it, kissed the blade, and handed it to his chief military aide, who promptly dropped it. Amid much fussing about, the offending general recovered it and handed it to a squad of soldiers who paraded it out of the room with great solemnity.

The first plenary meeting had gone as Churchill predicted, with issues identified, passed along to the military staffs, and discussed again at the second day's session. Stalin had quickly gone to the matter of a second front in France. Roosevelt made peripheral remarks that supported the proposed invasion, but otherwise left for Churchill the laborious task of explaining in detail the difficulties of mounting an amphibious assault, with landing craft being the pivotal issue.

Walking a fine line between direct and diplomatic tones and verbiage, Churchill explained that the problem was compounded by a commitment to General Chiang Kai-shek to commence amphibious operations in the Bay of Bengal at roughly the same time as the proposed invasion of France, now seen as being launched across the English Channel and dubbed Operation Overlord.

"We must first secure Greece and the Balkans, though," the prime minister insisted as he saw support growing for Overlord.

"You seem opposed to the operation," Roosevelt remarked archly. "Why?"

"It's not that I'm opposed to Overlord, Mr. President," Churchill replied. "Not only is timing important, but so is what is going on in other places. If we don't secure our southeastern flank, which we can do cheaply by supporting the Resistance movement in Yugoslavia led by that chap, Tito, our effort on the western front could be frustrated by a German drive through the Balkans. Before attempting a cross-channel assault into the heart of the Germans' defenses, we should mount a further supporting drive into the south of France."

Roosevelt mulled the statement. "You've always proposed an invasion in the south of France. Why?"

Churchill took a deep breath. "For the reasons stated, Mr. President." He fixed his eyes on Roosevelt. "From that bloodbath that was the raid on Dieppe, we learned the elements that must be present to have even a chance of success. I won't commit British troops to another Dieppe, and I'm sure you feel the same about how you send your American soldiers into harm's way."

Roosevelt regarded the prime minister with steely eyes. "But why southern France instead of in the vicinity of Calais? It's only twenty miles across the channel there."

"Which is why Hitler would expect us to invade there. An invasion in the south is more attainable. If we support the Resistance in the Balkans, we'll have our flank protected, we can launch from Italy after we've moved north of Rome, and we'll already have troops and landing craft in place."

"But the push to Paris and beyond to the German border would be much longer."

Stalin broke in. "I prefer an invasion in northwestern France, near Calais, as the president suggested, and the timing should be in May or June of next year." His iron tone bore no room for compromise.

Roosevelt turned to face Stalin directly. "We've already committed to those dates, and we'll meet them. The only question is where?"

The room descended into silence. Moments ticked by.

"What if we were to invade in both places?" the president mulled out loud.

The question hung in the air.

Churchill cleared his throat. "Mr. President, your factories are turning out new landing craft as fast as they can, and we're jointly repairing and shipping them from the Pacific as rapidly as is feasible. They are the crux of the matter, and we must meet our commitment to General Chiang Kai-shek in the Bay of Bengal. To bring off two operations on the shores of France simultaneously would require a dramatic shift in how we allocate those craft."

Roosevelt met Churchill's steady gaze and held it for a spell. "All right. Let's hand the question to our staffs for analysis. Perhaps we can reach decisions by tomorrow."

"Before we close for the day," Stalin said, intervening. He fixed his eyes on Churchill. "I have to direct a question to the prime minister about Overlord. Do you and your staff believe in that proposed operation?"

Churchill took his time to reply, and when he did, his voice carried the gravity of his response. "If the conditions are established, our stern duty requires us to hurl every sinew of our strength across the Channel against the Germans."

"How did it go?" Sarah asked when Churchill returned to the British legation.

Churchill shrugged. "Not well, from my view." He sighed. "The reality is that the center of influence in this war has shifted from Great Britain to the United States. On top of that, the Soviet Union is now a senior partner and we're junior in this unholy triumvirate." A bleak, angry look crossed his face. "Would to God that were not so," he growled, holding back fury, "but wars cannot be won without facing reality."

Sarah curled her fingers in her father's shirt just below his neck and leaned her head on his chest. "No one has fought harder than you, Father." She smiled up at him. "You might be the most pragmatic idealist who ever lived, and if I know you, you're not nearly prepared to be relegated to the scrapheap of history."

Churchill wrapped his arms around his daughter and squeezed her. "Yes, well, now I must prepare for one of those odious state dinners. Marshal Stalin is hosting it. Roosevelt's son, Elliott, arrives today, and Franklin proposed to make this a family affair. You're invited."

"Ooh. Lovely." Sarah giggled facetiously. "Whatever shall I wear?"

Despite the tensions of the day, the dinner proceeded with at least forced congeniality. The list of guests was short, consisting of the Big Three leaders, their immediate senior civilian advisers, and Sarah. As the banquet proceeded, Elliott showed up at the door. Roosevelt waved him in, and he took a seat at the end of the table.

Stalin was expansive in his cordiality, and as the evening and Stalin's wine consumption waxed, Churchill became the target of his humor. The prime minister took the jibes in stride, returning them when he chose. He remained good-natured until Stalin wondered out loud and in a convivial manner about what punishment should be meted out to Germany, flatly stating that the German General Staff must be liquidated. He observed that Hitler's entire army depended on the work of fifty thousand officers and technicians, and he suggested that when the war was won, they should be rounded up and executed by firing squad.

Astonished by the brutality of the comment, particularly to this gathering, Churchill leaned back in disbelief and replied immediately and firmly. "The British Parliament and public will never tolerate mass executions. Even in war passion, if our countrymen allowed them to begin, they would turn violently against those responsible after the first butchery had taken place. The Soviet Union must be under no delusion on this point."

Seeming not to perceive the prime minister's discomfiture or perhaps ignoring it, Stalin persisted. "Fifty thousand must be shot."

Churchill placed his fork down in the middle of his plate and glared at

Stalin, seething. "I would rather be taken out into the garden here and now and be shot myself than sully my own and my country's honor by such infamy."

Roosevelt's eyes alternated between the two men. He coughed and leaned back, forcing a smile onto his face. "I propose a compromise," he said in an apparent attempt to break the tension with levity. "Instead of fifty thousand, why not shoot just forty-nine thousand."

Churchill was not amused.

Suddenly, at the end of the table, Elliott, the president's son, rose to his feet. Holding up a glass of wine in a toast, he declared, "I agree with Marshal Stalin's plan, and I'm sure that the United States Army would support it."

Churchill's reaction was immediate. He stood abruptly, tossed his napkin in his chair, and strode into the next room.

Stunned at what Elliott had said, Sarah stared up him. For Elliott's part, realization dawned on him that he had overstepped diplomatic bounds, and he sank into his chair.

The light in the room that Churchill entered was dim. He walked to a window to stare out at the Soviet legation grounds. Barely a minute later, he heard a sound behind him and two hands gripped his shoulders.

He spun around to find Stalin and the Soviet foreign minister, Vyach-eslav Molotov, standing there. Both wore wide grins.

"I wasn't serious," Stalin said. "Something like that would never enter my head."

"He was only playing," Molotov chimed in.

Churchill studied the two men's faces but remained silent.

"Let's go back to the dinner," Stalin cajoled. "We're all good friends here, with a common purpose."

With no better alternatives, Churchill acceded and allowed himself to be escorted back to his seat. Stalin resumed his place at the head of the table. "Please, ladies, gentlemen, let's continue in the good spirit of this conference."

"Are you all right, Father," Sarah asked later as she and Churchill sat alone in the library of the British legation. "The president was embarrassed by what Elliott did and said. It was a stupid, immature act that reflects his ignorance of the values we fight for."

Churchill blew out a breath of air. "I understand. I couldn't let that comment pass. Stalin is a study in contrasts, sometimes a brute, sometimes incredibly articulate, and we know the ruthless cruelty he's brought down on his people.

"He makes a joke like that, and maybe that's all it was. Or perhaps he was testing us to see if we'd condone and perhaps even join in his level of barbarity. He uses a captivating manner when it suits him, and he was at his finest in that regard this evening when he came after me in that room. I'm not convinced he wasn't serious when he made that 'joke.'"

"We should get some sleep," Sarah said, yawning. "You've another full day tomorrow, and don't worry about the birthday arrangements. They're fully under control." She stood and gazed at him, seeing him still sitting, absorbed. "Ah, Father," she murmured, leaning over and kissing his forehead. "What must it be like to be you?"

He glanced up and grimaced. "Hmph. Daunting." He added with a chuckle, "Nevertheless, I remain undaunted."

"Well, here we are at our final session," Roosevelt declared as the third plenary session opened the next day, "and I think we might be closer to agreement on the big issues than we might have thought last evening. We still have a few matters to discuss that we haven't yet mentioned here, and I'll get to them. But"—he glanced around the room at the expectant faces of Churchill, Stalin, Eden, Molotov, and the other advisers in the room—"I had a conversation with my senior military staff this morning. I believe we have common ground." He directed his gaze at Stalin. "We are prepared to commit to Overlord in May of next year."

Churchill sat with a blank expression, listening.

"And we will support the Resistance in Greece and the Balkans," the president continued while turning to the prime minister, "as well as a second invasion into southern France. To accomplish that, I will direct the US Navy that only those landing craft in the Pacific that are absolutely necessary for operations in the Bay of Bengal should be kept there. My staff ran the numbers, and what's needed there is minimal. The rest are to be shipped to the European theater, starting immediately."

While Churchill sat absorbing what he had just heard, Stalin beamed. "That is good news. I think the end of this war might be in sight. What's the other matter?"

Roosevelt took his time to answer, taking note of Churchill's reticence to react to the compromise. "I've modified my position on Turkey. We must get her into this war," he said. "That's how we reinforce the eastern flank. We don't even need for them to engage in fighting, just let us base our aircraft there. Our bombing runs over the Baltics are coming from North Africa, but if we could launch them from Turkey, we'd cut off hundreds of miles and hours of flight time, save fuel, drop more bombs, and reach closer to the Soviet southern border."

Surprised at the proposal, Stalin furrowed his brow and rubbed his chin as he contemplated. "You know Turkey is formally neutral and is not friends with the Soviet Union. You want to coax them to join the Alliance?"

"Exactly," Roosevelt said, warming to his proposition.

"But Bulgaria is part of the Axis Powers. They might attack Turkey if it joins the war against Germany."

"Not if you, Marshal Stalin, commit to going to war with Bulgaria if it makes a move on Turkey."

Stalin sat back in his seat, mulling.

"It might work," Churchill interjected, "and before we leave the subject of Overlord and the other actions in Europe, let me say that I support them." Amidst murmurs of approval, he went on. "Regarding Overlord, we'll need a good deception plan, an expansion of what we did in North Africa and the Soviets did in Russia.

"With respect to the matter at hand"—he turned to Stalin—"the president and I are returning to Cairo after this conference. We've invited Turkey's President İsmet İnönü to meet with us there. Perhaps we can come to some agreement."

Stalin smiled broadly, and Churchill noticed the wolfish expression he had observed two days earlier. "In that case, you can tell him that the Soviet Union commits to attacking Bulgaria if it acts against Turkey. And further." Stalin revealed his broadest smile. "We will commit to another massive offensive against German forces, the largest yet by far, timed to coincide with your invasion of France in May."

Roosevelt leaned back, smiling in satisfaction. Churchill remained inscrutable.

"The next item I'd like to discuss is a new bombing concept. We call it 'flyover bombing.'" He directed his next remarks to Stalin. "To carry it out, we'd place American groundcrews on bases in Siberia. Then bombers from England would fly over Germany, drop their loads, and instead of flying immediately back to England, they'd continue on to the Siberian bases, re-load and re-fuel, and drop more bombs as they flew back to England." He looked around the room, apparently pleased with the suggestion. "Simple. We get double the payload drops for the same money. What do you say?"

Stalin exhaled. "Sounds reasonable." He turned to his military adviser. "Make it happen."

"We'll need to publish a statement," Churchill added.

43

December 4, 1943
Cairo, Egypt

Roosevelt and Churchill sat together on the roof terrace of the Mena House hotel looking out over the mystical Sphinx and the pyramids that had bewitched travelers for generations. "They are beautiful," the president observed. "You wonder at the history played out there. The sheer effort to build them. How did they do it? We still don't know. And the battles fought in their shadows."

He shifted in his chair to face Churchill as a warm breeze threatened to blow a hat from his head. "Honestly, I can't tell you which is more enchanting, the Atlas Mountains over the desert sunset we observed from Marrakech, or this." He swept his arms out across billowing sands caught in the waning rays of Egypt's sunlight.

"People talk about the wisdom of the ancients," Roosevelt went on, waxing philosophical. "I've wondered about that. If they were so wise, why are we still fighting wars in the same places they were? Why couldn't they learn to teach their descendants how to live in peace."

"You know the easy answer," Churchill responded. "Evil exists. As long as bad actors want and feel emboldened to take what other people have, there will be wars. The best we can do is try to keep our homelands free of them until the generations that come immediately behind are able to take up the mantle and fend for themselves."

"The threats are not getting smaller, that's for sure." The president swung his chair around to fully face the prime minister. "Take that Manhattan Project, for example. If we put the A-bomb together, we could end the war early. On the other hand, we don't have a monopoly on the knowledge of atomic energy. That technology in the hands of evildoers—"

"Like Stalin?" Churchill suggested.

"You're looking into the future, Winston. Yes, like Stalin. If Hitler hadn't preempted him, I have no doubt that Stalin would be the evil we'd be fighting today. His territorial ambitions don't stop at his borders. But at the moment, as you've reminded me many times, we need him to win this war."

Churchill took a deep breath. "Our discussions on post-war borders were not encouraging. He's insisting on the return of the Baltic states to the Soviet Union based on coerced elections before the war. Also, he wants the Kuriles in the northern Pacific. And he doesn't stop there. He's using his negotiating position resulting from his victories over the *Wehrmacht* to wheedle us into agreements we find abhorrent."

"He's a master at it."

"That he is." Churchill looked at Roosevelt quizzically. "I thought you liked him. The two of you got along famously in Tehran."

"You noticed." The president grinned as he pulled out two cigars from his pocket and handed one to Churchill. "But we never smoked any of these together."

"You hardly spoke to me. The notion of the Big Three came into serious doubt, from my view."

"I had to hold you at arm's length in Tehran so I could get close to him. He had to perceive that we regarded him as an equal or his suspicions of us would only have deepened. We couldn't expect to conduct our normal friendship there and think he would open up to either of us. Surely, you see that."

"You could have given me notice that you were going to take that stance."

"Yes, I suppose I could have. Should have, really, but the thought came to me only as we were first meeting with him."

"Well, it's neither here nor there now. In any event, the way things played out was probably more genuine anyway."

Roosevelt puffed on his cigar until it was fully lit, and then he let out a stream of fragrant smoke. "I'll tell you, Winston. I heard a rumor shortly before the Tehran Conference. Ordinarily I don't pay attention to rumor, but coming from the source, prudence dictated that I should at least listen. It pertained to a secret British document, and the essence of it was that while you gave lip service to the cross-channel invasion, Operation Overlord, your true intent was to undermine it in favor of Operation Anvil on the Mediterranean coast of France. The amazing thing was that Comrade Stalin seems to have gotten wind of that document too. I recall how he quizzed you directly regarding your dedication to Overlord."

The prime minister sat back in his chair, puffing on his cigar. When he didn't reply, Roosevelt tossed his head and gazed back across the desert. "The world that will emerge from success with the Manhattan Project is a fearsome one. I'm not sure I want to live to see it."

"I'll give you a response regarding Overlord," Churchill said gruffly.

Roosevelt turned toward him without speaking.

"Mr. President, you have your responsibilities to your country, and I have mine to Great Britain. We're both doing our best to carry them out under trying circumstances.

"I won't deny that I have strong doubts about a cross-channel invasion or that a document such as the one you mentioned exists. I will tell you this. If you read it, the verbiage leaves open the possibility of interpreting it either way: in support of Overlord or undermining it."

"You didn't read it before you issued it?"

"Of course I did, Franklin, but look where we are." He swept his hand across the vista. "In Egypt. And before that in Tehran. And before that, here in Cairo. We met in Casablanca at the beginning of the year, and in Washington at mid-year."

"What's your point, Winston?"

"We're running a bloody war, Franklin." Churchill barely contained his exasperation. "Those documents are written by bureaucrats, some of them with 'dogs in the fight,' as you Americans like to say. I read voraciously, but I lay no claim to catching every detail. When Stalin asked me pointedly if I supported Overlord, there in front of God, him, and you, I committed to it."

Churchill's face had turned red, and now he raised a finger in the air. "But I'll tell you, sir, I will not have another Dieppe with greater than sixty percent casualties. Either we do this right, or I will pull my support and my British boys from the operation and throw them aggressively into Operation Anvil."

Roosevelt met Churchill's vehemence with equal severity. "Our boys, yours and mine, are right now slogging their way up the back of Italy under blistering gunfire, Winston. That Nazi crocodile you're fond of referring to has a rather stiff and prickly spine extending up from its soft North African underbelly, and it's called the mountains of Italy."

Churchill's eyes opened wide. "And need I remind you that it was General Eisenhower's public announcement that blew the surprise on the landing at Salerno? Otherwise, the story might be very different."

Roosevelt stared at Churchill, studying his face. Then his lips broke into a small, irrepressible smile before he chuckled. "Ah, Winston, God broke the mold after he made you." He laughed again as he puffed on his cigar. "Maybe God erred." He reached over and touched the prime minister's arm. "Let's not fight among ourselves."

As Churchill stared back, Roosevelt laughed again, deeper and longer. "I do believe, Mr. Prime Minister, that this the first time I've seen you at a loss for words."

A slow smile crossed Churchill's face, his belly jiggled, and he lapsed into an involuntary chuckle. "I'll drink to that," he quipped. Then he added seriously, "The fact is that we took Salerno, at a high price, but we're progressing up Italy's spine." He looked around for a drink table. "Hmph, they didn't bring the tray yet."

While he looked around, Roosevelt launched into another subject. "Our boys just took Tarawa in the Pacific. That might be the most horrific battle we've fought in any theater to date." The president took a deep breath and stared into the desert. "You know, sometimes I try to imagine what our boys go through in those battles. They're all terrible, but this one was particularly gruesome.

"Our signals intelligence in the Pacific picked up a message from Admiral Shibazaki where he bragged before the assault that he was so well dug in that if we attacked with a million men, it would take a hundred years to dislodge his troops."

He arched a brow and caught Churchill's eye with unfiltered pride. "Winston, our Marines did it in three days." He stared again into the desert. "They were magnificent. We should drink to them too."

Churchill climbed to his feet. "I'll go get some brandy."

Moments later, he returned carrying two glasses with the golden liquid. He handed one to Roosevelt as the scent floated on the evening air. After they toasted, Roosevelt said, "That battle at Tarawa sends chills up my spine. The Japs were dug in a lot better than we knew, and when the Marines went ashore, they had nowhere else to go but straight into a barrage of machine gun fire—and they did it. There was a Marine scout platoon commander who single-handedly attacked and subdued six machine gun nests. Hawkins, his name is. He was wounded twice, once in the chest, but he kept going. His own men are clamoring for him to receive the Medal of Honor, and I think we might do that.

"There was this other guy, some actor I'd never heard of, a Navy man, Lieutenant Eddie Heimberger. He was the coxswain of a salvage boat, and he risked his life saving thirty-six Marines who'd been stranded offshore on a coral reef and were taking enemy machinegun fire. When his boat was shot up, he commandeered another one to continue the rescues, and he coaxed two other landing craft drivers to follow him and rescue still more men."

He shook his head in amazement. "Where do we get these magnificent fighters?" He leaned forward. "I've read the reports, Winston. What those boys faced—"

His voice trailed off. He sniffed and sipped his brandy. "You know, the Japanese figured this battle would come. They employed a strategy they call Yogaki—that means 'waylaying attack.' They wanted to demonstrate to us the folly of attacking their mainland."

His voice became more intense as he spoke. "They had built a maze of concrete tetrahedrons to scuttle our landing craft, and they strung barbed wire and planted underwater mines between them. At last count, they had sixty-two heavy machine guns and forty-four light ones, as well as fourteen tanks pointing offshore with 36 mm cannons."

He nudged Churchill. "You can read the reports, so I won't go into it all, but they even had four British 8-inch Vickers coastal guns they had captured in Singapore. And then there was their command bunker that had withstood all the artillery and bombs dropped on them for four hours. Our Marines went in there with hand grenades and flame-throwers and cleaned 'em out."

He took another sip of his brandy and once again stared across the desert. "Like I said," he murmured in a hushed tone, "magnificent."

He reflected for a moment and then continued. "That battle was a tragedy, there's no other way to look at it. But our Marines, supported by our Navy, fought brilliantly against Japan's battle-hardened veterans. They never gave up, and they delivered the victory we needed to open up Japan to a campaign against their homeland. Like Germany, Japan's days are numbered.

"We learned some hard lessons at Tarawa. Our amphibious troops must have waterproof radios, and there must be a dedicated communications ship to organize and coordinate radio traffic. Our staffs will be busy studying those and other aspects to make sure our men are always fully supported."

"No argument there," Churchill broke in. "And that success is a great story to tell. Our chaps deserve every help we can give."

"It's served another purpose too," Roosevelt said, "one I regret but that was necessary. Americans were shocked at the number of casualties. In three days, we lost as many men on Tarawa as we lost during the six-month Battle of Guadalcanal." He sighed. "I think our people are now seeing that this is a long war, and what it will take to win it. It was a decisive battle."

"It was at that."

The two men sat in silence for several minutes. Then Churchill took a sip of his brandy. "To change the subject to another pressing matter, have you decided on a commander for Overlord yet? We promised Stalin we'd let him know this week."

"It's a hard choice, Winston. My first instinct is to go with General Marshall."

"You sound like you have doubts."

"About Marshall?" Roosevelt waved away the comment. "He's excellent. But I rely on him for so much in Washington. I couldn't bear to have him away indefinitely. So, I'm going with Ike."

"Eisenhower is also an excellent choice. He's diplomatic, tough—"

"It's his diplomatic talent we need to hold together this Alliance of very different cultures. You made a comment once that with General Brooke to do his planning, the two of them could pull off a particular operation. Husky, I believe it was. Between you and me, we'll make sure he has the right planners."

Then the president leaned toward Churchill and grasped his hand. "And I make this promise, Winston. Not a single Allied soldier will be sent across that channel until we are absolutely prepared."

Churchill pulled his shoulders back, sniffed, and wiped his eyes. "Thank you for that, Mr. President." He took a sip of his brandy and stared out toward the Sphynx. "To that end, I want one more commitment from you."

Roosevelt's head tossed up. "Only one?"

Churchill smiled roguishly. "For now." He took a puff on his cigar. "If we are to launch our boys to Europe across the channel, they'll need every advantage we can give them. I want your promise that no assets will move out of the European theater to the Pacific until Overlord is complete."

Roosevelt puffed long and deep on his cigar and then gazed again at the pyramids, just visible in the day's last light. "All right, Winston. I promise."

Churchill breathed a long sigh of relief. "We have our differences, Franklin, we know that. Your main objective is to win this war as fast as possible. Am I correct?"

"Absolutely. I said so to Elliott before we left Tehran."

"Mine is too, you must believe that, but it's not the far-out objective. We'll win next year or the year after, but what comes then? I know you and your staff still harbor thoughts that I'm more interested in saving the British Empire than defeating Hitler quickly, but nothing could be more untrue. The fact is, that ship has sailed, and nothing I can do will reverse it. But we must save western civilization as we know and love it.

"I fear that by conducting two simultaneous invasions into France, we'll divide German forces. On paper, that sounds good, but by doing that, we force Hitler to move divisions out of Central Europe, leaving a vacuum that Stalin will be happy to fill. That's why he supported the plan, not because he believed in the military strategy."

Roosevelt dragged deeply on his cigar. "You might be right, Winston, but if we go north through the Balkans, we'd be fighting in much rougher, channelized terrain, more difficult to support. We'd still need a massive amphibious assault launched from greater distances into cramped beaches in the Adriatic.

"Our own folks at home would be less than supportive. They're looking to liberate France, remove the threat to Great Britain, defeat the Germans, and then take out the Japs. On that last point, they're not happy about putting Japan in last priority. They haven't forgotten Pearl Harbor."

"We already got them Italy," Churchill broke in. "That ought to count for something. One month to the date after surrendering unconditionally, the Italians declared war on Germany." He halted a moment as a thought crossed his mind. "By the way, how do you think the Italians will measure up as our allies?"

The president took a moment to gather his thoughts. "You'd probably know the answer better than I. I think you said they were good fighters in Albania, but the soldiers never had their hearts in the battle, they were under-equipped, poorly trained, and badly led."

Churchill nodded in agreement. "The Italian war channeled Mussolini's dream of restoring the grandeur of the Roman Empire, but he never had the people with him as evidenced by how jubilant they were at his downfall. Besides that, he never had the industrial base to support the war, and his officers were appointed and promoted by patronage, not by competence."

"Agreed, Winston, we fight the battles we can, and if others appear before us in the future, such as the ones you alluded to a moment ago with the Soviets, we'll have to fight those, too. In any event, we're both committed to Overlord and Anvil, and plans are active to execute them." He savored his cigar and took a sip of brandy. "Speaking of potential battles, when do we meet with President İnönü?"

"In the morning," Churchill replied, "but before we go into that, there was one other subject I wanted to ask you about. Your Army Air Corps has developed what they call 'flight nurses.' How is that working out? Is the concept proving worthwhile?"

"I think so. We just started the program at the beginning of this year. The nurses go through rigorous physical, weapons, and survival training, and they are specially taught to treat wounds. The first ones went to the Pacific, but I hear we had some deployed and taking care of patients coming out of Sicily. The idea is to take the worst wounded out of the combat areas aboard evacuation flights and give them palliative care in flight until they reach a full field hospital. I think the program has already saved a lot of lives."

Churchill contemplated for a moment. "That sounds like something the British military should be doing. I'll get my staff on it." He took a small notebook from his jacket pocket and scribbled some words. "Now, if you're ready to retire, I shall call our orderlies and help you down to your room."

"Two more things, Winston. First, how successful were your discussions with the Portuguese on closing the Azores Gap?"

"As predicted," Churchill replied. "The Portuguese president readily acceded to his obligation to back Great Britain under the Windsor Treaty provisions."

"I heard that he balked on supporting my country in the same way."

"True. But we made clear that the US was coming in regardless of his support or opposition. When your engineers promised to build a huge air base at Terceira that Portugal will be able to use after the war, that cheered him up. That was a good move on your part." Churchill chuckled. "The day after we landed there, we caught the *Kriegsmarine* by complete surprise and sent a German U-boat to the bottom of the Atlantic."

"So the Azores Gap is firmly closed?"

"It is, and we are operating quite effectively from there."

"What's your other question?" Churchill inquired.

"Ah. Yes." A concerned expression crossed Roosevelt's face. "This might seem like an odd question, but are you hearing anything about concentration camps for Jews and Gypsies and anyone else Hitler doesn't like, and the particularly gruesome treatment of them?"

Churchill took a deep breath. "We are, sir. They've trickled in, and the reports are coming from various parts of Europe and they're fairly consistent in describing acts of unimaginable cruelty. I shudder to think of what we'll find there when this war is over."

"We're receiving similar reports," Roosevelt muttered. "Another element we'll have to contend with. And all because one man fancies himself a god." He sighed as he took one last glimpse at the pyramids. "All right, Mr. Churchill. I'm done for the evening. Lead away." He slapped the arm of his wheelchair. "In maneuvering this contraption to my room, I am decidedly at your mercy."

44

Churchill and Roosevelt sat together again over breakfast in the president's suite the next morning before the arrival of Turkey's leader, President İnönü. "Before he gets here," Roosevelt said, "we really should talk about the Italian campaign."

Churchill regarded him in surprise. "I thought that was settled. We attack Anzio next. We're not making progress fast enough up Italy's back, and we must be finished with Rome by spring to position the landing craft for the cross-channel invasion."

"Yes, yes," the president agreed while nodding and waving a hand, "but I'm not sure that Eisenhower is all that keen on Anzio as an objective. It's a hell of a risk."

"But one we must take if we're to have a chance of taking Rome and the airfields north of there. We've been over this." Frustration crept into Churchill's tone. "Without those airfields, we can't threaten Germany directly anytime soon."

"I understand, Winston, but since Salerno, our troops, yours and ours—"

"Allied troops," Churchill interjected gruffly.

"Yes. Allied troops. As you pointed out, they've been slogging up Italy's spiny crocodile backbone for months now, and the casualties are piling up.

Some say we should be bypassing Italy in favor of an invasion into southern France."

"Don't forget," Churchill replied with a frown, "that one of our major objectives for going into Italy was to draw as many German troops as we could into Italy from the Soviet Union and the south of France. Granted, we wanted to liberate the people of Italy, but that kind sentiment was not the military reason for going into Italy first.

"And if we divert and go to southern France first," the prime minister continued, "we'll have a strong army on our flank capable of hitting us from those same airfields we hope to take in northern Italy and use against the *Wehrmacht* in the same place, southern France." He choked down evident exasperation. "We have a strategy, Franklin. Eisenhower is in London now planning the next part of it, the cross-channel invasion next year, which you know I'm not entirely in favor of; and General Alexander is now in charge of the Italian campaign and drawing up the details for the Anzio operation. We can't second-guess either of them."

Roosevelt put his palms up in a pacifying gesture. "I understand, Winston. But let me be plain. I know you want to capture Rome. Badly. Some say that is your current main objective, but achieving it will be costly." The president's fervor rose. "Before we commit to that, we'd better be sure that we are looking at every detail and considering every alternative, and if we go forward, it's only because we can't find a better way. Don't forget that all of Italy is not with us, despite its surrender and flipping to our side. Some Italian units are fighting with the Germans."

"Do you want me to admit that I might enjoy some personal pleasure in taking Rome?" Despite the mid-morning hour, Churchill's demeanor changed to one of fatigue. "I do so freely, just as I will rejoice when we've achieved final victory over Berlin.

"But surely you know that I would never put personal interests ahead of national interests or the Allies' interests." He drew himself to full height, and anger sparked in his eyes. "And I certainly will not waste the lives of our young men for personal aims, be they British, American, or any other nationality."

Roosevelt folded his hands in front of his mouth and nodded slightly. "I know you wouldn't, Winston. But General Kesselring is in charge of the

Wehrmacht in Italy now, and he's fighting a war of attrition. He's done it brilliantly, keeping us bogged down in Italy for the same reason we've bogged them down in other places—to get us to use up our men and resources while they regroup."

The president's passion rose to meet the prime minister's. "You worry about the bloodbath we'll visit on French civilians when we invade there, but that is exactly what's happening in Italy right now. That will be particularly true in a few days at a village called San Pietro in the Fifth Army's sector. That's where the Germans straddle the main highway leading to Rome.

"We're crawling north over the mountains of Italy inch by inch, wearing out whatever equipment that's not outright destroyed, and sending our dead home to grieving families by the boatload. And winter is setting in."

"I know," Churchill murmured, chagrinned. The two were quiet for an extended time, and then the prime minister asked, "So where do we stand on the subject? If we are going to change the plan, we'd better do it soon. Our men are already heavily entrenched inland along both the east and the west coasts, and as you pointed out, the Anzio operation is set to launch at the beginning of next month."

Roosevelt sighed. "What a way to begin a new year. Let's just hope the operation relieves pressure on our men further south and sets us up for an easier ride to Rome."

He paused in contemplation. "I understand your concerns. I'm saying to let the planning go forward, but let's be sure to consider every possibility before we execute—satisfy ourselves that there really isn't a better way. And if we go forward at Anzio, we had better be prepared to explain the high casualties at home, because they are bound to go higher."

The two men's eyes met and held. "Agreed," Churchill said at last. He stood quietly in thought, and then added, "I'm reluctant to mention this, Franklin, but the large number of casualties at Tarawa must have awakened your public to the difficulties ahead. The people of Britain are already accustomed to such high numbers, many of them from among civilians."

"Valid point," Roosevelt intoned grimly. "A sad one, but a valid one."

Churchill looked tiredly at his watch. "We had better prepare to meet President İnönü. He'll be here momentarily. I'm afraid he's a bit put out at me. When he and I met in Turkey back in January after the Casablanca Conference—you know we got together in a deserted railroad car at Yenice Station thirteen miles outside of Adana—"

Roosevelt's head swung up in surprise. "I didn't know that. You took a hell of a chance."

Churchill grunted. "Are you serious? And what am I doing in Cairo with you right now?" He chuckled at the irony. "In any event, I promised him financial assistance and military equipment, as I told you I would. In the interim, I had to reduce the aid. As a result, I'm sure he believes he made the right choice, to remain neutral. But we need him in this war."

Roosevelt took a moment to think through his response. "Winston, despite telling Stalin that I wanted Turkey in the war, I have my doubts. As long as İnönü maintains neutrality, that part of our flank is secured. Hitler might like to take that country, but he'd spread his forces even thinner, and he can no longer readily replenish them the way we can—not the men and not the equipment. He's pulling from the dregs for new recruits, and his war manufacturing base can't keep up. He reached the peak of his power at the beginning of this year, and it's downhill all the way for him from here on out. Even he must see that." He took a sip of coffee and added, "I'll be interested to hear Mr. İnönü's views."

President Ismet İnönü was a tall, slender man, impeccably dressed and courteous to a fault. He was known throughout Turkey and internationally as the right hand of the legendary Mustafa Kemal Atatürk, the man who had brought democracy to the seat of the former Ottoman Empire. Having served in the army for a full career, İnönü knew the ravages of war and the suffering of people living through it.

"As I told you last year, Mr. Prime Minister," he said as he, Roosevelt, and Churchill gathered in a conference room at the hotel, "I'm not anxious to get into this one." He locked his eyes directly on Churchill's. "I don't mean to be rude, but my reluctance to join the Allies grew in proportion to the reduction of your promised aid."

"I understand," Churchill said. "Unfortunately, that became necessary.

Our pockets are not bottomless, and the war is consuming massive resources. I didn't cut the aid out of whimsy, I assure you. We need you in the Alliance. I'd like to see you open another front in the Balkans too."

İnönü shook his head slowly, his eyes unwavering. "I'm on your side in spirit," he said softly, "but I cannot subject my people to more misery from war." He paused, and his forehead wrinkled. "As I understand matters, more than needing Turkey in the war, you need airbases on our territory. Do I grasp that correctly?"

"You do," Roosevelt interjected. "What are you thinking?"

İnönü took his time to respond. "Until the Allies took over the Azores, Portugal provided fuel and supplies to German submarines there and at Goa, in India. It received no repercussions for doing so from the Axis. I could look at the feasibility of providing the facilities you need in Turkey on the same basis. Having security guarantees would be helpful in addition to continued self-defense aid."

Roosevelt pulled a sheet of paper from his pocket and handed it to İnönü. "We just met with Marshal Stalin in Tehran. He is prepared to declare publicly that he will regard an attack on Turkey by Bulgaria as an attack on the Soviet Union and will consider itself to be in an immediate state of war with that country." He gestured at the document. "This is our joint statement from the conference. Read point number three."

İnönü scanned the paper and studied section three intently. It read:

"Took note of Marshal Stalin's statement that if Turkey found herself at war with Germany, and as a result Bulgaria declared war on Turkey or attacked her, the Soviet Union would immediately be at war with Bulgaria. The Conference further took note that this fact would be explicitly stated in the forthcoming negotiations to bring Turkey into the war."

"Stalin's prepared to declare that publicly," Churchill said.

İnönü raised his eyebrows. "I see that you're increasing support to Tito and the Resistance in Yugoslavia too. That and the statement by Stalin puts a new light on the subject." He studied the document a few moments more. "Let me confer with my advisers and get back to you. We might be able to arrange something."

December 6, 1943

Roosevelt and Churchill met in the grand foyer of the Mena House hotel to say their farewells. Before parting, they took to a quiet corner made available by their security detail and away from listening ears, where they talked in hushed tones. "This has been a good two weeks, Winston. I feel that we've accomplished a lot."

"I know you were dead set on the operations in the Bay of Bengal," the prime minister replied. "In canceling them, I think you made a wise choice."

"Couldn't be helped. We need the landing craft in the European theater, and the numbers that Lord Mountbatten provided as necessary to pull off the operation in Bengal were just too high. I read his rationale and understand his desire to make his first amphibious assault a successful one, but given the other priorities, canceling that operation was the only thing to do. I still believe we must find an active way to support Chiang Kai-shek, but it'll have to wait." He half-grinned at Churchill. "So, we both come away with some things we wanted, and we were disappointed in others."

"That's why it's called war," Churchill said with a mischievous smile. Then he added, "This has been a good year, Franklin, in spite of all the setbacks. At the beginning of it, Hitler was at the height of his military power, and now in December, he is decidedly on the decline."

Roosevelt arched his brows for a second and pursed his lips. "Vemork is once again producing heavy water. And a raid on the plant by our US bombers two months ago barely dented the place."

Churchill chuckled. "I know. Well, you had to have your go at it. We didn't do any better in our bombing run last year. The plant is well built and too deeply entrenched in the valley for an air raid to be effective." He added with a sly smile, "But we're hearing through Bletchley that your raid convinced the Germans to move the facility to Germany. When they do that, we might encounter some opportunities. We can hope."

"Of course. And at least we got that physicist, Niels Bohr, out of Denmark—or rather your commandos did. Losing him was a big blow to German atomic ambitions."

Churchill agreed, nodding gravely. "That was a sad affair, though. The radio operator who flew into Denmark on the same flight that brought Bohr out was captured by the *Gestapo*. Her codename was Trudi, and apparently she never revealed the fact that she was King George's first cousin. She had been the Morse-code operator on the London end of a Danish Resistance network.

"The operator on the Denmark side had been found out and executed. Trudi was so distraught that she insisted on replacing him. She helped put Bohr on the return flight to England and was captured soon afterward. We still don't know her whereabouts and assume that she's dead."

The prime minister's head dropped, and when he raised it again, his eyes were pained, his voice hollow. "No one will ever be able to tell of all the bravery exhibited by people of all sorts in this war, nor will we be able to adequately recognize them."

The president nodded silently, and then he said in a broken voice. "You're right, Winston, and if for no other reason, that's why we must win."

As if to break the somber mood after another quiet interval, Churchill smiled while taking a deep breath. "Well, as they say, upward and onward." Then he added seriously, "I saw the note from İnönü. We get the airfields, but Turkey maintains neutrality under Soviet protection. I can live with that."

45

December 14, 1943
San Pietro Infine, Italy

Sergeant First Class Zack Littlefield peered west over the eastern edge of a long ridge. Far in the distance, on the opposite end of the valley below, San Pietro appeared serene. Along the village's right and left, two more mountain ranges running parallel to each other boxed in the community that was protected on all sides from the weather, remaining green with vegetation despite its fallow fields.

With an estimated population of fourteen hundred people, the notion that this spot on the road held any strategic value seemed farfetched. A story circulating among the troops in Zack's platoon, however, held that the ancient Apian Way ran through the village, which had originated on that spot as a waystation along the famous Roman road.

One of Zack's men, Corporal Enzo Bonetti, had been an archaeological student before enlisting in the Army and had studied the works of a contemporary professor of Roman topography, Giuseppe Lugli, of the University of Rome. The professor had used recent technology to map the ancient thoroughfare, and Enzo had studied his work as a matter of personal interest.

Enzo had been invaluable to Zack as they had fought up the Italian coast with a national guard unit from Texas, the 753rd Armored Battalion of the 36th Division, after the near disaster that had been Salerno. Enzo's parents had emigrated to the US from San Pietro, precisely where the division now sought to engage the *Wehrmacht* and break General Kesselring's defensive line.

Two roads led into San Pietro, both from the south, one through a narrow pass, the other over the high mountain ridges. They converged in this tiny village and proceeded north as Highway 6 to the next major objective, Rome.

Like many Americans born to Italian parents, Enzo felt an obligation to fight for the "old country," and there was no shortage among the ranks of Italian-speaking soldiers of like minds. Enzo was bilingual, and Zack had therefore kept him within arm's reach ever since the squad had taken its first objective, the hilltop at the south end of the beach at Salerno.

The landings had been hard fought, much more deadly than anticipated, with the Germans sending in ample reinforcements. At one critical point, Zack sensed that his squad was about to be overrun from the rear, and at that point, Enzo appeared with a local partisan. The man gestured wildly in the air, his eyes wide, and he spoke in a high-pitched whisper while looking back fearfully the way he had come.

"We have guardian angels," Enzo told Zack. "This man and his friends have been watching from several hundred yards back. They came to warn us when they saw German mechanized vehicles coming our way. *Wehrmacht* troops have dismounted and are maneuvering through the trees."

That bit of information saved the invasion's right flank. A quick radio message up the line brought in additional naval gun strikes and air bombardments that blunted the German advance, but it could not save Zack's platoon sergeant, who was killed in the battle. Zack had been promoted in the field to replace him.

The death of the noncom hit Zack hard. The two men had been part of a reorganized company formed from the remnants of other devastated units within the 36th Division while still in North Africa. Although the new company received veterans from a variety of occupational specialties, it reorganized as an infantry unit. The platoon sergeant of one of the battalion's line platoons noticed Zack's strong leadership skills and therefore requested Zack's reassignment to that platoon and promotion to squad leader.

The idea had never crossed Zack's mind that he might one day replace the man he had come to regard as a mentor, and certainly not so soon. Now, looking over the ridge into Liri Valley, the thought flashed through his mind of how fleeting time was. The image of the platoon sergeant's face was fading in his memory, merging with those of so many others who had become casualties in this war. Centuries seemed to have passed since Zack had found himself alone on the sands of the Kasserine Pass when, in fact, only nine months had gone by: only five months since Sicily, and only three months since the landing at Salerno.

Meanwhile, the grind northward along Italy's mountainous spine had been mind-numbingly arduous, becoming worse as winter approached and rainy weather set in. As soon as the division's tanks had landed in full force at Salerno and the beachhead had been established and secured, Zack had requested a transfer back to tanks on the basis that he had trained in armor and that was where his skill was better developed. The division being short of tanks and tankers, he met no resistance, and because of his promotions, he found himself in an acting capacity once again as a platoon sergeant in Company C of the 753rd Armor Battalion.

The role was not one he cherished as he took on the duties of ensuring that food, ammunition, supplies, and replacements got to the front and that casualties were cared for or sent back to field hospitals. While he did not relish being in combat, he nonetheless felt in his gut that he shirked his duty by working in the rear.

After consolidating the Salerno beachhead, the Allies had fought north through Naples, securing its port and continuing the advance through one small village after another. And always, as successive battles drove the Germans north across deep ravines and fast-flowing rivers, desolation lay in the wake. Stone houses and village buildings were reduced to rubble, and roads made impassable to everyday vehicles.

Yet, after the *Wehrmacht* had gone, townspeople poured from the bombed-out doorways and precarious cracks and crevices into street debris to celebrate their regained freedom and the departure of their oppressors. They welcomed their liberators with flowers, showering them with embraces and kisses.

As the division had headed into the mountains, Zack wondered about the role of tanks in the upcoming battle, particularly as the rain fell more frequently, in greater volumes, muddying the roads and bringing whole columns of the armored behemoths to a halt. He had entertained thoughts of requesting to go back to a frontline infantry unit. That thought became more pressing as the higher he went into the mountains, the more he learned of the conditions under which the infantry lived and operated.

By the time the tanks had labored up the steep slopes, the infantry had already secured high ridges and mountaintops, but the effort to sustain the soldiers on the rims with food, water, ammunition, and the other sundries critical to staying alive and holding off a determined enemy across an army-wide front proved to be monumental. To accomplish the task, any available US soldiers and paid local Italians organized into "mule skinner" teams.

Each night hundreds of mules burdened with supplies were led by the skinners a third of the way up the mountain. There, the loads were transferred to the backs of many more men who carried the cargoes the remaining distance to the troops in the defensive positions on the ridges. Often, the troops themselves participated in lugging the supplies up.

Zack was weary to the bone most of the time, as were all the soldiers he knew. Yet, when he saw the haggard faces of these infantrymen on the ridges, he had to control his emotions tightly so as not to show pity or revulsion. They were haggard beyond belief, filthy for having insufficient water and hygiene supplies, and cold for spending so much time in wet, blustery weather with insufficient warm clothing. And on any given day, German artillery levied blistering barrages on their positions.

Zack wondered which elements generated the most casualties: enemy fire, exposure, hunger, or infection. He was astounded to learn that many of the soldiers, as they descended the mountains for medical care, served as night guides to keep the mule skinners from getting lost.

Unbelievably, though, the infantry's morale remained high, despite their poor conditions. Zack was most struck by how appreciative they were for every effort and provision extended to support them.

Zack ascended the ridge on this day to observe the lay of the land. Leaders of infantry and artillery units of the 36th Division had already made such treks, but as no one had anticipated tanks being in the mix of elements to climb these heights and then descend into the Liri Valley, he had not previously been there.

He sucked in his breath as he gazed across the valley. Far in the distance on the left flank to the west, on the other side of San Pietro, Mount Lungo rose over seven hundred and fifty feet high. Germans occupied the heights there.

On the opposite side of the valley, the *Wehrmacht* still occupied the highest ground, on Mount Sammucro, at a height of over twelve hundred feet. It held a commanding position over the ridgeline where Zack now lay prone, looking through binoculars at the prospective battlefield.

He had already read the intelligence and battle reports to date. The 2nd Battalion/15th *Panzergrenadier* Regiment of the 29th *Panzergrenadier* Division defended San Pietro. Also, 3rd Battalion/15th *Panzergrenadier* Regiment occupied Monte Lungo. But fortunately, American troops had ousted the 2nd Battalion/71st *Panzergrenadier* Regiment from the heights of Monte Sammucro.

San Pietro itself, the obstacle blocking a northward push to Rome, sat on high ground above the valley floor. The Germans garrisoned the village, defended it with mortars, machine guns, and heavy weapons, and fortified it with barbed wire, minefields, and interconnecting trenches and pillboxes.

Zack had read in operations reports that an Allied action conducted a week earlier had gone badly. The Italians had executed it as its first battle on the side of the Allies and as a morale-boosting campaign. They had envisioned an easy victory.

Two of their battalions had scrambled up Monte Lungo's slopes abreast of each other. Expecting light resistance, they all but marched straight into prepared positions of the 3rd Battalion/15th *Panzergrenadier* Regiment. The Germans had zeroed their guns on the avenues of approach. Very quickly, the Italians were in retreat and took high casualties.

At dawn on that same day, a combined force of the 1st battalion of the 143rd Infantry Regiment, 504th Infantry Regiment, and the 3rd Ranger Battalion swept the German defenders off Monte Sammucro. Despite German counterattacks over the next few days, the Americans held and expanded their positions to include Hills 1205 and 950, to the west of San Pietro.

Again, the Germans counterattacked and succeeded in re-taking Hill 950 from the 3rd Rangers, but they, in turn, were driven off by the Rangers the following day.

In the valley below, the 2nd and 3rd battalions of the 143rd Infantry Regiment mounted their drive toward San Pietro. Rain had fallen all night and continued as the attack began. The thick, muddy earth on the approaches was rolling and uneven, tripping soldiers into the ooze as they ran into minefields, while mortars and field artillery directed from Mount Lungo took a deadly toll.

By the second day of battle, the two infantry battalions had succeeded in advancing only four hundred yards, and on Mount Sammucro, casualties had reduced the 1st battalion's strength by fifty percent, to three hundred and forty capable fighters. The 36th Division's commander, General Walker, ordered a withdrawal of the attacking forces to their original positions to plan for a new assault.

Zack's company commander, Captain Lazard, attended the battalion brief for the new operation and then prepared his lieutenants. Zack had attended Lazard's subsequent briefing with his platoon leader, Lieutenant Joe Hunter. "It's grim," Lazard had said. "We're short on platoon leaders, so we're combining our tanks into two platoons of eight tanks each. Lieutenant Hunter, you've got first platoon, and Lieutenant Brown, you've got second platoon. The CG wants to put our tanks in that valley. The attack goes in two days."

Zack respected both Lazard and Hunter, though he had not known them long. Very few men in the unit had been together for much time, all having survived the hard slog up the Italian boot thus far, and most having been reassigned to new units as old ones became combat ineffective. As replacements arrived, hardened veterans maintained a distance, not for lack of friendliness but to safeguard against painful emotions from losing yet another close comrade.

Zack had developed a particular fondness for Lieutenant Hunter. The lanky, dark-haired officer of serious countenance kept his distance but took care of his men. He knew each soldier's name, background, and hometown, and he provided ample words of encouragement. Most important, he ensured that every last one was rested, fed, and as fully equipped as possible.

Zack knew little about Hunter, only that he came from a tiny town in west Texas. The platoon leader had been married a year and recently received news of a newborn baby daughter.

On hearing Lazard state the H-hour of the attack on San Pietro, Zack stared up the steep slope where the village seemed peacefully nestled. "How are we going in?"

"Over the high ridge."

A collective gasp had escaped from the group. "The CG is going to put tanks over that?" Lieutenant Brown asked, aghast. He had gestured toward the steep grade. "We'll be lucky to get them up on this side, much less get them over the top in sufficient strength to be effective on the other side."

"I know." The captain shook his head. "We'll do a recon from the ridge before we go in." He breathed in heavily. "It's like this. General Clark wants tanks in the fight as soon as possible. He sent Fifth Army's ops officer, Brigadier General Brann, to talk with our commanding general, Walker, about the feasibility. From what I gather, Brann impressed on Walker that Clark really wants this done—tanks in the battle. He thinks they'll add to field artillery suppressive fire when we get close to the village."

"And Walker gave in," someone interjected.

"Careful," Lazard cautioned. "We have orders and we're going to carry them out." Over a dirt model of the terrain carved into the ground, he laid out the plan to his fatigued, steely-eyed subordinates. "With the exception of Mount Lungo, we now occupy the high ground around San Pietro. Two battalions of the 143rd Infantry will advance from the northeast on our right flank.

"Meanwhile, two infantry battalions, the 141st, the 142nd, the remaining elements of the 143rd, and another element of the 504th will enter the valley via the lower pass in the south. Their objectives are these three hillocks west of the village." He pointed them out on the dirt model. "They're between San Pietro and Mount Lungo. Walker believes that if we strike fast and hard, he'll seize those hillocks and overwhelm the troops in the village, isolating the guns on Mount Lungo before they can react. Then, the 141st will attack San Pietro, and the 142nd will attack the units on Mount Lungo to seize that high ground and neutralize their guns."

"And our role?" a lieutenant asked, his voice laced with skepticism.

The CO took a deep breath. "We'll descend into the valley on this road —" He pointed it out.

"Sir," Hunter said. "I've been up there for recon already. I've seen that road. It's narrow. The ground is terraced above and below that route. Ya can't see beyond what's right in front of you. We already know that the Germans have plotted aiming points in that area. Getting to our objective is a suicide mission. And what are we supposed to do? What's our objective?"

Lazard cast him a castigating glance and then held up a placating palm. "Calm yourselves, gentlemen. We're soldiers. The combat engineers are going in ahead of us to blow out some of the retaining walls holding up those terraces and widen the road as much as possible."

"Oh great," Lieutenant Brown remarked. "So now we get to line up tanks in a row like in a carnival shoot. Or we get to have tons of dirt slide down to smother us or roll us downhill."

"That isn't tank country," Hunter added.

"Enough," the CO said sharply. "Our orders are set. As I was saying, our mission is to descend into the valley on that approach, spread out when we get to the flat ground, support the field artillery with suppressing fire until the infantry has taken those three hillocks and cleared a path through the minefields, and then attack and enter San Pietro from two directions. Once there, we'll search out and destroy enemy heavy weapons and set up blocking positions on the far side of the village against counterattack."

"Is that all, sir?" a disgruntled platoon sergeant said. "Meanwhile, if the plan doesn't work, we'll be out in the open, easy targets for fire from Mount Lungo."

"Cut the crap," the CO said. "That's our cross to bear. The infantry has its own. They'll attack in broad daylight across ground that's already ranged by German artillery and heavy machine guns. Before this operation, their assaults were at night. And they'll be crawling on their bellies through minefields, trenches, and barbed-wire barriers.

"Now, on to command and control. We're short an exec and a first sergeant, so if I go down, the senior man takes charge." He paused and rubbed his eyes tiredly. "I'll take pertinent questions only." Turning to Hunter and Brown, he instructed, "First platoon leads off. Brown, yours will follow." He shifted his eyes to take in the full group. "No more bellyaching. It's time to recon, plan, coordinate, and prepare to march."

As Zack continued studying Liri Valley, Hunter sidled up next to him. "This is even worse than what I thought, sir," Zack said. "That road can barely hold a car, much less a tank." He rolled over to lean his back against the hillside just below the rim. "Whoever came up with this plan either has never seen the terrain or doesn't understand tanks."

"Yep. That's the way I see things." The lieutenant peered over the valley. "Ours is but to do and die." He continued his gaze, and then asked, "Have you reconned from the other positions?"

"This is my first. I'll spend the day up here seeing as much as I can from every angle. We can compare notes tonight."

As Hunter started to move away, Zack stopped him with an appeal. "Sir, I can't sit in the rear while our men go into that inferno. I know you'll lead from the front. You always do. Request to be in the tank right behind yours."

The lieutenant turned and gave him a long, sad look, and then nodded. "Organize for it. Make sure we have a good acting platoon sergeant getting grub and bullets to the front." He broke a grim smile. "Maybe we'll catch some luck."

He started away again, stopped, and faced Zack. "I need a favor." He reached into his jacket pocket and pulled out a crinkled, sealed envelope. A name and address were scrawled on the front.

Dread seized Zack, and his throat caught.

"Will you do me the honors?" Hunter said. He turned his head. "I'd like to know that my new daughter will grow up knowing her father loved her." He added, sniffing, "My wife too." The lieutenant's head dropped momentarily, and then he said with a forlorn half-smile, "I don't know anyone else well enough to ask."

Zack stared, frozen. Then he reached for the envelope. "I'll be happy to hold it, sir. But you won't be needing it. Not just yet. I'll give it back after we've taken San Pietro."

46

December 15, 1943
San Pietro Infine, Italy

The thunderous concussion of heavy guns had been deafening throughout the night as hour after hour, field artillery units pummeled San Pietro and Mount Lungo while the other combat elements moved into place. And the rain still fell.

At mid-morning, with Hunter's tank in front and Zack's a healthy distance behind him, sixteen tanks started down the narrow road into Liri Valley. As they descended the steep track, Zack wondered at the sense of sending armor on a narrow channel through the mountains. He blocked questions regarding the senior leadership's judgment from his mind.

The rain had cleared, and the day was beautiful. Sitting in the commander's hatch, Zack marveled at the stunning landscape. Even from this distance, he saw that olive groves and vineyards along the valley's floor and walls had been left unattended for an extended time and were fallow. But Enzo had told him that Liri Valley remained green year-round, and below the tree line, wild vegetation grew in profusion, overwhelming areas that had been cultivated fields and orchards.

As the tanks descended, the rise in temperature was dramatic, resulting from protection by the mountains on all sides from the blustery wind east of the ridgeline. Despite the improved weather conditions, Zack suppressed his reverie. He clearly saw the tactical situation on the ground, and it did not bode well for his unit.

As Hunter had noted, the road barely accommodated the width of the war machines, and looking up from lower ground to the commanding heights of Mount Lungo to the southwest, he sensed the visceral threat of being in the open with no cover. The vehicles were presently out of range of the German guns, but soon his tanks would be targeted by heavy artillery.

The platoon moved to the assembly area short of the line of departure. Final recon reports arrived, equipment was checked, and repairs made.

Intelligence reports received overnight gave no room for optimism. The Germans had counterattacked in force on Hills 509 and 1205, and with the 143rd's depleted numbers, the division's ability to hold those positions was tenuous.

Preparatory to the attack, the full force of US Fifth Army's heavy guns again unleashed barrage after barrage. Overhead, heavy bombers flew in mass formations, dropping tons of high explosives. The hiss of artillery rounds through the air and the whoosh of dropped bombs followed by the dull thuds and concussive detonations thundered across the western landscape from the top of Mount Lungo, across the three hillocks southwest of San Pietro, to the base of the high ground north of the village. Zack watched through binoculars as homes, shops, and the cathedral were obliterated. Then thick smoke and debris obscured his view.

At noon, on schedule, the ground attack began. The heavy gun and air bombardment continued, but ranged closer to the village and away from ground that American troops would traverse. Zack hoped they had taken out most of the minefields.

Hunter's tank suddenly roared, spewed black exhaust, and emerged from the deep shadows of a tree line onto the narrow road leading down into the valley. Zack's Sherman followed.

Turning around in his cupola, Zack watched the other six tanks of first platoon fall into a line behind him, spaced out a distance to avoid more than one vehicle being taken out by a single artillery round. Overhead,

American bombers disappeared to be replaced by fighter aircraft protecting against enemy strafing and bombing.

Zack ducked under the commander's hatch and pulled it closed. Together, his driver and his machine gunner now performed as his eyes. Otherwise, he was blind.

The Shermans proceeded along the road, encountering the places where combat engineers had demolished retaining walls and removed the threat of landslides. Zack assumed, but could not see, that the infantry moved abreast of them on the uphill terraces to the right.

The units advanced almost to the German forward defensive lines reached in battle a few days earlier, roughly four hundred yards from this morning's line of departure. Meanwhile, US artillery fire continued, pounding targets inside the village and on Mount Lungo.

Then suddenly, the German lines erupted with fire, and the big guns on Mount Lungo rained artillery down on the tank column and the infantry to the right. The thump-thump-thump and woodpecker-staccato of heavy and light machine guns broke through the air with bullets hissing by. Zack found himself strangely thankful for the noise and the obscured view that prevented his seeing and hearing the anguished cries of infantrymen being cut down to his right from the withering onslaught.

Then he heard the plink-plink-plink of bullets striking the skin of his tank.

Before Zack could absorb the implications of being hit by crew-served direct-fire weapons, he felt and heard an enormous boom to his front and his driver called urgently over the intercom, "Hunter's been hit. He's down."

Zack jerked the handle securing the hatch and raised it sufficiently to see the road ahead. Hunter's tank straddled it, a mangled hulk spewing flames, its ammunition load exploding amid black smoke.

Recalling the scenes at the Kasserine Pass of sprawling and burned bodies spread over the battlefield amid torched war machines, he closed down the memory and the obvious implication of the horrific scene ahead of him. He called down to the driver, "The rear of Hunter's tank isn't burning. Can you get close to it?"

"I think so, Sarge."

"All right. Pop some smoke and wait till the ammo stops burning off."

He turned the dial to the company net on his radio. "This is Charlie 2. Charlie 6 is down. No survivors. I'm senior. Will clear road and proceed unless otherwise ordered."

The response from Lazard came almost immediately, but the lull seemed to last an age. Meanwhile, Zack fingered the letter Hunter had entrusted to him.

"Roger. Proceed. Your call-sign is now Charlie 6."

Disregarding a heavy heart and a churning gut, Zack switched to the platoon net. "This is Charlie 6. Hunter is down. We proceed. Acknowledge."

He heard the replies within seconds, and once again called over his tank's intercom to the driver. "Close on that tank and shove it over the side."

"Sarge?"

"Do it," Zack snapped, "unless you want us to be next. We can't turn around. The only way for us is forward."

The tank lurched and the sounds of battle continued outside unabated. Another call came in from a tank over the company net from one in second platoon. Recognizing the call-sign, Zack's heart sank. "Brown and Lazard are dead," came the panicked report in the clear. "We're the fourth tank forward at the rear of second platoon. Seven tanks ahead of me are in flames. You're senior man in the whole company. What are your orders?"

Zack stared at the mic in disbelief. Doing a quick mental calculation, he came to an inescapable conclusion. Of the sixteen tanks that had started down the road, only eight remained. Four of those were from his own platoon; the four from second platoon were blocked. Only his own tank and three behind him were intact and in a position to move forward.

"Return your tanks to the assembly area," he barked to the second platoon. "Await further orders. Out."

From the front of the tank, Zack felt a thump as his tank jolted against the smoldering carcass of Hunter's vehicle. Once again, Zack opened the cupola a crack to watch. He heard the engine rev, the ground scraped as the tracks slipped and gained traction, and then his tank strained as it pushed and finally lurched forward. The doomed war-machine slid over the bank and rolled out of sight.

"Keep moving," Zack called. "Take the next turn to the left. Our spot to spread out is down there. We'll be off this infernal road."

He called to the three vehicles behind him, "Follow me. It's just us four."

The gunfire lulled.

Zack opened the hatch wider, spinning in the cupola to make sure his remaining tanks trailed behind him as his driver made the sharp turn. The tank accelerated as Zack realized that the platoon's situation had worsened. They had even less cover, and they could be targeted broadside.

A massive explosion shook the ground. Spinning in the cupola, he saw that a Panzer IV had turned in the road to his rear, but apparently had not seen the other three Shermans coming behind. Before the Panzer could shoot, the lead Sherman made short work of it. However, now it blocked the road. The three tanks of first platoon could not follow Zack.

Surveying both sides, he studied the terraces. They were too steep for the three tanks behind to follow in parallel above him. Only the terrace next to him offered sufficient flat ground. His tank's only recourse was to turn onto it and proceed west.

"Go back to the main road," he ordered the trailing tanks. "Seek cover. Shell the town at will and maneuver toward it when you can. We'll link up there."

To the driver, he yelled, "Turn onto that terrace and hug the retaining wall. Make your way forward. Carefully."

The tank rumbled along the terrace, bulldozing ancient olive trees and every form of vegetation in its path. The soil, still wet from days of rain, made traction sporadic, the heavy tracks spinning in places until they had plowed into firmer ground.

Then, as Zack and his crew drew closer to the village amid continued heavy shelling from Mount Lungo, another threat manifested, one that Zack knew well: direct-fire anti-tank guns, shooting from San Pietro. Unable to turn in any direction from its current path, the tank rumbled on, slowly, toward its death trap.

An explosive jolt hit the left side of the tank, and a flash of searing heat stabbed through the turret. Spalling caused by the impact bounced jagged pieces of metal around the interior, ripped from the inside walls by the impact. The vehicle lifted momentarily, and when it settled, smoke rose from its stricken side. Inside, the entire crew lay still.

47

December 16, 1943
Tunis, Tunisia

Captain Sherry Littlefield heard the clanging bell that always caused her gut to tighten. The sound alerted her and the other flight nurses that more Douglas C-47 Skytrain evacuation aircraft, dubbed "Dakotas," were inbound with severely wounded soldiers. She would accompany some of them on their flight to Great Britain.

Sherry had been in one of the first classes to enter training at Bowman Field in Kentucky early that year. So great was the need in North Africa and the Pacific, however, that she and her classmates graduated ahead of schedule and shipped out to both theaters. Sherry had been assigned to the Mediterranean.

Since Allied troops had landed in Italy, flights had arrived with disturbing frequency. Primarily Allied soldiers and Marines were onboard with traumatic wounds that, if not treated immediately, would result in death.

Little in Sherry's training had prepared her for many of the traumatic injuries that confronted her. Men with missing arms or legs, sometimes both, the grisly stubs wrapped in bandages that then had to be removed for cleaning and further treatment. Others with gaping wounds to the abdomen or chest, and still more men with their faces blown away or with ghastly wounds in their extremities.

Just as disconcerting were the patients who appeared perfectly normal with no visible signs of injury. They were victims of artillery detonations or bombs dropped from the air. Often, they had been missed by flying shrapnel, but the shockwaves had caused concussion and/or damage to internal organs that were not discernable without X-rays or surgery.

Some of these latter wounded arrived unconscious and remained that way for their entire transport to military hospitals in Great Britain. Others were awake and even friendly, conversing with the flight nurses and grateful for the care bestowed on them.

Sherry recalled one such soldier who had been wounded during Operation Torch in North Africa. He seemed barely out of his teens, and having been cleaned up on arrival, his tan skin almost glowed. Hailing from Ohio, he could be any mother's son, one who was at once respectful and charming.

"I got a girl back home in Loudonville. Louisa," he told Sherry. "We been goin' together since high school. We aim t' get married when I git home." His face took on a forlorn look. "Well we was. She might change her mind, thinkin' I'm a coward."

He gestured with one hand indicating the length of his body, and then winced at obviously excruciating pain. "Look at me," he gasped. "Not a mark on me."

"Do you need more pain medicine?" Sherry asked.

"Nah. It's gone now. As I was sayin' about Louisa. We both like canoein'. Ya know, Loudonville is the canoe manufacturing capital of Ohio. It sets right on the Mohican River, an' we used t' sneak out at night or skip school t' go down t' the river." He snickered and winced again as pain overcame him. "Of course, we wasn't always canoin'. Sometimes we was smoochin'."

His grin transformed to pain evident in his eyes, and he looked up into Sherry's. "I'm not feelin' so good." He coughed. "Could you hold my hand? I'll pretend it's Louisa's."

A lump formed in Sherry's throat as she took the young soldier's palm.

"You're going to be all right," she said with forced warmth, knowing otherwise and repressing tears.

He smiled. "Thanks," and squeezed her palm. Moments later, his grip loosened as he let out his last breath.

Hiding her emotions from the other patients in the closely stacked racks of the cargo area, Sherry tucked the blankets around him. "Get some rest," she said, forcing normal calm into her voice. "I'll just close this curtain to make it easier to sleep."

She made her way to the galley behind the cockpit, stopping along the way to comfort the other wounded soldiers. Then, out of sight, hidden in shadows, she wept. But only for a minute. She dried her eyes, took a deep breath, and returned to her duties of tending to the physical and emotional wounds of the men in her care. She knew her role: to provide immediate medical care and stand in for the mothers, wives, girlfriends, sisters, daughters, or any other woman whose memory gave comfort to Sherry's broken patients.

Another soldier who haunted her was wounded in battle north of Salerno. A volley of machine gun fire had grazed his upper extremities, taking his face with it. He had been a handsome man, and whenever Sherry drew near, he had shown her a photograph of himself, as if to say, "I didn't always look like this." Other wounded soldiers tried to encourage him with assurances that plastic surgeons would reconstruct his face, which was so torn that he could not drink, not even with a straw. All that Sherry could do for him was render pain medicine and keep him hydrated intravenously.

Working in the field hospitals provided no respite. Because of the steady inflow of wounded men, the exhausted state of those tending to them, and the small support staff to handle logistical and administrative duties, opportunities to rest were scarce. On more than one occasion, with no time to move the dead from the hospital to the morgue, the stench of death permeated all quarters.

Sherry understood that similar scenes played out at other airfields across the Mediterranean and in the Pacific theater. In her mind's eye, she saw thousands of Dakota aircraft flying across the skies. They carried cargo on their outbound trips, so they bore no Red Cross insignia traveling in either direction, thus making them legitimate targets for enemy fire. And on their return flights, they transported the most seriously wounded—thousands upon thousands of stricken men who might never return to normal life, if they survived at all.

When the visions appeared, Sherry shuddered and closed them out.

At night, when her nightmares played out in vivid color, she awoke sweating and shaking and praying to God to stop the carnage.

Once the incoming Dakotas had taxied to a stop, Sherry and the other nurses snapped into action, boarding the planes, screening the patients, and directing corpsmen regarding which ones to carry out first. In some instances, they administered treatment immediately, allowing the patients to deplane only when sufficiently stable and sedated, and often grabbing the ends of the litters themselves to move the patients.

The nurses, as they had been trained, interacted with the wounded men with warm friendliness, offering cigarettes, chocolate, and hot coffee when appropriate, and providing encouraging words. They moved swiftly and efficiently, establishing priority for those most in need and watching stoically as those who had died were transferred for burial.

Then, larger, four-engine Douglas C-54 Skymasters, with ranges of three thousand miles, were loaded and prepared for the flight to England, with a flight nurse assigned to each plane. Her authority was unsurpassed in matters of medical care during flight and until patients were delivered to a medical staff on the ground. More than one such nurse had found herself performing surgery in flight.

Sherry knew of an instance when a Dakota had crash-landed, and a propeller had ripped through the fuselage and lacerated the trachea of a wounded soldier. The flight nurse had fashioned an air tube from pieces of the aircraft's systems, fed it into her patient's airway, and kept him alive. Sherry had heard other stories equally tragic and heroic, hoping, as she imagined all her colleagues did, that she would be spared such exigencies.

She boarded the Skymaster assigned to her, strapped herself in, and waited, preparing herself for the emotional toll of caring for her wards for the next six hours. The plane rumbled down the runway, lifted its nose, and lumbered into the air. When it reached its assigned altitude and leveled off, she started forward to meet her twenty-eight patients, stacked in racks, four high, along the interior walls of the aircraft.

The first man had suffered a shoulder wound. The round had shattered his shoulder blade. He was in a cast. "This dang thing itches," he told Sherry, obviously in good spirits. "The bullet missed my heart by three inches. Wasn't my time to go." He squirmed uncomfortably. "Can you scratch inside my cast? Just below my shoulder blade."

"I'll try," Sherry said. "Let me know if I'm hurting you." The soldier twisted as best he could. She inserted her fingers between his skin and the plaster, found the area, and gently scratched.

"Ahh," the man exclaimed in obvious relief. "No wonder we call you flying angels."

The second soldier was also in good spirits, but they seemed forced. "I'm going home," he said. Then he indicated his lower body. "Minus a leg. But hey, I got another one. Just keep that morphine comin'."

The third man lay still, with his eyes closed, and before Sherry looked closely at him, she gazed at his chart. He had a few lacerations from flying metal, but no serious surface wounds. Damage to his internal organs was not yet known. He was in a coma, the victim of a shockwave from a direct hit by an anti-tank round.

Sherry glanced up at the soldier's face. An involuntary gasp escaped her lips, and she nearly fainted. With her eyes locked on the young man, she took a deep breath, steadied her wobbly knees, and while still clasping the chart, she staggered to her seat.

There, out of sight of her patients, she took deep breaths and fanned herself while tears rolled down her cheeks. She stifled cries of agony, and then stared once again at the chart. After some minutes, Sherry stood, straightened her uniform, and continued about her duties. As she passed by the soldier who had caused such an emotional reaction, she returned his chart to its holder by the bunk. Across the top, large block letters spelled out her patient's name: Sergeant First Class Zack Littlefield.

EPILOGUE

December 17, 1943
Bletchley, Park

"Sir, you asked to be briefed on what we hear coming out of Berlin regarding the battle around San Pietro in Liri Valley, Italy?"

Commander Travis looked up at Claire and waved her through the door to her usual seat. "Yes. It's grim on both sides of that country. The PM wants to be kept fully informed. What have you got?"

"From our vantage, there's been a bit of a breakthrough in that valley. It's near the west coast. From the German view in Berlin, it's not so good. The *Wehrmacht* had stalled the US Fifth Army on the east end. They attacked on the 10th, but were driven back. Over the next several days, they took the high ground around San Pietro. It's on the main approach to Rome. The US attacked again on the 15th and were successful in taking the village and Mount Lungo, a mountain to the west where the *Wehrmacht* had placed heavy artillery.

"The Germans counterattacked the next day—yesterday—but they did so as a prelude to withdrawing. They were repulsed, and today their forces are moving northward to prepared positions on the Gustav Line."

Travis sighed heavily. "That withdrawal makes sense, from their perspective. They know they're losing Italy, and they're bleeding us while buying time to re-build their forces. For the life of me, I don't understand why we went that route. We could have cut German supply lines to Italy by cordoning it off in the north. Now we're taking so many casualties, and at the rate we're crawling up those mountains, they could succeed." He sighed again. "But those decisions are made far above my head." He was silent a moment, and then added, "And we can't stop what the Germans are doing in Norway. So far, neither we nor the US has stopped their production of heavy water."

Claire gazed at him with a bemused expression. "Sir, I'm afraid I don't know the term 'heavy water.'"

"What, oh, I spoke out of turn. Disregard that. Forget I mentioned it. What about Montgomery and Italy's east coast."

"Probably nothing startling that you don't already know from the operations side. The Gustav Line extends across the country south of Rome. On the British end in the east, our soldiers are inching northward. Orders from Berlin are for the *Wehrmacht* to reinforce the defensive line over the winter, during which time the Germans expect the Allied forces to be slowed by the weather and to use the lull in battle to rest and refit their forces."

"Have you heard any mention of Anzio?"

"None, sir. Is that something we should be listening for?"

Travis nodded as he rose from his seat. "Yes. Please let me know if any decoded messages mention Anzio. And now, I must go to a briefing. Thank you, Miss Littlefield. Your information corroborates what we're hearing from the operations side."

Stony Stratford, England

The nanny saw Claire through the sitting room window and hurried out to meet her on the gravel path. "I'm sorry to worry you, mum," she said. "I've just had a message from your cousin, Sherry. She's quite distraught and left a number for you to ring her as soon as you came in."

Claire thanked the nanny and headed inside to the kitchen to return the call. On the way down the hall, she was surprised to see Chantal. "I'm sorry," Claire said, hurrying past her. "I must phone my cousin. She left an urgent message. I need to find out what that's about."

Chantal gave her a sympathetic smile and moved aside to let her pass. As Claire picked up the receiver, through a window, she saw Amélie entertaining Timmy in the back garden. Moments later, Sherry greeted her hoarsely over the phone.

"What is it?" Claire asked. "The nanny said you were rather upset."

"It's Zack." Sherry's voice sounded like it might break. "He's been wounded. He's in a coma."

"Where are you? I'll come there immediately."

"Could you? I feel alone and helpless. He's just lying there—"

"Just tell me where you are, and I'll come as quickly as possible."

"A US Army evacuation hospital in Wraxall. In North Somerset, near Bristol. The most severe cases come here."

"I'll be there. Stay with him."

When Claire hung up, Chantal watched her closely, joined by the nanny and Amélie. Timmy ran to her and threw his arms around her legs. "Gigi," he yelped excitedly.

Claire stooped and hugged him. "I must go," she said. "Miss Amélie will care for you with Miss Chantal." She looked up at the younger Boulier sister. "I was surprised to see you this early. I thought you'd arrive later. Welcome."

As Claire crossed the kitchen to greet her, Chantal burst out, "We finished training today. I'm done." She flashed her eyes toward Amélie and then back at Claire. "Aren't you going to tell us what's going on?"

"My cousin Zack's been wounded and he's in hospital. Sherry is with him. She's beside herself with worry. I must go to her."

"How will you get there? Amélie asked.

"I'll see if my landlord will lend me one of his motorcars. I'll explain the matter to him. I'm sure he won't mind."

"Would you like company?" Amélie said.

Claire shook her head. "I'd love it, but that's probably not best. I'm going to a crowded US Army hospital. Getting in could be difficult. Now I must be going."

The landlord proved eager to help, insisting that his chauffeur drive Claire, despite the distance being greater than Claire had thought, a hundred and thirty miles each way. Nevertheless, three hours after speaking with Sherry, Claire showed her credentials at the hospital's front gate and was admitted through the various checkpoints to the intensive care ward.

As she made her way through the corridors laden with the smell of antiseptics, she was struck with both horror and admiration. Soldiers on crutches, in wheelchairs, or walking with missing limbs or arms in casts roamed the halls. Some staggered, some limped, some appeared as living cadavers, while others, further along in treatment, looked comparatively robust. Some wore smiles and greeted Claire as she passed by.

She heard Christmas music playing as she approached a corner, and when she rounded it, she encountered a group of patients decorating a tree. They greeted her with smiles and friendly calls as she passed by, lifting her spirits.

Directed by staff along the way, she found Sherry in a staff office, leaned over in a chair, half asleep, her elbows resting on her knees, her hands cradling her face. When she looked up on hearing Claire's voice, tears rimmed her hollowed-out eyes.

"How is he?" Claire asked anxiously.

"Still the same," Sherry replied in a ghost of a voice. Her shoulders shook. "My little brother..." Her voice trailed off, and she sobbed.

Claire stooped and placed her arms around Sherry. "He'll be all right. You'll see."

The two cousins sat together through the long night. "I'd all but forgotten that Christmas was coming," Claire said at one point.

Sherry sat up straight and stared. "I had too. I'm trying to remember the last Christmas we celebrated. That must have been in 1940. Three years ago. Josh was home. Zack was still in school, and Mom—" Tears welled in her eyes. "That was the last time we were all together."

Claire clasped her hand and squeezed it. "It's painful, I know."

"I don't mean to feel sorry for myself, and really, I don't. Others have suffered far worse. It's the thought of Zack lying in there. Will he live? Will he be normal? And coming just a year after Mom died."

"It's all right, that's why I'm here. We'll get through this war together."

Sherry replied in a broken whisper, "Thank you for coming. I'm not sure I could get through this alone. To be honest, I'm not sure I can go back to nursing." She related how she had discovered Zack on the evacuation flight. "And there he was, asleep like a baby, but I had the chart of his injuries in my hand with his name on it."

"You poor dear," Claire said. "I can't imagine." She once again wrapped an arm around Sherry's shoulders. "Let's deal with what we must at present, and the rest later. Have you heard from Josh?"

Sherry nodded. "He's in the Central Pacific somewhere." She pulled a letter from her handbag. "He says in here that he was saved by a famous actor. I think that was supposed to impress me, but all it means is that he was somehow in mortal danger. Anyway, he says that this actor is changing his name. It's Eddie Heimberger, but people keep mispronouncing it as 'Hamburger,' so he's changing it."

They both laughed, a welcome relief. "What's he changing it to?" Claire asked.

"He mentions it in here," Sherry said, scanning the letter again. "He says that the actor's middle name is Albert, so that's what he's changing his last name to. Albert. He'll be Eddie Albert. That's it."

"Never heard of him, but I'll be sure to look for his movies now. After all, he saved your brother's life."

They laughed again, and then Sherry asked, "What about your family? Do you know how and where everyone is?"

Claire shook her head and sniffed. "Now it's my turn to hold back tears. I know where my father is, but I don't hear from him directly. Mother is alone and contending with the Germans on Sark. The good news is that both are alive and well, relatively speaking.

"Lance is back in the same POW camp he was in before his escape, Colditz Castle. More worrisome is that he's been classified as a *prominente*. My imagination goes a little crazy with what that could mean."

"In what way?"

"I don't see any way for it to be good. The war is turning bad for the Germans. At least that's what the newspapers are saying. *Prominentes* are prominent persons.

Apparently, being the Dame of Sark's son qualifies him. The Germans have gathered some of them together, and my fear is that if the *Reich* attempts a negotiated peace and their conditions are not met, the Germans will try to use them as bargaining chips, essentially holding them for ransom with potentially disastrous consequences."

"That's terrible," Sherry said. The two were silent for a few moments, and then she asked, "And what about Paul?"

Claire heaved a sigh. "Who knows what Paul is doing at any given time. He is such a cerebral man. When we were growing up, he joined in our adventures, and he's athletic enough, but his aspirations were along analytical lines. And in fact, he started as an intelligence analyst. Now he looks like a lean, battle-hardened soldier, and we never know what he's doing.

"I did hear from him a few weeks ago, and somehow, he's worked his way into ground combat in Italy. He was in the invasion at Salerno with a British unit under the command of that American general, the flamboyant one. Patton, I think his name is. Anyway, he's had a fast rise in rank. He's a lieutenant colonel now."

"That's impressive," Sherry remarked. "Where is he now?"

"Somewhere in Italy. That's all I know." She sighed again.

"And what about Jeremy? Is he still in France?"

Claire shook her head, strain showing on her face. "No. He's here in England somewhere, either training or preparing for another foray into France. I expect that he'll go back soon, probably in the new year. His fiancée and her sister are staying at my house right now. When he goes, my guess is that the sisters will go as well." She related how Jeremy had met the Bouliers.

"What a sweet and sour story," Sherry exclaimed when Claire had finished.

Claire nodded with a slight smile. "You should see Jeremy and Amélie together. They are so good for each other. And Amélie's younger sister has her heart set on a chap by the name of Horton. Sergeant Derek Horton. He escaped Dunkirk with Lance and then worked with Jeremy in France. That's how he knows the Boulier sisters. He's an impressive man, and funny, but he sees Chantal only as a little girl. She was fourteen when they first met, but she's nearly eighteen now, and he's not much older."

"Do you think anything will ever come of it?"

Claire shrugged. "Who knows? Chantal can always hope or set her sights elsewhere."

They laughed together. Then Sherry observed, "You've had your share of challenges. How did you ever get through them?"

Claire chuckled. "With that famous British stiff upper lip," she replied. "But I do know how you feel. Jeremy was shot down twice—"

Sherry's head snapped sharply toward Claire. "I didn't know—"

Claire nodded. "During the Battle of Britain. He was shot down once and parachuted to safety on a farm. The second time, he lost a lot of blood before any help could get to him. We nearly lost him. And Paul was shot up quite badly in Italy."

Tears rimmed Sherry's eyes. "Then you do know..." She sniffed and left the sentence unfinished.

A nurse appeared in the office door. "Captain Littlefield?"

"Yes," Sherry replied anxiously, standing up while wiping her eyes.

"Your brother is awake and stable. You may go in to see him if you like, but just for a few minutes. He needs his rest."

The light in the room was dim as the two women entered and approached the bed. Zack lay still, but as Sherry leaned over his head, his eyes opened slightly, and a smile formed on his lips. He said nothing, but when Sherry took his hand, he squeezed it. She let out a small gasp and kissed his forehead gently while Claire looked on.

"His heart is strong," the nurse said quietly. "His organs were swollen, but they're returning to normal. His surface wounds are slight other than a laceration in his right calf. He's out of danger, and with any luck, he'll be up and about in a few days and make a full recovery. His head took a wallop, though. He's suffering from a concussion, so he'll need to take things easy for a few weeks."

Sherry stood by Zack's bed, listening. As she did, her shoulders squared, she stood erect, her tears dried, and she smiled. "Thank you," she said with the practiced warmth of a flight nurse. "I can't put into words what your care for my brother has meant to me."

Claire stepped forward. "I'm Sergeant Littlefield's British cousin, and I have a question." The nurse turned to her. "Is it possible that he'll be well enough that we could take him to my house north of London next week for Christmas?"

"That's a wonderful idea," Sherry enthused, suddenly enlivened. "I'm a flight nurse on two weeks of leave to be with him. I won't take risks that would endanger him."

Taken aback, the nurse did not immediately respond. "Of course, that will depend on his progress," she said at last. "His doctor would have to approve, but we could ask."

As the chauffeur drove the two cousins back to Stony Stratford in the early hours of the next morning, Sherry said, "That was nice of you to offer your home. You've already got a full house."

"The more the merrier, and anyway, I'm being selfish, taking advantage of the time to become better acquainted with my American cousins. And with any luck, Jeremy will be there too. You'll have a chance to meet him."

"I'd like that," Sherry said. Then she studied Claire quizzically. "I'm a US Army officer, a flight nurse, and I still had to go through careful checking before being allowed inside the American compound. How did you clear security so easily and move about the hospital? Most Brits are not allowed on post without special clearance."

Taken by surprise, Claire took a moment to respond as her face turned rosy. She shrugged, and then she displayed her best dazzling smile and pointed at it with her index finger. "I guess this did it."

Sherry regarded her skeptically, but did not press the matter.

***

Christmas Day, 1943
Sark, Channel Islands

Dame Marian Littlefield stared at the letter in her hand, conveyed by the Red Cross. It was from her husband, Stephen. Constrained by German proscriptions to twenty-eight words, it said little, but enough to provide slight relief.

"Darling Marian, I'm fine, or I wouldn't say so. You know that's true. The scenery is beautiful, the camp not, and the ersatz tea... I love you, Stephen."

Wondering how many iterations he had drafted before deciding on which twenty-eight words to send, she lifted her eyes to stare out her sitting room window and over the fallow fields across the road beyond the gate. "I miss you, Stephen," she murmured. "I miss you so much."

A knock at the front entrance startled her. She quickly dried her eyes in deference to a self-imposed stricture that the Nazis would never see her cry. Her two poodles, barking despite their skeletal frames, wagged their tails as she made her way into the foyer. Opening the door, she found Ethan Boggs, the man who had driven the horse cart that had carried her and Stephen to the quay on the day he had been deported.

"Good day, mum," he said. "Me and the missus was just checking in on you and want to invite you to spend the day with us. We hate to think of you being here all alone on Christmas Day."

"Thank you, Ethan, but I'll be all right. I don't feel much like celebrating today."

"Then no need to celebrate, mum," he said gently. "Let's just be together." His eyes beseeched her. "Please come."

Marian gazed into Ethan's face and felt her resolve dissipating. Her chest heaved as she choked back tears. "All right," she whispered. "Just let me get my coat."

Stony Stratford, England

"Why do I have to get all dressed up?" Chantal complained.

"It's Christmas," Amélie said with a slightly scolding tone. "Claire has been good to us, and she's trying to make things as normal as possible for those around her, especially little Timmy. She's pulling together what she can for a Christmas celebration, and the least we can do is help her along. If she wants us to dress up, then we should dress up."

While she spoke, Amélie moved to a wardrobe and removed a garment on a hanger. "Look, she's given you this beautiful blue dress that she can't wear anymore. You and I are the same size now. I altered it while you were in training. It should fit you."

Chantal eyed it dubiously.

"I'll fix your hair and we'll put on makeup," Amélie went on. "It should be fun."

"Yes, but what's the point? No one's going to see me all dressed up except for those of us here."

"Who are also dressing up. Just do it."

"I will," Chantal retorted crossly, "but I'm not going to like doing it."

Jeremy sat on the divan in the sitting room in deep discussion with Zack apart from the others. He had arrived that morning, and Zack the previous evening. Meanwhile, Claire and the nanny were in the kitchen preparing as sumptuous a Christmas dinner as was possible under wartime rationing. "Things are better now than at any time during the past three years," Claire had reminded everyone, referring to the Battle of Britain, the *blitz*, and the attendant blackouts.

"I got word of the battle results from my unit," Zack told Jeremy. He had immediately been drawn to Jeremy, not only because of the family relationship but also because both had been in heavy combat. Jeremy gathered very quickly that the young sergeant needed someone to speak with about his latest experience.

Jeremy felt for his cousin. Zack walked with a limp from the laceration in his calf, but his other surface wounds had healed nicely. His body was still sore, particularly in his abdomen, and occasionally he had stabbing headaches that could last from a few seconds to several hours, but otherwise, he carried himself normally and recognized improvements in his condition daily.

"I don't know why I'm alive," Zack said, his voice pained. "Out of my entire platoon, I'm the only one who survived the battle at Kasserine. The same thing happened at San Pietro. For a short while, I was the acting company commander, and all but four of our tanks and crews were destroyed. By rights, I shouldn't be here."

"Ah, but you are here, Zack, and we're very glad of that." He leaned over in his seat. "But I do understand the feeling. I was stranded in Dunkirk after the evacuation. I was on the beach, weaponless, with Germans all around. Yet somehow, I escaped, while my brother was taken prisoner. He escaped and made it home last year, but then he was recaptured on a commando mission, and he's back there now at Colditz.

"I jumped from a sinking ship holding Timmy and the hand of his mother. She never surfaced, and I don't know what happened to her. I'm here, and so is Timmy, but she's not. How can anyone explain that?

"I flew in the Battle of Britain with five of the Eagles, those American pilots who came to fight for us before the US entered the war. They're all dead, and I'm not.

"I think about those things sometimes, but let me tell you what saves me from sinking into a sense of guilt." Jeremy pointed across the garden to where Timmy played alone in a sandbox with several of his bright Dinky trucks.

"It's him, Zack. The children deserve the lives we had before the war began. We love our families, but if you and I die now, we've already had good lives. Timmy hasn't, and neither has his generation. If we stop fighting, they don't stand a chance. If I wallow in guilt, I can't do my best, and they need for me to do just that.

"I'll tell you what else keeps me going—"

For the first time, Zack grinned. "Amélie?"

Jeremy stared at him in surprise. "Is it that obvious?"

Zack laughed. "It's only the main topic of conversation between our two sisters." He mimicked Claire and Sherry. "'They should go ahead and get married.' 'Do you think they'll wait until after the war?' 'I do want them to have a normal life together.' It goes on and on."

Laughing with him, Jeremy clapped Zack's shoulder. "Amélie and I will marry," he said with a determined air. "On Sark, and you're invited to the wedding."

"And I'll do my best to be there," Zack promised with a smile.

Jeremy shoved his shoulder playfully. "Don't you have a girlfriend back home in New Jersey?"

Zack reddened. "I do. Sonja." He pulled a photo from his wallet and handed it to Jeremy. "We were high school sweethearts. I hope she's still around when I get home."

Jeremy took the color photo and studied it. A girl with blue eyes, full lips, and long, straight blonde hair smiled out from it. "She's beautiful," he told Zack. Then he laughed and clapped his cousin's shoulder again. "And don't worry too much about her staying around for you. Jody can't get all the girlfriends."

At that moment, Claire appeared, waving frantically.

"Excuse me," Jeremy said. "I've invited another guest, and I think he's just arrived. I must greet him. You're welcome to join us."

The man Jeremy greeted at the door was stocky, medium height, and dressed in a British Army uniform with sergeant stripes. He was in his early twenties, looked like he might have played rugby while in school, and bore a perpetual half-grin that hinted at a jovial nature. When he saw Jeremy, he extended his hand. "It's so good of you to invite me for Christmas, sir," he said.

"Derek Horton," Jeremy said, his voice booming. "Welcome. There's no rank in this house. Drop the sirs."

"I'll try, sir, but old habits die hard."

In the bedroom she shared with Amélie, Chantal first recognized Horton's voice, and her heart took a leap. Then she clearly heard Jeremy all but shout out the sergeant's name, and her head popped around. She stared wide-eyed at her sister.

"Surprise!" Amélie exclaimed.

"He's here? Horton's here?" Chantal cried in disbelief.

"You made Jeremy promise to try to get him here."

Chantal fanned her face with her palms as the blood rose in her cheeks. She looked about wildly. "How do I look?"

Amélie laughed. "I thought you didn't care how you look."

"Yes, but..." Chantal stammered. "He's here?" She rushed to a mirror, examined herself from head to toe, straightened out wrinkles, and fixed her hair. "How's my makeup?"

"You look gorgeous," Amélie assured her, barely able to restrain her amusement. "With that face, those eyes, and the way that dress shows off your figure, if Horton's still aloof when you go out there, he needs to be checked for a pulse."

As Chantal headed for the door, Amélie stopped her. "Don't go and throw yourself at him. That didn't work so well before. Stay calm. Be demure."

"Demure? What does that mean?"

"Be a little bit reserved. Almost standoffish, but not quite. Be friendly but mix around the room with others. I'll let you know how you're doing."

Horton was being introduced to Zack when Chantal emerged. He stopped in mid-sentence to stare, and then caught his breath.

Chantal appeared not to have seen him at first, weaving her way through the others in the room, stooping to kiss Timmy, and finally allowing her eyes to rest on Horton. "Ah, Sergeant Horton, what a surprise, and how nice to see you."

She walked toward him, her hand extended. "It's been so long, at least a year. I think the last time I saw you was as I was leaving Cherbourg after our trip to the beach below that quaint little hotel where we stayed together at Bruneval."

Horton turned crimson. "Y-yes," he stammered. "That's been awhile." He looked about, self-consciously. "We stayed in separate rooms."

Genuinely amused, Chantal laughed softly. "Yes, we did at that."

Horton's eyes trailed over her. "You look lovely," he rasped.

"And you look so handsome," Chantal said, smiling coquettishly. He started to respond, but she moved away to converse with others in the room.

Amélie sidled up next to Chantal. "He can't take his eyes off you," she whispered.

Chantal chuckled. "He's remembering the show we put on to distract the German guards in France—our kiss on the beach. Serves him right. What I remember is that he only shook my hand as I departed after we had risked our lives together on that reconnaissance mission. He knew how I felt about him. I could've strangled him."

Dinner proceeded into the evening with a slice of ham, potatoes, and some Brussels sprouts. Claire and the nanny sat with Chantal between them on one side of the table while Horton was seated directly opposite Chantal, between Jeremy and Zack.

After dinner, and while darkness settled into night, the party moved into the sitting room for drinks and conversation. A while later, the nanny left for home, and Horton took that as a cue that he should make his departure.

He stood. "Thank you for includin' me in this celebration," he said, addressing everyone. "I really should be goin'." His lips widened into his characteristic grin. "The war's not waitin', and I've got trainin' early tomorrow mornin'."

"I'll see you out," Chantal exclaimed, rising to her feet, slight alarm in her eyes.

An awkward hush fell over the room.

"Well then, I'll take my leave," Horton said, and started for the door.

Her cheeks turning crimson from so many eyes suddenly on her, Chantal followed. The pair stepped through the doorway, and she closed it behind them.

"I really was very happy to see you again, Sergeant Horton."

"Likewise, mum." Once again, his eyes strayed over her, and he took a deep breath. "You really are lovely. You've come a long way since that little girl—"

"I'm not a little girl anymore, Sergeant Horton."

"I should say not. You've... well, you—"

Chantal suddenly stepped close to Horton, wrapped her arms around his neck, and pressed against him tenderly. "You fool," she whispered into his ear. "Shut up and kiss me."

DRIVING THE TIDE
Book #6 in the After Dunkirk series

As the Allies prepare to liberate France at the height of World War II, one family will do everything within their power to end the war—even when it calls for the ultimate sacrifice...

The liberation of occupied France is long overdue, but the magnitude of the operation requires the combined efforts of the Resistance groups across Europe. Jeremy Littlefield returns to France to prepare for the Allied invasion, Operation Overlord. An occupied country is a dangerous terrain to navigate, and as Jeremy works with his fiancée to set the plan in motion, even the smallest mistake can come at a fatal price.

At Bletchley Park, Claire Littlefield decodes a troubling message from German high command. Hitler is moving his secret weapons development resource from Norway to Bavaria. Previous attempts to stop production in Norway have failed, and now the Allies must launch another mission before they lose their chance—and they're counting on Claire to deliver the right information to ensure their success.

After making his mark in fierce combat against Rommel's army in North Africa, Paul Littlefield is dispatched to Italy as his battalion prepares to take the country. Many days of exhausting ground combat push Paul to his limits, and soon he realizes that this victory will require a greater sacrifice than ever before.

Lance Littlefield has been recaptured and sent back to the POW camp in Colditz Castle. His first escape was improbable; his chances of escaping a second time are slim to none. Luckily, Lance has never been afraid of taking big risks.

And in the Pacific, an amphibious landing as ambitious as the one in Europe is in the works, with Cousin Josh Littlefield at its center.

DRIVING THE TIDE is the riveting sixth installment in the After Dunkirk family saga, bringing to life the darkest pages of World War II —and the unflinching bravery of regular people who rose to the challenges of their times.

Get your copy today at
severnriverbooks.com/series/after-dunkirk

ACKNOWLEDGMENTS

As with all my books, the list of people to whom I owe gratitude for providing help, advice, and encouragement is long. For fear of leaving anyone out, I prefer to acknowledge them here as a group. The After Dunkirk Series has enjoyed tremendous success that would not have been possible but for their generous insights. Hopefully, in thanking each of them personally, I've left no one out.

Choosing to whom to dedicate any particular book to is as sensitive as whom to acknowledge. Of course, there is always my wife and family, but given my intent to recognize heroes and heroines of the war, just a listing of those who deserve such a dedication would take another book. Therefore, I choose to highlight individuals whose actions caused a turning point in WWII. Such was certainly the case with the Norwegian men of Operation Gunnerside. The world came too close for comfort to apocalypse. That said, for some, the mission to destroy the heavy water produced at Norway's Vemork Hydroelectric Power Plant was not yet over, so my quandary became whether to recognize them in this book or the next.

A similar quandary surrounds Jeannie Rousseau. Her perspicacity led to a major change in the direction of the war. However, her greatest sacrifices still lay ahead. I will only state here that she deserves the most profound admiration and respect, and my next book, Driving The Tide, will be dedicated to her memory.

ABOUT THE AUTHOR

Lee Jackson is the Wall Street Journal bestselling author of The Reluctant Assassin series and the After Dunkirk series. He graduated from West Point and is a former Infantry Officer of the US Army. Lee deployed to Iraq and Afghanistan, splitting 38 months between them as a senior intelligence supervisor for the Department of the Army. Lee lives and works with his wife in Texas, and his novels are enjoyed by readers around the world.

Sign up for Lee Jackson's newsletter at
severnriverbooks.com/authors/lee-jackson

LeeJackson@SevernRiverBooks.com